THE TURTLE WARRIOR

THE
TURTLE
WARRIOR

Mary Relindes Ellis

VIKING

VIKING
Published by the Penguin Group
Penguin Group (USA) Inc., 375 Hudson Street,
New York, New York 10014, U.S.A.
Penguin Books Ltd, 80 Strand,
LondonWC2R 0RL, England
Penguin Books Australia Ltd. 250 Camberwell Road, Camberwell
Victoria 3124, Australia
Penguin Books Canada Ltd, 10 Alcorn Avenue,
Toronto, Ontario, Canada M4V 3B2
Penguin Books India (P) Ltd, 11 Community Centre, Panchsheel Park,
New Delhi - 110 017, India
Penguin Books (N.Z.) Ltd, Cnr Rosedale and Airborne Roads, Albany,
Auckland, NewZealand
Penguin Books (South Africa) (Pty) Ltd, 24 Sturdee Avenue,
Rosebank, Johannesburg 2196, South Africa

Penguin Books Ltd, Registered Offices:
80 Strand, London WC2R 0RL, England

First published in 2004 by Viking Penguin,
a member of Penguin Group (USA) Inc.

1   3   5   7   9   10   8   6   4   2

Grateful acknowledgment is made for permission to reprint excerpts from the following copyrighted works:
"A Song for What Never Arrives" from *Star Quilt* by Roberta Hill (Holy Cow! Press, 1994). Copyright © 1994 by Roberta Hill. Reprinted by permission of the author and publisher.
"Avoiding News by the River" by W. S. Merwin. Copyright © 1967 W. S. Merwin. Reprinted with permission of The Wylie Agency, Inc.
"The Sound of Silence" by Paul Simon. Copyright © 1964 Paul Simon. Used by permission of the publisher, Paul Simon Music.

Publisher's Note
This is a work of fiction. Names, characters, places, and incidents either are the product of the author's imagination or are used fictitiously, and any resemblance to actual persons, living or dead, business establishments, events, or locales is entirely coincidental.

Library of Congress Cataloging-in-Publication Data

Ellis, Mary Relindes, 1960–
The turtle warrior / Mary Relindes Ellis.
p.   cm.
ISBN 0-670-03265-4
1. Vietnamese Conflict, 1961–1975—Wisconsin—Fiction. 2. Wisconsin—Fiction.
3. Boys—Fiction. I. Title.

PS3605.L468T87 2004
813'.6—dc21   2003057167

This book is printed on acid-free paper.

Printed in the United States of America
Set in Bembo with Cheltenham Light   Designed by Daniel Lagin

For my brother

Paul Alexander Ellis

Acknowledgments

This is a book of fiction, hence any resemblance to persons living or deceased is purely coincidental. The VFW Hall on East Wisconsin Avenue in Milwaukee and the Heron Reservation are completely fictional and were created for the sole purpose of the novel.

While the battle of Khe Sanh actually did take place in late January 1968—the beginning of the Tet Offensive—and proceeded to escalate as the fighting continued toward Hue, the characters are fictional as are some of the events created around the Khe Sanh Combat Base. The soldiers are all fictional characters and hence their opinions and feelings concerning the Vietnam conflict and more importantly the immediate battles they fought in are also fictional. While there were combat chaplains in Vietnam, the chaplain in this book is fictional and his predicament and actions that deviate somewhat from official military policy are those of a fictional priest/chaplain suffering a crisis of faith. What is not fiction is that the battle of Khe Sanh, like the rest of our involvement in Vietnam, was terrible and lives were lost on both sides of the conflict. What is not fiction is that the United States' role in Vietnam will forever haunt every American, especially those men that fought and survived, and the families of those men who were killed. We tragically fail, as a nation, to learn from our mistakes.

In addition to my own experience as a girl whose older brother served in Vietnam and who endured a long night with my siblings and mother concerning that wounded brother, I am very indebted to many books that were important to me in my research. I tried to study the Vietnam War from many perspectives. Those books are:

Dispatches, by Michael Herr; *The End of the Line,* by Robert Pisor; *Fire in the Lake,* by Frances FitzGerald; *Semper Fidelis: The History of the United States Marine Corps,* by Allan R. Millett; *The Pacific War,* by John Costello; *Operation Buffalo: USMC Fight for the DMZ,* by Keith William Nolan; *Combat Chaplain: A Thirty-Year Vietnam Battle,* by James D. Johnson; *Chaplains with Marines in Vietnam, 1962–1971,* by Commander Herbert L. Bergsma, CHC, U.S. Navy; *Valley of Decision: The Siege of Khe Sanh,* by John Prados and Ray W. Stubbe; *Free in the Forest: Ethnohistory of the Vietnamese Central Highlands, 1954–1976,* by Gerald Cannon Hickey; *The Montagnards of South Vietnam: A Study of Nine Tribes,* by Robert L. Mole; *Reading Athena's Dance Card: Men Against Fire in Vietnam,* by Russell W. Glenn; *The Battle of Leyte Gulf: 23–26 October 1944,* by Thomas J. Cutler; *Turbulent Times and Enduring Peoples,* edited by Jean Michaud; *Vietnam: A History,* by Stanley Karnow; *Our Vietnam,* by A. J. Langguth; *The Encyclopedia of the Vietnam War: A Political, Social and Military History,* edited by Spencer C. Tucker; *They Called Them Angels: American Military Nurses of World War II,* by Kathi Jackson; *A Chorus of Stones,* by Susan Griffin; *No Time for Fear: Voices of American Military Nurses in World War II,* by Diane Burke Fessler; *Ojibway Heritage,* by Basil Johnson; and *Farming the Cutover; A Social History of Northern Wisconsin, 1900–1940,* by Robert Gough. I am also grateful for the terminology provided by the Vietnam Project.

A very special thank-you to the editor and staff of *Leatherneck* magazine (the official magazine of the United States Marine Corps), for their thoughtful and sensitive answers to painful questions I posed regarding the care taken to identify those Marines killed and the Marine Corps policy of notifying the families of those deceased men; and to Professor Edward Griffin, for his reading of the manuscript and for his own perspective based on military service.

Parts of the novel also appeared in slightly altered form in *The Bellingham Review* and *Glimmer Train.* I received wonderful support and encouragement from the owners and editors of *Glimmer Train,* Linda B. Swanson-Davies and Susan Burmeister-Brown, who have created an enduring literary journal that embraces stories that might not otherwise get published.

I am grateful to Marly Rusoff, my agent, for her enthusiasm and belief in this book, and to Kathryn Court and Ali Bothwell, at Viking Penguin, for their editorial help, support, and enthusiasm. Many thanks as well to Steven Barclay and Kathryn Barcos, for their advice and unfailing kindness; and to William Merwin for his generous advice.

I should like to thank the following for their faith, love, and continual support: Peg Johnson, Heather McIver, Dawn York, W. Kent Krueger, Trudy Lapic, Scott and Lisa King, Craig and Sal Johnson, Deb Swackhamer, Jan Philibert, Gwen Ellis, Paul Ellis and Viola Kien, Barbara Stoltz, Tracy Ellis and family, Edith Mucke, Betty Johnson, Alan and Jeannie Steffen, Theresa Durand, Patricia Galiger Schoenborn; my "other" parents, Darlene and Miles Galiger; Brian and Jody Hayman, William and Margaret Hunt, Doris and David Preus, Dan Guenther and Margaret Pennings, Patti Brierbauer, and Donna Cotter. I received mentoring and guidance as an undergraduate from Professors Charles Sugnet and Michael Dennis Browne, and more recently, extraordinary assistance from Professors Shirley Nelson Garner, Toni McNaron, and Madelon Sprengnether. Also, a special thank-you to the staff and the chair, Kent Bales, of the English Department at the University of Minnesota, and Margaret Yzaguirre of the College of Liberal Arts. I am also grateful to my mother, Relindes Catherine Alexander Berg, and all the women who helped raise me and who were/are warriors in their own right.

Tragically, Tom Lapic, senior aide to Senator Paul Wellstone and husband to Trudy Lapic, died in the plane crash on October 25, 2002, and hence did not live to see this book, which he so supported and did not get to read in its entirety. But he knew the conflicts, philosophically and morally, concerning all the issues involved in this novel and worked constantly toward righting those wrongs until the day he died.

The writing of this novel was assisted by the financial support of a 1997 Minnesota State Arts Board Grant.

AVOIDING NEWS BY THE RIVER

As the stars hide in the light before daybreak
Reed warblers hunt along the narrow stream
Trout rise to their shadows
Milky light flows through the branches
Fills with blood
Men will be waking

In an hour it will be summer
I dreamed that the heavens were eating the earth
Waking it is not so
Not the heavens
I am not ashamed of the wren's murders
Nor the badger's dinners
On which all worldly good depends
If I were not human I would not be ashamed of anything

W. S. Merwin

October 2000

✖✖✖✖ HE STOOD NEXT TO HIS yard light and looked at his watch. It was 8:00 P.M., and he did not want to wait a moment longer, to cause them worry. He turned the light switch on and then off, waiting for a few seconds before doing it again: on and off. It was a signal to his younger neighbor that all was well at the Morriseau farm. A nightly ritual.

It was dark and cold, but rather than go into the house, he leaned against the light post. Autumn again. It was the season in which the memories of his father were most visceral. His father had been dead for fifty years. Ernie was now seventy-six. Autumn made him more aware of his mortality, yet his chest swelled with excitement, with the change arousing his senses. The spice and funk of wet bark and wet leaves, the papery fertility of dried grass and the astringency of pine. The leaves like varying shades of fire. The first October storm that released them like smoke. The surprising loveliness of bare branches reaching upward as though the sky had pulled their shirts off to get them ready for bed.

Autumn briefly transcended the truth of his age and allowed him to dwell in the memory of being a treasured late-in-life child. He had loved and respected his mother and father; had been the child of, and witness to, an extraordinary marriage. In trying to be what he thought was a good son, a citizen of the world, he had made choices that hurt his parents and caused them worry and pain, some of them inevitable but others selfishly ill considered. He hadn't paid attention. He only half listened in the evenings when his father told stories and anecdotes while they did chores. Stories of his father's life on the reservation, stories of why the moon was full once a month, why birds go south, the creation of butterflies. He understood and listened to his parents speak in what should have been his first language, Ojibwe. Ernie knew only a half dozen words, as his generation was not allowed to speak their native language in school. If he had listened more closely and learned, he might have solved the riddle that his father unwittingly left him with and that troubled him for years.

✕✦✦✦✦✦✦✦✕

They had been deer hunting that day and had stopped to drink some water and eat their packed sandwiches.

"Spring," his father commented out of the blue, looking up at the treetops, "is the season of women and birth. Fall is the season of men and hunting."

Ernie was sixteen then and did not think to question its meaning, but it was odd enough for him to remember.

His father suffered a stroke two weeks after Ernie came home from fighting in the Pacific in 1944. Ernie had gotten married just before returning to Olina. Rather than have a honeymoon, he and his wife were suddenly faced with the responsibility of his family's subsistence farm and the care of his aging parents as well. In those long days of work there never seemed to be time to discuss much of anything except what was necessary. He was hesitant to do so anyway; afraid that he might upset the old man by forcing him to speak when it was so difficult for his father to ask for the simplest needs and wants. His wife's nursing of his father and her patience with the daily physical therapy required appeared to have nearly restored him. Just when it seemed his father had regained all of his speech and could walk without help, he suffered a fatal stroke one night in his sleep.

Ernie told his mother, not long before she died two years later, what his father had said, in the hopes that she would know the intent of the words. Her usually good-humored face folded in confusion.

"I don't know." She shook her head. "I don't know what he meant."

He would have given anything to talk to his father again. To ask the older man if he had really understood what he had said: that women belonged to life and that men belonged to death and that men killed in the fall what women gave birth to in the spring. Even if it was not literally true, the metaphor was a terrifying one.

He put his bare hands in his coat pockets and looked up at the night sky with its many stars and constellations. He shivered. Peace did not come with old age. The new millennium meant nothing to him. He and his wife had gone to bed early on New Year's Eve, ignoring the national fear of being bombed, of terrorism striking anywhere and everywhere. They did not, as some of their neighbors did, buy cases of water, load up on canned goods, buy huge power generators, or turn their basement into a bunker. They slept, knowing that whatever would happen would happen regardless of what they did.

His right hand fingered the handkerchief in his pocket. If he had learned something profound in his life, it was this: that to ask a question could be the most rebellious of acts and the most necessary. That allowing words to go unspoken could cause not only harm to oneself but harm to another.

He tasted it every day in his mouth. As though he had bitten down on a prickly ash berry. The sudden infusion of wild citrus flavor before it numbed his gums and tongue. Not even water seemed to wash it away.

Bitterness.

June 1967

XXXX SOMETHING NUDGED BILL WHEN THE firecrackers went off in the snapper's jaws. It told him to pay attention to the queasy feeling in his stomach and remember. Bill saw his brother and his brother's best friend, Terry, laughing at the turtle's gaping mouth and mutilated jaws. His brother's hand was clutched around a Pabst beer. Blood from his bitten thumb trickled across the blue ribbon on the brown bottle and dripped onto the sand as they stood on the shore of the Chippewa River near the old logging bridge.

"Damn! That sucker nearly took my thumb off." James raised his hand to his mouth and began licking the blood.

"Don't lick your own blood!" Terry said, his lips wrinkled with disgust. He took a swig of beer from his own bottle.

"You lick it then!" James held out his bloodied thumb, taunting his friend.

"Get away from me! I ain't no vampire."

James walked toward him and jabbed his thumb into Terry's face, causing him to back up awkwardly. The older boys jostled up the bank away from the river, shouting and laughing at each other.

Bill watched them goof around for a while before turning his attention back to the snapper. It was a big female. She moved laboriously toward the river, her front claws digging into the sand to pull her forward. Her lower jaw dragged, and pieces of it fell away as she crawled. Then she stopped and dropped her head upon the sand. She made a strange noise. Not a cry like many other animals would make in pain. More like an anguished groan. Tears watered Bill's eyes.

Snapping turtles were like nothing else Bill knew. Not like humans or animals. Not even like their cousins the box and mud turtles. Snappers were sometimes algae-covered or muddy or even mossy-looking at times. They appeared ugly, wise, and ancient all at once. The combination lifted them to a transcendent beauty, an otherworldly magnificence that thrilled Bill. They were the nearest thing to a dragon that he would ever experience. They couldn't move their bodies very fast on the ground. It was their heads and jaws that gave them their name. The head could suddenly shoot forward and snap down on prey with jaws that could not be pried apart. Bill liked to put his bare feet on top of the empty shells of the turtles his mother had used to make soup and feel with his toes the ridges and leathery points of the carapaces. Like most turtle shells, snapping turtle's shells were not round but slightly oval, some of them with one distinct ridge running straight down the middle from the head opening to the rear of the shell, where the turtle's tail protruded. He had picked the largest shell and asked his brother to drill a hole on the right and left side of the shell, where it was the widest to protect the vulnerable skin between the turtle's front and back feet. Bill threaded and knotted one end of a rope through the one hole, then pulled the rest of the rope across the interior of the shell and through the opposite hole so that it was taut. He cut off the excess rope and knotted it. He could then insert his left arm up through the inside of the shell so that it functioned as a shield.

His small feet danced and dodged around his imaginary enemies on the packed-down dirt of the barnyard. He held the turtle shield high to keep the sun out of his eyes, and its jagged edges cast a shadow over his face. He rarely had to use his shield as protection for his face and chest. His sword moved too fast for him to learn the names of his enemies before they died. But they knew his name. Bill imagined that his enemies called him the Turtle Warrior, and swinging the wooden sword that James had made for him, he punctured their chests and sliced their hearts in two. Bill knew that almost nothing, not even bears, bothered a snapping turtle. So, he reasoned, nothing would mess with the Turtle Warrior either.

The snapper began moving again. He grabbed the back of her shell and pulled her away from the water. There was a large stain of blood from where she had laid her head. He didn't know why he pulled her away from the water. Whether she was in or out of the water didn't matter. She was going to die. Without her powerful beaked jaws, she had no way of catching fish or eating carrion or any other food the river had to offer. Four firecrackers had doomed her to a slow death from starvation if they left her here. The turtle groaned again. Bill helplessly watched as she crawled toward the river.

✕✦✦✦✦✦✦✕

James was baby-sitting his younger brother that June day just a week after school had let out. It was warm but not hot yet, and James had just finished his chores on their farm when his friend Terry Baker stopped by.

"Mom?" James yelled, poking his head inside the kitchen door. "I'm done with my chores. Can I go fishing with Terry at the river?"

Bill was sitting at the kitchen table, drinking a glass of milk. Their mother was washing dishes, and she didn't turn around at the sound of her older son's voice. Bill saw Terry standing behind his brother. Terry tapped James on the shoulder.

"Beer," he mouthed silently. He grinned and raised his eyebrows up and down like Groucho Marx.

"If," their mother answered over her shoulder, "you take Bill with you."

She turned around from the sink. Claire Lucas had bluish winged shadows under her brown eyes that made them appear larger. The corners of her mouth sagged, and her lips were pale except for the faded red lipstick along the lip line. She wiped her hands on the dish towel hanging from the belt of her blue house-dress and stared at James. Bill didn't want to go with his brother and Terry, but instead of protesting, he gazed absently at his mother's onionskin hands. If he whined, she might slap him across the face in front of the big boys. The sting would go away, but the embarrass-ment and smell of dirty dishwater would linger for a long time. James nodded reluctantly. Bill slid off the chair and followed his brother outside.

"Come home before dinner. Do you hear me?" she yelled after them.

When they had walked a quarter of a mile down the dirt road away from the Lucas farm, James turned around and savagely shook his little brother.

"Don't you tell Mom we're drinking beer or we'll hang you from a bridge again. Only this time we'll let go." He bent down and pushed his face into Bill's.

"I won't. I promise."

Out the corner of his eye, Bill could see Terry grin. He hated Terry, hated his shit-stinking cigarette breath and large beaver teeth. Bill could still see the jagged rocks loom before him and feel the thundering of blood in his ears as James and Terry had held him by his ankles and dipped him up and down over the side of the rust-colored bridge. He halfheartedly believed that they weren't going to let go of his legs, but they'd been drinking that day too, and their grip wasn't as tight as it could have been. At one point when Bill thought his eardrums were going to explode from the pressure of blood in his ears, he saw the river beckon to him. Her watery arms splashed upward when the fast-moving current hit the rocks, and he felt the spray on his face. He thought the river might grab his head, disengaging it from the rest of his body with a quick yank. But then James and Terry swung him over the bridge and onto the road, dropping him so that he fell painfully onto the gravel. They laughed as Bill's arms frantically clawed the air before he hit the ground.

"It's a bird! It's a plane! It's . . . it's . . . it's Billy Baboon!" they shouted in unison before howling with more laughter.

As Bill lay on the dirt, trying to catch his breath and establish his bearings, he saw his brother gradually stop laughing. James dropped his beer bottle and walked toward him. A frightened look came over his brother's face, and he hoisted Bill up, roughly grabbing him under his armpits. Bill knew then that James would never have let go of his ankles. What he didn't know was what caused his brother to do it in the first place.

James did not treat him that way when Bill was very small. But as James grew older and especially when he spent time with Terry and his other friends, he entered blind periods of cruelty. When Bill was thrown in with his brother and his friends, the dark and unseeing maliciousness of his brother encircled him. During those times James seemed to forget who Bill was and even that he loved him. Bill could see his brother's jaw jut out and set, the small muscles knotting along the bone. His face looked as though winter had passed and crusted it with ice. Still, Bill sought out his brother when their father's drinking became severe and their mother's sorrowful anger ricocheted through the house.

✗✗✗✗✗✗✗✗✗✗

The snapper was almost to the river when Terry shouted, "Hey! Don't let her get away!"

The older boys raced down the bank. James grabbed the turtle's thick, rough tail and dragged her back, her claws raking at the sand. He placed one boot on top of the snapper's back and pressed down.

"What are you gonna do with her?" Terry asked.

James stared down at the turtle, absently chewing on the soft end of a timothy weed stalk. "Take her home maybe. Mom can make soup outta her."

"Got any more firecrackers? Maybe we could put 'em up her

other end," Terry suggested gleefully. Bill instinctively squeezed his buttocks together with horror. Just watching James and Terry the first time was bad enough.

✕✦✦✦✦✦✦✦✕

They had spotted the big snapper as she was climbing down the bank after having deposited her eggs. James teased her with a stick the size of his wrists, and it was then he got the idea of using his firecrackers. He stood up and reached into the back pocket of his Levi's, produced a packet of red and white striped tubes the size of cigarettes.

"You don't tell Mom I've got these either," he warned Bill, his eyes slightly bloodshot from the four beers he had chugged.

James taunted the turtle with the stick; her head darted forward, and her jaws snapped at the wood waving in front of her. Then she bit down on the stick and hung on. The size of the stick made her jaws spread far apart, and Terry quickly inserted six firecrackers in the gaps. James struck a farmer's match against the silver metal buckle on his belt and, reaching forward with his other hand, lit them. The snapper surprised him by letting go of the stick and lunged toward him. She razored part of his thumb, and if it hadn't been for the firecrackers protruding from her mouth, she might have bitten down fully, severing his thumb from his hand.

"Jesus Christ!" He yanked back his hand. Then the firecrackers went off. Bill automatically jerked an arm up to protect his face. When the white smoke had cleared seconds later, his stomach rolled at what the small explosion had done to her jaws.

✕✦✦✦✦✦✦✦✕

"No!" Bill surprised himself by yelling. "How'd you like your butt blown apart!"

But rather than look at Terry, Bill stared at his brother. He'd seen James do some mean things, but this was the worst. His brother picked up his bottle of beer and held his arm away from his body as though he could not believe the limb belonged to him. He seemed shocked at the blood dripping from his thumb and flexed it slightly across the bottle's label. The turtle had only managed to cut through skin and veins, not the bone or tendons that enabled James to move his thumb.

"You—" Bill shouted again, so angry that he felt the spit gather and build into foam in his mouth—"had it comin'! She didn't do anything to you!"

His brother's mouth fell open, and he stared back at Bill. He let his arm fall limply to his side, and he shifted his gaze toward the turtle. She groaned, and his brother's face darkened with shame. Rather than feel kindly toward his brother, Bill became even angrier.

"You! You!" Bill searched for the right words, the worst words he had heard. Words that would damn his brother to hell. "*YOU . . . GOD . . . DAMNED . . . BASTARD!*"

"Are you gonna let him talk to you like that?" Terry asked incredulously. When James continued to stare wordlessly at his younger brother, Terry spun around and, opening his big tobacco-stained mouth, began to yell.

"You little shit! It's just a fuckin' turtle!"

Bill immediately backed up, knowing Terry would try to grab him. Terry had calloused palms and stubby fingers that were as stained by tobacco as his mouth. He extended his hands toward Bill, ready to pound him into the sand next to the turtle.

"Knock it off!"

His brother suddenly came to life again and pushed Terry back. "I'll beat on my little brother if I feel like it, but not you."

Terry hiked up the steep bank toward the road, cuffing the sand now and then with his boots.

"Listen," James said, bending over so that he was eye level with Bill, "I'm sorry, okay. I'm *sorry*. It was a stupid thing to do," he whispered hoarsely, his breath sour with beer.

He wiped his eyes with the back of his uninjured hand.

"I need your red bandanna to wrap my thumb," he said, his voice cracking.

Bill pulled his bandanna from his pocket and gave it to James. His brother wrapped the red cloth around his thumb before reaching down and grabbing the snapper by the tail.

"I can't take it back. It's done now. When we get home, I'll shoot her so she doesn't suffer anymore. Maybe Mom can use her for soup, so she doesn't go to waste."

"Mom is gonna know what happened to her," Bill said hesitantly.

"I know. But *you* don't tell her. That's my job. I'll tell her what I did. Just shut up about the beer."

His brother glanced up at the road where Terry was waiting. "C'mon. We gotta start home or Mom will really get pissed. And just don't say anything more to Terry, okay? I don't want him to sock you."

Bill nodded.

James began hiking up the steep bank. The turtle's head swung just above the ground, and blood from her jaws splattered his jeans. Bill hung back, waiting for the two older boys to get ahead of him. He looked back at the shore. Brown beer bottles were scattered across the grass, and there was a trail of clawed-up sand and blood. He stared at the rippling surface of the river. *We never did go fishing,* Bill thought. He wondered if his mother would notice that they had left the house without rods and reels or that they had come home with no fish. He began to walk up the bank.

He continued to trail behind his brother and Terry, already about fifty feet in front of him, when they reached the gravel road that led to the Lucas farm. Bill could hear the low sounds of their talking and occasional laughter, but he couldn't hear the words. James didn't turn around to see if Bill was following them. So Bill studied his brother as he walked, his own black high-topped sneakers kicking up the brown dust of the road.

The sun arched steadily downward in the sky. He wished that James and Terry weren't ahead of him and that he had his turtle shield and wooden sword. He would fight his enemies here, hidden in the bright rays of the afternoon sun and the grassy ditch along-side the road. And when he was through fighting, his enemies blood-ied and littered in the gravel, he would run back to the Chippewa and dive beneath the water's surface to join the other Turtle War-riors, lying beneath the lily pads. Only he was special. He would keep his human form and still be able to live in or out of water.

James and Terry began to sing "My baby does the hanky panky." Then they switched to an Elvis tune that Bill didn't know the name of. But he knew it was an Elvis tune because James sang it all the time. Watching them scuffle the dust into knee-high clouds ahead of him, Bill saw how much they tried to look like Elvis. Both of them wore their hair slicked back with Brylcreem, ridged on ei-ther side of their heads and combed toward the middle so that the ridges came together and formed ducktails at the nape of their necks. They both wore white T-shirts with sleeves rolled up to the shoulder except that Terry had a pack of Camels tucked into the right arm sleeve.

"The doctor says his lungs are black from all the smoking he does," James whispered to Bill once. After that, all Bill could think of when he saw Terry was his black lungs shrunken into dried mushrooms and how much he hated him.

Then Bill looked at the lower half of their bodies. Both wore tight Levi's jeans with rockabilly black boots to complete the Presley look. But his brother looked more like Elvis than Terry did. Bill momentarily swelled with pride. James had silky black hair and their mother's dark brown, almost black eyes. He could rotate his hips, rising up so that his boot-covered feet balanced on the tip of his toes while he jerked his knees obscenely back and forth just like Elvis. Throwing his already deep voice down even deeper, James warbled the songs out of his throat just like the King, using an old dried corncob for a microphone.

It was 1967. The Beatles had already invaded the United States, but time moved so stubbornly in the Olina community of six hundred that it was as though they didn't exist yet. Not just in Olina but in the whole of northern Wisconsin. James stuck by Elvis, Roy Orbison, and Jerry Lee Lewis. Sometimes the Big Bopper, Ritchie Valens, and Buddy Holly. He played them so often, the music blaring out of the hayloft of the barn where their mother had banished the record player to, that Bill knew all the lyrics to James's records and sang them while fighting his enemies in the barnyard.

He sang "Don't Be Cruel" and raised his wooden sword. Swish! Another enemy was dead. He sang "Love Me Tender" loudly and out of tune, speeding up the beat while cutting off the purple tops of thistles by the chicken coop with a few sweeps of his sword. He screamed the words to "Great Balls of Fire" while pretending their mutt dog, Beans, was one of his archenemies and chased him around and around the outside of the barn and sometimes into the field. And when Bill got tired of playing, he sang "Blue Angel" and sat on the wooden fence post behind the barn while the dog retreated to a safe distance to rest, his tongue lolling and dripping out of his mouth but his eyes kept warily on Bill.

Once when James was dancing to his music in the hayloft and Bill was fighting and singing below in the toolshed, their father furiously loped around the corner of the barn. He pushed open the sliding red barn door and yelled up into the hayloft, "Will you shut off that goddamn wango-bango music! Shut it off! Do you hear me! Shut it off!"

Then he ducked into the toolshed and grabbed Bill's sword out of his hand. He dragged Bill by his arm out into the yard, and while his son stood violently trembling, John Lucas flung the sword into the field next to the barn.

"Now quit dreamin' and do some chores!" his father yelled, lifting him off the ground by the neck of his shirt. Bill's arm dangled inside the turtle shell. He held his breath. His father stank of tractor oil, sweat, and Jim Beam whiskey. Then he dropped Bill and strode just as furiously back to the tractor he was supposedly repairing behind the barn.

"Christ, he's hung over. Probably woke him up," James muttered, having climbed down from the loft to stand near Bill. Bill watched as James turned in the direction their father had gone. His brother raised one brown muscled arm and, closing his hand into a fist, lifted only his middle finger. Bill watched that bird fly.

✕✖✦✦✦✦✦✦✖✕

"Hey!"

Bill looked up.

"Get over here!"

Bill broke into a reluctant jog until he caught up with them. The snapper's flow of blood had slowed to a trickle. She appeared almost dead except for the rhythmic clawing of her legs.

"Quit being so poky, and c'mon," James said irritably, shifting the turtle to his left hand. Bill could tell James and Terry were coming off their beer buzz because their shoulders slumped and they weren't talking anymore. They barely lifted their feet, shuffling like elderly men.

Minutes later they were walking out of the curve that hid the Lucas farm from the road when they heard the low hum of a vehicle coming up behind them.

"Wonder who it is. Your old man?" Terry asked.

James stopped and listened, his head cocked toward the sound. "Nah. My old man is in town. I'll bet it's Ernie Morriseau. Sounds like his truck. Can you hear that knock?"

The hum and knock became louder. Bill hoped it was Ernie Morriseau, and when he turned around, his hope was confirmed as the gray '64 Ford truck appeared behind them. Ernie Morriseau slowed down behind the boys and brought his truck to an idling halt beside them. He eyed the turtle in James's hands.

"Did you get that snapper down at the river?" He leaned out of his truck window for a better look.

"Yeah . . . we're taking her home to Mom for soup," James answered stiffly.

Ernie glanced at all three boys. "What happened to her jaws?" He said it quietly, but they heard him despite the idling engine.

"Nothin'," Terry answered sullenly. "We were just havin' a little fun."

Bill watched Ernie's eyes narrow toward his brother and Terry. The turtle let out a groan. Bill's eyes watered again. Ernie cut the engine.

"How bad does your mom need a turtle for soup?"

Bill could tell Ernie was mad. The skin on Ernie's neck was a sun-weathered red-brown, and when he was angry, it turned bronze.

"Not bad." James shifted the turtle back to his right hand.

"I'll buy it from you." Ernie reached into his back pocket.

"Ten bucks!" Terry suddenly demanded. For a few precious moments Bill thought Ernie was going to reach out of his truck window and grab Terry by his greased-down hair. His heart beat faster. *Maybe,* Bill thought with no small amount of joy, *he'll slam his head into the door.* Bill looked up at James. His brother had that cocky look on his face that really meant that he was scared.

"Okay," Ernie answered coolly, "ten bucks it is."

He got out of his truck and handed the ten-dollar bill to James instead of Terry. James extended the hand holding the turtle's tail toward Ernie.

"Wait."

Ernie grabbed some tarpaulin from the bed of the truck. He lined the floor on the passenger side with it. Then he took hold of the turtle hanging from James's hand by both sides of her shell and placed the almost dead animal on top of the tarpaulin. After stepping onto the running board, Ernie swung back into truck's cab and started the engine. He looked back at the silent boys.

"Billy," he said, hooking his thumb toward Bill, "how'd you like to come over for supper? Rosemary would love to have you."

Bill looked at his brother. James wasn't cocky anymore. He

dropped his head and stared at his boots. "Go ahead," he mumbled to Bill. "I'll tell Mom where you are."

Bill hesitated. Ernie reached over to open the passenger side door. Bill walked slowly around the front of the truck.

"Better take care of that thumb. It looks pretty nasty," Ernie commented to James as Bill climbed into the truck; he kept his feet on the seat instead of resting them on the snapper's back. Then Ernie revved the engine, and the truck rolled forward. Bill twisted his head around to stare out the cab window. Just above the brown dust of the road, he saw James's startled face staring after them, his other hand holding the bitten thumb.

✖✦✦✦✦✦✦✦✖

When they pulled up close to the yellow farmhouse, Bill saw Rosemary Morriseau's face appear in the kitchen window. She vigorously waved when she saw that Bill was in the truck too.

"Rose! We've got company for dinner!" Ernie called from the open window of the truck. Bill got out and walked around to Ernie's side.

"Billy!"

Rosemary Morriseau flung open the screen door and almost skipped down the porch steps. She reached forward and hugged him, his face nestled just under her breasts. Bill's guilt at leaving James washed away in the luxury of her hug and smile. He could not recall a time when his mother greeted him the way Rosemary Morriseau did, nor did his mother smell like her. He pressed his nose into the bottom crest of her ribs and inhaled. She wore lily of the valley perfume and that other smell of her body. He could not name it. He only knew it as her smell. It gave him joy and made him feel safe.

"Dinner will be ready in forty-five minutes," she said, stepping back and ruffling his hair.

"We'll be in the house in a bit."

Rosemary ruffled his hair again before stepping back inside the house to finish cooking dinner. Bill hoisted himself over the tailgate to sit in the box of the truck. Ernie drove the truck to the back of the barn. He got out of the driver's side, walked around the front of the truck, opened the passenger side door, and lifted the turtle out of the truck. Bill swung himself over the tailgate and onto the ground. He watched as Ernie placed the turtle on a small bed of straw. The snapper clawed the loose straw but could not lift her head. One glassy eye seemed riveted on Bill's face.

"What did James do to her jaws?"

"Terry too!"

"Terry too," Ernie echoed, and then repeated, "What did they do to her jaws?"

Bill didn't know if he could say. "Our neighbors don't need to know what goes on in our home," his mother always said, looking at Bill and James nervously after they had been at the Morriseau farm. But this had happened at the river, not at home. Bill suddenly felt very tired.

"Firecrackers."

"Huh," Ernie grunted. He bent down to take a closer look at the snapper. "I thought I could wire her lower jaw back together, but it's too bad even for that."

He stood up and stepped back so that he could lean against the truck. Bill joined him, sitting on the running board.

"Are you gonna make soup outta her?" Bill asked tentatively.

"No."

Bill inhaled deeply. He could smell the sweat of hard work and the mint-flavored gum that Ernie always carried in his shirt pocket.

"That," Ernie explained quietly, "is the last of the dinosaurs. You know why snappers keep moving even after they're dead?"

Bill shook his head. He just assumed snappers were that way, and no one at home told him differently. When his father beheaded one, the body continued to crawl around the yard until his father nailed the turtle by its tail to the light post so that the body would bleed out. After a few hours his father cut the turtle free from the base of its tail and, after flipping the animal over, unhinged it to get at the meat. The tail continued to move for days before becoming motionless. Until Bill touched it. Then the tail reflexed as though it were still alive.

"Well, scientifically speaking, they are considered primitive. Their nerve endings take a lot longer to die. This one is very old," he added. "You can tell by the shape and size of her shell. At least it looks as though she's laid her eggs already. You boys didn't bother the nest, did you?"

"No." Bill could answer that truthfully.

Ernie looked up, his gaze focused on the waving oats in his field. "If my father was here," he commented, "he'd tell you differently. He would tell you that turtle created the world."

They watched the snapper for a minute more until Ernie pushed himself off the truck.

"You better run up to the house and help Rose with supper. I'll take care of the snapper."

He gave Bill a small nudge. Bill knew what that meant. Ernie would take the .22 rifle he kept in the barn and shoot the turtle behind the head.

✖✖✖✖✖✖✖✖✖

They were just finishing dessert when they heard a car pull into the driveway and heard the dog bark. Ernie pushed back his chair and stood up from the table to look out the kitchen window.

"Billy, it's your dad."

Bill stiffened, unable to swallow the chocolate cake lumped on his tongue. He wiped his mouth and, guided by Rosemary, followed Ernie out of the porch door. He could hear Ernie calling their dog, Angel, away from the station wagon so that John Lucas could get out. Bill watched as Ernie caught the dog from lunging, holding him by his collar until Rosemary knelt down and wrapped her arms around the dog to physically restrain him. Ernie stood up.

"John." He extended his hand toward Bill's father.

John Lucas shook Ernie's hand as though it were covered with shit but unavoidable and said coldly, "I came to pick up Bill."

"Did Jimmy tell you we invited Bill to dinner?" Ernie asked.

John Lucas nodded. "We need him at home now. C'mon, Bill." John Lucas motioned to his younger son.

Ernie laid a hand on Bill's shoulder and let it slide off as Bill walked by him.

"Say, John, if you don't need Jimmy this summer, I'll pay him to work over here. I could use some help this summer."

John Lucas released his hand from the handle on the door, caught by Ernie's request. "Well, he can't do that. He won't be here this summer. James enlisted. He's leaving tomorrow."

Bill stopped before opening the passenger side door to the station wagon. *Enlisted.* Bill didn't understand what his father was talking about. He waited and listened for Ernie's response. But Ernie appeared stunned. Bill shifted his eyes to stare at his father.

John Lucas was a tall man with sparrow-colored hair and sallow skin. He towered over Ernie Morriseau, but Bill noticed that Ernie was more muscular, more compact than his father. He wondered which man would win, if it ever came to fists. But he didn't have to wonder long because he could see that Ernie would be able to drop his father despite John Lucas's height. All Ernie would have to do is punch John Lucas's soft white belly and the tall man would fall like a chain-sawed pine in the woods.

"Enlisted," Ernie repeated as though he hadn't heard right. "There's a *war* going on."

"Yeah," John Lucas snorted. "There usually is when you enlist. If you're a real man. James is gonna serve in the Marines like I did."

With that said, John Lucas's chest puffed out arrogantly, and he stared down at Ernie Morriseau before opening his car door and sliding into the driver's seat. Ernie looked as though he were going to say something, but he only nodded his head and walked back to the steps where his wife was standing. Bill did not see the dog, but he heard him, hysterically barking just inside the door.

✖✖✦✦✦✦✦✦✖✖

Bill waited tensely for the barrage of yelling to begin, but his father stayed silent during the short mile home.

"Do you want me to do somethin'?" he asked timidly when they got out of the car.

"Nah. Go play." Bill watched his father saunter into the house. Then he ran toward the lyrics of "Only the Lonely" streaming out of the hayloft.

✖✖✦✦✦✦✦✦✖✖

James wasn't dancing. He sat on a yellow hay bale, staring out the small window he had installed when he moved his record player into the loft. The smoke from his home-rolled cigarette anchored between his fingers drifted toward the barn rafters, and the ashes fell in gray clumps onto the wooden floor. An open Pabst bottle was next to his feet. Bill took a few steps forward and then waited to see if James would notice him. His brother's face was so blank, staring off in the distance at the house, that Bill couldn't tell what mood James was in. Bill decided to chance it.

"Your lungs are gonna turn black like Terry's."

James turned his head and stared at Bill. Stared through him. Bill shivered. Then his brother smiled. "How was dinner?"

Bill skipped over and sat on the hay bale next to James. "Great!"

"Yeah. Rosemary Morriseau sure is a good cook." He rubbed his chin with his free hand. He didn't seem hurt anymore. Bill waited for him to ask about the snapper. But James only took a drag on his cigarette, reaching over to flip the record before exhaling the smoke. Roy Orbison's melodious voice surrounded the space around them. Bill silently sang along to "In Dreams."

They sat for a while and listened to the music. Finally Bill couldn't wait any longer.

"Dad says you enlisted."

"Yup." James picked up his beer and took a long swallow.

"What does that mean?"

James glanced at him, his eyebrows pulled together over his eyes. "You know. *Enlisted*," he answered irritably, and looked again at Bill to see if he understood.

Bill still didn't understand.

"It means," his brother explained, "that I joined the military of my own free will instead of being drafted. You know. Forced to go."

Bill kicked a dried chunk of manure off the toe of one of his sneakers.

"I'm leaving tomorrow," James said, dropping his cigarette on the floor and smashing it with the heel of one boot. "Mom and the old man are driving me to the bus station."

"How come you didn't tell me?" Bill's chest quivered, and his eyes watered.

"I dunno," James answered. "I guess after I signed up, I couldn't believe I did it. I signed up last winter, and it just didn't seem like the day would come when I'd have to leave."

Bill began to shake.

"Oh, Christ. Don't cry. I meant to tell you."

Bill's chest hammered even though he heard the words. James tensed and then relaxed. He ran one hand through his slicked hair before flinging it and his arm around Bill's shoulders.

"Hey!" he said, shaking Bill gently. "Is this the same kid that chases everything with that stupid sword? The dog can't even take a piss when he sees you comin' with that turtle shell and hunk of wood. Hell," he added with a strange laugh. "Maybe you oughta join the Marines with me. I'll just tell them you're a midget or somethin' like that."

Bill giggled.

"Here," James said, holding the bottle toward Bill. "Have a sip of my beer."

Bill looked at his brother's long fingers wrapped around the bottle. His fingernails were transparently white even though his hands had been covered with dirt and blood that afternoon. Even the bandage on his thumb was still clean and white. But that was his brother. James was fastidious about his appearance right down to the intricate and unseen details like the perfectly clipped toenails on his feet. Bill couldn't imagine James as a solider, like the soldiers they watched in the WW II movies on TV, trudging through the muddy jungles of the Pacific or bunkered up in a bombed-out café in Italy. Bill took a small sip of beer, swallowing it quickly to get rid of the bitter taste. He gave the bottle back to his brother and wiped his nose on the front of his T-shirt.

"Well, the old man is happy. He's finally getting rid of me. After basic training in San Diego, they'll probably send me to Vietnam." He took another long swig of beer, the condensation from the cold bottle wetting his fingers.

"Dad was in the Marines. In World War Two," Bill said, thinking their father was happy because James was doing what he had done.

His brother snorted with disgust. "The old man was only in for the last few months of the war." James sneered, rolling another cigarette.

"Ernie Morriseau is a different story." James spoke again, tilting his head in the direction of the Morriseau farm. "Ernie saw a lotta action in WW Two, in the Philippines. He's still got shrapnel in him. You know those blue bumps on his back?"

Bill nodded.

"Well, that's metal working its way to the surface. That metal is twenty-some years old."

Bill remembered seeing those bumps when Ernie worked shirtless in the heat.

"Rosemary cuts out the shrapnel closest to the skin with a razor blade," James added.

He didn't put on another record and instead puffed away on his cigarette. Bill chewed on a piece of straw. Shadows descended across the diminishing light from the window, and the thin strands of sunlight that had shone through the cracks in the rafters were gone.

"We better go in," James said, and stood up.

They walked to the ladder, and James motioned for Bill to go down first. When Bill was halfway down, James spoke, his deep voice echoing above Bill's head. "You comin' to the bus station tomorrow?"

Bill paused, one leg already down on the next rung, and looked up. He was dumbfounded. Of course he would go because James was leaving and Bill wanted to see him off. And he was only eight. Where else would he be since he was still too young to be left at home alone?

"Yeah, I'm comin'."

In the brief moment before he released his other leg, Bill thought he saw a shining glint in his brother's eyes, but James looked away, so all Bill could see was his shadow-covered Elvis head.

✕✦✦✦✦✦✦✦✦✕

The next morning Bill crept out of the house in his pajamas and ran for the toolshed. He scooped the turtle shell and sword out of the woodbin and raced around to the back side of the barn, where he couldn't be seen. He had heard his enemies calling him and taunting him all night to come out. Come out and fight them. He kicked off his sneakers, already soaked by the early-morning dew, and positioned his bare feet on the dusty ground. He raised his turtle shield so that it covered the left side of his chest and, with his right hand, gripped the sword.

Swish! One came at him almost before he was ready, but Bill managed to dance aside, catching his enemy in the neck. He heard the footsteps of another behind him and swung around very fast, extending his sword out so that it sliced that enemy in half. Bill weaved backward and forward, sideways and back, while his enemies came at him with the unnatural energy of those who did not need sleep. He heard them call his name, and he raised his shield to identify himself. But he was too fast for them, and they began to pile up like dead flies. Then, while Bill was in the middle of a battle that was forcing him up against the barn, he heard one of them call his brother's name.

James.

Bill lowered his sword, and the enemy in front of him disappeared. They all disappeared. Bill was listening for the voice again when he heard his mother calling him.

"William Lucas! Get in here and get ready for breakfast!"

Bill reluctantly walked around the barn to the toolshed. He opened the woodbin and placed his sword and shield on top of the cut wood. He briefly wondered where Ernie had buried the snapper and if it would be a sin to dig up the grave so that he could have the shell.

"Bill! Quit dawdling and get in here! Now!"

He trotted back to the house.

◆◆◆◆◆◆◆◆◆

James was okay through breakfast, even joking with their mother, and he was okay when they loaded his duffel bag into the backseat before he got into the station wagon. Bill noticed that James really looked like Elvis that morning. His hair was ridged especially high, and his rockabilly black boots shone with new polish. He winked at Bill when their father swore at the truck in front of them for going so slow. But when they pulled into the Standard gas station that doubled as the bus stop in the middle of town, James's face went blank, and he got out of the station wagon stiffly.

The bus wasn't due for another half an hour, so they waited inside the station on rickety green plastic chairs. Bill passed the time by pushing his nose up against the dirty picture window, allowing him to see the cars that drove up next to the gas pumps for refueling. Their father leaned back in his chair and dozed, the bristly hair in his nostrils quivering every time he inhaled and exhaled. Their mother nervously fanned herself with a tattered Wisconsin road map even though it wasn't that hot, and James sat as though frozen to his chair. Bill watched the two service station attendants scurry between the cars before fixing his eyes on a Volkswagen parked behind the station's red tow truck.

It was the third time he'd seen one of those little cars that did indeed look like beetles. Nobody in town owned one. "Hippie cars," his father sneered once. It was covered, front to back, with bumper stickers and Bill squinted to catch the print on some of them. One said "I don't wanna know your name 'cause I don't like your game," and another one said "Flower Power."

Bill thought that one was pretty funny. "Flower Power." He giggled, and his mother momentarily stopped fanning herself to see what amused her son. He squinted again. Some of the stickers were too small for him to make out. Then for the first time, he noticed the huge sticker on the driver's door: "Get Out of Vietnam!"

Vietnam. That's where James was going. He tugged on his brother's sleeve and pointed to the car. "The door," he whispered.

James craned his neck around Bill's head and stared. He stared for a long time.

When James finally pulled his head back, it was in slow motion, as though his eyes had had to take minutes each to look from the car to the glass wall, to the gas station attendants still hurrying between cars, and finally, to resting upon a pile of magazines stacked up against the glass in front of him. Bill watched as his brother swallowed, his Adam's apple rising and dropping like a fishing bobber.

"The bus," their mother said, pointing with the map at the gray whale-size vehicle turning into the station. Bill hopped up and followed his parents to the door. He was almost out of the door when he realized that James was still sitting in his chair. He squeezed through the rapidly closing door and ran back to his brother.

"C'mon! You'll miss your bus!" Bill grabbed James's bandaged hand. His brother got up slowly. Bill felt his brother's hand tighten around his own, and he tugged insistently, leading James out of the door. Their father stood by the gas pumps.

"Better move along now. I already gave your duffel bag to the driver."

Their mother hugged James, secretly slipping a twenty-dollar bill into his jacket pocket. Bill watched as James returned the hug with such vigor that it lifted their mother off her feet.

The bus driver motioned that he had to get going.

"You'll be okay," John Lucas said, stifling a yawn.

"Send us your picture and address," their mother added tearfully.

James released his arms from around their mother. He turned to Bill and abruptly swept him up into his arms, squeezing Bill's chest so hard that he could barely breathe.

"I told Terry and the other guys that if they touched you at all, I'd beat their heads in," he whispered. Bill could feel the hot breath from his brother in his ear. "And listen," he whispered again, "*don't be like me.*"

Then he lowered Bill to the ground and walked toward the bus.

James put one foot up on the first step when he turned around and waved. Bill raised his hand to wave back but stopped when he spotted something shadowing his brother's head. Bill stepped forward and tilted his head. He quickly turned around to see if his father and mother appeared to notice anything. They didn't seem to and continued waving. Bill thought the bright morning sun was playing tricks on his eyes or that it was the rays shining off James's greased black hair. When Bill looked back at his brother, it was gone.

James got on the bus, and they watched him select a seat, waving again once he was seated. "Go Greyhound," the panel on the side of the bus stated, and Bill looked at the skinny gray dog running in front of the words. With an eruption of black diesel exhaust, the bus began its roll south down the highway. The excitement he had felt moments before had chilled, and his stomach felt queasy.

Bill and his mother continued to stare at the bus until it became a speck on the black and yellow-ribboned highway. They waited until it finally disappeared from their sight.

"C'mon. I don't have all day," John Lucas muttered irritably.

Bill's mother took his hand, and they walked slowly to the car.

Bill paused before opening the car door and watched his mother open hers.

"Yeah, they'll probably ship him out to Vietnam after six weeks. He'll be okay," his father was saying when Bill crawled into the backseat.

Bill looked over at his mother. Her eyes were shut, and she was slumped down in the front seat as though asleep, but Bill could see her lower lip trembling. He lay across the backseat to settle his upset stomach.

"He'll be okay. He always is," his father drawled again to no one in particular, draping one arm across the top of the steering wheel.

Bill folded his arms over his chest and watched the blurred green scenery go by as they sped down the highway. He shut his eyes.

When the car stopped moving, he opened them and realized they were home. Without a word to his parents, he scrambled out of the car and ran to the toolshed for his sword and shield. He lured the dog into the shed with a dog biscuit and locked him inside so that he wouldn't follow Bill. Then he cut through the woods, staying off the gravel road and following the edge of the big swamp until he reached the Chippewa River. The sand had remained clawed up, and the blood was still there, soaked into the sand. A red-brown stain. Bill scooped up the bloody sand and put it inside the shell. He threaded his sword under the rope lengthwise, front to end, on the carapace.

He picked up the shell filled with the bloody sand and balanced with his sword and waded into the river up to his knees. He placed the upturned shell in the water and watched as it bobbed in the strong current. It floated toward the middle of the river where the watery movement was the strongest. There the current seized the shell and pushed it down the middle of the river, going south.

◆◆◆◆ MY HUSBAND PARKED THE STATION wagon underneath the elm by the chicken coop. The moment the car came to a halt, I felt Bill come to life in the backseat. I watched as my younger son scrambled out of the station wagon and ran toward the barn. I did not have the energy to call after him, to find out where he was going. It took everything I had just to clasp the door handle, to push open the door. Before I could swing my legs out, my husband reached over and tapped me on the shoulder.

"He has to do this, you know. He has to serve his country. He can't be your mamma's boy anymore. Vietnam," he said, exhaling smoke, "will make him grow up."

He waited to see my reaction. His face cracked into that grin that always followed after he tried to hurt me. On a small child such a smile would be welcome—the happiness of having accomplished something after a lot of hard work, such as working round blocks into round holes and square blocks into square holes—but such a smile on a grown man is sinister and foreboding. He had played tricks like this before, trying to provoke a fight. It took me a few years, but I had learned to display nothing of what I was feeling. I had learned the passive tactics of defense.

When no reaction appeared, he sat as though pondering what he thought was the wisdom of his own words, smoking his cigarette and flicking the ashes out of the window.

The exhaustion I felt disappeared. My husband's words thundered and struck like lightning, leaving the burned remains of his twisted logic tattooed on my brain. They opened a vein of strength I had no idea existed within me until that moment.

I looked at my hands. I felt the clarity of purpose in my hands.

I opened the door but held on to the top edge to steady myself. Then I began to walk alongside the car. One hand over the other, each hand placed palm side down and flat against the hot hood of the blue station wagon. I leaned my head back and stared at my husband through the windshield but did not stop the cat walk of my hands. John pulled his cigarette from his mouth and let his arm and hand dangle outside the door. His mouth fell open. I turned so that I faced the front of the station wagon and pawed my way across it, my eyes never shifting from their focus. He squinted and tilted his head back. His fingers dropped the cigarette on the ground.

When I reached his door, I bent down so that my face was level with his. At the same time I ground the burning cigarette into the gravel of the driveway with the toe of my shoe.

"What in Christ's name is wrong with you all of a sudden?"

"Be careful," I warned him in a voice so low that it sounded like the territorial rumbling in a cat's chest.

I stood up and looked down at him.

"Be careful."

I took the chance and waited. He could have opened the door and slammed it into me. Grabbed me by my hair. But he was spooked. He moved away from the window, and I saw his shaking hands pull out another cigarette from the pack of Salems on the dashboard.

"You're crazy!"

I turned around and walked toward the house. He had started the engine before I even reached the door, and I watched as he backed the car out the driveway. One straight and fast shot backward, then the squeal of tires as he straightened the car out of the driveway entrance and gunned it for town. I knew I had scared him. At least for a while.

I went in the house, got a cup of coffee, and then sat on the porch steps. I wondered where Bill had gone, and I decided I would give him an hour. Then I would get up and look for him.

I tried to remember when things were different. When I first saw my husband.

✖✦✦✦✦✦✦✖

I met John at a dance. It was after the war, and it seemed like everybody met their future husbands and wives at a VFW dance. He was tall and blond and handsome in his uniform, as all the men were. He leaned forward when he talked to me, as though my answers to his questions were as deeply meaningful as Aristotle's. He had big plans. He was intent, he told me, on going to college on the GI Bill. I mistook that for a healthy ambition, and so I said yes to his proposal. I thought I was in love. He said our marriage vows almost tearfully, as though I were the greatest gift he could ever have been given. I believed that I was set for life and that he would fulfill his prescribed role as provider and loving husband just as I would be a loving wife and good mother. But he quit college after a year, and it was a year into our marriage. I had a college degree and had taught high school for two years. He resented it although he wouldn't come out and say so. His rationale for my quitting teaching was that I didn't make enough money at it and we would be better served by my staying at home. He laughed at my visits to the library, how many books I read, the kinds of books I read, and made fun of my expensive liberal education. Within six months of our marriage his voice gradually stopped being loving, and as he spoke, his words became more and more coated with sarcasm. Only when he wanted to move up north did some of his former charm return, and he continually worked on me until I gave in. I told myself that our marriage would become better and that farming might bring forth some of my own hidden desires as well as some much-needed space from my mother, who had made my life in Milwaukee, in some ways, as unendurable as John's father had made his.

✕✦✦✦✦✦✦✦✕

I remember when I first saw the farm. It seemed so *northern*. So *wild*. It was early fall, and I walked the place with old Mrs. Hausherr. I gasped when I saw the giant white pine stumps in the fencerow.

"Ja," she said, acknowledging my shock. "This place once had big pine. But it needed to be cleared so we could farm it. Those big timbers in the barn are white pine."

Some of the pine stumps were six feet in diameter. They shocked me as much as if I had witnessed an execution, and my recollection of French history suddenly became vivid. The stumpy remains of the white pine resembled the eighteenth-century illustrations of men and women after their heads had been sliced off by the guillotine. The bloody, pulpy necks. The sap had oozed up just as blood would have and had covered the stumps' surfaces. Much of it was no longer sticky but hard and brown and on its way to becoming amber.

The Hausherrs were in their seventies, and their sorrow at leaving was visible. Their children wanted them to come to Milwaukee because they were tired of making the long trip back and forth to make sure their parents were all right. I thought it was ironic that we were trading directions. They were going south for an easier life, and we supposedly were headed north for an easier life.

While Emil Hausherr talked to John, Anna Hausherr showed me the house and surrounding yard. "There is new plumbing!" she proudly announced.

"Oh. When did you have the plumbing replaced?"

"Replaced? We never had plumbing before that!"

She guided me to the porch, and we looked out of the window. That was when I noticed the tall and narrow shack not far from the chicken coop.

"Two years ago we were still using the outhouse. Or—" she joked, her hooded eyes crinkling—"the *Schmidt* house, as Emil calls it after we saw a cartoon in the *Milwaukee Journal*. It had Santa and all the reindeer perched on top of an outhouse and Santa was saying, 'Rudolph! I said the Schmidt house. Not the shit house!' We laughed pretty hard over that one. You see, our neighbors to the south are the Schmidts. We never did get along with them." She gestured with her head toward the south.

"You should keep it," she added, "in case of emergencies. I'm still not sure about that plumbing . . . our kids chipped in and had it done for us, but I didn't mind using the outhouse."

She was proud of her house, but it was when she showed me her garden that her voice caught and she covered her mouth from time to time.

"There is rocks," she said. "Always rocks. I think they grow here. Every year I had to rake out more rocks, and the children, when they were younger, hated picking rock. But I could grow good lettuce and tomatoes and good, good potatoes. Flowers too. Zinnias, marigold, some daisies. Imogene Morriseau showed me how to use a cold frame to get them started early. Her husband, Claude, showed Emil how to do maple syruping."

When we went back inside the house, she took me downstairs into the basement to show me the housewarming gift she had left for us: rows and rows of canned vegetables, pickles, maple syrup, and berries. The jars glistened like jewels even under the dull light of a single bulb. Dark blueberries, ruby-colored beets, and the green of pickled cucumbers.

"Oh, my," I said, overwhelmed and thinking of my mother's advice never to take food from people I didn't know, "don't you want to take these with you? Your husband will want them and your children too."

"*Ach!*" she exclaimed. "My children only like store-bought food. It is good food," she said as though reading my mind. She smiled proudly. "I have a cabinet shelf full of ribbons from the county fair for my canned goods."

I knew she had many children—nine, I think—and so I wondered why none of them wanted the farm.

"Well, we did have a son," she said haltingly, "who wanted the farm. Our youngest boy, Joseph. He was my late-in-life baby, and he loved this place. But he enlisted and went to France. He died there."

"I'm sorry."

We stood in the basement for a long time in silence. Then she grabbed my hand and led me back upstairs and out of the house. She must have sensed my nervousness and my fear of so much wildness.

"It will come to you. You'll see." She patted my cheek. "Your children will love it, and so will you."

She turned away slightly and watched John as he talked to her husband in the driveway.

"Your husband," she commented dryly, "does he know much about farming?"

✕◆◆◆◆◆◆◆◆✕

I remembered her hands, so calloused and thick from hard work. Her legs were wrapped in Ace bandages to help ease the pressure from varicose veins. Her face was ruddy and full of little wrinkles that folded her skin inward. The blue plates of her eyes underneath the cowl of skin that draped over them. The look on her face when she spoke of her youngest son. She had probably said good-bye to her son on the very porch steps I was sitting on.

Does a house come with pain? I wondered, thinking of the way Anna Hausherr patted my face and looked at me so kindly as if to give me bread for a long journey.

I drank the rest of my coffee. I knew I would have to take a nap. I had not slept the night before, and I felt as tight as a bowstring ever since seeing Jimmy board the bus. My head hurt, and I heard a buzzing noise.

I thought of John's smile. That malevolent look on his face. I was so angry I thought I could almost smell the smoke from the in‑visible lightning that had struck me a half an hour before. I could not believe what my husband had said.

Vietnam will make him grow up.

I felt something snap.

✗✗✗✗ EVER SINCE HIS BROTHER LEFT for Vietnam, Bill had the same dream. Only it wasn't as much a dream so much as it was a sensation. It beat across the insides of his eyelids, and he could see the slits of sunlight as the white feathers expanded to soar on a current of air. He was underneath, but he couldn't see anything except the feathers. The wind whistled in his ears, and the feathers flapped against the bright yellow sunlight. He was being carried, but Bill could not see where, and he could not turn his head because it was held in a viselike, even painful grip. While he was listening intently to the melodious whistling, it became shrill, and he was suddenly dropped. His arms beat frantically against the wind, but they were useless. He heard the sound of his own voice, but it did not say what he had intended, what would have been natural. It did not say "Mamma!" or "Help!" It said:

"Billy!"

His mother's voice cut through his fall.

"Here," she said, shaking his shoulder. He strained to open his eyes, recognizing that it was still night. He could see the outline of his mother but not the details of her face. She was waving something white in front of him.

"From your brother," she said before dropping it on the covers and disappearing from his room. He pulled an arm out from underneath the covers and groped for the white thing. A letter. Still shaking from his dream, Bill crawled out of bed and onto the floor to the night-light by the closet. He sleepily crossed his legs and ripped the top of the letter open with his thumb. Then he held the seemingly fragile paper under the dim yellow light to read.

Camp Schwab, Okinawa, Sept-67

Dear Billy Baboon (just kidding),

I know it's been awhile since I wrote to you. We're stuck in the compound this week. It's been hard to get some time alone here. Seems like when that happens, the guys want to play poker or do something. I told them tonight, though, I had to write to my little brother. How are you doing? How's Beans? I just got a letter from Mom so I know she's doing okay. Well, okay enough I guess.

I'm doing okay. Man, you should see the weather here! I'll never complain about another Wisconsin summer again. It gets hotter than hell here, and so muggy that I feel like I'm wet all the time. If you were here, you'd be running around bare-ass naked—except it wouldn't be allowed 'cause you'd be a running target. My sergeant says I shoot pretty good. I don't give a damn if I shoot good or not anymore. When I come home, I don't want to see another gun again. Even if I have to bust the ones we have over the old man's head just to get rid of them. And him too.

Did I tell you they call me Elvis Jr? My buddy, Marv, even painted it on my helmet. I don't know why they call me that, all my hair is shaved off. Did you hide all my albums like I told you to? If it looks like the old man is getting close to finding them, take them over to the Morriseaus'. Mrs. Morriseau will keep them for me.

I better go. Keep writing and let me know what's going on there. I'll write again in a bit—hopefully before they send us up to somewhere near Laos—it's still a rumor, though. Don't worry, I'll be back soon.

Love James

P.S. I sent Mom some money—don't tell the old man. He'll take it
away from her and use it on a beer dream. I sent you some too. Keep
it under your mattress, or better yet, hide it in the barn in case of
emergencies.

Bill looked down at the two twenty-dollar bills that had slipped out
and fallen to the floor while he read the letter. He picked them up
and stared at them. He lifted his head, still in the trance of so much
money for an eight-year-old boy, and gazed at the twin bed across
from him. *James.* Bill's mother always called his brother "Jimmy," as
did their neighbors and the rest of the community, but Bill, looking
at his brother's empty bed, had always called him "James." Like
James Dean, another one of his brother's idols besides Elvis. Or Saint
James, although his brother was anything but a saint before he left.
There was the good and the bad James, but the letters Bill had gotten so far seemed full of the good James.

He crawled back to the bed, hefted the mattress up, and slipped
the letter underneath with the other letters his brother had sent.
This was the first time James had sent money, though. He folded the
bills in half and tucked them under his pillow. Tomorrow before
school he'd have to think about where in the barn to hide the
money and the letters. He climbed back into bed and pulled the covers up next to his chin. Feeling the coldness of the sheets at the
spooky end of the bed, he bent his legs and curled his toes. Since
James had left, he worried even more about the safety of his feet so
close to where *something* could reach up from underneath the bed and
grab them. And no one, not his mother in her few hours of peace, or
his father in his Pabst-saturated slumber, would hear him like James.

He turned on his side so he could look again at his brother's bed,
covered with a white crocheted spread and untouched now for five
months. He thought about the letters lying underneath him and the
ghostly way his mother always brought these letters to him in his
sleep. As though they didn't exist in the daytime. As though his
brother didn't exist except at night, a black inky voice on white paper.

The wind whispered through the pine boughs outside his window. He slowly dropped off to sleep again and waited for the feathers.

✕✦✦✦✦✦✦✦✕

The next morning he crept out of the house early, clutching a large blue mason jar in his arms and the letters and money stuffed inside his shirt. It was late October, and he'd forgotten his jacket in his desperation to get to the barn and back before his parents woke up. By the time he reached the creaky old barn door, he was shaking violently from the freezing morning whip of fall temperatures. He put the money and the letters in the jar and buried it deep in a corner of the barn where he knew the loose hay would be untouched by his father. After peeking out of the barn door to check for signs of life and seeing none, he streaked across the barnyard and slipped back into the house.

✕✦✦✦✦✦✦✦✕

"Billy, why don't you want to go outside and play? It's not that cold!" Sister Agnes questioned him at the beginning of the morning recess.

"Nooo." He faltered and, swallowing quickly, came up with an excuse. "I thought I'd practice my penmanship."

The excuse glided across his lips better than he thought, and Sister Agnes beamed with an approving smile. "All right then."

He watched the long black skirt of her habit glide as smoothly as his excuse out the door to the playground. He opened his notebook and began to write in his usual scrawl print.

Wednesday

Dear Elvis Jr (ha, ha),

I am doing okay to. I hid the money in the barn. Dad hasnt found your records. He has been pretti drunk. Mom and me found him on Saturday in the field sleepng. He ran over Beans to.

Bill stopped momentarily and stared out of the classroom window, the recent death of his dog causing beads of tears to escape. He wiped them away and continued to write.

> I buryd him behind the barn. Do you use bombs? Will you teech me how to shoot befor you bust our guns? I am writng this at school. Its been pretti cold. But no snow. We are havng turky for thanks givng. Mom says becase your not here to get a goose. I am going to help Mom bake cookes. So we can send them to you.

He heard the wild laughter of many children fill the hallway outside the door.

> Resess is over. I got to go.

> Love Bill

He quickly stuffed the letter inside his desk as the room filled with third graders.

"How's the penmanship?" Sister Agnes's voice loomed up behind him.

"Getting better," he answered in a small, tinny voice, and tried to shrink himself further down into his seat.

"That's good," she said, patting his shoulder, her long skirt brushing past him.

He let out a deep sigh, relief buoying him back up to his normal size.

When he got home from school, he'd ask his mother for an envelope and a stamp. He'd painstakingly write James's address in small letters so it didn't swamp the front of the envelope the way his writing usually did. Under his address, though, in the top left-hand corner, he would write "USA" in big block letters, and he did the same under James's address with the words "SOUTH VIETNAM." Then his mother would take the letter and correct the address, and it would mysteriously disappear until he saw her from the frosted bus windows in the morning thrust two letters (hers included) into the pale gray mailbox that said "LUCAS" on the side and jack the red flag up.

Every day, as the bus rumbled down the gravel road toward town, he watched her dwindling figure walk tiredly up the long driveway saluted by red pines until the bus rounded the curve in the road and he could see her no more. She wore the same thing—an old pair of green rubber hunting boots over her slippers and a black-and-white plaid jacket that covered a housedress of faded blue polka dots—and her black hair was still wound in foamy pink rollers that from a distance looked to Bill like newborn mice under the pale blue netting of her nylon scarf. The bus became hushed when he got on, and he fervently prayed every morning that she would wait until the bus rounded the curve before she began talking aloud to the pines as she walked back to the house. That she would keep her hands to her sides until then, before moving them through the cold air as if explaining *something*, as if to touch *someone* strolling beside her.

Then it would start up.

"Hey, Luuucassss," Merton Schmidt would tauntingly croon, sometimes putting a finger up his nose. "Hey, Puuccass! How come your mother's crazee and your dad's a stinkin' drunk? Maybe 'cause yer all LUC-ASSES. Hey! My brother says your brother *should* get a bullet between the ears jus' for bein' a dumb ass and enlistin'! But hey! He's a LUC-ASS, right!" And Merton would laugh so loudly it resonated through the bus like several jackhammers.

Merton Schmidt was thirteen and supernaturally big for his age, so big that the other kids called him Shit House Schmidt but never to his face unless they wanted to run for the rest of their tiny lives. Bill's brother called Merton the little Hun, but names didn't do Bill any good even though his hatred of Merton outdistanced even his hatred of his father on some days. Bill kept his face pressed to the cold bus window and tried to keep the crying safely down in his stomach or Merton would be on him. He vainly struggled to picture his brother's face, but all he could see was his walking, talking mother in the driveway. He bit his trembling lower lip and gazed out of the window. He ran the same gauntlet of teasing every day.

One morning, after a particularly severe verbal beating from Merton, he turned his face to the window only to see the family's blue Chevy station wagon lodged into the ditch by the curve and the upper torso of his father hanging out of the driver's window, a smiling haze over his unconscious face. The bus didn't stop.

"Hey, Billy," the bus driver yelled back, "I'll call somebody to haul him outta there when we get to town."

A grin broke across Merton's face, and the shots from his mouth began all over again. Bill's nine-year-old heart split open with pain. He stayed huddled in the bus seat, his eyes barely level with the bottom of the window. But he continued to peer out of the window, watching a scattered group of crows circle above the pines and wishing desperately that he were one of them.

Thankfully, Merton rarely rode the bus home from school, instead catching a ride with his father, who worked at the feed store. And Bill's mother did not walk down the driveway to greet him when the rattling black and orange bus brought him home.

✕✦✦✦✦✦✦✦✦✕

Bill ate his grayish brown oatmeal with an island of peanut butter in the middle. He watched as his mother leaned against the countertop, watched her eyes drift toward the kitchen window where she stared at the frozen fields and adjoining swamp and woods. He never forgot what he had overheard their neighbor Rosemary Morriseau say to her husband, although Bill knew it was not meant harshly, just sadly.

"Poor Claire." Rosemary sighed quietly to herself while she washed the supper dishes and her husband, Ernie, polished his boots.

Bill pretended to read a book in their living room, but he secretly watched Rosemary. She tapped the side of her head. "She's touched."

He thought he understood what that expression meant but not in reference to his mother. Sister Agnes often said it when she described the various saints. "They were touched," she said, meaning God touched them. Wasn't that a good thing? Did that mean his mother was a saint? Is that why his mother behaved the way she did?

On the weekends she wandered through the house during the day, talking and talking, her tired and haunted face appearing in one of the windows every so often when Bill was outside playing. She used to hit him. And shake him until he thought his head would snap off, rolling across the floor like a bowling ball and crashing into the legs of the furniture. That had changed after his brother left. When anger flushed her face, she kept her arms and fists locked to herself now and just yelled at him. Even the yelling had tapered off. She had become, gradually, his ally.

◆◆◆◆◆◆◆◆◆

He was being carried again. This time he could look down, and the Chippewa River was a black, wriggly cord in the landscape sweeping beneath him, and everything beside it was covered with snow. The whistling filled his head. The grip was not so tight now, but it held him firmly. He spread his bare toes and wiggled them in the rushing wind. But it was not cold; it was *warm,* like maple syrup was warm after it settled on his hot pancakes. He spread out his arms to catch the same feeling as his toes. The whistling slowly took on a familiar tune, something he'd heard in the not-too-distant past. He could see his brother's face, his Brylcreemed hair, his dark, narrowed eyes. What was it? He listened harder. It was . . . "My baby does the hanky panky"!

"James!" he shouted. It was his brother whistling "My baby does the hanky panky." Bill laughed. He laughed, and his heart felt whole. He laughed at the waves of wind pushing his hair off his face. And he began to sing. . . .

✸✸✸✸✸✸✸✸✸✸

"Shshsh. Wake up," she said, nudging his head. It was close to Christmas, and another letter floated out of the darkness and onto his blanket. He blinked, trying to catch the dim outline of his mother. She caressed his forehead and then was gone. He almost fell out of bed in his sleepy but hurried effort to get to the night-light. Then he opened the letter, the whistling still echoing in his ears.

Dec-67

Hey Bill,

I can't believe it's going to be Christmas soon. It doesn't snow here near Khe Sanh, but it rains. And rains and rains. It's a lot cooler than being in Okinawa. It looks like there is snow in the highlands, but it is hard to tell—they're mostly green with a little purple. I had a dream the other night that you and me were down at the river—I don't know—fishing or something. It was a good dream. I needed it 'cause it's been a bad week. I lost one of my best buddies, Rick. We were on recon patrol, and I heard the shot before I saw Rick go down. We all dropped into cover. I couldn't even cry. That's how fast it all happened. I know I rolled over twice, and then I lifted my rifle and saw the little bastard. Well, he is no more. I guess you could say that he wasn't by himself either. It's like Mom used to say: If you see one mouse, you know you've got twenty. 'Course you're the guy who brought them into the house (ha-ha).

I'm still not feeling so good. I got some kind of shit growing on my toes too—our medic says it's immersion foot—you know—like athlete's foot except it's worse over here. My feet look like Mom's bread dough. God, I can't wait to come home.

Say I'm sorry about Beans. Goddamn the old man. He's got to fucking destroy everything he touches. He should come over here and trade places with me. I'll bet he'd be one big chicken running through the rice paddies. You know why he's that way? Cause he's SCARED. I used to wonder about him, but since I've been in Nam, I've figured it out. He's fucking scared of everything, but he's really scared of Mom. Cause he knows she's better than he is. When I come home, he better watch out for me cause I'm gonna bust his fucking head.

I'm sorry I couldn't get you a Christmas present. But I sent along some money. I sent Mom some money too and told her to spend it on herself. Make sure she does it, okay? Thanks for the cookies, they were really good. My buddy Marv's sister sent him some cookies, but they were as hard as grenades. After I ate one, I felt like my stomach was gonna blow up too. We used the rest for target practice.

Pray for me. Some days I feel like I'm rotting. Probably cause it's my own damn fault. I guzzle beer over here as much as the old man when I get a chance to. I need to over here, to forget I'm here. Keep writing. The guys think your letters are great. Merry Christmas.

Love you, James

There were splotches in places, where the ink had run slightly. Bill traced a finger across the raised wrinkles in the paper where the splotches were. His brother had been crying. Bill shivered and looked up at the white winter moon framed in his window. Its light reflected off the snow-covered Norway pines next to the house and filled his room with its pale winter glow. He gazed at the moon, absently fingering the money James had sent, seventy-five dollars in all. Bill shivered again. His brother talked to him like he never had before. He talked to him like a *buddy* and not his little brother. He picked up the letter and held it up against the moonlight. It was written in late December, but he didn't know what day or time, and his brother was changing, and he couldn't see or touch him.

Bill crawled back over to the bed and lifted the mattress to stash the letter and money underneath until morning. Then he grabbed his notebook and pencil from where they lay on the floor at the foot of his bed and crawled back to the night-light. He would cheer his brother up.

Friday

Dear James Dean (ha-ha),

I had a dreem to. Just you and me and we was flying over the river. And you was singng to. And you had wings. But not chiken wings. Big wings. I saw Bunny at the store. She says hi you good lookng devil. Sister says my spellng is gettng beter. I have ben playng with Angel. He is a good dog and Mrs. Moriso says I can play with him all I want. But I cant bring him home becase you know. I am going to buy Mom some perfum for Christmas. We sent your presants out last week. Mom cut my hair. Now I dont have none to. My ears get cold. Can I have your red hat? I wont wreck it. I promise. I am writing this in the midle of the night. The moon is realy white. I member the foxs you showd me. Well its like that now. We got lots of snow. Me and Mom are going to church to pray for you. I will be good and pray doubly hard. I got to go to bed now.

Love from your brother,

Billy Baboon

P.S. I will pray for your buddy Rick.

Bill folded the letter and placed it on top of his notebook so he wouldn't forget it in the morning. He climbed into bed, curled himself into a fetal position, and stared at the shadows on the wall made by the snow-laden pine boughs in the moonlight. Christmas was going to be extra hard without James. But he sent money, and that would help some. Bill's father, John Lucas, had been drinking more and working less, but for the past two weeks he had been gone most of the time, logging for the lumber mill in Olina. He would be back for Christmas, however. Bill pulled the covers up over his face and shut his eyes tightly to bring back the dream. But water squeaked through, and he cried himself to sleep instead.

✕✦✦✦✦✦✦✦✦✕

"What does he write when he writes to you?"

Bill looked up from his oatmeal. It was Saturday, and he was in no hurry to eat his breakfast. His mother's face was hollow-looking and colorless as though she had not slept. She propped her elbows up on the table and rested her face in her hands.

"What does he write when he writes to you?" she repeated.

"Jus' letters," Bill mumbled. He swallowed another spoonful of his oatmeal.

His mother sighed heavily. "I know something isn't right. But he always says he's fine when he writes to me. And he sends so much *money*."

Bill almost stopped his spoon in midair but caught himself and neatly guided it into his mouth. He felt the blanket of his mother's gaze cover him.

"Billy. Can I read the letters he sends to you? I promise I won't say anything."

Bill quietly placed his spoon on the table. He was hoping she wouldn't ask that. He looked up and silently scrutinized his mother's face. He watched for any sign, a false smile, or too many tears, or even one tear, that might signal her betrayal, signal her old anger that would pull him across the kitchen by his hair if he said no. There was nothing. Nothing but exhaustion so pure it rendered his mother a sagging shell, and he thought he could almost see through her to the kitchen sink.

"I'll give 'em to you at lunch. But you gotta give 'em back before—"

But he didn't have to finish because his mother knew. She nodded, reaching out slowly to touch her small son's teak-colored hair. Bill's mouth fell open as he watched her arm extend itself toward him, toward his quivering face, and all he could see and feel was a thin finger of sunlight gently touch his head.

✕✦✦✦✦✦✦✦✕

Pray for me.

He always thought of the Sacred Heart Church as a large brick cave. Except that it was dry, not damp, and the cavernous ceiling was covered with frescoes of trumpeting angels and the ascension of the Virgin Mary into heaven, painted by the German immigrant artists who first settled Olina. It was surprisingly empty even for a Saturday afternoon. He tagged after his mother in the enormous hush of the empty church, trying to keep his bulky winter boots from thumping. There were two votive light stands on either side of the church, placed before the steps to the altar. Four rows of twelve short white candles, most of them unlit, filled the ornate wrought-iron stands. Each stand had a small iron box with a slit in it for dimes. A dime to light one candle, one lit candle to pray for a beloved's soul, a piece of fire to keep the prayer alive.

As if by silent agreement, Bill and his mother parted ways at the top of the aisle, and she went to the votive stand on the left while Bill knelt at the one on the right. He heard the clink of her dime as she inserted it into the box. She took a long, thin taper and held it in the flame of an already lit candle until it caught fire. Then she lit her own chosen candle. Bill listened to the low hum of her voice carry through the church as she began to chant the Hail Mary and Our Father. He waited until he was sure she was engrossed in prayer before pulling out a ten-dollar bill from his jeans pocket. He folded the bill into fourths and quickly tucked it through the slit in the box.

He glanced over at his mother. Her head was bent, and her

voice, although wavery, didn't stop. He took a taper and held it in the flame of the only lit candle at his stand. He let it burn while the words of Sister Agnes came to him: "These candles are for votive prayers. That means to pray or make a vow, usually for someone else, but you can pray for your own soul. The flame of these candles means your prayer burns eternal."

Eternal meant forever. He lifted his wooden taper and reached across the back row of candles. He lit one, two, three . . . and finally all twelve in that row. Then, after snuffing out the taper because it burned too close to his fingers, he reached for and lit another one. He lit the second row of twelve candles, then the third row, and finally, the fourth row of eleven. He snuffed out the last taper and clasped his hands. He squeezed his eyes shut and thought of his brother and his brother's buddies Rick and Marv. The whistling filled his head. He smiled. "My baby does the hanky panky." His face burned, and he stopped smiling. He tried to think of a prayer. But the formal prayers of the church didn't mean anything to him. Then it came to him. He whispered the only thing he could think to say. "Come home, come home, come home, come home—"

"Billy, did you have to light all of them?"

He lifted his head, his face flushed red from the heat of the candles, the eternal flame of forty-eight candles blurred in his eyes. "Pray for me," his brother had said.

"Yes," he answered, the s trailing through his teeth like a snake.

✕◆✕◆✕◆✕◆✕

The snowflakes skipped and skidded across the watery blue hood of the car on the way home. The sky was an ancient pearly gray, and Bill felt strangely happy. His mother drove, not saying a word, but he could sense that she too felt the same as her small son. They had stopped at the drugstore in Olina before driving back out to the farm. She bought him a new shirt and a pair of jeans and a giant solid chocolate Santa. It was as though she had read his mind when she gave the druggist, Bogey Johnson, a radiant smile and said, "Mr. Johnson, my son would like one of those Santas. Do you think we can oblige him?"

His mother hummed to herself. Bill bit into the fat arm of his Santa and watched the snow-covered fields and woods go slowly by as the car crunched over the new snow. Just as the chocolate elbow was melting into the roof of his mouth and they were nearing the farm, his mother braked the car in a series of small jerks and finally stopped it on the shoulder of the road right after they'd cleared the curve. She pulled the packet of letters out of her Wrigley's Doublemint-perfumed purse and laid them on the seat between herself and Bill. The chocolate trickled down the back of his throat.

"Thank you, sweetheart, for letting me read those," she said. She shifted in the car seat so that she faced him. Her face sparkled like the new snow, and for the first time that day he noticed that she had taken her pink rollers out. Her black hair was brushed and sprayed into full curls around her face. She could be, Bill realized, staring dumbfounded at his mother, very pretty.

"You know somethin'," she said matter-of-factly. "Jimmy is gonna come home. I feel it." She placed a clenched hand against her chest and repeated, *"I feel it."*

"You know somethin' else," she said almost gleefully, huddling down in the seat to look Bill in the face.

He shook his head, his eyes fixed on his illuminated mother. He absently bit off the tassel on his Santa's hat.

"Things—" she emphasized the word confidently—"are gonna get better. Lord, they can't get much worse. But you and me and Jimmy can run this farm and make it go. Don't you think so?"

Bill couldn't answer and quietly pushed his bitten-up Santa back into the bag. He cautiously looked back up at his mother. She didn't seem to notice his lack of response and had shifted forward in the car seat again. But her face was no longer jubilant; it was sad, and tears ran down her face.

"You know I love you boys . . . very much. But," she said

softly, looking through the windshield at their house in the distance nestled among the red pines, "if I'd have had wings, I would've been gone a long time ago."

Dec-67

Dear Bill,

I know this letter is coming pretty fast right after the last one, but Lt. Miller said there would be a special pickup for holiday mail. It's raining, and I'm writing this inside a bunker. Remember how much I used to love the sound of rain on the roof? Except Beans always howled like he was dying or something when it rained. I'm sorry that I threw my boot at him that time and hit him in the head. Then he really started howling, remember? Anyway, it rains like it's going to flood here. Listening to it makes me kind of sleepy. I pretend sometimes, when we can't hear any shooting or bombing, or even when the jets (we call them warbirds) are gone for a little while, that I'm home. Or when that doesn't work, I pretend this is a real country. It is a real country, but sometimes I feel like I'm floating just above the ground and I can't touch it. And other times I feel like I'm in a dollhouse—cause American soldiers are so big, me included. The Yards—the mountain people who live here and who help us and who are NOT Vietnamese—are the size of you, Bill. I'm a giant compared to them. I guess you could have joined the Marines with me after all (ha-ha). Speaking of big, you should see the RATS. I'm sorry I ever made fun of your mice. The rats here are like something out of the movies, and they BITE. Marv shoots any rats he sees with his .45. That's how much he hates them. So do I. Don't get upset. They'd EAT you.

We were cutting trail through some jungle two days ago, and I barely missed stepping into a punji pit. The North Vietnamese Army and the Viet Cong dig these holes and then put bamboo spikes in the bottom. They cover the holes up with leaves and even buffalo shit so you can't see them. If you step in one, the spikes go right up through the bottom of your boots and up into your legs. It scared the shit out of me.

Don't tell Mom, but I caught some shrapnel in my arm. The medic just cleaned it up and gave me a shot of penicillin. It's not that bad. Is Mom okay? Her last letter was strange.

Thanks for your letter—it was great! And it got here pretty fast too. You can wear my hat, and I don't care if you wreck it. I'm not going to wear it again anyway. Hey! I'm glad I don't have chicken wings—they'd never get me off the ground.

The other day I saw a really big bird flying. Like a heron, only bigger. I asked one of the ARVNs what it was. (ARVN stands for Army of the Republic of Vietnam—one of the Vietnamese fighting on our side.) He said it was a crane and laughed at me. He said didn't you ever see a crane before? I guess we have them in northern Wisconsin, but they usually stay in southern Wisconsin. They're beautiful, Bill. I hope I see more of them. But they must get hit in the crossfire and bombing. I wish I could have wings like a crane. Seeing that crane reminded me of the geese in the fall. I really missed seeing the geese this year.

Here's a picture of me. I look pretty dirty, but that's the way it is when we're out here. Thanks for the presents and the fruitcake. Well, little man, I've got to go. Give Mom a hug for me. Tell the old man to piss off (just kidding—don't do it). Say hi to the Morriseaus if you see them.

Love James

Bill stared at the Polaroid of his brother under the night-light. He had his helmet on, so Bill couldn't see how short his hair was, but the rest looked reasonably enough like James. Except his smile wasn't real. His mouth looked as though invisible fingers had taken his lips prisoner and pulled them sideways, the skin unnaturally tight underneath his nose. His eyes were sunken and dark, and it was clear that his brother had lost some weight. Besides the picture there was more money still, and Bill counted five ten-dollar bills. He leaned back against the wall. *Little man.* That's how he felt, as though when his brother left, all the unspoken reasons for James's leaving had suddenly descended upon Bill, and in his awareness of them, he had become old.

✕◆◆◆◆◆◆◆◆✕

It was a week past Christmas. Bill's father had come home, had drunk and slept through Christmas Eve and most of Christmas Day, getting up only to eat the holiday meal. It surprised Bill, covertly watching his father eat his turkey, how little he knew or cared about the tall, pasty-skinned man at the head of the table. His nine-year-old life had revolved so intensely lately around his daily struggle to survive at school, the strained wait for his brother's letters, the fields, the woods, the swamp, and the sky of their farm, and lastly, the fragile web of his mother's world that he had forgotten to be cautious around the beer-reeking presence that he'd been avoiding, it seemed, since he was born. He silently ate a forkful of stuffing before catching his mother's eye. A small conspiratorial smile passed across her lips. Her dark eyes had lost their dull captive look and shone. *Things are gonna get better.* He glanced down again to the far end of the table where his father sat and felt an unfamiliar stab of pity. James was thousands of miles away from them in a country that even Bill in his enormous capacity for imagination could not imagine but only carried with him in the word *Vietnam*. A country of purple mountains, man-made woodchuck holes that stabbed, wriggling barbed-wire bombs, a bird that flew bigger than a Canada goose, and hot metal that flew like a bird. Yet Bill knew it was his father, not his brother, who was in a strange country he'd never get out of, a country where only he thought as he did, and whose borders he broke through occasionally to hit his wife, to despise his sons.

Still, now that John Lucas was home for the holidays, Bill wondered how he was going to survive without his brother there to shield him, to shield her. But in his small head he knew, survive he must. James would come home. And James would tell the priest that what he preached at the Christmas mass was wrong. The loving brotherhood of man did not exist.

Sunday

Dear James,

Mom and me prayd for you. I ate alot of choclate at Christmas and got sick. Dad got fird and is home now. Me and Mom went sledding. She lost some of her curlers but did not get mad. She sat in front so I wouldnt get hit by snow. I am back at school. Sister says to look for Janury stars. Do you have stars over there? We saw a big white owl sittng on the fence by the barn. Mom says it is a snowi owl from canada. She says he came to visit us becase he ran out of food in canada. Mom cryd. She says you shoulda went to canada to. I said, mom, if they dont got any food, why should James go there.

Bill stopped. He could hear his mother shouting in the kitchen and the banging of pots and pans. His father's deep, rumbling voice answered her. Bill tensed up. Then he heard a heavy thump. His mother shouted some more. Bill sighed.

Can they let you out earli?

Bill raised his pencil from the paper. Now he could hear his mother sobbing.

Please come home. I am scard. I like your picture. Can I have your helmit when you come home? Mr. Moriso says he will take me and you to show us the crans. He says they fly by lake superier. They say

hi. If they let you out earli will you come home? I got to go to
bed now.

Love Bill

He put his notebook down. His mother's crying was ebbing. Bill
crawled back into bed and covered his ears against the muted notes
of her sorrow. It was the middle of January, the middle of a freak
midwinter thaw. The chickadees had broken into their spring song
that day. Bill had opened his window to the unseasonably warm
wind, and it blew the ivory curtains into midnight dancers. He felt
both elated and ashamed, having betrayed his fear to his brother. But
as much as he wanted to destroy what he had written, he also felt
sure that it would bring his brother home. Maybe, he thought, listening to the melting ice drip from the eaves, he could even persuade his mother to call the Marines and tell them that James was
needed at home. That he had made a mistake by enlisting.

Bill turned to lie on his right side. He tried not to think of tomorrow. Tomorrow was school. Tomorrow meant Merton. He
stared at the dancing curtains. Their fluttering hypnotized his already tired eyes, and combined with the soothing plunk, plunk of
the melting ice, his eyes closed. Tomorrow was not now.

✕◆◆◆◆◆◆◆◆✕

The wings flapped, enclosing Bill for a few seconds and brushing his
face and chest. They opened again, lifting upward against the surg-
ing wind, and he raised his eyes to see that the white wings spanned
an enormous length from side to side. His bare legs swung back and
forth, and he was held this time by his shoulders. The air was heavy
and moist, so moist that he felt slippery like a fish and as helpless as
one, clutched in the talons of an eagle. But his shoulders felt no
pain, just roped and secure. He dropped his head against his chest
and looked below.

They were passing over the Morriseau farm with its two silos and big duck pond. The eighty-acre field behind their house was filled with little clouds of dust, each one exploding like spores from the head of a smashed puffball mushroom. Poof! Poof! Poof! Little black specks were chaotically running through the field, and every time a speck hit one of the clouds, it burst into flames, becoming a ball of fire. He could hear shouting and the deep pop and zing of rifles going off. The air became thick and choking with dust. Bill's small chest caved in, and his lips quivered. He coughed hard, and his hands jerked up toward his mouth.

Then the wings came together again, enclosing his small body in a cocoon of feathers. When they opened, he saw that the field was clear and a cloud of cowbirds dipped and circled beneath them. His chest cleared, and he no longer felt like crying. He heard the high, clear notes of whistling and looked down. There was some-one standing in the middle of the grassy field, waving and waving. The wings caught an upcurrent of air, and they glided toward the far end of the field. They cruised its wide square edge before com-ing back around.

Bill cried out. It was James, wearing a dull green helmet that had "Elvis" painted in black letters on the side and balancing a ri-fle across his shoulders. He dropped the rifle and waved with both hands.

"Hey, Billy! Hey, Billy Baboon!"

"Jaaaamess! Jaaamess!" Bill shouted, but the wind took his voice and it disappeared in the rush of air between the feathers above him.

"Over there!" his brother shouted, and picked up his rifle and pointed with it toward their own field. A single black speck was running over the brown plowed earth. The wings caught the cue and flapped harder. They closed the distance in a few seconds and swept lower.

Bill screamed joyfully. "Shit house! You better run! You're up shit creek now!"

Merton was desperately running and tripping over the deep

furrows in the field. Bill pulled his legs up to his chest and curled his toes. They dropped altitude and cruised right up behind Merton. Bill lowered his legs and hooked his feet under Merton's arms. With legs suddenly as strong as steel cable, he lifted the squirming tonnage of a boy into the air twenty feet before dropping him.

"Don't hurt the little Hun! Jus' scare 'im!" his brother shouted.

Merton hit the soft plowed earth with a thump and a groan. But he got up and began running again, his head swiveling to pinpoint Bill's location. Bill whooped. Merton, his eyes rolling wildly, ran harder. Again they came off a large current of air to level themselves behind the nemesis of Bill's days. This time Bill did not pick him up but, with legs wound tight as springs against his chest, aimed and kicked, knocking Merton between the shoulder blades. Merton went down so hard he bit into the overturned field and ate dirt. He stayed down, breathing hard, grinding and spitting dirt. But he was not hurt, just scared. Bill stared at the sprawled-out boy as the wings lifted him back into the sky. Then, as quickly as the desire for revenge had come, it had gone, and they left the Lucas' field with its cleaved and unplanted earth and returned to his brother, standing almost perfectly camouflaged with his green jungle uniform in the middle of their neighbor's lush grassy field.

James had taken off his helmet and stood smiling broadly up at Bill. The wings, despite their massive size, lowered Bill until the bottoms of his feet touched his brother's shaved and bristly head. Bill could not speak. The wings didn't lower him any farther, and they hovered while Bill's feet curled around and hugged his brother's head. A look of pain crossed his brother's face. James reached up and encircled Bill's ankles with his hands, kissing the bottom of his little brother's feet.

"Man! It's really good to see you, Billy Baboon," his brother said softly. "Really good."

James released one of Bill's ankles and swept his arm in a semicircle around him. "I dream about this place all the time . . . yeah, all the time."

He kissed Bill's foot again. "Don't ever leave here, Bill. You and me . . . we'll have some fun when I come home."

The wings flapped. Bill strained, stretching his legs as far as he could to touch his brother's head. But the wings lifted him higher and higher. His brother put his helmet back on and picked up his rifle. He wiped his face on his sleeve and stared past Bill to the wings. James opened his mouth as if to say something but shut it again, raising his hand slightly.

"I gotta go. But don't worry. I love you, Billy! And Elvis," James said, pointing to his helmet, "loves you too!"

Bill watched James run from the field and disappear into the swamp on the edge. His heart beat against the wall of his chest. He heard the high notes of whistling echo from the swamp and smiled through his tears. "My baby does the hanky panky." He tried to cry out. Nothing. He listened to the lingering sound of whistling, and then it struck him. If his brother had been down there, who was above him, carrying him?

He stretched his neck to look up, but all he saw was sunlight, bright yellow and blinding. The wings flapped, covering his face, tickling and brushing his cheeks. A high guttural call pierced the air around him. The wings swept forward and covered him for the last time, enveloping him with the more familiar feel of his sheets and blankets, and with the descending silence of dreamless sleep.

XXXX SO MUCH I DIDN'T KNOW when I left home.

So much I did know.

I never used to write letters. Mom would get on my back about writing thank-you notes to relatives for birthday and Christmas gifts. The relatives that never visited us and those we never visited. But in Nam it became the thing you hoped for. Wished for. There weren't any phone booths. If you wanted a letter, you had to write one. I was careful when I wrote to my mother. I didn't want her to worry. What I couldn't write to her, I wrote to Bill. And I did something I never did before. I signed my letters "love."

I didn't write to Rosemary and Ernie. I didn't even say goodbye. It was a rotten thing to do. After all they'd done for me. I just knew when I signed up that they would talk me out of it. And I didn't want that. I didn't have any money, and I had to get the hell out of Olina somehow.

I could never get them to talk much about their time in the service. Rosemary talked some. Ernie almost never. I knew he had medals but I never saw them. I tried to picture Ernie like those guys in the WW II movies Bill and I watched. John Wayne fighting his way out of Bataan. Guts and glory.

There is a lot of guts but no fuckin' glory. Flies on guts. Rain on guts. Bloody guts. Ropes and ropes of guts. Being wet all the time. My feet swollen inside my boots and bleeding. But if you looked out from the base and didn't see it all close up, you'd think those hills were beautiful. Like the Garden of Eden. And it was at one time for the people who live here, who try to live here. Now

63

it's one fuckin' dangerous place. It's what Lieutenant Miller called surreal. I love that word. That feeling of being between what was real and what was unreal.

Maybe, I said to Miller, it's not so much SUR-real, but SO-real. He laughed. Nothing is as it seems.

Once I reached up to pick a purple orchid hanging from a vine. Our Bru scout, Kho, jabbed me in the belly so that my arm automatically reflexed down.

"No, no," he whispered. "Look."

Christ. Tied to the orchid and almost invisible was a home-made grenade.

What would I write to Ernie and Rosemary? How do you write, "Oh, yeah. I'm doing well. How are you?" after something like that? What if Kho hadn't stopped me? How could I write, "I blew my hand off picking a goddamn flower"? They were different. I could have written that to them, and they would have known. That was what stopped me. I couldn't write it, and I couldn't lie. They would see through that. I couldn't hurt them like that. I didn't know what to do, so I just stayed silent. No letters. Even when I wrote to Mom and Bill, signing my letters with the word *love* just didn't seem like enough. That was what I didn't know. That you could love someone so much that nothing you said could say it.

But what I did know prepared me even though I didn't realize it until it happened.

We were out on patrol for the last half of November. Me, Lieutenant Miller, Rick, Marv, Kho, and Cracker Jack, our radioman and Motown medic, whose real name was Solomon Jackson and who loved the Motown sound but did not come from Detroit. It came down the wire that the NVA was building up.

"Fuckin' shit, man. Just in time for Christmas," Cracker Jack said, pissed because he hated reconnaissance patrol. Hated the week rotations we were out there.

We were supposed to look for signs of them and to determine by the signs how many of them were out there. How many remains of camps did we find? Disturbed ground that might indicate a punji pit or piles of shit, human or elephant. Any dead? Any wounded? Any blood trails? We also had to radio in every time we got shot at. If we got shot at a lot, then the rumors were true.

"What the hell," I whispered to Rick so Marv wouldn't hear, "we aren't doing recon. We're fuckin' worms on a hook."

We had days of just hearing our footsteps. Then out of the blue we would hit the ground because of sudden rifle fire. It was my job as point man to keep my eyes up, to locate a possible muzzle flash, if any could be seen in the daylight. But even if I didn't see the flash, I could pinpoint the direction just by hearing it. I almost never used my grenade launcher. My own arm was much better. I'd pull the pin and throw that first grenade. Blam! Then that pop! pop! pop! pop! of an AK-47 as if I'd asked a question and they'd answered back. *That was what I wanted.* I threw a few more grenades in the same direction. By that time Cracker Jack had radioed in our position, and we stayed put until we could hear a Cobra or a Skyhawk overhead. We always prayed that the pilots got it right and fired or dropped a bomb where they were supposed to and not on us.

It wasn't the firefights that shook us up. It was the quiet in between. Marv drummed his fingers on his chest and bit his nails down. When his nails were gone, he chewed on the tips of his fingers. Rick ground his teeth. Cracker Jack just hung tight, and Lieutenant Miller rubbed his grenade launcher as though it were his dick. But eventually they'd all stop because you couldn't stay jittery for long. After a while you became tired. That was what I remember the most. Exhaustion. It works on you. That terror of never knowing what's going to happen next, of feeling surrounded, of being watched. If you weren't careful, you'd get stupid with it. Miller's eyes glazed over, and he walked as though his battery were running down. It got to me but not as bad. Cracker Jack handled it better too. I was trained for it, and from what little he told me, I suspect Cracker Jack was used to it too, from growing up in Chicago. My whole damn childhood had been like that. Never knowing what to expect next but to expect the unexpected.

We'd come out of the trees from time to time and walk into stands of elephant grass. Grass that was way over our heads. Blades of grass that were just that: blades. Our arms looked as though they'd been nicked by razors, and sometimes our faces too. Those cuts would get infected, and whenever we took a rest, we would lift the scabs off and squeeze out the pus. Cracker Jack put ointment on them.

Rick was from Austin, Minnesota. He said they had a prairie grass called cordgrass that grew in wet sloughs and that was almost as sharp. It scraped the skin instead of cut it. But it wasn't as tall. No wonder they called it elephant grass. Only an elephant could walk through it and see above it without trouble, without feeling anything because elephant skin is so thick.

We were two days away from going back to the base when Rick was shot.

✕✦✦✦✦✦✦✦✕

I could not get over Rick's death. I was the point man. I was the one responsible for making sure the rest of the recon team did not get hurt. There was so much thick cover, and we were big waddling geese going through it. The jungle was not for Americans. We were too tall, too big. The Yards were small. The NVAs were too, and even before we found the holes they had dug or smelled the fish sauce they ate, I could sense them. They were everywhere, and with so much dense cover, it was dark and spooky. I'd never felt that way before. I'd grown up feeling so at home in the woods. I looked at the trees, and I had to look at the branches to make sure that one of those balled-up hunks of leaves and vines wasn't a sniper. We were so tired that day that we could barely pick up our feet. It finally got to me. Living in fear day after day after day, even when nothing happened, stripped me down. I lost my appetite, which was just as well. We were eating fuckin' C rations only once a day, and for some strange reason variety wasn't in the packed menu plan. Wieners and beans, and ham and lima beans.

"Cracker," I asked, watching my C ration of ham and lima beans cook over a piece of C-4 explosive, "what the hell? Was this all you could pack?"

"That's all that was in supply bunker, man," he said with a shrug. "Dick and beans and ham and motherfuckers. Sorry, man. Pretend it's a steak."

❊❊❊❊❊❊❊❊❊

It was later that day. I heard the pop of the AK-47. We all hit the ground and rolled under the nearest cover. Except for Rick. As I was falling, I saw Rick jerk back and forth in a weird kind of dance, saw a red tulip sprout over his chest. That gook was a stupid sniper. He kept firing as though he were hell-bent on pumping an entire magazine into Rick. I rolled over twice and brought my rifle up to where I'd seen the flash. What looked like a mass of vines around a branch was really a man. The first bullet must have caught him in the throat. We heard a gurgle and what seemed to be a deep breath that ended in a hysterical sigh. I emptied a magazine into the guy, and only then did he fall to the ground. As though I'd shot a roosting grouse.

"Stay down!" I hissed when I saw Marv try to reach for Rick. I heard Cracker Jack radio in for help. I was so sure that there were more of them out there and that we were all going to get wasted. But nothing happened. I could not believe it was one lone bastard firing at us. And I didn't believe it. But for some strange reason they didn't consider us worth opening a fight over. Normally I would have crept ahead and checked my aim, checked the body for anything that might be of use. Maps, pictures, even what uniform he was wearing. But Marv was gasping as though he could not get enough air.

❊❊❊❊❊❊❊❊❊

After Rick was killed, Marv would just stare off into space, and sometimes I had to thump him on the back to make him pay attention. Marv was the guy responsible for painting "Elvis" on my helmet, not only making me a visible target for a mile but costing me a dressing down because it targeted everyone else as well. He painted it over for me. He laughed a lot. He made us laugh a lot. Until Rick was shot. He kept hugging the body bag that Rick was in, and I thought I'd have to break his arms so that he'd let go, let them load Rick onto an H–34 copter and take him home.

✕✦✦✦✦✦✦✦✕

Marv cried for a long time, off and on at night. It seemed to help him, but it got to me and made me feel pissed instead of sad.

There were two nights near Christmas when it was so quiet we held our breath to make sure it was as silent as it seemed. I shouldn't say quiet. The bugs made a lot of noise in the jungle around the base, but we accepted it, like the buzzing of mosquitoes, as part of the regular noise.

Around Christmas Marv got a guitar from some black-market papa-san. I don't know how he did it or what he traded it for in the Khe Sanh village, but it was a fairly decent guitar. I didn't even know he could play. One night I was reading and lying on top of some sandbags inside our bunker. Marv took out his forbidden guitar and began to sing softly.

"What's that?" I asked, not recognizing the song.

He stopped. "You really *are* from the backwoods, aren't you?" he said. Marv was from Philadelphia. "There *is* other music in the world. Have you heard of the Beatles?"

"Shut up. Of course I have."

"What about Beethoven?"

"Now you can really shut the fuck up there. My mother *loves* Beethoven. My mother used to be a teacher. She went to a private college in Milwaukee. Shit. I grew up listening to Beethoven, Tchaikovsky, and Debussy. You know. The classics."

"The classics." He smirked. "Where did *you* go wrong?"

I threw an empty beer can at him. He ducked and laughed. It was good to hear him laugh again after what happened to Rick. Then he started to sing.

Hello darkness, my old friend,
I've come to talk with you again,
Because a vision softly creeping,
Left its seeds while I was sleeping,
And the vision that was planted in my brain
Still remains
Within the sound of silence.

That was the first time I really paid attention to Simon and Garfunkel. That song stuck to me. For the rest of January I sang it under my breath like a prayer.

I THOUGHT 1967 WOULD NEVER END. December held with such ferocity that it became officially memorable, creating temperatures and conditions that meteorologists would use as a yardstick in the coming years. The winter began with an avalanche of snow from the November skies and unusually large gales on Lake Superior. When December came, the temperature became a steady twenty-five degrees below zero. The wind only made it worse, possessing the days with its icy force and torturing even such winter-hardy animals as coyotes, sometimes forcing them to find shelter in a surprised farmer's hay barn.

Then January 1968 arrived, and it cracked open that cold blue sky. A warm and wet wind came out of Canada and gave northern Wisconsin a most startling midwinter thaw. The chickadees sang their spring love songs and collected twigs and exposed grass for building nests. I hung laundry outside one day. After pinning the last shirt to the line, I turned into the wind and let my bathrobe flap open.

When we moved up from Milwaukee to this 250-acre farmstead filled with swamps, rocks, and pines in northern Wisconsin seventeen years ago, I didn't know the history or understand why the land was so cheap. I didn't think to ask Emil and Anna Hausherr because it was clear they had been happy here. We moved near a town with a Swedish woman's name, Olina, even though almost everyone was German in origin. I went from being surrounded by people, close to most of my own family and friends, to nearly complete isolation. Not only isolation but also a journey back into time.

The rural area of Olina was inhabited by the grandsons and granddaughters of immigrants who had been lied to by the Department of Agriculture and the lumber industry. By the time they discovered the logged-over soil and cold temperatures could not support big farming, they had drained all their savings and had no money to leave. Their children and the children after them learned to live on very little, and it became a twisted kind of life. They stoically toughed it out and spent their Sunday mornings listening to Father Wallace intone the master plan of God and pontificate his own views that people often brought tragedy upon themselves because of their lack of, or their misguided, spiritual lives. By Father Wallace's definition, sinners were people who did not conform to Olina's standards and traditions, the main tradition being depression. It was a sin, for example, to expect or want happiness. To expect love. I went to church because it had been fed to me since birth and had become as instinctual as breathing. I was afraid that if I missed a mass, something terrible would happen. It was a kind of voodoo that my mother had frightened me into believing, and she had done a good job. Although I sat in the pew and listened, I refused to believe that bad things happened only to people the church saw or defined as sinful.

Father Wallace was a good example of church hypocrisy. Our priest did not sip the blood of Christ but drank it by the bottle before, during, and after mass. It was not Mogen David wine either but a rather expensive French merlot. I had suspected it, and Jimmy confirmed it during the two years he was an altar boy. He brought home one of the empty wine bottles to show me. Like most self-righteous people, Father Wallace railed against the very thing he practiced. Sin. I wondered why the rest of the parish never thought to question why the priest had a large color TV and drove a Cadillac or that the name Wilson—Elizabeth Wilson, Robert Wilson, Mr. and Mrs. John Wilson, Alvira Wilson—scripted nearly all of the stained glass windows might have something to do with it. Wilson Lumber owned a large portion of our lives, the mill being the only place to work in the area and then only seasonally.

Our first year here I went to mass as a way of feeling at home, a ritual that was familiar to me and gave me the only place to wear the closetful of pretty dresses, suits, shoes, and hats. Olina didn't have any social occasions that demanded such attire. I bundled Jimmy up and went to mass every morning at six-thirty, just to get out of the house before my husband did. At that hour there were very few men in church. It was mostly women, sitting in the back pews, their rosaries wound through their hands. Many of them belonged to the Daughters of Isabella, a charitable group that attended every funeral mass, even for the most wretched and forsaken. They said the Hail Mary and Our Father, chanting in rhythm until the priest nodded and the funeral mass could begin.

Jimmy slept on the pew next to me. Sometimes the older women would peek at him and softly coo over his curly black hair and red cheeks. I took a rosary out of my purse. I was not as skilled as some of those stocky German and Slavic women. Their hands were the opposite of their bodies. They worked the beads through their fingertips with the agility they possessed in crocheting and knitting. Knit ten Marys, purl one Father. Their dry and pleated lips moved silently as they sat in trances, their eyes focused on the huge crucifix hanging on the wall behind the altar. I did not think they were fools. Or particularly faithful. It was the only time of the day those women could have an hour to themselves. The church was impenetrable except in cases of extreme emergency. No husband or child dared violate the sanctity of their time in church. Although those women would never admit it, they were praying to keep their minds and to avoid dwelling on their daily unhappiness. I knew this because my mother had gone to church every day when I growing up. And I knew why.

✖◆◆◆◆◆◆◆◆✖

When the weather shifted in January from what was normal, I did not see it as an omen but as a celestial gift that might indicate that the New Year of 1968 would bring a sense of peace and milder winters unlike the previous years.

I lifted my face to the wind and shut my eyes. I was Catholic in my habits only. That first year, home alone with a toddler during the week, I became aware of a breath. Of breathing. I walked in the interior of it, and it became the sound against which all other sounds were placed. I would hear crows cawing back and forth as I pushed the buggy up and down the dirt road in an effort to get Jimmy to sleep. One family in one tree and what appeared to be another but related family in another tree. Sometimes their cawing became intense and sharp as though they were quarreling. Other times their voices took on a comic ha-ha-ha as though one of them had told a joke. But at least once a day and often more I heard a deeper voice. A rattling but deep croak that scattered the crows. A raven. Its voice always cleaved the quiet as if it were a pronouncement, sometimes spoken in a frightening and foreboding tone, sometimes a hoarse chuckle, but mostly in a comforting manner as the large, black bird, perched high up in a white pine like a northern wizard, told the rest of us that all was well. A deep gong to announce sunrise, noon, and sunset.

Then the call of a barred owl at dusk. *Who cooks for you? Who cooks for you?* Some nights the howling of coyotes. The dog we had then would get excited and try to announce his own presence. His poor voice, a crackling howl, could never reach the higher, purer octaves of the coyotes. He tried and tried until they stopped, probably disgusted that our lowly dog had ruined their reverent song to the moon.

But always that breathing. Always that pulse.

The year Jimmy was four, I went to the bookmobile in Olina as usual, but this time I signed out books on the flora and fauna of where we lived, the geology of where we lived. I wanted to know what was underneath my feet when I walked down the driveway to collect our mail. I wanted to know what I heard and what I felt. I knew Jimmy felt it too. The way he cocked his little head and stared at the trees before slipping his thumb into his mouth as if to think on it.

What an enormous comfort it was when I found it. We lived on the Canadian Shield, a thick layer of rock so old and tough that not even the last glacier scouring its surface could reach down and break it. It was what some geologists called the ancient heart of North America. No wonder northern Wisconsin couldn't be farmed on a big scale. There was very little soil between that tablet of rock and my feet. It was not meant for farming but for praying. I stopped going to church during the week. When the weather was mild, I waited until my husband left for work. Then I took Jimmy outside with me, and together we would press our hands against the ground and I would explain to him how that ground was created. About the heart underneath our feet. Sometimes after I put him down for his afternoon nap, I would go outside and do it again. Press my hands to the ground. Beneath that bedrock heart, I imagined the soul. Liquid and fiery. How it warmed that enormous tablet and the unseen commandments written there so that those voices could rise to the surface. That was where the pulse and the breath came from. The heart and the soul.

It was this place, this boreal forest and stumpy cedar bogland, that eroded my city girl ways. That exposed the artifice of my religion. That gave me the mothering I never had. My trips to Milwaukee to visit my mother and relatives became less frequent because I could not stand the pity in their eyes and at the same time their refusal to acknowledge my pain or to help me with what had turned out to be a disastrous choice in husbands. I needed help that was older and wiser and not judgmental when I did not feel brave. When I cried. When I confessed my fears and my sins. The breath did not lie, did not tell me to say ten Hail Marys and everything will be all right. The pulse radiated up through the house on nights when I was tired of fighting loneliness, despair, and what I saw as a life wasted. When I felt lost. On those nights I looked at the veins in my wrists and thought of how easy it would be. But that larger pulse penetrated through the quiet of the house and reminded me that I had one of my own and that it was too sacred to cut. The tributaries of my veins flowed into the river in my body. My life had some value, some meaning, however small it seemed.

That was when I knew that the power of life was something bigger than a man-made God even when it tested me beyond reasonable endurance. It was evidenced once again by that untimely January warmth, by the smell of soil thawing. I took a deep breath. It was a good sign that the weather had let up and let us breathe without freezing our lungs.

XXXXXXXXX

A week later I was head deep into scrubbing out the oven, listening and simultaneously pooh-poohing the radio announcer's proclamation of the weather as unnatural when my younger son ran into the house.

"Mamma! There's a fox sitting by the barn! Just sitting there! C'mon!"

Bill grabbed my hand and pulled me outside. Both of us stumbled over the muddy ruts in the yard until we reached the barn. There next to the fence post by the southeast corner of the barn sat the fox as though it were a farm dog. I walked hesitantly toward the animal, keeping my son behind me. It occurred to me too late that I should have brought a gun in case the animal was sick. The fox appeared indifferent to my approach. When I was close enough to see better but far enough away to remain safe, I saw why.

Rather than the luxurious red-brown winter coat of fur it should have had, the fox had patches of fur missing. Even its tail was ratlike and scaly. I was sure I could have walked right up to it and grabbed the animal by the scruff of its neck, the fox so weak with hunger, so sick with mange that it would have shown no resistance. The fox was not the only one suffering.

Just before Christmas, Bill and I had seen a snowy owl perched on the snow fence along the driveway. We rarely saw those big white birds, and I knew immediately what it meant. The owl was having trouble finding food in Canada, its normal terrain, and had ventured south in an effort to survive. I shuddered. Something was wrong if a fox and an owl were starving during what was a rich season for predators. The fox's obvious hunger began to ruin my rare good spirits.

"Poor thing," I said to my son, peering out from behind me. "I think it must be a young one that is having a hard time hunting. But we can't help it. We have to let nature take its course."

My son didn't answer, his face pulled down with sadness. I stroked the top of his head with the fascination I had so often felt in the past at the difference between my younger and older sons. My older son would have shot the fox, kindly ending the animal's suffering. He would have been justified, merely expediting the process of nature. But Bill's heart beat for the wounded and the very young. He believed with a comic book hero's vision that he could rescue anything from the brink of death, and his bedroom in the spring and summer was living proof that he often could. It overflowed with orphaned and injured birds, mice, rabbits, and once a ball of entwined, newly hatched garter snakes that needed no care and proved it by disentangling themselves and spreading throughout the house. I was in a constant state of anxiety for months, once reaching into the sugar jar only to find a snake coiled there. My older son barely tolerated the zoo that their bedroom had become, and fights broke out frequently. I always listened from wherever I was in the house. If I thought the fight was rising to a level of physical danger, I would run upstairs and into their bedroom to break it up. They were often so mad at each other that they didn't notice me until I inadvertently became the target of something flying through the air. Once it was a balled-up sock that struck me in the head. A shoe in my backside another time.

I tugged on his hand. "Let's go."

That night I pretended that I didn't see Bill take leftovers out of the refrigerator and stuff them inside his jacket before silently ducking out of the house. For the next three days I cooked a steady supply of venison Jimmy had stored in our freezer from the winter before until the refrigerator bulged with an abundance of meat. Over a period of days the refrigerator gradually lost its contents.

I stopped myself from asking Bill if the fox ate the food, if it was lulled into brief domesticity by his kindness, and I wondered, noting his bare head and hands, where he had left his red stocking cap and mittens. Instead I waited until my son left the house. Then I watched him from the back porch window, watched as my nine-year-old ran toward the barn, his hands cradling the bottom of the jacket. He did not speak of the fox again. I was sure that it had died and that all the food Bill had piled out behind the barn had gone to waste or been eaten by coyotes.

XXXXX THE SUNSET HAD BEEN AN unusually spectacular orange-red like the sunsets of late summer that day and was streaked with clouds shaped like scattered fleece. He had been shoveling manure for about an hour behind the barn, adding to the pile already banked up against the outside wall, when he stopped to have a smoke and ponder the sunset. The temperatures during the day had reached the low forties for the past week. But now dusk was rapidly taking over, and the temperature was dropping. Ernie put out his cigarette and hurried to get the job done because in another half hour he wouldn't be able to see or feel his hands on the shovel. As he worked, he could hear the family dog inspecting and exploring the thick wet snow around the barn.

Ernie was straining to lift an enormous shovelful of shit when he heard the dog stop prowling and give a quick snort. Thinking the dog had just found an unlucky mouse under the snow, Ernie tossed the manure onto the pile and was about to shovel up some more when he realized that the dog had stopped moving completely. He straightened up and was trying to locate the dog when he heard him. A long, high howl broke the farmyard quiet. Ernie shivered and involuntarily dropped the shovel. Then the dog streaked right past him, jumping over the shovel, and ran about fifty yards into the snow-crusted field behind the barn. Ernie had turned in the direction the dog took, wondering what had spooked him, when he saw that the large black animal had stopped again and stood rigidly still with his head and nose held high. He looked beyond the dog, and that was when he saw Jimmy Lucas.

At first Ernie thought that Jimmy had been discharged early from the Marines and was finally home from fighting in Vietnam. But he was wearing his combat helmet and fatigues and carrying an M-16 rifle. Ernie stepped forward, sinking into the deep snow, and raised his arm.

"Jimmy!" he yelled, and waved his hand.

Jimmy Lucas didn't answer and instead reached up and took off his helmet, which he dropped into the snow. The helmet rolled as though it had hit hard ground instead of snow, and Ernie noticed that Jimmy was standing on top of the snow instead of sinking into it the way Ernie and the dog had. Suddenly Ernie knew it was and wasn't Jimmy Lucas and why he was standing in the Morriseau eighty-acre field behind the barn.

Ernie sank to his knees. "Oh, no, Jimmy," he whispered. "No, no."

Jimmy dropped his rifle too and slowly turned around. The dog snorted again but did not move. Then Jimmy walked away from them and continued walking until he reached the big swamp that bordered the Morriseau and Lucas farms. The very moment that Jimmy disappeared into the swamp, the dog howled again and took off running, floundering through the snow until he too reached the swamp.

An hour went by before Ernie was able to rise to his feet. He threw the shovel into the toolshed and reluctantly approached the house. He ate dinner methodically and silently before trudging up the stairs to bed. Thinking it was exhaustion, his wife only asked where the dog was and didn't question her husband's decision to go to sleep early.

When he woke up the next morning, Ernie surrendered what he had seen to the effects of working too hard. He'd been tricked by the warm weather and from working outside without a jacket or gloves. His hands had gone numb, and he reasoned that he'd had the beginnings of hypothermia, which always made a person feel dreamy. He looked out his bedroom window. It was another freakishly warm day. Water dripped from the eaves of the house.

His wife made breakfast and then kissed him good-bye because she had errands to run in town. He spread hay for his beef cattle, watered and fed the chickens, changed the filter and oil on his truck, and went back to work on the manure pile.

It was near noon, and Rosemary hadn't come back yet. Ernie was making himself a bologna sandwich and brewing another pot of coffee when the phone rang. He thought it might be Rosemary, calling to ask if there was anything he needed from town, so he picked up the phone casually.

"Morriseau's."

"Is this Ernest Morriseau?"

"It is."

"Mr. Morriseau, my name is Lieutenant Hildebrandt. I'm from the Naval Chaplain Corps. I'm calling from the reserve base in Madison. I'm calling you at the request of Private James Lucas, who listed you as the contact on his record of emergency form."

Ernie's chest constricted, and he began breathing as though he had been running. He stretched the phone cord so that he could pull a chair over from the kitchen table. He sat down.

"Mr. Morriseau, are you still there?"

"I am."

Ernie paused, then said, "Jimmy's dead, isn't he?"

"No, Mr. Morriseau. Private Lucas is missing in action."

"That means he could be alive?"

"That is our hope. They haven't found him yet. I will be driving up with another officer tomorrow to notify his family—" he paused, and Ernie could hear the rustling of papers—"and he requested that you accompany us. Do you live near the Lucas home?"

"Farm. They have a farm. I own the farm next to theirs."

"Private Lucas left very detailed instructions on his form. He specifically requested you. And he didn't want us to visit the family in the evening but rather during the day. Can you go with us tomorrow?"

"Yes. Of course I can."

"I will need directions to your farm, and we'll meet you at your place tomorrow at about ten A.M."

Ernie gave the officer directions and hung up the phone. His hands were shaking. He thought of the way the helmet had hit the snow, how it had rolled but had not tipped upright.

When Rosemary came home half an hour later she found Ernie still sitting by the phone.

"I've been yelling from outside. Didn't you hear me? I needed help carrying in the groceries," she said, dumping two bags on the kitchen table.

He turned to look at her. It took him a minute to hear the irritation in her voice, even to recognize that she had come home.

"I just got a call," he said.

⬥⬥⬥⬥⬥⬥⬥

His wife stiffly walked to the kitchen sink and, leaning over it, stared out of the window. He gazed at her and at the expression on her face. His thoughts shifted so that he concentrated on her. He knew what was happening in himself, how the body protected itself against this kind of injury. This was the kind of news that caused a shock, which quickly turned into denial. He understood denial as a biological response, a survival tactic. It was necessary at first so that the unspeakable could be absorbed more slowly. He looked at his wife and thought of something else. What seemed an inappropriate thought at such a time was indeed appropriate. His mind filtered past the news as if to seek a safer place to stay, and it settled upon one of his happiest memories.

Of the night he met his wife.

⬥⬥⬥⬥⬥⬥⬥

After he was released from the hospital in Hawaii, he flew to San Diego and took the train from there. He got off the train in Milwaukee for a short hiatus before the final leg home. He had no civilian clothes with him, only a second, dressier uniform, which the Pfister Hotel promised it would have cleaned and pressed by that evening. He wanted to hunt up some old friends or news of them, hoping that they had come home alive. When he heard about the VFW Hall dance on East Wisconsin Avenue just a couple of blocks from the hotel, he went there, thinking he might run into someone familiar. The large rectangular hall was packed. He pushed through the crowd of dancers, bought a beer, and sat down at a table in the corner. He immersed himself in the anonymity of the crowd. In the general joy bordering on much-needed amnesia, which alcohol and a local swing band, in imitation of Benny Goodman, helped instill.

It took him a while to get used to seeing so much color and so much activity that was happy. There were many pretty women and most of them were dancing, if not with men, then with one another. The hall was well lubed with three bar counters, one at each end of the room and a large one against the back wall. He didn't see anyone who looked familiar. He was making a third visual sweep across the crowd when he caught sight of her.

She was leaning against the largest bar. Unlike the other women, she had on a black satin dress with spaghetti straps and a low heart-shaped neckline. A dress that was not meant to twirl away from the body but to hug it. While the other women had mimicked the look of stockings, having drawn seams up the back of their legs with eyebrow pencils, she wore the real thing. He wondered how she had found a pair of stockings when so many women could not. Even from a distance, he could see that they were silk and not orange rayon. Even more impossible than finding them she had evidently found a pair that fitted what appeared to be the longest legs he'd ever seen on a woman. She was tall, and the open-toed heels with black ankle straps made her even taller. Her toenails were painted red. Her lips were red. And her black hair was pinned into a chignon.

She was not from Wisconsin. He was sure of it. He watched as she turned around, bent over the bar—Jesus!—and paid for another drink. She slid onto the empty barstool next to her and, with a kind of tipsy movie star bravado, pushed herself so that she swiveled around to face the crowd of dancers. She crossed her legs, and it was then that Ernie became aware of the vacuum around her.

None of the available men was flirting with her. He tried to catch her eye so that he could test the waters of her mood with a wink, but she was drunk and didn't appear to focus on a single individual, staring out over the crowd instead.

What the hell, he thought. He'd be leaving Milwaukee in a few days. He got up and walked toward her, his legs feeling wobbly and treacherous. He lightly tapped her bare arm and set his jaw against the anticipated rejection. When she turned and looked at him, he caught his breath. Her face mirrored the same disillusionment and weariness that he felt, that look of something lost, something that could never be returned. He knew what it was. He'd seen it when he shaved a few hours before in the hotel's bathroom. They would never be young again.

It was unsettling to see the anger and sorrow he felt reflected back at him from a woman. She wasn't vulnerable, though. That dress. You had to have guts and the body to wear a dress like that. Even if her mood had been visibly sweet and inviting, the men still wouldn't have flirted with her. The incongruity of her threw them off-balance, and in their confusion they stayed away from her.

He swallowed and tried to smile his best smile. "War's over. Wanna dance?" he asked. She put her drink down and slid off the barstool. He could smell the gin and tonic on her breath. The sharpness of juniper berries. He tried to keep from shuddering as she ran one hand across the top of his shoulders.

They danced for hours. At one point he pulled slightly away from her.

"You're a nurse, aren't you?"

"I was a nurse," she answered, leaning her head back to appraise him. "In the Army. I was in the Philippines. I just got back."

"I was in the Army too."

"I know," she said, tapping his uniform shirt with one finger.

When the VFW Hall closed, they went back to his room at the Pfister. It was an expensive hotel, filled with marble and brass. He had, in a moment of recklessness, decided to treat himself, having heard that the Pfister was *the* Milwaukee hotel to stay in. He regretted it at first after having settled into his room, feeling that it was too much luxury until he saw Rosemary. Then he was grateful for his recklessness and considered it fateful. She sat on the edge of the bed, and he knelt down and undid the ankle straps on her shoes. He got up and sat on the bed next to her, watched as she pulled up the hem of her dress, undid her garters, and rolled the precious stockings down her legs. He unbuttoned her dress. When she was free of her clothes, he ceremoniously took the pins out of her chignon, placing each pin on the bedside table before removing another one. The coil of thick black hair unraveled in his hands and he let it go so that it fell in one long wave down her back. He could not stop touching her hair, mesmerized by the weight of it, the length. All the nurses he had seen in the Philippines had had short hair.

"Your hair."

"Because it's long?"

"Yeah. You didn't cut it?"

"No. It's like an arm, you know? Can't cut it off."

He pulled his fingers through it. Lifted it and let it fall in fans across her face. That night he was grateful for the streetlight shining through the windows. He wanted to see her. When he swung her above him, he saw what the wounded men in their hallucinatory pain had seen as she bent over them to check their pulses and palm their foreheads. The large brown eyes with long lashes. Her pale throat beaded with sweat. The black hair slipping from the pins, strands of it pasted to her neck.

She swept her right hand across his chest, and he shivered. Then she did it again with her left hand, her fingertips pressing down as though to feel his heartbeat.

✕✕◆◆◆◆◆◆◆✕

At breakfast the next morning in the hotel café, he asked her to marry him. Then he asked her where she was from. "I know you're not from around here," he added.

She grinned impishly. He noticed a dimple indenting one cheek.

"What makes you think that?"

"Nobody wears a dress like that around here."

"That's why I like it. I bought it and the shoes in San Diego. And one of the doctors I worked with gave me the stockings as a good-bye gift. In case," she added, "you were wondering where I got them."

He lit a cigarette, remembering how the slow unrolling of her stockings had resembled the unveiling of a marble statue. The stockings were a serious gift. He wondered about the doctor. Wondered if it was wise to ask. She spoke again before he could risk it.

"My mother will shit peanuts when she sees this dress."

Ernie exhaled and laughed at the same time.

"You didn't answer my questions," he said.

He took a sip from his coffee.

"Yes. I'll marry you. And," she said, "I'm from Cedar Bend."

Ernie choked, nearly spraying her with his mouthful of coffee.

"I was about to ask you the same question," she said, taking the cigarette from his hand. He wiped his face and the front of his shirt with a napkin while she took a drag from his cigarette. "What's so bad about being from Cedar Bend?"

"Not bad." He coughed and then cleared his throat. "I'm from Olina."

"No! Really?"

The comedy of fate. He had fallen in love with a woman who not only had been in the Army and in the Philippines at the same time he'd been but also had grown up in a small town only twenty miles away from his own. *Jesus,* he thought. *Cedar Bend.* Why hadn't he seen her before?

They exhausted themselves with laughter and listened to each other until their voices diminished into occasional chuckles and, in Rosemary's case, incredibly charming hiccups. Then they sat wordlessly and studied each other. He forgot to consider that she might really be from somewhere else. That to have her might mean leaving northern Wisconsin. It was a thought that he'd never entertained once in the service. It was home. Just as certain animals returned to habitual nesting grounds, he too could not imagine going anywhere else except to the boreal bogs, forests, and the Lake Superior of his youth.

Before last night, he had felt grief, fear, terror, and finally numbness. When he woke up, he remembered her sweeping his chest. How she'd opened it without breaking the skin, the palm of her hand parting the pectoral tissue as if it were water, and indeed, when he woke up, he breathed and felt his lungs expand freely for the first time in a year. He knew that if she asked, that if she didn't want to go home, he would leave northern Wisconsin for her. He was shocked at what his body knew before he even thought it. Of how the instinctual in him gravitated toward that which unconsciously was home. He realized, watching her smoke his cigarette, that she had physically articulated for him something that he knew but could not have described. That home was not always familiar or easy. That the land of his youth was sometimes neither of those, and that was why he loved it so. She was like that. A surviving and survivable beauty. She had enough of what he knew in her. And more of what he didn't. He wanted that. He wanted to hunt for that mystery.

He dropped some money on the table and stood up. Held out his hand. She hiccuped.

"Let's go back to bed."

He got up from his chair and wrapped his arms around his wife. She took a deep breath, turned, and buried her face into his chest.

She had told him a few weeks into their marriage that she hadn't wanted to marry someone who had been in the war. She hadn't wanted a military man. She had wanted someone free from all that knowledge. But when she met Ernie, she knew that it would never have worked that way, that what she initially wanted was the opposite of what she needed. Who else would believe some of the things she had seen, endured, and done but another veteran?

Ernie looked around the kitchen. Although it had been re-modeled after his parents had died, it was still the same room where his mother and father had received the telegram notifying them that their son had been wounded in the Pacific. That was all they'd known until they received a letter from him a couple of weeks later, postmarked Hawaii. The telegram hadn't given them any details. They did not know how badly their son was wounded or if he would live.

He had never really thought about those days. How wretched they must have been for his parents. But they were fortunate in one way. Their ignorance of modern warfare protected them from even more pain.

His shoulders sagged. He could feel the palsy of his wife's crying in his chest. There was nothing to protect them.

XXXXX THE WARM AND CLOUDY WEATHER held, and on a Saturday in late January I began to contemplate the possibility of an early spring. I was staring out the dining room window, envisioning where to plant my marigolds, my petunias, and my morning glories, when I saw Ernie Morriseau's gray truck coming toward the farm, a cloud of white exhaust billowing behind it. When the truck turned into our driveway, I saw that a car was following it, veiled and hidden in the trail of Ernie's exhaust. I didn't know that my cup had tipped in my hand until I felt the warm coffee spilling down the front of my housedress. I didn't make a sound until I saw the insignia on the sedan's driver's door. I sucked air in so fast that it whistled before I dropped my coffee cup and ran into the living room.

"Go upstairs to play," I said, roughly lifting Bill to his feet and pushing him toward the stair.

"What's wrong?"

"Now!" I shouted.

I waited and watched Bill scamper up the stairs before I ran into the kitchen. I didn't know what to do. I ran to the table and then to the refrigerator, jigsawing around the room, my hands touching every surface until I stopped at the kitchen sink. I gripped the edge of the stainless steel sink and listened for the first knock at the back door. It came and went and then again. Minutes passed, and still the insistent knock on the back door. I opened the door slowly and saw Ernie's face before I saw the two uniformed men behind him.

"Claire. We need to talk to you. Can we come in?"

I motioned them in. They all walked into the kitchen.

"Claire," Ernie said again, "this is Lieutenant Hildebrandt, who is with the United States Navy Chaplain Corps, and this is Lieutenant Schlessinger, also with the Navy. They are from the reserve base in Madison. May we sit down?"

"Yes."

All three of them pulled out chairs and sat down at the table. I did not sit down, choosing instead to lean against the countertop.

"Won't you sit down, Mrs. Lucas?" Lieutenant Hildebrandt urged. I shook my head and stared at him. I shoved my hands into my pockets and picked at the lint gathered in the seams. The three men tried not to stare back. I knew what they were looking at. I was a mess. My pink foam rollers were loose and unraveling in some places on my head, my housedress was stained with coffee, and even I could smell the dishwater, coffee, and the musty remnants of sleep on my body. I could see that the officers were afraid of putting their immaculate uniformed arms on the kitchen table. Besides having stacks of magazines and newspapers crowding the center, there were breadcrumbs and smears of peanut butter and grape jelly from where Bill had made his own lunch.

"Is John home?"

"He's at the mill," I answered Ernie. I saw the one officer part his lips, and I knew what he was going to ask. So I cut him off at the pass. "And won't come home even if I call him."

"Where's Billy?"

"Upstairs. I made him go upstairs. Please don't talk loud."

"Claire, we're here because—"

"I know, Ernie," I said, interrupting him. Then I could not shut up, my mouth running on a single breath of air. "I know because the military only visits for a reason. And that car . . . I know what that car means. Didn't you guys used to drive black sedans during World War Two? It's a good thing it's not summer. Otherwise every farmer in the field from town to here would know. Everyone knows what your car means. *Everyone.*"

It was as though the pain had lifted me above myself, above the men in the kitchen, and kept me hovering close to the ceiling. Although I could feel it, some part of me moved away from it, and I could be calm. I know it surprised them. The men were so startled that they remained speechless. So I asked them.

"What has happened to my son?"

Lieutenant Hildebrandt leaned forward and looked up. She was direct. His instinct, honed by his own tour of duty in Vietnam, was that this was not a woman easily deceived. She had the blank stare of an insomniac and skin so milky white that she was nearly transparent. He had seen that look before, that look of endurance sustained by desperation and hope. She appeared to be reduced to the same basic elements as the men he'd seen at the end of their calendars, counting the days till their tours were up.

He was not supposed to tell the specifics. But the higher-echelon assholes in Washington who made such policies weren't sitting in this woman's kitchen three miles outside the tiny farming and logging community of Olina, Wisconsin. He'd been in so many kitchens. Yellow kitchens, blue and white kitchens, kitchens with rooster plates lining the walls. He had come to realize that it did worse damage not to tell the families at least some of the details. Especially to those families where a body wasn't shipped home. When it was an MIA.

She waited.

He nervously fingered the envelope in his hands, aware of Lieutenant Schlessinger's by-the-book righteousness. So what if they heard all the way back to Quantico that he had disobeyed the policy? Fuck the policy. He had been a theology student and then an ordained priest before he had become an officer, and his tour of duty in 1965 and part of 1966 had been in the same area where her son had been killed. His thirteen-month roll through Vietnam had obliterated any foolish idealism he had ever spouted or believed in, any of the big world concepts about peace. He could no longer sleep through the night, and his thoughts were anything but pure. It had even changed the way he talked.

He had never heard the word *fuck* used so often or in as many contradictory combinations. *Fuckin' Fantastic.* Or *we're fucked. Fuck off. That's fuckin' A-okay with me. Cute little fuckers.* Every now and then the men remembered who he was and what he stood for. Then they apologized for swearing in front of him. But after a while he ceased to hear the language, considering it background noise like the wind. It had even become part of his vocabulary. *What a blessed fuckin' mess.* But he would never say "motherfucker." That was more profane than taking the Lord's name in vain.

His time in Vietnam had altered every cell in his body. He could still smell it on his skin: lime-covered shit and the puking odor when they burned the latrine waste, fresh blood, and the gutty smell of ruptured abdomens. Blood. He'd never forget the smell of blood. Or the heavy greasiness of it on his hands, slippery between his fingers.

He stayed in the reserves as an act of contrition, a penance for what he witnessed, and to do the best he could as a chaplain and a casualty officer in notifying families. He was a United States Naval Chaplain, assigned, as all Naval Chaplains were, to the Marine Corps for duty. The Marines did not want anyone but someone from the Corps itself or from the U.S. Navy Chaplain Corps to notify the families. In all the sickness that was Vietnam, it was one of the few things that made sense. It was a perverse kind of honesty that he could not help admiring. If the Marine Corps took sons and husbands, if those sons and husbands died, then the Corps had an obligation and a duty to see it through to the end. If there was anger or hatred, it was to be absorbed by the Corps as well.

"Your son was in the Fifth Marine Division and a member of India Company, Third Battalion, Twenty-sixth Marines. The Fifth Marine Division was based near Laos at the Khe Sanh Combat Base. India Company was aiding the Fifth Division, Bravo Company, in trying to regain control of a hill called Eight-eighty-one North when they encountered a heavy concentration of North Vietnamese. Apparently the reports were in error about the number of enemy forces there although they knew the NVA was building up. They just didn't know how many or where and when they could expect some action."

He paused. He wanted her to sit down. Hildebrandt had the uncomfortable feeling that she was taller than he was and that she actually looked down at him. He was prepared for any kind of reaction, as was Schlessinger. One father had threatened them with a shotgun, but most often they were either greeted with strained silence or engulfed with hysterical hugs from grieving family members.

"Khe Sanh isn't that far from the DMZ. In Vietnam the DMZ is an allied military term. The Vietnamese call it the highlands, and it is hilly country, some of it covered with jungle that is extremely dense. It is suppose to be a demilitarized zone according to the Geneva Convention, but nothing in Vietnam goes by the Geneva Convention."

The other officer coughed.

"There is a tribe of people that live in the highlands that are not considered to be Vietnamese by either the North or the South. They know that area better than anyone, and they are allies of the United States."

They are called the Montagnards, he nearly added. He would never forget the Montagnards. They were the smallest people he'd ever seen, with tribal markings on some of their faces. They were persecuted and unwanted by the Vietnamese. The Vietnamese called them *moi.* Savages. The Marines and other Special Forces units re-lied upon the Montagnards for intelligence and for guiding them through elephant grass, through jungle and plant cover so heavy that an average-size American was handicapped. Almost all of the men referred to them affectionately as the Yards. Yard scouts were essen-tial. They could spot NVA booby traps. Modified grenades camouflaged in the vines. The vines would swing with their fatal fruit into a soldier's face or chest, detonating upon impact. Punji stakes and pits. He often visited several Yard villages with one of the medics and assisted in giving vaccinations and cleaning up minor shrapnel wounds. They were not of Vietnamese or Chinese descent and they consisted of several tribal groups, each with a specific name. They were in fact the indigenous people of Vietnam. The American Indians of Vietnam.

Schlessinger coughed again.

"On January twentieth, the Fifth Marine Division stormed the western side of Hill Eight-eighty-one North. The commanding officer was killed. Your son was running after his CO when they last saw him. Until we can verify his death, we cannot officially say that he was killed, and so he is listed as missing in action. I have brought you a copy of the official report. His trunk with his personal belongings is being sent from Okinawa."

He placed an envelope on the table.

"I'm sorry, Mrs. Lucas. On behalf of the United States Navy Chaplain Corps and the United States Marine Corps, I'm very sorry."

It was selfish, but he hoped she wouldn't ask any questions. Hildebrandt was exhausted. What he was prevented from telling her, and could not tell her, was that an F-4 Phantom had dropped a load of napalm so close to the Marines on Hill 881N that it was likely that her son had been caught in it and roasted alive. He prayed that Private Lucas had been shot before that happened. That he had died before being burned. Otherwise her son would have danced like a mythical but crazed fairy in the woods, glowing with flames.

I couldn't quite grasp what he was saying. *Jungle.* Jimmy wrote home about the jungle, how it was thicker than the thickest forest we had here at home, how it was unbelievably humid and full of bugs almost as big as his hand. How frogs, bugs, and fish were eaten by some of the rural people called the Yards. How they scavenged through the combat base's dump for food and how they even ate rats. How the jungle camouflaged some of the deadliest snakes in the world and how at night they sometimes heard the chattering of monkeys and once the roaring of a tiger. I read between the lines of his letters: the suffocating terror my son thought he was concealing. His letters to Bill were somewhat guarded even if they said a bit more. He never directly wrote of anything bad happening except for the death of his friend. Maybe this was military policy. *Never tell your mother the truth.*

I tilted my head to one side like a chickadee. *Missing in action.* Had I heard right?

"They can't find him?" I felt myself begin to descend.

"Not yet."

"There must be a way!" My voice rose while the rest of me came down. Something had gotten hold of my ankles. I was not dropping but was being steadily pulled down.

"Mrs. Lucas," Lieutenant Hildebrandt answered, his voice so low that it fluctuated with hesitancy and made it hard for me to hear him, "I know this is terrible news. The Marines never leave their casualties behind even at the risk of losing more men in retrieving the dead. They will keep looking until they find your son."

Ernie leaned forward. "He's right, Claire. Jimmy may have been taken prisoner. He's missing in action. That doesn't necessarily mean that he is dead. His division will find him. They will search until they have exhausted all their options."

Whatever it was gave me a quick yank, and I came down the rest of the way into a tintinnabulation of pain. Eight months ago in the early June heat, I had stood on the cracked asphalt of the Standard station in Olina and watched my eighteen-year-old son board the Greyhound bus. He hugged me so hard that my feet left the ground. I felt his heart beat as though it were straining to escape his ribs and get back inside me. I couldn't think of what advice to give him. And now it was too late. I should have whispered, "Stay scared and run like a rabbit."

I expected him to come back. If not a live son, then a dead son. That was part of the unspeakable deal. He had to come home either way. It had never occurred to me that he would simply vanish. That he would be missing. I needed his body. To kiss Jimmy's eyes shut like I used to do when he was a small boy being tucked into bed, telling him that my kisses would prevent bad dreams. I thought of Bill upstairs. How was I going to explain to my younger son that his brother was missing, that the only evidence we had of him were words hanging in the air and typed on a piece of paper?

I stared past Ernie at Lieutenant Hildebrandt, at the small crucifix pinned to his uniform jacket.

"This is easy for you," I replied hoarsely. "You're a priest or a chaplain or whatever. You don't have to carry a gun. You are," I said meanly, wanting to poke him in the chest, "safe."

Ernie intervened. "Do you and Bill want to stay with us?"

"No."

"Are you sure you don't want me to call John?"

"*No.*"

I heard a sound from upstairs.

"You can go now. All of you, please."

The men awkwardly stood up from their chairs. The chaplain was red as though he'd been sunburned.

The two officers left the house, but Ernie hesitated at the door. I looked at him, and it dawned on me that our neighbor actually knew Jimmy was missing before I did.

"How did you know?" I asked.

He turned around. "I knew because Jimmy had listed me as the first contact on his record of emergency form. And he requested that I come with them. I don't think he wanted you to take this alone."

He shoved his hands into his pockets. "Call us, Claire. Let us help you."

I shook my head. I had nothing to say, and I felt there was nothing they could do to help us.

Then Ernie left too.

I waited until I heard them start their engines, and I watched from the storm door as Ernie did a U-turn in the yard so that he could head back down the driveway, followed by the dark blue sedan.

✖◆◆◆◆◆◆◆◆◆✖

Once they cleared the Lucas driveway, Schlessinger started.

"*What* is wrong with you? You are *never* supposed to tell them all that. You *keep* doing this. You better hope she doesn't call Quantico."

Hildebrandt could still feel her voice, gravelly and rough. The verbal finger jabbed into his forehead.

He suddenly remembered the first lengthy conversation he had had with Private Marcus, a beachboy blond twenty-year-old who had come to Vietnam happy-go-lucky and had joined Hildebrandt's company as a sole survivor of battalion that was, as Marcus put it, *annihilated*. Marcus would never be happy or pretty again. The one piece of shrapnel that hit him had sliced into his face and barely missed his right eye. The burned and jagged scar that ran from the outside of his right eye curved slightly down and then across his right cheek, denting one nostril of his nose. It was a million-dollar wound. He could have gone home. But he refused because a facial wound was nothing compared with the vengeance he wanted to seek.

Marcus was a renegade. The Marines tolerated him because he was an excellent reconnaissance and point man. They overlooked his deviations from what would have been deemed appropriate Marine behavior, although even Hildebrandt had to admit that being based at Khe Sanh was so uncertain that there was no such thing as appropriate behavior, even for a priest at times. He'd seen the Special Forces men who were on their second and sometimes third tours, some of them silent and brooding after spending so much time in the highlands, wary of anything that remotely resembled civilization and wary of prolonged conversation. Their eyes appeared huge inside the frames of their faces until he realized that some of them were dilated. He didn't know what they had swallowed, only that it made them spooky. They did not want him or need him. The Marines he worked with appeared normal in comparison, and they avoided the long-range reconnaissance patrol men as much as Hildebrandt did. Most of the men regarded Hildebrandt's presence as chaplain essential, and he had a warm relationship with most of them. But not Marcus.

Hildebrandt watched as the twenty-year-old swallowed a handful of Dexedrine and chased the pills with a long drink of beer. Hildebrandt considered it ironic that Marcus swallowed a fistful of speed with the very thing that would slow it down.

"Let me ask you somethin', Hildebrandt. Or should I say *Father Hildebrandt*? How can you believe in God after seeing this shit? Did you ever stop to consider that God *sent* his only son down to earth, knowing they were going to kill him? What father does that? What right did he have to send his kid? Why the hell didn't he have the balls to come down to earth himself? Tell me, *Father* Hildebrandt—" Marcus sneered before leaning back for another swallow of beer, "how you can believe in such fucked-up shit as that?"

"That's the mystery of it, Marcus," he answered lamely. "We just have to believe He knew what He was doing."

Marcus stared at him. "Mystery, huh?" he commented. He got up and tossed the beer can so that it nearly struck Hildebrandt in the head. "Is that what you're gonna tell the next guy who gets his brains spilled? Or his mother?"

Marcus lowered his voice and made it go *Dragnet* flat. "Sorry, ma'am. Your son's head was blown off. It's a mystery."

Then Marcus lit a joint. "You're a piece of work." He laughed sarcastically.

"Tell me somethin'," he added, speaking through his teeth so as to keep the hit of smoke in as long as possible. He exhaled. "Are you a man of God who can fuck women or one of those who can't? Or maybe," he added with a sneer, "you don't even *like* women."

His laughter trailed after him as he walked away. Just as the smoke from his joint did. Taunting solidified by the sweet and nauseating smell of dew.

Two days later he watched as Marcus dug trenches with the rest of Bravo Company and they uncovered a mass grave, part of which was old and part of which still carried a heavy stench of rotting corpses. Almost all of them wore pieces of cloth or handkerchiefs tied around their noses and mouths. Some of them vomited before they could rip the cloths from their faces. Hildebrandt wore one too. Marcus was the only one who didn't wear a cloth. Hildebrandt thought it was because Marcus's fragment wounds had damaged his sense of smell. Later that day he watched as Marcus squatted down near the perimeter of the base camp, just inside the razor wire, and rocked back and forth on his feet. Humming. Hildebrandt turned to Lieutenant Abramson.

"Can't you order him to stay away from there? What about that sniper?"

"That gook's cock is off. He can't hit a damn thing. I could order him, but Marcus wouldn't obey me. He doesn't give a shit about command. And he likes that little gook. Although," Abramson remarked casually, "Marcus might just get it into his head to take that little shit out. On the very principle that he shoots so badly and shouldn't be called a sniper at all."

They heard the shot in the middle of the night. Hildebrandt was shaken awake, and he stumbled into a wall of sandbags in his effort to keep up with the medic. At first he thought the NVA sniper had finally succeeded. Marcus was lying in the same place by the razor wire that he had been the day before. But it wasn't the NVA sniper. His own .45 had instantly killed him. His palate was split, and the back of his skull blown open. Two privates lifted and carried him away from the razor wire, running awkwardly with the body until they were behind the protection of sandbags.

✖✖✖✖✖✖✖✖✖✖

Just before he made the sign of the cross and began to recite the last rites, Hildebrandt stopped. He had no idea what Marcus's first name was.

"Steven," Abramson said.

There could be no last confession, no completion of earthly affairs. Even the last rites Hildebrandt had been taught to practice underwent a kind of triage to fit any and all situations. There was the long version that included extreme unction, the short version, and what he thought of as the flying-by-the-pants version, otherwise known as cases of special need. He began with verses 14 and 15 of James V. "Is any man sick among you? Let him bring in the priests of the church and let them pray over him, anointing him with oil in the name of the Lord. And the prayer of faith shall save the sick man and the Lord shall raise him up; and if he be in sins they shall be forgiven him."

"Into thy hands, Lord, I commend the spirit of Steven Marcus. Please receive his spirit."

He paused.

"Mary, Mother of grace, Mother of mercy, protect thy son, Steven Marcus, from the enemy and receive him at his hour of death."

Hildebrandt watched himself go through the motions of sending the dead to God, knowing that Marcus would have sneered at the ritual, that Marcus had achieved what he had wanted all along. He was no longer the survivor of his battalion. With his death, they all were *annihilated*.

✖✖✖✖✖✖✖✖✖✖

There was something about Claire Lucas. He thought about her face. The whiteness of it. The dark circles under her eyes and her skinny neck. Just before she verbally jabbed him, she had moved slightly as if to poke him physically too. The top two buttons on her faded housedress were unbuttoned, and the right side limply flapped open. She was such a thin woman that he remembered thinking that it was strange he couldn't see her clavicle. The skin was purple there. He had dismissed it earlier as a birthmark.

He placed his right hand on the dashboard and lowered his head. He had seen the gross manifestation of bullet-torn flesh, spurting blood, heads blown open by grenades, legs and arms that twitched after being severed. Fingers that closed and opened on a lone hand in the middle of a road while Vietnamese women bicycled past. Holding a bandage on a severed artery in a soldier's groin. The blood left the body with such force that it spurted over his fingers at first. He recognized the butterfly fluttering of the eyelids and the gradual relaxing of the jaws signifying the slow loss of consciousness as the man bled out. Being back in the States for a year hadn't touched that deadening of the senses to horror. Until now. He missed it because it had become a regular feature on the human body in Vietnam and an acceptable aspect of war. But he was home now, and he saw what was supposed to be unacceptable in his own culture. The deep bruise of a punch. The swelling that hid the beauty of a woman's collarbone.

✖◆◆◆◆◆◆◆✖

Hildebrandt lifted his hand, clenched it, and hit the dashboard with his fist.

"Don't tell me what to say! See this?" He pushed his thumb underneath his lapel so that his chaplain's insignia was thrust forward. "I'm not supposed to lie! I'm fucking sick of lying to people. I *am* the chaplain! I'm supposed to tell the truth. I'm going to tell the fucking truth! That woman," he continued yelling, "was not stupid! She knew! She has nothing! *Nothing!*"

Schlessinger had been about to apologize for his own outburst when Hildebrandt went off. He had never heard Hildebrandt swear and had never seen him so angry. He was simultaneously startled and remorseful. Just as he was about to attempt another apology, Hildebrandt shocked him by suddenly weeping.

Schlessinger pulled into the Morriseau driveway, parked the sedan, and got out. Hildebrandt could hear him thanking Mr. Morriseau. Could hear him making apologies for Hildebrandt's absence. Hildebrandt kept his face down. He could not get out of the car.

They drove in silence the rest of the way to Madison.

Thirty miles into their road trip Hildebrandt realized that Marcus had spoken a truth that Hildebrandt refused to acknowledge to himself. Since landing in Nam, he didn't believe in God. If he had gone through the motions of the Father, Son, and Holy Spirit, it was to ease the men against the very real knowledge that they were fighting for nothing but some old men's dreams of winning the invisible. There were no holy wars. There was nothing but money and games and betrayal at the top. But at ground level, *out there,* brotherhood was at its finest. They would die protecting each other. He could believe in that.

✕◆◆◆◆◆◆◆◆✕

Bill had heard everything from the top of the stairs. When he heard their vehicles start up, he quietly crept to his bedroom and pressed his face to the window, watching the exhaust trail behind Ernie's truck and then the officers' sedan. Bill had just gotten a letter from his brother dated January 10, 1968. It was still January 1968. If the soldiers couldn't find his brother's body, then that meant that James was not dead. James was hiding somewhere on that hillside until it was safe to leave. Or maybe the soldiers couldn't find his brother because the Viet Cong had taken him prisoner.

No, Bill thought, shaking his head. His brother had been too good at navigating the woods. James knew just where to hide and where to find what had been hidden. Even their neighbor Ernie Morriseau said that James was one of the best woodsmen he'd ever seen. He just now heard Ernie say that it didn't mean that James was dead. It was a matter of waiting, even if that meant years before the war was over. Before his brother was able to come home.

His nose dribbled on the glass. He was wiping the window clean with his shirtsleeve when a sudden movement from across the driveway snagged his attention. Sitting behind the faded red snow fence that separated the driveway from the oat field next to it was Angel, their neighbor's black dog. Bill pounded lightly on the window, hoping to scare the dog away before Bill's father came home from work. The dog peered up through a hole in the snow fence to locate the noise. Bill watched as the dog focused on the window and then on him. He pressed his flat hand against the glass in greeting. Angel lifted his muzzle as if to scent Bill through the glass.

❌❌❌ I LEANED AGAINST THE DOOR and closed my eyes. I had to think. Think about what to do. My husband would or would not be home. It was hard to tell. It might be his night to spend at Pete's Bar and Grill, and if so, he would be there until the early-morning hours. I prayed that he would stick to his usual routine and not come home. There was some relief in that, one less thing to think about, to consider.

I heard the stairs creak and opened my eyes. Bill had crept down the stairs and was sitting on the bottom step.

"Is James coming home?"

I opened my mouth to frame the words carefully so that they wouldn't be so rough. But my mouth hung open, and I grew desperate, unable to explain what I could barely understand.

"I don't think so," I said, and walked toward my younger son.

Bill didn't cry. Nor did he talk. No whys, no hows, no ifs. Just a blank speechlessness. I rocked him in my arms at the kitchen table, his body stiff and uncomprehending. He would not eat any supper, and finally, I picked him up, bulky and unevenly heavy in my arms. I negotiated the stairs slowly, reaching the top with barely enough energy to carry him into his bedroom. Bill was asleep by the time I reached his bed. I was too exhausted to undress him, so I tucked his limp body underneath the sheets and blankets, his head falling into the pillow. Placing my cheek next to his mouth, I waited until I felt the proof of warm breath upon my skin. When I lifted my head away from his face, I could detect the faint smell of mouse urine even though I had scrubbed the bedroom with bleach that fall. Much to Jimmy's relief, I had forbidden the housing of animals in the boys' bedroom in the winter. With Jimmy gone, the room seemed cold and lonely without the rustling of mice and gerbils in their cages.

I padded down the hallway and began to open the door to each room upstairs, looking in, sometimes walking to a window. In addition to the bedroom I shared with my husband and the boys' room, there were two other bedrooms and a bathroom on the second floor of our old farmhouse. The last door I opened was the bedroom that still housed the crib, now standing in the middle of boxes containing old clothes. Terrified of imaginary feet pinchers under the bed and the shadows cast on the walls by the pines outside, Bill had not wanted his own bedroom. As soon as Bill could learn to walk, he clung to Jimmy. They ended up sharing a bedroom, its walls witness to the angry words of brotherly fights, long pauses of quiet petulance, and often laughter. I stood in the doorway and stared at the peeling teddy bear appliqué on the headboard of the crib.

Just over a year ago Jimmy and I had attempted to clean out this room, going through odds and ends, throwing away clothes too old and too worn, and packing those still useful into boxes for the church charity drive. Normally Jimmy would not have helped me, preferring instead to go fishing or hunting or to listen to his records in the barn loft. He would do anything to get away from the house. He suffered from the sporadic and nearly uncontrollable anger of adolescence, and anything I said set him off. Even the most innocent words acted like a match on the gasoline of his hormones. I used my words sparingly, flinging them out into the air like a lasso in a last attempt to get him to do his chores, to show respect, and to behave like his size: big-shouldered and grown. He bucked my words, my wishes. We fought and retreated, fought and retreated, our wills battering each other like bulls. Periodically we reached a point of mutual exhaustion, and a lull in our fighting took place. It was during such a lull on a quiet Saturday morning that Jimmy offered to help me clean out the room. I had been sitting on the floor, sorting through baby clothes, when I heard the clank of metal and looked up to see Jimmy trying to pry open a green tin box with his jackknife.

"Where'd you find that?"

"Up there." Jimmy nodded toward the closet. "On the shelf."

The lock on the box was old, and it didn't take long for him to spring it. I continued to fold baby clothes but listened as Jimmy sorted through the contents. Then my son whistled.

"What?"

"Read this," he said, handing me a sheaf of yellowing papers.

They were my husband's discharge papers from the military. He had received an honorable discharge, but not, as he had led us to believe, from fighting in World War II and not as a Marine. He had been in the Army for the last six months of the war, and he had never left the States. The third page of the papers praised him for his skills as a quarterback, playing for the Army team. I was dumbfounded. What of the medals he dangled in front of us when he was drunk? The Bronze Star? The Purple Heart? The stories of fighting in Europe?

Jimmy slapped one of his thighs. "Can you believe it?" He howled with laughter. "Dad played *football*! No wonder he can't shoot straight. They must have stood by the goalpost with a beer and said, 'C'mere, boy, here it is. Jus' throw us the football and we'll give you the bottle.' "

"But the medals?"

"Don't you get it, Mom?"

I shook my head.

My son gasped between bouts of red-faced laughter. "He must have bought those medals in a pawnshop. Or stole them off of some other guy."

I watched my son laugh himself into a fetal position on the floor and was astonished that he took it so well. After all, my husband had dangled those medals plenty of times in front of Jimmy, always drunkenly insinuating that Jimmy would never amount to

what those medals represented. I had painfully endured those epi-
sodes with Jimmy, winking at him behind John's back when Jimmy's
face became tight and flushed. I had mouthed the words *Ignore him.*

I listened as Jimmy's merriment slowly diminished.

My husband couldn't have been a soldier. We moved to the
tiny German Catholic town of Olina because land was cheap and
because John's father thought that northern Wisconsin was where
the good life was. It was a twist on Basil Lucas's definition of *Gemütlichkeit,* that life was good as long as the beer was flowing and
somebody else was doing the work. As though the north were a big
beer garden where dreams could be obtained easily. I could hear my
father-in-law in my husband as he argued for what he thought was
the one true life for a man: farming, hunting, fishing, and, unspoken at the time, drinking. John failed dismally at his dream, flopping
as a farmer. His hunting and fishing skills meant shooting the bark
off trees and catching nothing but lily pads and the occasional sun-
fish. How could he have farmed, hunted, and fished? Nobody had
taught him how. All three required work of some sort, work that
my husband wasn't prepared to do. But he kept up his belief in his
rural dream, fortified by a growing dependence on Pete's Bar and a
temper turned physical. Jimmy, on the other hand, seemed born
with an innate ability and desire for rural life, his instincts guided
by our neighbor Ernie Morriseau. While my husband's paycheck
seemed to dwindle, Jimmy kept our freezer filled with ruffed grouse,
venison, ducks, geese, and fish. The older and better skilled he became, the more Jimmy grated against my husband like a steel file. I
was terrified. Such knowledge would provoke a violent fight between my son and my husband. If something happened, Jimmy
would be the one to pay. Not my husband.

"Jimmy," I warned, "there must be some reason for this. You
have to promise me that you won't say anything about this. Not to
your father, not to Bill, not to anyone. Please. Promise me."

"I promise," he said, his cheeks wet from tears of laughter. He
wiped his face on his shirtsleeve. We silently resumed our work of

sorting through boxes. But the next time I glanced over at him, Jimmy was studying the green metal box. I could see he was working a thought, his dark brown eyes full of wondering.

We never did finish cleaning out the room, spending the last moments of our time putting the green box together the way we found it and tucking it as far back on the closet shelf as possible. I reached for the doorknob. I had almost closed the door when the realization hit me.

I pushed the door open again and stared back into the room.

Jimmy *had* warned me. He *had* threatened many times to leave home, and I blatantly dismissed it as being the angst of a teenager.

"I've had it!" he yelled during one of our fights. "After I graduate, I'll be gone. The old man will be happy! And you won't have to nag me anymore!"

"Where are you going to go?" I challenged him. "You need money! Training! A job! If you think it's that easy, then you've got another guess coming! You think"—I threatened back—"that you're the first one around here to think of leaving?"

Why hadn't I paid attention to the way his eyes contemplated the green box, the tremendous *aha!* of his laughter? What a glorious way for Jimmy to leave home, to humiliate his father as his father had humiliated him. He would join one of the toughest branches of the military. He would go to war and, having all the confidence of a teenager, be convinced that he would come home not only alive but as a hero who had earned his medals. He would return a soldier who had actually hit the ground because of combat and not because he was sliding across some manicured grass field making a touchdown. Not only would he humiliate his father, but he would become the opposite of him. Jimmy would come home with respect. With honor.

I shut the door so hard that the sound startled me. I waited. Nothing stirred from Bill's room. My stomach reared, throwing bile and bits of food up to burn the back of my throat and coat my tongue.

I moved blindly toward the staircase and completely miscalculated the distance. I missed the first step and stumbled down the next three steps before catching myself on the railing. I kept both hands on the railing like a toddler and placed my feet slowly down on each step. When I reached the bottom, I stretched my arms out in front of me and followed the marker of light radiating from the kitchen. I grabbed the nearest chair, my fingers suckering tight to the wood.

I sat at the kitchen table under the yolk-colored light and waited for the tears to come. My head ached, swollen with the relentless replay of that afternoon's visit. From time to time I fingered the report, tried to keep it from brushing against the peanut butter smears on the table, and listened for the small noises of the house: the clank of the furnace, the whining of the pipes when I stood up and turned on the kitchen faucet to make more coffee. Listened for the small footsteps of my son should he wake up.

I leaned forward and cupped my head in my hands. If I forgot about the events of the day, it could have been any night from years ago when Jimmy and Bill were babies. My breasts swollen and wet from nightly feedings. Chicken pox or measles. My hands caked with calamine lotion. My fingernails stained pink for days afterward. The parental magic of making the monsters of night dreams disappear. Exhaustion so deep that it made my hearing acute, my ears pricked to the slightest whimper, the creak of bedsprings above my head. The call for Mamma firing through any light sleep, producing a sudden hit of energy to my veins and causing me to leap out of bed with maternal devotion. I stared down at the mottled Formica specks on the table's surface and concentrated on my breathing, on the sound of it in my ears. I thought I could hear the house itself breathing, creaking as though it shifted on the foundation with each breath taken. I could smell the mustiness of my housedress and the earthy smell of my skin. No wonder the officers had cringed at my appearance. I had given up looking at myself, and it was only when

I was mirrored in the face of others that I thought about how I looked.

I rubbed my forehead. My son had kept everything from me.

✕✕✦✦✦✦✦✦✕✕

"You weren't old enough last winter. Why did you have *him* sign those papers?" I demanded of Jimmy the night before he was to board the bus.

"Because," Jimmy said, snapping his fingers. "I knew he'd do it just like that. I *used* him. Dad thinks he's getting rid of me. But he's not. I'm comin' back. Besides," he said, breaking into a disarming grin, "Elvis was in the Army, and nothin' happened to him."

"That's because there wasn't a war going on when Elvis was in the Army! I thought you said," I added, forcing some humor, "that you were leaving and never coming back."

"Oh, Mom." He feigned exasperation. "I was just mad when I said that. I would never leave you and Bill for long. Don't worry." He joked, jostling my arm. "Nothin' is gonna happen to me. I'll be okay. I really will. Don't be mad. Laugh."

"Laugh!" I pinched one of his ears hard enough to hurt. "This isn't funny, Jimmy. This isn't like going duck hunting."

My son just fell back on the bed, rubbing his ear and giggling as if nothing truly were going to happen to him. As if he *were* Elvis, and this was a brief but necessary stint in the career of his life.

✕✕✦✦✦✦✦✦✕✕

For a few months after he left, I tried to believe in Jimmy's optimism. I worked outside, weeding and troweling in my flower beds and my vegetable garden. I listened intently for all signs of life: the frogs at twilight in the pothole at the east end of the forty acres nearest the house; the swallows chattering in the barn; Bill, as he shouted threats and stirred up dust with his bare feet, engaging in imaginary fistfights. My husband put in overtime at the mill and was gone so much that I didn't feel he lived with us anymore except for the meager amount of money I wrestled from what was left of his paycheck and the inevitable fights that followed.

The optimism began to ebb when September came. I stood outside with Bill fretfully hugging my waist and watched the geese pass over, crying over the trumpeting of their calls. All the birds flocked up and left; the swallows first, then the blackbirds, the wrens, and finally the robins. October was the month and color of dying leaves falling easily some days and ripped from the trees by strong winds on others.

November arrived, producing unexpected snowstorms, dumping five feet of snow, and leaving a shock of plunging temperatures in their wake. The snowstorms felt violent to me after the cocoon of summer and fall. The weather hermetically sealed me inside the house and not only turned the world outside uninhabitable but also rendered my inside world devoid of humanity. Bill was in school all day. The small sounds of housecleaning could not overcome the ominous silence that made my mind twist with worries. In desperation to hear a human voice, I made the mistake of turning on our rickety black-and-white TV in the hopes of having something cheery to watch while I cleaned. The black screen lightened to gray, and then Dan Rather's face loomed before me with the United States flag on one side of him and the Republic of Vietnam flag on the other side. He was standing in front of a large building that I dimly recognized as the United States Embassy in Saigon. His face was barely shaved, but I didn't listen to what he was saying because I was staring at the flags. As they could only do on TV, little boxes of information were superimposed on them. I looked closer. On the American flag was a box with the growing number of dead American soldiers. On the Vietnamese flag was a box listing the mounting number of dead Vietnamese Republic soldiers. And then a third box marked "Enemy" contained the number of their dead. For a brief moment the TV screen looked as though it was a board game like *Monopoly*. No money in the bank though. No investments. All dead. I pulled so hard on the switch that it snapped off into my hand. I didn't want the TV to be turned on ever again. I removed one of the vacuum tubes from the back of the set and hid it in the porch closet. Later that night I explained to Bill that the television set was broken and that we couldn't afford to fix it.

"We'll get more library books from town," I said curtly when Bill whined. "Reading is better than watching TV anyway." I watched as my son silently and sadly clocked off the shows he would miss: *Petticoat Junction, Flipper, Mutual of Omaha's Wild Kingdom, Jonny Quest*.

Life inside the house became suffocating. I found myself one morning sitting in front of the living room window, tapping the glass with the heel of one of my Sunday pumps, wanting to see how hard I could hit the window before it would crack. I stopped after the fifth tap, realizing that a broken window might mean a broken arm. So I got up and went to the closet and wrapped myself in warm clothes. I left the house and began to walk up and down our long driveway, hearing that necessary breath again and talking to the air and to the Norway pines that lined the driveway.

It became a habit. I volunteered to walk Bill out to the bus in the morning, ignoring his protests and the pained and embarrassed look on his face. When he was safely on board the bus, I would turn around and begin walking and talking my way back to the house. I waited impatiently to walk down the driveway again at noon, when I saw the mailman's white Chevy Impala pull away from the mailbox.

A letter from Jimmy would send me into happy action, storming through the house in a fit of housecleaning and cooking, dreaming of his final trip home. I believed that everything would change when Jimmy came home. I repeated it like a prayer, taking my rollers out and brushing my hair into curls like a normal woman. I was making plans.

"Just hang in there, kiddo," I said to the air and the pines along the driveway. The farm would be worked by family and not rented out to our neighbors the Edelmans for planting and grazing. I would hire a lawyer and end the farce that was my marriage, peel it off my body like my musty, dusty housedresses and have it judicially burned. I would get a job in town, hold picnics, and visit my neighbors more often. Maybe develop some real friendships.

But when there hadn't been a letter since January 2, my hopeful enthusiasm had died down. I couldn't remember the last time I'd washed my housedress, and my hair rollers felt as natural on my head as my ears or nose.

✕✖✦✦✦✦✦✖✕

I crossed my arms on the table and rested my head on them, intending to nap for a few minutes.

The next time I looked up, it was 11:00 P.M. My husband hadn't come home. The wind whistled as it cut around the corners of the house. I had hurt that officer. His words would have given any normal person hope. *Missing in action* could mean that Jimmy was alive and taken prisoner. But that officer flinched several times as though he could disguise the doubt on his face. Ernie's hands were shaking. I knew the odds were too high to have any hope.

"The Marines!" I said to Jimmy. "Couldn't you have picked the Navy or the Army? Or even the Coast Guard? The Marines!"

"They offered the best package," was his response. Then he added, and I didn't think about it until later, "The Marines take care of their own."

I was not stupid or naive. The chances of Jimmy's being alive were nil. Missing in action was the bureaucratic middle ground. A comma indicating a pause until they could finish the sentence with his remains. When the wind whistled again, it occurred to me that I was waiting out of habit and that this paper in front of me told me that the waiting was done now.

I picked up the report, folded it, and tucked it into the pocket of my housedress before pushing back my chair. I walked to the back door with such deliberateness that it wasn't until I had put on my socks, boots, and winter coat that I thought of Bill sleeping upstairs. I paused, listened for sounds of his young body: a thrashing of legs against the sheets, a crusty cough, maybe a murmur that said Mamma. I heard nothing. Deciding it was safe to leave him, I gathered the tools I would need: a kerosene lamp, a handful of wooden matches, and a long, wood-handled spade. I lit the kerosene lamp and let the flame lap at the glass before turning it down to a small arc of yellow. Then I opened the door.

Even late at night it was still surprisingly warm. I heard the drip of melting ice falling from the eaves of the house. The path to the barn was muddy, and my boots sank down with each step, mud cresting over the green, rubbery toes. The kerosene lamp swung like a warning in my hand, the yellow light rhythmically flashing upon the barn before casting its light behind me on the return swing.

I did not stop until I was directly behind the barn. Twenty feet behind me was the wooden fence separating the barnyard from our forty-acre field to the northeast. The boys considered it a good spot. Both my children played there, close enough to hear my calling voice, yet blocked from my vision so that they could conduct whatever mischief seized them that day. When Jimmy became a teenager, he moved inward and upward, creating his own hideaway in the barn loft. He wired in a stereo and speakers and hauled up the ladder three chairs that he had found at the town dump, one of which still bore the teeth marks of a hungry black bear.

I looked at the upper part of the red barn. Jimmy didn't need to tell me what he wanted to be when he grew up. It blared out of the barn loft. The culture and music lagged behind the rest of the world in our small town of Olina. If it was 1968 elsewhere, it was 1958 in Olina. The stereo loudly announced what Jimmy could not say, and the stereo had only one volume setting. Jimmy called it high and I called it impossible. I'd hear Jerry Lee Lewis howl "Grrrreat BALLS of FIRE!" and before I could finish clipping two shirts to the clothesline, all the small brown bats that should have been sleeping in the barn rafters came flying out of the broken upper windows in panicked droves. While the music only irritated me, it made my husband furious. John would run toward the barn with every intention of catching Jimmy in the act of disrupting the peace, only to find the hayloft empty and the records gone, Jimmy having slipped away and laughing at his own slyness.

The music even caused our dog to act strangely. Every time Jimmy played "Jailhouse Rock," the dog would chase his tail, whirling like a tornado across the yard until the song ended. Then he'd drop to his belly by the porch door, sucking in air and wheezing as though his lungs were collapsing. The funny thing about it was that my son did look a lot like Elvis, and he could sing too. I discovered after Jimmy had left that I missed hearing the harmoniously joined voices of Jimmy and Elvis crooning a love song that sailed in waves across our fields.

I set the kerosene lamp down on a bare patch of ground before grabbing the spade with two hands and wedging the tip of it into the ground. With one foot on the shoulder of the spade's blade, I shoved it deep, then bit and lifted the first clump of dirt out. I kept at it, stopping only once to take off my winter coat and to pin three rollers back into place on my sweaty head. I had to quit digging when I couldn't reach the layer beyond two feet because the warm weather had not penetrated the frost line that far. I dropped the spade and reached into my housedress pocket for the report. I knelt beside the lamp, opened the folded papers, and read them one more time. Not a clipping of his hair, a fingernail, or a smear of blood. Just ink on paper, words that by their presence tried to prove everything yet could not prove anything. Those officers had come all that way from Madison to carry a report that was supposed to substitute for Jimmy.

A report.

I folded the papers into thirds and tucked them into the bottom of the hole. They gleamed against the black soil, so falsely pure in color that I didn't wait to use the spade. I grabbed handfuls of dirt and furiously filled in the hole.

Those stupid advertisements. "Serve your country and see the world at the same time. Experience new cultures." The one I hated most was the recruiting poster I found in his bedroom not long after he left. "The Marine Corps Builds Men." The irony of it. As though my purpose in life was simply to give birth to him and they of course would *build* him into being a man. Made him believe that he was less of a man because he was not in the Marine Corps.

Well, my son hadn't seen the whole world, but he did experience a new culture, and it killed him.

"The Marines take care of their own." Jimmy had said more than he realized. He wanted to belong. So he joined an even tougher family. A brotherhood that his family could not provide, that promised him a place in the world with a name that was not his father's.

I stood up and tamped down the dirt with my feet. I stepped off the mound and stood beside it, lifted my head to the sky, and opened my mouth. What came out sounded unearthly even to my ears: a long, thin moan. When the first cry ended, I opened my mouth again and again. I cried until I was exhausted. My skin tingled. I remembered my coat only when I looked down and saw that my hands had become grayish white with cold. I put it on but did not make any effort to leave, slipping instead into a numbing euphoria of feeling nothing. It felt so good to feel nothing that I almost got trapped by it. I turned to look at the snow-covered forty acres. I could walk the field until I felt sleepy. Then I would nest myself into a bed of snow. Once asleep, I would be able to step out of my frozen body, and the sky that brought all of that warm wind would take me. I would fly over to the highlands in Vietnam, a frozen Wisconsin mother looking for her disappeared son. I let my coat drop from my shoulders and used the sleeves to tie it around my waist. Then I began to walk toward the melting whiteness of the field.

But before I had walked twenty feet, my swollen eyes caught the hint of something red perched on top of the fence post at the entrance to the field. It jarred me awake. I reached forward and

snatched the cap that belonged to my younger son, spun around and
ran toward the house, slipping and falling twice into the icy mud. I
was so mad that I swore at his waste of a good piece of clothing. If
it hadn't been for the day we'd had, I would have yanked him out of
his bed to yell at him.

I heard it after I opened the screen door. Something. Enough
to make me stop. I listened, trying to hear above the pulsing sound
of my own heart, my own breathing. I thought the sound had come
from the house, from Bill sleeping upstairs. But the house was quiet.
I turned around and looked back at the barn and field. At first it was
that old sound, what I'd heard a thousand times in past winters: the
high cry of a cold and forceful wind as it swept across the field
and negotiated a path through the big red pines next to the house.
Somewhere in the threads of its current was a higher, sharper cry.
The wind made another go-around, picking up speed as it crossed
the field and cut through the pines. I heard it again, a short yelp that
resonated like the cry of a child. *Mamma.* I had one of those sudden
pains in my chest, the kind that holds your breath for a few minutes.
When I could breathe again, I let go of the door and walked
halfway into the yard, staring at the barn and field.

I was on the verge of yelling, "Who's out there?" when a flicker
of motion appeared near the lamppost by the barn. Another flicker,
then a third. What moved flirted briefly with the light a fourth time
before stepping fully inside the illuminated circle.

Billy's fox. The animal returned my stare, its black tufted ears
framing its luminescent eyes. Tentatively placing one paw forward,
the fox lifted its narrow muzzle to scent me. Its fur was still mangy,
but the bare patches were growing back, and the animal had put on
weight, its eyes bright and alert. It had also regained some of its
natural wariness, its head cocked sharply for any sound that might
indicate danger.

When the animal continued to sniff the air, the purpose of the
stocking cap in my hand became clear. Bill had left an article of
clothing, a territorial marker of goodwill so that the fox would as-

sociate the scent with the bearer of food. Despite my grief, I was amazed at the animal's survival and my son's ingenuity.

When Bill woke up in the morning, I would have something to tell him, however small a victory it would be in the enormity of our pain. He would be upset that I had removed the cap, and I briefly considered returning it to the fence post. I could almost hear Jimmy's voice, his repeated counsel that a wild animal grown used to people was a dead animal, that the DNR routinely had to kill some of the black bears at the town dump when they became aggressive and moved beyond the dump, showing up at houses, looking for food. When Bill objected to his brother's advice, Jimmy caustically told him that not everyone treated wild animals with his same good intentions.

"But I don't kill them!" Bill had shouted at his older brother. "They don't attack *me*!"

The fox sat on its haunches. I gazed at the fox and thought about what I would say. I would tell Bill that I had seen the fox, that he had saved it and that it would survive on its own now without his red stocking cap, without the food Bill had so patiently placed behind the barn. I would tell him that he would have to believe that the fox survived even if he never saw it again.

I tucked the cap into my coat pocket before stepping forward and waving my arms. "Pssssst!" I hissed loudly.

I began running toward the fox, waving my arms. "Run!" I shouted. "Run!"

The fox appeared so startled by my sudden and rapid approach that it didn't move, and I thought I was going to run right into it. But in a movement so sleek and calm that it appeared magical, the fox lifted itself up from its haunches, turned, and slipped away into the darkness.

ERNIE COULD NOT SLEEP. He walked outside without a jacket but went as far as his toolshed and no farther.

He gazed through the dark at the Lucas farm and noticed a light bobbing back and forth, moving with whoever was carrying it. It was near midnight. Normally he would call or drive over to any of their neighbors if he suspected something was wrong. But Claire's silence that day was final. She would not ask for help and made it clear that it was not wanted. His wife was right. There was privacy, and then there was a freakish need to keep secrets that were visible anyway.

Ernie owned and rented many fields. He turned and looked at the field most familiar to him. Everything he had seen, touched, smelled, or found in that field since he was born was real. If the field and the land around it were unpredictable, they were only so much as the weather was unpredictable and the animals that lived in their area were occasionally unpredictable. But natural.

When he was seven years old, he had witnessed at the far end of the field two bucks that had locked antlers in their duel over a doe and had spent hours trying to disengage from their combat. He disobeyed his father and followed his father and his uncle as they approached the two deer. The bucks were exhausted and down on their front knees, their eyes bulging and their tongues lolling. The two men carried long iron poles taken from one of the hay wagons. They put a pole to the shoulder of each buck and shoved so that the animals went down on their sides. Then his father and uncle walked around to the animals' backsides so as to avoid being kicked. Ernie's mouth fell open as he watched his father pull a handsaw out of his hunting jacket and work the teeth back and forth through the tangled forks holding the two sets of antlers together. When his father finished cutting through, the two men stepped away slowly, keeping their eyes on the two rutting bucks just in case they found the energy to rise and charge. After twenty minutes the winded bucks realized they were free from each other and scrambled up. His uncle shouted a long "HEYYYYY!" and the bucks scattered, one bounding into the nearby white pines and the other clearing the fence to the adjacent north field.

He popped up from the grass, curiosity overriding his father's authority. "Why didn't you shoot them?"

His father frowned at his son's obvious disobedience, but his uncle laughed and winked at Ernie. "We've got more than enough venison. You gotta have bucks if you want more deer next year!"

✕✕✦✦✦✦✦✦✕✕

He took a pack of Camels from his coat pocket and tapped one out, then raised his shaking hands to light it. Ernie watched the smoke blow out of his mouth and nostrils. He'd been trying to quit, but did it matter anymore? He looked up at the sky. He still had not told Rosemary what he had seen. Ernie had kept only one other thing from Rosemary in all the years of their marriage, and that was his grief and anger over her inability to bear children. He knew it wasn't right, that it wasn't her fault and that it grieved her worse than it did him. But he couldn't let go of the resentment of having been cheated out of being a father.

Now for the second time in his life he would be unable to tell his wife something so important to him. He tried to understand what he had seen three days ago, but it was the confused yet questioning expression on the young man's face that Ernie could not interpret. Or the way Jimmy took off his helmet—and did Ernie imagine it, or did Jimmy momentarily hold the helmet as though saluting Ernie before he dropped it? Then the way Jimmy turned and walked away from Ernie without speaking.

The pain of that day suddenly struck his chest, and he bent over for a few minutes. Ernie took deep breaths and after a few minutes slowly straightened up. He dropped the cigarette to the ground and smashed it with his boot.

He felt betrayed. His own land had produced something beyond the unusual and explainable. He would never be able to work that field without sweaty palms and without looking over his shoulder. He could not know it then, but his dread would slowly deepen in the coming years. He wanted to tell Rosemary, but he suddenly wasn't sure that she would believe him. There was only one person he could think of who might have been able to help him, who would have been able to explain what it was Ernie saw and what he should do. But Claude Morriseau was long dead.

✕✕✕✕ WHEN MY LITTLE BROTHER WAS four, he became fascinated by the way the burners on our gas stove burst into blue flames when he turned the dials and how he could adjust the flames with a slight turn of the dials. I caught him one day and shook him.

"Your face could get burned!" I yelled. "Do you know what would happen if the stove suddenly went nuts? It would blow up on you!"

Then I turned on one of the burners and stuck my finger in the flame for a second. It hurt. *Christ, it hurt,* but it did what I wanted it to. I had scared Bill enough to make him cry.

Then I put my finger in my mouth to cool it off. I pulled it out and showed Bill the blistering skin on the tip of my finger and the blackened fingernail.

"This is what happens. Only *worse.*" I shook my finger in front of his face. I could smell my own burned flesh, and I could tell the smell got to him too. Bill gagged and threw up on the floor before he started crying like he always did. A deep breath and then a drumroll building up.

"You're scaring me!" he cried.

"You damn right I'm scarin' you. I'm doin' it for your own good. Don't play with the stove! I better never catch you doing it again or I'll stick *your* finger in the burner!"

✕✕✕✕✕✕✕✕✕

For some odd reason this is what I thought about when I first became aware that I was on fire. I was burning, and not even screaming can make the sound that would tell someone how terrible it feels. How napalm is like being covered with scalding jelly and how it sticks to the skin, burning and burning until there is nothing left. Then that sudden rise, as though the ground had become a trampoline. It wasn't a bouncing Betty. I had been thrown too high into the air for one of those evil fuckers. I don't know if I was hit by one of our own shells or if I stepped on an NVA land mine. It was definitely a lot bigger than a grenade and gave off a cloud and a familiar smell. White phosphorus. All I know is that I was shot straight up into the air. The rush of air felt good, and the burning stopped instantly. I saw the flaming boot from my right foot, and it took me a few seconds to realize that my right leg was attached to it, glowing like a fluorescent lightbulb. It flipped end over end like a stick tossed through the air for a dog to retrieve. I looked down at myself, and everything that was me was no longer. Pieces of my body were blown *everywhere*. I didn't think I'd leave Vietnam without some kind of wound, but I had hoped it would be a million-dollar one. I didn't even get *peanuts*, our word for wounded in action. I got Kool-Aid. Killed in action. And I was doing what we joked about when we were stoned or drunk. When we were scared but wouldn't admit to it. I was fertilizing Hill 881N. I could look down and see Lieutenant Miller's body. I could see my buddy Marv. I could hear him screaming until the rest of the guys from the Fifth Division tackled him so that he'd shut up. "I lost Lucas! I can't find Lucas! Goddamn motherfucker! He ran ahead of me!"

Actually I was running after Lieutenant Miller, who got a sudden case of buck fever. I knew he had stood up too soon, and I ran after him to knock him to the ground. He insisted that we charge the hill and reclaim it and proved it by being the first one. We only had one M-60 and not enough linked ammo for it. My M-16 kept jamming. I hated that fuckin' gun. No matter how many times I cleaned it, took it apart, and put it back together, that damn thing jammed if you breathed on it. I wanted an M-14, but they wouldn't give us any. I would have given anything for the Marlin I'd left at home. Our column had moved west on the hill in dense fog. Then, early in the afternoon, the fog lifted like a curtain on a stage, and we were surrounded by a mean audience of the NVA. We were too few in number and should have retreated until we got more reinforcements, but our orders were to stay. Miller took a round in the chest and another in his head. I felt a spray of something on my face, and then I tripped over him as he fell. I got up and tried to wipe my eyes so I could see, but it was as though I'd covered them with grease. Then I looked down at my hands, and the gray greasy stuff covering my hands and my face was from Miller's head. I freaked out, and instead of running backward, I ran forward.

Cracker Jack had radioed in for air support when we realized the joke of our position in the clearing fog. I could barely hear him. The last thing I heard was Cracker Jack yelling:

"Ricky-tick! Most fuckin' ricky-tick!"

Some help did come from overhead. An F-4 Phantom suddenly appeared and dropped the napalm that rose like a giant arm of fire. The napalm that hit me.

I wondered: *How is it I can still hear myself? How is it I can still think?* I didn't see or hear Lieutenant Miller. I was floating in the sky, but I existed. I was conscious of *being*.

Just as I watched and felt my body tear apart, I then felt something else. A gathering of my senses. As though the invisible molecules that had belonged to me came together again. I remained above Khe Sanh for a day, saw the A-4 Skyhawks and the F-4s as they shelled around our sister Hill 881S and around the perimeter of the Khe Sanh Combat Base. There was a shitload of the NVA out there, but even with heavy bombing, they were hard to find. It didn't matter how many of them were killed by bombs. Ol' General Giap always had more. He opened his platoons like cages so that like an endless supply of mice, they kept coming and coming and coming.

Eventually everything that was green and beautiful would be bombed beyond recognition. The dead NVA soldiers would simmer and bloat in the sun, peel away and rot in the rain. The smell would be god-awful, like the spring pileup of winter kill from a large lake during a hard winter.

✕✕✕✕✕✕✕✕✕✕

We were hunkered down on Hill 881S on the night before I bought it and joking about the movie we'd miss on Saturday night: *Paradise, Hawaiian Style.*

"Ha!" Marv said with a grin. "We are in a movie. *Paradise Khe Sanh Style.*"

"Fuck," Charlie Matheson said, "some paradise. Did you guys see Miss January?"

"The oh yeah, oh yeah Miss January that you left back at the base? How could you leave Miss January?" Marv joked. "We could use her pillows right now. Imagine resting your head on those babies."

They laughed for a while and then were quiet. I crawled over to where Lieutenant Miller was sitting alone. Brooding. He asked me if I thought the sensors were off, that maybe there weren't that many NVAs because they weren't visible from the air.

I puckered my lips like some of the righteous old women I'd grown up with and pretended to be shocked. "You mean the sensors that we're not supposed to know about?"

He laughed, and it made me feel good that I had cheered him up. It was supposedly top secret. *But come on.* All those Air Force jets dropping something in December and January. Something that we could barely see and that didn't explode. It was clearly intelligence equipment of some kind, and it was more accurate than counting piles of elephant shit. Since we couldn't stand up on patrol and yell, "Okay. Time's up. How many of you little yellow fuckers are out there?" there had to be a way they knew the NVA was massing up. They always assumed that we couldn't figure it out. But we knew. The Bru tribe of highland people that picked over the food in the base's garbage dump suddenly disappeared the week before we bivouacked on Hill 881S. If you didn't have to fight, then was the time to get the hell out. Miller found out what it was they dropped even though it was supposedly *classified*. The equipment was called ASIDS. Air-delivered seismic intrusion devices. In other words, tiny microphones draped over tree branches that detected enemy sound and movement. Did that sound like James Bond or what? *How lucky we were.* Even John Wayne never had ASIDS.

It always pissed me off when our own higher-ups thought we were stupid. I think when some of those officers work their way to the top, they lose their fighting intuition. They had experience but no sense. Hell, they lost all five of them and often that extra sense that comes from fear. Your face buried in mud, your knees pulled up to your chest, your neck hunched down. Squeezing your eyes shut against tears and praying that your flak jacket and helmet would do what they said they would: protect you from flying shrapnel. I felt like I had eyes in the back of my head. Just like Mom did when she caught me doing something and I couldn't figure how the hell she saw me or knew. There was never just one NVA. If you saw one, you calculated fifty to that one.

"You know we never get an accurate description," I said. "Those five officers that were shot just after New Year's were wearing uniforms that look a lot like ours."

"Yeah," he said, "but you've been out there. What do *you* think?"

I thought about the green hills around us and what it must have been like for the Bru and the other Yard tribes who lived there a hundred, maybe two hundred years ago. How Kho's family found everything to eat, in addition to the rice they grew, in those hills. What I would do if I had been born there.

"I think that they know this fuckin' place a lot better than we do."

✕✦✦✦✦✦✦✦✕

I tried to stay above the smoke filling the sky. I remembered thinking how much it looked like the smoke spewed out of the stacks from the Wilson paper mill. I looked down at all my friends. I knew the stubbornness of those guys, and I was both proud and pissed at them. They would look for me no matter what. Even if it killed them just looking for my dog tags. I also knew that they'd stay trenched in that shithole known officially as the KSCB until they were ordered out. Some of us called it Private Piles' Plateau. Just like a bad case of hemorrhoids, the base would bleed and bleed until almost no one was left.

I could look down and see it all. What many of us had suspected was true. We were fuckin' bait for a battle that never should have been. Those fuckin' old men in Washington didn't give a shit about us and argued while we sat there. Some of our own COs were trying to move some asses to protect us, but they were in the field too and a long way from Washington. All that reading I did about the history of Vietnam paid off. I put it together. It was about history. About losing a garrison and losing face like the French did with Dienbienphu. While General West-who-wanted-More-Land argued for his chance to invade Laos and then Cambodia—the Big Time, we called it—with Johnson, we didn't get the supplies we needed because the NVA had cut off Route 9 and everything had to be flown in. That was blood in the eyes too. Our airstrip had become a kill zone. Any pilot who could land and take off without being hit by a mortar round was not just close to God. He was God. It seemed like every other copter that tried to land on the airstrip was doomed to be shot out of the sky.

That short period of time around Christmas when we went

into the village and went to a restaurant that everybody called
Howard Johnson's was just that: short. Everything after that went
downhill. We were ordered to wear our flak jackets and helmets at
all times.

✕◆◆◆◆◆◆◆◆✕

Early the next day we were told to move toward Hill 881 N because
it had been taken by the NVA and we were to help Bravo Company
take it back. Just before we started humping through elephant grass
to the other hill, Cracker Jack surprised all of us when he pulled out
a miniature Bible with pieces of paper stuck in it. He had a deep
voice when he became serious. His voice could make a sick Yard
baby stop crying. It came right up through your feet and into your
head. A rocking chair voice. He began to read, our medic turned
Baptist minister.

"Young men, listen to me as you would your father. Listen,
and grow wise, for I speak the truth—don't turn away. For I too was
once a son, tenderly loved by my mother as an only child and the
companion of my father. He told me never to forget his words. 'If
you follow them,' he said, 'you will have a long and happy life.
Learn to be wise,' he said, 'and develop good judgment and common sense! I cannot overemphasize this point.' Cling to wisdom—
she will protect you. Love her—she will guard you."

Cracker Jack said it was a proverb of Solomon. His namesake.
If anyone else had read it, I would have said it was bullshit. I'd never
listen to my old man. But it was comforting coming from Cracker
Jack. For a week we had that awful feeling of being sitting ducks.
Of being cut off and not wanted. Charlie Matheson was right when
he said we were orphanage kids on a government camping trip, left
behind on purpose.

I watched Cracker Jack's back as we walked in a column
through the grass, and I noticed the ripple of muscle above the collar of his jacket at the back of his neck. *I'd believe in God again*, I
thought, *if Cracker Jack was my minister.*

XXXXXXXXX

None of it mattered anymore when I looked down at all of it. I was a fastball of energy. At the end of that day I realized that I could will myself to move. That I could go anywhere I wanted to.

XXXXXXXXX

I wanted to go home.

XXXX IN THE IMMEDIATE DAYS THAT followed, Claire and Bill experienced nightly sleep absent of any sensation or movement. They did not speak of it to each other. At daybreak Bill crawled toward the surface of consciousness. He struggled to open his eyes, and when his eyes did open to the light, all the swollen visions of his brother entered, so he shut them. His mother must have felt the same way because it was noon before she roused herself and Bill out of bed. The phone went unanswered. The one time his mother picked up the receiver, it was the priest asking her about holding a mass.

"You can say a prayer for him or dedicate a mass to him. But we just can't attend right now."

Bill became aware that other people knew because of the cars that drove slowly into their driveway for a week afterward. Their various neighbors discreetly left casseroles, potato bread, cakes, Swiss steak, frozen vegetables, jam, venison sausage, and other food wedged between the screen door and the storm door.

During that week Bill and Claire sat at the kitchen table in a silent stupor from noon until suppertime. Only then did his mother rise and heat some of the food left on the porch. She filled her plate but did not eat, nursing a cup of coffee instead. Her bloodshot eyes watched Bill's hands as they moved the food from his plate to his mouth. All that could be heard was the sound Bill made chewing his food. On Sunday night he put his fork down midway through the meal.

"I missed school this week. Can I stay home tomorrow too?"

"No." Her voice sounded strangled. "I want you to go to school tomorrow."

"Bill—" she began more fluidly—"Your brother is—"

"No," Bill shook his head. He stared at his mother, silently raging at her easy acquiescence. At her betrayal of his brother. "You *don't* know."

✕◆◆◆◆◆◆◆◆◆✕

Bill could confidently maintain his belief during the day. It was the night that frightened him. He fell into a deep but strange sleep. Whatever lived under the bed, whatever had pinched his toes had moved up his legs. He could not open his eyes to see what it was, to cry out for help because his sleep was like being beneath water. Every time he neared the surface to break it, he saw a glowing light before something pulled him down. One night he tied a corner of his brother's white crocheted bedspread to the bedpost on his brother's headboard and stretched it across the room to his own bed. He held a loose corner in his fist. It was the only way he could go to sleep. But when he woke up in the mornings, he had a burning sensation in his groin, and with deep shame, he discovered he had wet the bed.

Like everything else his brother had touched or used, the bedspread that had once covered him cloaked Bill with its growing imaginary powers. He cut off some of the fringe bordering the bedspread and put it into a small leather pouch. He carried the pouch with him in his pants pocket. If he was struggling through another bad day at school, Bill would discreetly shove his hand into his pocket and hold the leather pouch with the tips of his fingers.

In the weeks after the news, Bill's father was almost never home. When he did make an appearance, it was to raise his big bark-peeling fists. John Lucas walked, talked, and even slept as though he'd been permanently wronged. Bill had never been able to determine what cross his father had to bear when his life appeared to be identical to that of other men in Olina. Men who worked even harder but who did not drink or beat their wives. Bill did not understand why his father, so apparently aggrieved with having to support a family, did not run off like so many men who discovered that *wanting* and *having* a family meant *working* for one. But John Lucas doggedly stayed as if to punish them. Even with overtime pay at the mill, he barely earned a living and spent a third of those earnings on the beer and liquor he consumed at Pete's Bar or kept stashed in numerous hiding places all over their farm. He drank with the unmistakable aura of defeat that hours later would ferment and bubble up to his brain as a killing rage.

Bill thought it was common for all fathers to get so angry until he started school and discovered otherwise. He intuited that most mothers did not wear sunglasses on cloudy days or all day long. He listened to the chatter of the other children as they related what their parents had done and with whom, the vacations they went on as families and the TV shows they all watched. The other mothers belonged to bridge groups or baked cakes and cookies for the church's bake sales.

The awareness pushed him out of the garden of his imagination and simultaneously caused him to dwell deeper in it. He had only one clear memory from the year he was six years old, a memory so permanently fixed in his consciousness that not even denial overrode it.

✕◆◆◆◆◆◆◆◆✕

Sitting on the staircase. It was night, and he was looking down through the railing bars at his parents. His father had pinned his mother's arms and hands above her head on the floor with his left hand while his right hand waved the blunt tip of a screwdriver above her face. Her yellow housedress was bunched up around her waist. Bill could see the purple grooves of garter marks in the white skin of her thighs. Saw the tears streaming into her black hair and heard the odd rasping sound from her mouth. His father's pants were down around his calves. One booted foot covered his mother's bare ankle and the black dirt from the sole looked like pepper on her toes. Bill shook. Not knowing what else to do, he let loose a wail reminiscent of an ambulance siren. It caused his father to turn around and loosen his hold on Bill's mother. She threw the big man off-balance and struggled to her feet. In her frantic run up the stairs, she swept down and grabbed Bill under his armpits, dragging him with her until she reached the top. His brother, awakened by Bill's cry, ran out of their bedroom just in time to see their mother carry Bill into the bathroom and lock the door.

"Jimmy! He's gonna kill me!" she screamed through the door while Bill hunched down in the corner by the toilet. He peed involuntarily, and it pooled underneath his butt cheeks, soaking his pajama bottoms.

His brother was sixteen then but nearly full grown at six feet three. He stood at the top of the stairs and watched as their father attempted to climb the steps. Bill held his breath, and even his mother became silent, pressing her head against the door. They could hear his brother's voice through the door. It was his deadliest voice. Even and quiet.

"Better stop right there. Or I'll beat the shit outta you if you come up here," his brother said. "And you know I can do it."

They heard John Lucas stumble back down the steps. Listened as he groped through the unlit kitchen for the back porch door, opening and slamming it with such force that the tremors shook the beams up in the bathroom.

Bill's mother pulled him out of the corner and picked him up by the waist like a sackful of chicken feed. She carried him out of the bathroom and into her bedroom. She dropped him before standing in front of the window but kept one clenched and trembling hand wound in the fabric of Bill's pajama top, pulling his small chest out at a painful angle. Bill watched as she rested her forehead against the glass and began weeping.

"Mamma."

As if recognizing him for the first time, she turned from the window and in a burst of sudden anger viciously shook him.

"What were you doing out of bed? Huh?"

She grabbed his hair in her fist and pulled his head back so that his trembling face was exposed.

"I wanted-d a glass of water-r-r," he stuttered, his chest heaving between hiccups.

She slapped his face and shoved him toward the door. "Go to bed now! And quit crying or I'll give you something to cry about!"

Bill stumbled out of the room and into the hallway, where he fell into his brother's arms. His brother lifted him and carried him into their bedroom. He remembered James stripping him of his wet pajama bottoms before tucking him into bed. Remembered the feel of cold sheets against his wet butt. He watched as his brother reached into their closet and pulled out his Marlin .30-30 rifle with a scope mounted on top. He reached into the closet again and pulled a box of bullets from the top shelf. Bill watched as James knocked the lever up and opened the chamber. He listened as his brother loaded the rifle with seven long-nosed bullets. He would never forget that peculiar clink as they fell into place in the gun's chamber.

"Where are you going?"

"Shsh. Go to sleep. I'll see you in the morning."

His brother carried the rifle with the barrel pointed to the floor, cautiously opened the door, and vanished from the room. Bill later learned that James, perched on the lid of the woodbox, sat up for the rest of the night near the back porch door.

After his brother left, Bill did his best to protect her. When his father's wood-nicked hands began to strike his mother, Bill ran in between them, slapping and kicking his old man into chasing him around the house and away from her. With his father thundering up the stairs behind him, Bill would dash into his room, lock the door, and push a chair against it. Then he would wrap his brother's bed-spread around him, even covering his head with it to muffle his father's yelling and pounding on the door. The bedspread would protect him even if his father managed to break down the door. Bill wrapped himself around and around into a cotton cocoon. Even if his father did break down the door, he would not be able to find a beginning or end to yank his son out of his protective shroud. Bill didn't even think his father would try. The bedspread's whiteness glowed. His drunken father would be frightened of such an ethereal illumination, the way people long ago had been frightened by the paleness of the moon.

IT WAS TEMPTING TO KEEP Bill home from school, to ease the intensity of those days and break the jags of crying. It was my motherly sense of doing what was right for Bill even though I could not participate in it myself. I forced my son back into the outside world. On weekends I looked out the living room window and watched Bill play by himself, building snow forts. Sometimes he just sat on the snowbanks and stared at some destination beyond the house.

Our neighbor Rosemary Morriseau called several times, inviting us both over for dinner. She repeatedly offered help, but I declined. Jimmy had spent so much time over at the Morriseaus' that it hurt me. He admired Rosemary Morriseau in a way that I could not compete with. He did not see my short experience as a teacher as comparable to her experiences as a wartime nurse. Bill had begun to spend time over there as well, as though I didn't exist and was not his mother. I insisted he stay at home. I would not lose another son in that way. But there was a deeper motive in my not keeping contact with Ernie and Rosemary Morriseau. I wanted to keep at bay the questions I could not answer, did not want to talk about the voices I thought I heard and talked back to. I did not want Rosemary, a sharp and intuitive woman, to read what I suspected was true.

I was not just going crazy. *I was crazy.*

✖✖✖✖ LIKE AN ANNUAL APRIL FOOL'S day joke, the first gnats of the season came out in black clouds. Bill could not play outside without being tormented by them. Black and small. Biting. Always biting. He spent a day or so swiping them with his hands, blowing them out of his nose before resigning himself to them as he did every year. He ignored them as they tried to crawl into his eyes and crowded together in the wells of his ears, biting and then dying in clumps. Bill was so overjoyed with the early miraculous warmth of spring that tolerating the bugs was made easier in the late orange light. He stole one of his mother's gossamerlike hairnets that she used to hold her hair in place before going somewhere, covered his face with it, and pinned it to his short hair with a few of her black bobby pins. In this way he could walk through the woods and swamp with some protection as the fine netting shielded his mouth, nose, and eyes.

On April 4 he joyfully jumped from the school bus and ran toward the house to change into play clothes for another evening outside. He was out of breath by the time he reached the kitchen and so did not hear her at first. He was halfway up the stairs when he became aware of the radio's drone and of her weeping somewhere downstairs. He found her in the living room, lying on the davenport. The radio on the end table produced mostly static. He could discern a faint voice, could tell it was the afternoon news, but the static was so bad that he turned the radio off.

"Mamma," he said, shaking her shoulder. "What's wrong?"

She pushed herself up just enough to rest on one elbow. He

saw the ribbing from the brown davenport cushions imprinted on her face.

"Dr. King has been shot."

The pressure from her crying raised the blue veins in her forehead. Not knowing what else to do, Bill wedged his butt between his mother's legs and the edge of the davenport and patted her shoulder. He sat with her for an hour, listening to her deep sobs, feeling them as they racked her chest and tunneled up through her shoulder into his hand. He stared out of the window at the bird feeder, at the warm and sun-filled yard beyond the bird feeder, the deep green pine boughs dusted with the incandescent light of a falling sun. He could dimly understand the significance of what had happened, but Dr. King was not related to them. He could not understand his mother's intense reaction.

When she became too exhausted to cry any longer, he nudged and prodded her into sitting up and finally into standing. He wrapped one arm around her waist and helped her climb the stairs. He maneuvered her until she was in front of the bed, and then he gently pushed her until she sat down. He pulled off her house slippers and tucked her under the blankets. He ran back downstairs, made toast, and heated up a can of chicken soup with mushy noodles. He put the bowl of soup and toast on a tray that was meant for the luxury of eating in bed but had never been used for that. He gingerly carried the tray upstairs. She swallowed the spoonfuls he offered her. Chewed on the pieces of bread that Bill broke apart and fed to her in bits as though she were a pigeon. When she would eat no more, he took the tray back to the kitchen. Climbed the stairs again. This time he wet a clean washcloth with cold water and wiped his mother's face, holding it against her swollen eyelids. After she gradually fell asleep, Bill got up from the bed and stood in front of the bedroom window. He stared at the setting sun behind the barn.

✕◆◆◆◆◆◆◆◆✕

Bill spent the next few weeks getting up an hour earlier than what was normal for him. He dressed and then slipped into her bedroom to shake her awake. Every morning he cajoled her out of bed, pushed her pink bedroom slippers onto her feet, and guided her downstairs to the kitchen. She sat while Bill made toast and oatmeal and coffee. That was when he learned to make coffee, to drink coffee, and to love coffee. His mother drank her coffee black but appeared not even to smell its presence until he pressed the edge of the cup against her lips to make her drink. He poured coffee into his cup halfway, filling the rest of the cup with evaporated milk. The milk became less and less of a component until he was drinking his coffee black as well. Bill made sandwiches at night, taping notes to the refrigerator so that she would eat them while he was at school.

By the middle of May she could get up by herself in the mornings although she still relied on Bill at night. He washed her hair as she bent over the bathroom sink, rinsing it and then toweling it dry. She sat on the toilet seat, holding a jar of Dippity-Do in her lap while Bill combed and parted her hair into thin sections. He held each section with one hand while dipping the tips of his fingers from his other hand into the jar of green gel. He smeared it onto the section of hair to be rolled around the pink sponge curlers his mother always used. When he was finished and her hair was wound into neat pink rows on her head, he tied on the blue hairnet that would hold them in place while she slept. Then Bill helped his mother into bed and talked to her until she fell asleep.

✖◆◆◆◆◆◆◆✖

"What the hell is wrong with your mother!" his father bellowed one evening, angry over another dinner of Campbell's soup.

"She's just tired and kinda sick," Bill answered, bent over his bowl of soup. "I'm taking care of her."

His father brooded for a few minutes. Bill felt his father's bloodshot eyes bore into him. Bill knew that if his mother stayed sick, his father would keep away from the bedroom. His father hated illness.

"So you think you're the man of the house now," he rasped, reaching over and poking Bill disdainfully in the arm.

Bill lowered his head and didn't answer. To say something would only enrage his father and give him reason for taking further action. Bill silently ate his soup and prayed that his father would leave the house soon.

✕◆◆◆◆◆◆◆◆◆✕

The last day of school did not bring its customary release of screaming-with-joy children. They heard muffled crying and even some wailing from the hallway. The children fearfully looked at one another. Sister Agnes walked to the front of the classroom.

"Children—" she wavered, her face wet with tears "—we must go to church and pray. Senator Kennedy has been shot."

Bill solemnly walked with the other children to the Sacred Heart Church a block away. He felt sick to his stomach and worried that he might throw up in the pew.

When he got home, he found his mother spread out on the davenport again, facedown into the cushions. He pushed her over and saw that she had been crying. But she was not asleep. She was drunk.

✕◆◆◆◆◆◆◆◆✕

Bill repeated his routine of early April, adding to it housework. He vacuumed floors, washed dishes, dusted, washed windows, stripped beds, and learned how to operate the washer and dryer. Once a day he pulled his mother out of the house and, holding her hand, took her on a walk through the woods, hoping that the summer warmth would crack her catatonic state. He learned how to drive that summer, putting two pillows on the driver's seat so that he could see above the wheel of the station wagon. They exchanged places just before they reached town. Once his mother was done with her grocery shopping, she drove a half mile outside town, where they exchanged places again. Bill drove the rest of the way home.

By the beginning of August his mother seemed to revive and take her place in the day. Bill was free to play for a few hours. He ran for the woods, the swamp, and the river with the desperation of regaining some of his former life. On rainy days he hid in the barn loft and occasionally pulled out his jar of money. He had once been elated over how much money the jar contained, thrilled that his brother had entrusted him with holding the money. He wearily fingered the bills before stuffing them back into the jar. He could not think of what to do with them.

He stuck the jar of money back into the corner of the barn and piled the loose hay on top of it. He climbed down from the top of the stacked hay bales and sat on the very hay bale where his brother and he had sat the night before his brother left. The ashtray was still full of his brother's cigarette stubs. He dipped one finger into the ashes and ran it across his forehead. He dipped his finger three times more, creating a slash of ashes down each of his cheeks and across his chin. Then he fell asleep.

✖✖✖✖ THAT STRANGE WEATHER OF JANUARY *was* an omen.

Anyone who might have brought peace was killed. To strive to be good and to do good were dangerous. It was as though an undeclared hunting season had been established. In April of that year it was the shooting of Martin Luther King. Then in June, Robert Kennedy was shot in California. I crumbled, sensing that it was not just my life, but that life in general was out of control on a grand scale, and nothing I did or said could stop it.

✖✦✦✦✦✦✦✖

I made it through the rest of that winter and spring because of my son. I had taught Bill too, as soon as he could walk, to listen for that breath and pulse that were outside. He had absorbed it even better than Jimmy had. Knowing that walking, just walking, might make me feel more alive, he dragged me outside even when I didn't want to go. Some days I couldn't hear anything, stumbling along the path that the boys had made in the woods. But I was always aware of his small hand, warm and moist, clutched tightly around my own hand. Tugging me along like a listing ocean liner when I slowed down or tried to stop.

One morning I sat at the kitchen table and watched as Bill made coffee and breakfast. As he pressed the cup to my lips and the hot coffee spilled into my mouth, it was as though I had been slapped. I woke up and saw what I was doing to Bill. How tired he looked. How ashamed I felt. I had to get better. By early August the tide of my grief had gone down enough so that I could do basic chores and Bill could play once again.

When I could not do housework, the long days of light allowed me to walk the perimeter of our field. Sometimes I walked it twice until my legs felt rubbery, until I was exhausted from talking aloud. I would walk home with a hoarse voice, climb into bed, and fall asleep instantly.

⬧⬧⬧⬧⬧⬧⬧⬧⬧

One evening I was scrubbing the porch floor and trying to find some breathable air above the ammonia fumes and the suffocating humidity and heat of August when I thought I heard someone talking. Thinking I had unexpected company and not wanting any, I raised my head just enough to peep out the porch window. There was no one out there. I stood up and peered out the window at the rest of the yard.

It was seven-thirty, and Bill was already in bed, suffering from a mild case of heat stroke from having been out all day without a hat or enough water. I looked beyond the yard and at the forty-acre field behind the barn.

Our neighbor to the south of us hadn't cut the field yet for a second baling of hay, and the tall grasses, dry and wheat-colored from the sun, rippled in waves as though the wind were skimming water. I leaned over the sill.

I had helped hay that field dozens of times. Looked at it every day during the boredom of household chores and gratefully walked its edges. I thought I knew every inch of that ground, but it didn't look the same. The field appeared to flow from the setting sun and toward me, announcing itself. My mind emptied itself of everything: of Jimmy's death, of Bill floating through his days in make-believe, of the loneliness I'd grown used to, and of the sweat trickling between my breasts and down my face. I dropped the ammonia-soaked rag in my hand and opened the porch door.

By the time I reached the barn, I had unbuttoned my cotton shirt and pulled it free from the waistband of my baggy khaki pants. I stood by the fence post for only a moment. Using my arms to sweep aside the grass in front of me, I plunged into the field as though wading into a deep lake. Timothy weed and brome seeds scattered themselves across my sweaty belly, and some of the grass slapped back hard enough to deposit some of their seeds on my face.

I heard a whoosh of exhaled air and then a bleat before I saw her. I froze. A doe scrambled up from the anonymity of the grass thirty feet in front of me. I held my breath and waited, waited for the brief whistle, the stamp of a hoof, and the white flagging of the tail. The doe remained standing although her flanks rippled with muscular tension.

I had seen plenty of deer before, sometimes as close as the doe. But after the initial moment of discovery, they bounded into the woods within seconds of having been seen. Never had I seen one this close for so long.

The long lashes. The eyes reflecting blue inside their blackness. The velvet and tawny brown ears, brown flanks, and white under-side. The muscles and cabled tendons in her slender legs that appeared so thin as to be brittle when in fact they were strong and with deceptively dainty black hooves that could slice like a knife. Jimmy had killed does as well as bucks during deer season. I had eaten such beauty. I had longed for such beauty. I did not have it and did not have to look at myself to know what was there.

My shirt flapping open in the wind. The overwashed bra that trapped sagging breasts and shaped them into torpedoes, holding them up with a Cross Your Heart elastic that pinched. My head, covered with ridiculous pink sponge curlers, and my hands, wrinkled and peeling from scrubbing the porch floor. The small ring of fat that would never go away and rode my hips and waist like a tricycle tire. The slightly pouched belly that would never give birth again. My own face. I had lost so much weight that every bone in my face threatened to cut itself out of my skin, and my skin was as waxy and as pale as a diabetic's. My eyes were sunken, the eyeballs appearing to float in ponds surrounded by ocular bone cliffs.

"Did you call me?" I opened my mouth to ask, but I reacted instead by stepping forward. That was when I saw the fawn. It scrambled to its feet, and I could see the fading spots on its body. The doe whistled and flagged her tail, leaping across the field in bursts with her fawn following her. She chose a section of the fence that was down so that her baby could clear it and not become entangled in wire. They both disappeared into the white cedars that bordered the swamp. I walked to where they had bedded down in the grass and knelt. With the palms of my hands, I touched the flattened grass and felt the warmth from their bodies. Rocking forward, I pressed the side of my face into the grass. Then I remembered Bill. He was alone and sleeping in the house. This time I wouldn't forget him.

◆◆◆◆◆◆◆◆◆

Before entering his bedroom, I went down the hallway to the bathroom. I leaned over the sink and stared into the mirror. In the artificial light, my eyes were the flat black of an ancient flint arrowhead, the same color as Jimmy's eyes in the Polaroid picture he had sent home the month before he died.

"Soldier eyes," Bill had said with all his TV wisdom, fingering the photo. "Like in the movies, Mom."

My face. Wrinkles wound like ivy around my eyes. Those pink curlers that held my hair like mousetraps.

I was sick of those curlers.

"For chrissakes," my husband had sneered a few days before, "don't you ever take those things out?"

Yes, I thought. *I'll take them out.*

I reached into the medicine chest for a pair of barber's scissors. After grabbing one curler and pulling it up, I cut it free from my head. One by one, curlers of my hair fell into the wastebasket until I was left with a jagged crop of hair barely an inch long and a scalp that finally breathed.

I slipped into Bill's room and stood over his small body. It amazed me that he could sleep in pajamas and with all those blankets when it was so hot, that he could still sleep so deeply after the loss of his brother whereas my insomnia had returned. I wouldn't realize until years later that it didn't matter where he slept or how many blankets he had wrapped around him or whether it was hot or cold. His was a dreamless sleep, the deepest sleep of all. But as I looked down at him, he appeared as though he had had a bellyful of my milk and was gone from the world until the next feeding.

I lifted and carried him as if he were a toddler again, on one hip with an arm wrapped underneath his rump, his feet touching the middle of my calves. I scooped up the cotton blanket at the foot of his bed with my other hand.

My arms were stiff with pain by the time we reached the doe's bed in the field. I dropped the blanket and spread it flat with my foot before easing Bill onto the ground. Then I lay down next to him. Bill had not stirred or made a sound in our journey from the house to the field. I put one hand up near his mouth and felt the warm air from his nose. I studied the way his breathing caused a small tremor in his chest every time he inhaled and exhaled. I lifted his hands and looked at each of his fingers and at the dirt underneath his nails. His palms were as calloused as his feet from climbing trees. I could tell from his long legs that he would be taller than his brother. His toes flexed and curled in his sleep.

I was brushing the hair away from Bill's forehead when I heard a car pull into the driveway and park. I crouched over Bill and lifted my head just enough so that I could see through the grass without being seen. My husband had come home.

He staggered into the house. I prayed that he was drunk enough to fall into bed and go to sleep. But every light went on, and ten minutes later John came out of the house. He shuffled until he stood underneath the yard lamp. I could tell by the way his shoulders were hunched forward that he was squinting his eyes as though trying to see in what little natural light was left.

"Ca-laire! Bill! Where the hell are you!"

I listened to his repeated call for us. The words were slurred, but with each effort his voice rose to the boiling point I knew so well. The doe had bedded down just close enough to have full view of the comings and goings from the house and barn while staying in the dark, beyond the rim of the barn and yard lights. I could see my husband, but he could not see me.

Only last week he had shoved me against the refrigerator, his hands around my neck, choking me. "Why did you do that? I told you that would make me mad!"

Why did I do what? What had made him mad? I didn't know what I'd done wrong. And really I had done nothing wrong. He had just come home in a bad mood, ready to burn the house down if that was what it took to make him feel better.

Bill had run outside and gathered rocks from the driveway. As if to break up a dogfight from a safe distance, Bill pelted his father with rocks, striking him in the head twice so that he would release his hold on my neck. My son's aim was perfect. I didn't get hit once by one of those rocks. I instinctively reached up to my neck at the memory of it. The bruises were yellowing now.

I stared at my husband. He weaved and reached out to grab the lamppost to steady himself. I opened my eyes and tried to make them as big and as dark as the doe's, tunneling my rage and hatred through the dark and into the light. And into him.

Then something warm covered my back and traveled down my arms to my hands. There was a voice again, not from my head but from behind my left ear.

"Laugh," it whispered. I felt a warm breath on my neck.

I hesitated. I wasn't sure of what I heard. Then it came out of the dark again.

Laugh.

So I did. I laughed. It came out of my mouth in a way that my crying never did. It pierced the darkness naturally, hauntingly high like the scream of a bobcat in heat. Suddenly everything seemed funny: my husband, our marriage, life in Olina, and the craziness of my drifting days. I laughed harder, my voice dropping in pitch so that it squalled.

My husband stumbled backward from the post. "Jesus!"

I laughed again. But this time like the raven. With a deep pitch and rattle in my throat. It worked. My husband ran, tripped, fell down, and stumbled back up in his desperation to reach the car. The rumble and then roar of the engine. The tires spitting rocks.

I waited until it was quiet. Stroked Bill's face and smiled at the fact that he had slept through it. That I had protected him and he didn't know it. Smiled for myself. I was *not* crazy. There *was* a voice out there somewhere in the field. I listened, hoping to hear him again, and turned around to see if I could glimpse him. The sun had gone down, and it was completely dark. All I heard was the rustling of grass, but I wasn't afraid. After fifteen minutes of hearing nothing, I decided to take the first step. I sat up and held out my hand, hoping to feel that warm breath again. Then I called out, "Sweetheart. Mamma's here."

1976

✕✕✕✕ HE HAD TAKEN THE STEERING wheel off of the green Oliver tractor but for no other reason than to do it and to give the impression that he was working even if he had been making the same tinkering noise for twenty years. The tractor had started once during their first year on the farm, and John had driven it for a mere ten feet before the engine killed and stayed dead.

"Cracked manifold" was the diagnosis from the local snuff-chewing farm mechanic, and then he named his price for fixing it. Of course John would not pay it then just as he would not pay for it now. His older son had put it in plainer terms not long before he left for Vietnam.

"The engine's fucked!" his son had called out from a window in the upper level of the barn. "And has been for twenty years! Besides," his son sneered, his cigarette ash drifting to the grass below, "you wouldn't know how to drive it anyway. Who do you think you're foolin'?"

John Lucas stared up with hatred at his son but made no move to go after him. Nothing John did made the kid obey him, and when Jimmy got older, it became dangerous even to try. But as a young boy Jimmy was immune to his father's punishment. It didn't matter how many times he told the boy he was stupid or hit him with a belt, the kid just laughed. If Jimmy hadn't been conceived so early in their marriage, John Lucas would not have considered Jimmy his because there was nothing of the Lucases in his looks except his height. He was dark like his French-Irish mother. Jimmy had her black hair and deep brown eyes, and he could tan up in the summer as brown as an Indian. John grimaced, thinking of their neighbor Ernie Morriseau.

He could hear his wife singing as she hung clothes on the line. He threw the wrench against the wheel and then settled himself down next to the hub to rest. Earlier that day he had purchased a bottle of Wild Turkey bourbon. A treat, he told himself, for working so hard at the mill lately. He drank straight from the bottle. Claire's voice drifted over the top of the barn, and he shifted uncomfortably against the wheel. He had awakened that morning in a strange mood, an almost oily feeling that made his limbs feel disconnected. He slithered out of bed, and he noticed that his brain felt the same way. It slid inside his skull like kneaded but well-greased bread dough. His head grew heavier as the day went on, as though his brain were expanding. Things he had not remembered for years bubbled up, warm and yeasty. Until his wife began singing something familiar that punctured the bubbles.

✖◆◆◆◆◆◆◆✖

"Are you sure she's not somethin' else," his father had whispered, pulling John aside at his wedding reception, "besides being a mick and a frog? And," his father added, puffing on his cigar, "a little princess?"

John was in love then, proud of his lovely and well-educated wife.

"Shut up, Pa."

Basil Lucas blinked several times in astonishment, his broad fatback face turning red as though slapped into a hot frying pan.

"Don't think," he slurred, repeating what he had grown fond of saying to his tall son, "that I can't reach up and pull you down, big-shot soldier. Height's nothin.' "

"Here," John said, grabbing a stein from a passing waiter and pushing his corpulent father down into a nearby chair, "drink another beer and sit tight for a while."

Basil Lucas downed half his stein and stared after his son dancing with his new wife. "Height's nothin'!" he roared, and they danced farther away from him, ignoring him. "You gotta have muscle too," Basil muttered to himself.

✕✦✦✦✦✦✦✕

John couldn't figure out why his wife seemed so happy today. He took another drink. What the hell did she have to sing about? At least it wasn't crying, though. He hated it when she cried, and he remembered her blubbering the day they had taken Jimmy to the bus station. She had only made things worse by doing that, and their son was just doing what other people's sons had done for hundreds of years. Served their country. *Hell,* John snorted, feeling the bourbon in his nose, *he* didn't have a mother to see *him* off when he enlisted. Had circumstances been different, he might have been killed too.

God, he had a sudden terrible pain in his head. He put his head between his knees to relieve some of the pressure. He sniffed again, and he thought he smelled blood, and then, oh, God, that was another memory he thought he had buried.

The truth was it never left him. The sight and smell of those blood-soaked bed sheets or how the smell of blood mingled with the odor that was always in their Milwaukee neighborhood, living as they did four blocks away from the Schlitz brewery. That dank primeval smell of blood mixed with the odor of fermenting hops and yeast. Because it was too late to transport her to the hospital, the doctor did what he could in their home. But his mother died in childbirth anyway, the baby girl dying with her as well. He and his sister, Edna, sat on the parlor sofa and listened to the frenzied sounds of footsteps and watched as two neighborhood women ran back and forth from the kitchen to his parents' bedroom. Then it became quiet except for the low, moaning sobs of the women.

His mother's labor had come on with sudden force while she was preparing breakfast for eight-year-old John and his younger sister. His mother hadn't been feeling well for the last month of her pregnancy, but nothing prepared him for her collapse next to the stove and the sight of all that pinkish fluid that flushed out from beneath her skirts followed by a river of blood. He ran to their next-door neighbor, the Krugs, and Gertrude Krug called for Dr. Horowitz before running over to the Lucas house. She sent John to the brewery to get his father, but Basil Lucas sent his son home, saying there was nothing to worry about as women had babies all the time and he was needed more at work than he was at home.

His father remained speechless for a few minutes upon his arrival home hours later. John thought it was grief, the way his father bent over and moaned, smacking his hands against his thighs. But then he started shouting.

He had no wife! How the hell was he supposed to work and raise two kids? "What was wrong with her? What was wrong with *you*? Why the hell didn't you do something!" he yelled at the doctor. "She didn't have any trouble before! They slid out like butter!" How the hell could she do this to him?

Dr. Horowitz stared at Basil Lucas. He was wet with sweat, and the front of his shirt was soaked with blood. If he had not been a medical doctor, John knew Basil Lucas would never have let him in their home because he was Jewish.

"You thickheaded ass!" Horowitz shouted back. "She had high blood pressure! She's always had high blood pressure, and your son and daughter did not slide out like butter! Your wife had a massive stroke! The placenta detached too soon, and the baby died before it could breathe."

Horowitz wiped his forehead against his shirtsleeve.

"Mr. Lucas! Mrs. Krug says your wife hadn't been feeling well for a while. It was not your wife's fault! Why didn't you bring her in to see me? She never regained consciousness, the poor woman."

"Damn it all!" John and his sister heard their father say as Gertrude Krug was pushing them out the door toward her own home. "It was that goddamn baby! A girl! What a waste!"

Gertrude Krug fed John and his sister pork roast with heavy

gravy and onions, poured over boiled potatoes. Henry Krug, over his wife's protest, put two large glasses of lager in front of John and his sister and told them to drink it. His sister refused, hating the taste of beer, but John drank it and was grateful for the numbness it brought him. Henry Krug filled the glass up a second time and a third time until the boy was nearly incoherent. Then they were put to bed, John with the Krug boys and Edna with the Krug girls. He dimly recollected hearing the conversation between Henry and Gertrude Krug float up from the kitchen, as the boys' bedroom was directly above the kitchen.

"The cheap bastard. He wouldn't pay for Amelia to go to the doctor." To which her husband responded, "Enough, Gertie. The man has just lost his wife."

"Well!" Gertrude Krug cried. "He might not have lost her now, would he, if he'd have dished out some money? You yell about the Jews being cheap? They take better care of their women!"

Rather than mourn his wife, Basil Lucas bore a grudge toward her until he died. It never occurred to John to be angry with his father. In his family's particular German culture, obedience to a father and a husband was absolute and remained the highest value, above love and respect. His mother had disobeyed her husband by dying. Without his wife, Basil Lucas seemed to forget about things his children needed, such as new socks and decent shoes and boots. He and his sister did without or quietly accepted the clothing neighbors gave them. Their humiliation deepened when their neighbors' children recognized their own cast-off clothing on the Lucas children and teased them relentlessly. John and his sister stayed miserably silent. His father would not tolerate complaining. In this way he was just like the other working-class German fathers in their neighborhood.

Whenever his father beat him, John cried with anger at his mother. He silently agreed with his father. His mother should have been stronger. His father labored fourteen hours, sometimes eighteen hours a day. The other German women in the neighborhood were as tough as horses, and many of them had more than five children. Why not his mother? It was Basil Lucas's excuse whenever he thought his children were faltering.

"You're weak!' he would yell. "Like your mother! I'm doing this," he often added, hitting his children with the belt and the belt buckle, "to toughen you up. You won't make it in this world if you cry all the time!"

In his child's mind, John concluded that his mother wanted to leave them, and without realizing it, he nursed this thought his entire life. When later asked about his mother, he would feign to have no recollection of her and would simply say she died.

Gertrude Krug and two other neighborhood women took turns cooking the family meals and cleaning the house, having Edna work alongside them so that when his sister turned ten, she became responsible for the housekeeping. Their father continued to work at the Schlitz brewery despite his loud opinions and garrulous nature. Basil Lucas was the physical epitome of the beer-drinking, working-class German man: big-chested, thick-waisted, and ham-fisted with graying blond hair and watery blue eyes. Unlike a baker who spends his days so drenched with the smell of sugar and spices and cream fillings that he cannot eat his own creations, Basil Lucas drank his company's product with pride and as frequently as if it had been water. He puffed on nothing less than Cuban cigars. It was not uncommon for his father to come home from the brewery with a bucket of beer, its sides smeared with butter to keep the foam down. He drank the entire bucket with his heavy meals of pork, sausage, or beef and fried cabbage or potatoes. His skin reflected the basics of his diet, and his red face had the corrugated consistency of a tire tread. He might have retained his pride in being a German had it not been for the backlash and prejudice during the First World War. Basil Lucas bristled anytime his loyalty to America was called into question. He could not have proved his loyalty, as he was just a hair too young to fight in the First World War, but *oh,* what he would have given to have the chance. He was a fighter. There was no one that could stand up to Basil Lucas's fist, and he carried out his job as a foreman at the Schlitz brewery just by the threat of that fist.

While Edna maintained their house, John Lucas got a job at the brewery during high school by the force of his father's will. Basil Lucas did not want anyone to think he favored his own kid, so he worked his son to exhaustion, running errands, filling in for a sick worker in any one of the sections of the brewery. If he made a mistake, his father's punishment was immediate. Once he hit his son so hard in the head that it nearly shattered his eardrum. John hated working at the brewery. It was the local priest's intervention that allowed John Lucas to participate in the school sport he loved the most, football. For three nights of the week he trained with his high school football team.

John Lucas did not want to enlist. He wanted to serve the war effort by working as a merchant marine on the Great Lakes, but his old man was adamant. Basil Lucas made it clear during their Christmas dinner of 1944.

"I'm gonna go with you tomorrow. You're gonna sign up," he said, gazing at his son across the dinner table with hard-boiled eyes and pointing to him with a mustard-covered butter knife. "We are Americans, and it is your duty to serve your country. You can fight the Germans because you are an American first."

John Lucas thought about his father's handshake before he boarded the train for basic training. That stubby-fingered paw that threatened to crush the bones in his son's hand.

"Make sure they send you to Europe," his father said gruffly. And then he walked away from the train platform.

John Lucas almost didn't pass basic training when it became apparent that anything beyond fistfighting was hopeless. He was so cockeyed in shooting a rifle that they had his vision tested several times, and they discovered, after his initial physical, that the hearing in his left ear was impaired. But an opportunity arose and he tried out for and was accepted into the Army football team. He rationalized that his playing football for the Army was a contribution as well, to lift morale. He never wrote home, fearful of his father's response to a letter postmarked in the United States. He also dreaded the day of his release from military service because he had no stories or medals, only a letter praising him for his skills as a quarterback and one of the tallest quarterbacks ever at that. He did mingle with some of the returning veterans, working part-time at a VA hospital, and escorted them on various outings. Disabled or not, they all found a way to hit the local bars and taverns, and John went with them, quietly listening to their stories of hand-to-hand combat, the types of bombs, the snipers, the various landscapes they had been in and the various strategies of fighting. They weren't all enlisted men. One man who frequently joined them was an Army officer, and John often felt the man's dark eyes rest on him while they played cards. The officer usually didn't say much, but John knew that he had fought in Europe and that his wounds were less physical and more mental. Shell shock.

"I thought you were a doctor or an orderly," the officer commented one evening, "until they told me that you were a football star. At least in the Army. How did you manage that?"

"I applied several times to be sent overseas, and they wouldn't send me," John lied. "Do you think," he added, his temper rising, "that I should've gotten my own rowboat and gone over?"

"No, I guess not. Pretty peachy, though, that you got to play football. I guess," the officer drawled out, "you *can* get injured that way. Too bad, huh? Big German fellow like you. We could have used you on the front lines."

"I said I wanted to be there. It's not my fuckin' fault I didn't go."

John got up from the table and threw some bills down. Striking an officer when he was so close to being discharged would be stupid, but his temper often got the best of him, and so he decided it was safer to leave. John could see the contempt on the man's face.

"It's none of your fuckin' business anyway," he said, and, dramatically clicking his heels together, saluted the officer just as contemptuously.

Two days before John was to go home, they all went out for another evening of cards and beers. The Army officer remained quiet during the entire evening and finally slumped over in his chair. He'd been drinking bourbon while the rest of them had stuck to beer.

"Jesus Christ," said the sergeant they called Limb Limkowski because he was missing his entire left arm, "he's gonna take a leak soon, and it's gonna be over our fuckin' shoes."

"I'll take him to the biff. I have to get back to the base anyway."

John hoisted the officer up and managed to get him to half stumble, half walk, leaning heavily on John's shoulder, as they made the trip through the dark and narrow hallway behind the bar to the men's room. John kicked open the stall door, yanked down the man's pants and underwear, and pushed him down on the toilet. The officer's upper torso leaned sideways like a branch heavy with fruit until one stubbled cheek was resting against a stall wall. John listened as the urine hit the side of the toilet, and he briefly considered pulling the bastard off the seat and shoving his head into the toilet bowl. He noted that the officer was not circumcised and that his previous assumption that the man was Italian was probably not right. He was dark-skinned in a funny way. It was hard to deduce from the name. Captain Waterston.

The guy was taking a long time to piss.

Fuck 'im, John thought.

He opened the stall door and looked around. Nobody else was in the bathroom, which was unusual, given the amount of drinking going on in the bar.

He shut the stall door again. He grabbed the officer's head by his hair and rammed it into the stall wall at least three times until John was sure the officer was unconscious. He held his breath and stood still to listen for any other noise. Then he unpinned the man's Purple Heart and Bronze Star from his uniform and shoved them into his own pants pocket. He slipped from the bathroom, left the bar from the nearby back door, and ran down the alley.

Before John was discharged two days later, it was with only a minimum amount of questions about the incident from his CO.

"He was drunk but okay when I left him in the bathroom."

"You left him? Was he conscious?"

"Yeah. He told me to beat it because he could go to the pisser by himself. So I left him and went out of the back door of the bar," John lied, "because I was on my way out anyway."

When he disembarked from the train, his father was waiting. Basil Lucas stared in wonder at the medals pinned on his son's chest. Then he did something he had never done before in John's memory. He embraced his son.

"No letters? *Ach!* You were probably too busy fighting."

"Yeah, it got pretty rough out there. But boy, can I tell you some stories." And John proceeded to tell his father the stories he had heard, embroidering them so that his father's face flushed with more and more pride every time.

Then John met Claire at a VFW dance and told his father he wanted to go to college on the GI Bill.

"You think you're a Uihlein? Or a Pabst or Miller? That fancy fiancée of yours has filled your head with corncob dreams. A workingman doesn't need an education beyond reading, writing, and arithmetic. If I was your age again, I'd go north. The land is cheap there, and the only reason some of those poor SOBs ended up back here in Milwaukee is that they didn't work hard enough or weren't smart enough. Uncle Sam still giving GIs house loans?"

John nodded.

"Then get that loan and go north. When you own your own land, you are your own boss. And you have more freedom. The secret is to make the land work for you! Then you can go hunting and fishing all you want. You'll be a happy man then. You will have," his father said, slapping him heartily on the back, "*Gemütlichkeit!* Unless," his father added shrewdly, "you want to stay here and work at the brewery."

〉◆◆◆◆◆◆◆◆◆〈

John looked at the 40-acre field in front of him. It was but a portion of the 250 acres he owned, and although it was paid off, he was just a hop ahead of losing it because he was always late paying his property taxes. His father didn't know what he was talking about. Sure, it was beautiful, but the joke was on him. Just like his wife. How proud he had been that such a petite dark-haired beauty had chosen him, a lowbrow German boy with only a high school education. She had been beautiful in the beginning too. But like the land, she was mostly swamp and rock now. Farming this far north required an innate sense of what to do, and John clearly didn't have it. It didn't matter how hard he worked, he couldn't make a living off the place like some of his neighbors. He was sure they had family money of some kind, and that was how they did it. Or like his neighbor Morriseau, who probably got a government subsidy because he was a timber nigger. Within a year of their moving north, John knew he was licked and got a job with the lumber company instead

He was grateful that his father died five years after they had left Milwaukee and had never come up to visit them. Just picturing his shriveled white-haired father in the hospital made the tears start up in his eyes.

His old man never understood. None of them understood. He *was* a good man, but the world had always been against him. What had been hard for some was harder for him. He worked, didn't he? He raised a family and didn't run out on them, did he? Yet they weren't grateful at all. People in Olina looked at him as though he were eight years old again and wearing hand-me-down clothing. Shit, his son was dead, but Jimmy was talked about like a hero. Why the hell was that?

John had been secretly relieved when Jimmy had asked for his help in signing the enlistment papers because Jimmy was underage at the time. *Thank God,* he remembered thinking, signing the papers in the Cedar Bend recruitment office, *the kid is finally going to do something besides listen to records.* He was grateful that Jimmy was leaving. The kid had been nothing but trouble and was too smart for his own good. Just like his mother. *Well, smart-ass,* he thought smugly as the bus drove away from the Olina Standard station, *welcome to the real world. Life won't be so easy anymore. You're gonna get what's comin' to you. They'll dress that fathead of yours down. That's what happens when you disobey your father, when you point a gun at your father, when you humiliate your own father.*

On the way home from seeing Jimmy off, John whistled a tuneless song and, glancing back at his younger son lying across the backseat, began to make some plans. Now that Jimmy was gone, John was going to make sure his younger son didn't grow up as cocky as his older brother. John wasn't sure how he was going to do it, but Bill was not going to point a rifle at him. That pipsqueak in the back of the car was going to grow up knowing the normal order of things. Father first. Then son.

✕◆◆◆◆◆◆◆◆◆✕

He sucked at the bottle's glass lip, tilting it every now and then for a small dribble to make it last longer. A sudden chuffing breath came from the field, and he put the bottle down. Something black was moving within the tall grass. His head hurt again, and this time his chest chimed in and his heart *coughed* so that he held his breath. Then he saw the thick, long tail and realized it was just his neighbor's busybody dog. He had wanted to shoot that goddamn dog so many times for roaming over to their place. But despite his racial disdain for his neighbor, John Lucas was wary of him. Ernie *had* fought in the war. John knew that Ernie was considered a premier hunter and marksman, even by some of the most racist men in Olina. He had no idea that Ernie had taught Jimmy how to shoot until someone at Pete's Bar and Grill mentioned seeing Ernie and Jimmy duck hunting on the Chippewa. Although drunk, John drove home as though on fire. He knew Claire had something to do with it. He had split her lip and thrown her across the kitchen until she hit the refrigerator before feeling the steel of a double-barreled shotgun pushed into the small of his back. His son said nothing. He didn't have to. John raised his hands in the air, and his thirteen-year-old son pushed him outside with the gun barrel jammed into John's back. Then he gave John a frightening demonstration by moving the barrel only slightly past his father's waist, and firing until the old outhouse door was full of holes. The last thing John heard before passing out dead drunk was the sound of his son reloading.

✖◆◆◆◆◆◆◆✖

His wife was humming now. How dare she sing while he was sitting in the hot sun? He had tried to make her happy, but she didn't listen to him. She never did anything he wanted, and it seemed she deliberately did the opposite, often acting like a crazy woman. He used to warn her ahead of time. "I told you that makes me angry," he'd say, and she'd go and do it anyway. His father was right. Women could make a man feel bad about himself. It was their small and sneaky way of bringing a man down. They didn't have a bit of sense, and his wife was worse in that she thought she knew more than he did because she had a fancy degree and had once taught school. All that book learning had only made her crazy. He thought it was just a phase of grief until she began to walk at all hours of the day and night. Before she began talking to invisible people. And then that night when he heard her and could have sworn that she surrounded him on all sides, even floating above him and laughing hysterically. Jesus Christ! The woman was a bitch *and* a witch. He stayed away from her after that.

But he was angry now. She had the nerve to sing while he worked. He started to rise, bracing his free hand against the tractor tire.

His wife had once told him that he went about it all wrong and that he didn't understand where they lived. The fury he felt at her criticism came out swinging until he had knocked her down. They hardly talked anymore, but he was going to talk to her now in a way he felt she best understood. She deserved to be hit just for the audacity she had in singing while he was out there trying to fix the damn tractor and for the way she looked at him sometimes. His older son had that same look, and now his younger son too stared at him as his brother once did. On the rare occasion when he ran into Ernie Morriseau, he saw the same look. Through their eyes came Captain Waterston's cold stare.

"Liar," it said.

"What?" he asked, because he could have sworn he heard it spoken aloud.

Then his chest seized up, and he was falling down, the bottle slipping from his hand so that he could grab his chest.

✕✕✕✕ THERE WAS NO INDICATION IN his mother's voice about why he had to come home in the middle of his shift as a mechanic at the Standard station. Bill had just gotten the job after school let out that May and was still thrilled, although not outwardly so. He was seventeen and had a natural knack for fixing engines. It was the perfect job for him. It allowed him to work and not have to talk to people. That was the owner's job. Wally Wykowski explained to the car owners what needed fixing on their vehicles, how much it was going to cost, and when the cars would be ready. Wally praised him every other day, slapping him on the back. Bill swelled under the rare light of being told he was good at something. Now it was July 5, and his mother had called the station in the middle of the afternoon.

"Come home."

"Now?" he asked irritably. "My shift isn't over. What's so important that I have to come home now?"

"Come home," she repeated. "Now."

He bristled after hanging up the phone. His mother could be maddeningly taciturn. Yet Bill was just as reserved as his mother, just as reluctant to give words away or any hint to what he was feeling, keeping his voice flat like his mother's when she spoke the language of everyday needs and wants. He had seen his mother unhappy, seen and heard her sob uncontrollably, and experienced her voice raised in anger. But it was mostly her choice of words that conveyed what action she wished him to take. *Now* meant "right away."

So Bill drove the six miles home in the battered '67 dull blue

Ford Falcon that he had purchased for a hundred dollars and arrived in time to see the Olina ambulance unobtrusively depart from the Lucas's long driveway. He pulled his car onto the shoulder to let the ambulance pass and waited until it was well on its way down the gravel road toward town before he turned into the driveway. His mother, dressed in her slippers and her blue polka-dot housedress, stood near the back porch of the house. Standing on one side of her was their neighbor Ernie Morriseau. Standing on the other side of her was the very fat Alfred Meyer, the sheriff who doubled as the coroner and was a parody of a small-town sheriff. Someone who didn't have to chase, and couldn't have chased, crooks. He was merely a waddling presence, wearing a uniform to signify law and order. He called upon the state troopers for any chasing that needed to be done.

About forty feet behind them and apparently unnoticed by everyone except Bill sat the Morriseaus' dog, Angel. When Bill parked his car alongside Ernie's truck, the dog silently loped into the tall grass next to the barn.

"I'll be all right," Bill heard his mother say to the two men as he got out of the car. "Bill's home now."

"Are you sure?" Al Meyer asked.

"I'm sure. We'll be all right."

"Billy," Ernie Morriseau said, lightly clasping Bill's upper arm, "call us anytime if you or your mother need help."

It was only after the two men had left, their vehicles spewing pillows of dust as they drove away from the Lucas farmhouse, that Bill's mother spoke to him.

"Your father is dead. Ernie found him. He came over to talk to your father. I told him I didn't know where he was. But I said to check behind the barn. And sure enough," his mother said, shrugging her shoulders, "that's where he was. Heart attack, they think. Maybe a stroke too," she added as though Bill had asked.

She stood next to Bill with a tired but composed face. Bill had already known it was his father when he saw the ambulance lumber out of the driveway. What was inevitable had finally happened. Bill was unable to react because he had no emotions to react with except one. He glanced at his mother with curiosity.

"Well, Mom," he asked hesitantly, digging the heel of his boot into the ground, "do you want me to do something?"

"You don't have to do anything," she answered matter-of-factly. "Neither do I. It's already been done."

****

That night Bill opened his bottom dresser drawer and pulled out a shoebox of childhood memorabilia. He sat on the floor next to his brother's bed and habitually wrapped one arm up into a corner of the bedspread. He rifled through the box's contents with his other hand until he found what he wanted. It was the last picture he had of his brother, the one James had sent Bill from Vietnam. Bill turned the Polaroid over and reread the message he knew by heart.

"These are the highlands I was telling you about—a lot bigger than our ridge, huh? They're pretty, though," James had written in his heavy block-style print. "It's too bad they're in Vietnam. I'll tell you more about them when I come home. Love, James."

The picture helped Bill remember the movie star sensuousness of his brother's full lips and the flint-colored eyes, so like their mother's. But he could no longer recall his brother's voice.

He lay on his bed for a couple of hours but could not sleep. Leaning over the side, he reached under the bed and pulled out a six-pack of beer that he had filched from his father's stash in the barn a month ago. Bill drank all six cans. Instead of causing the dreamy stupor that he had hoped for, the beer hooked him, creating for Bill an illusion of clear thinking.

The last American troops were pulled out in 1973. President Ford had announced last year that the war in Vietnam was finished. Their father was now dead. There was nothing to keep his brother away from home.

His brother *was* back, Bill drunkenly reasoned, because he felt him. But Bill never sensed him near the house. James would not come near the house because it was stained with their father's presence, even after death. Away from the house, though, Bill had a hunch that he was being watched and even touched. He could smell something, too. On a clear morning in the woods or on a hot and dry summer's day his face would become cold and moist as though mist had fallen. Or fishing off the bridge at the river, he would smell smoke and, walking up and down both sides of the river for a ways, could not find the source of it.

He would go looking for his brother tonight. But where would James be? He might be down at the Chippewa River, among the big birches bordering the water there. Bill ruminated on several favorite spots along the river and then reconsidered. It was too far away from the farm. James wouldn't go there. Bill picked up the Polaroid picture and looked at it again. There was only one place his brother could be.

He put the picture back into the shoebox and thrust the box into the dresser drawer. One by one, he quietly placed the empty beer cans back underneath the bed. Then he padded out of the bedroom and down the stairs, stopping for a few seconds to listen for any sounds that might indicate that his mother was awake. Donning his blue sweatshirt and green rubber boots, he slipped through the barely opened screen door and walked just outside the perimeter of the yard light. Once his eyes adjusted to the dark, Bill broke into a dogtrot and headed toward the hump of land that rose out of the middle of the swamp on the edge of their farm.

I HEARD BILL WALK DOWN the stairs and watched out my bedroom window as he left the house. I would have been worried if we had lived in a city like Chicago or Milwaukee, where I had grown up and gone to college. But he was seventeen, a big boy, and there was nothing in the swamp or woods that he did not know about or that would hurt him. It didn't bother me either that it was midnight or that Bill appeared a little unsteady on his feet. He had gotten hold of something to drink, and it was more than likely that it came from our own land, which was pockmarked with my dead husband's hidden caches, bottles of beer and whiskey that he hid in the barn or buried in various spots, squirreling them away just in case he couldn't get to town. Although his death that day was a jolt to both of us, I was sure that it did not cause my son's drinking. Or my insomnia. It did not cause us grief. Bill's face registered relief almost immediately when I confirmed his father's death. I too felt only relief and could not summon any appropriate feeling about my husband of twenty-eight years. There was not the expected emotion such as tears or the howling of grief, the fear of an unknown future or compassion. I could not even draw up pity. I felt hot and sticky. It was nearly ninety degrees. My hair was wet, and it dripped perspiration into my eyes. The relief of John's death subsided much quicker than I would have ever thought. In my many years of wishing him dead, I dreamed of savoring the relief for days and months. But it arrived fleetingly and went. In its place came desire.

169

Ernie Morriseau had driven over that afternoon because he was having his land reassessed and did not want John to mistake the surveyors working along our shared fence line for trespassers. I had been hanging bedsheets on the line and humming a vague rendition of "Moon River," made even more vague by the two clothespins stuffed into my mouth. The moment his truck pulled up, I stopped humming and did not reach down to the basket for another sheet.

"Hello, Claire. Is John around?"

That sonorous and silky voice. I pulled the clothespins out of my mouth.

"Behind the barn."

I watched him walk to the barn. Put one clothespin back in my mouth and bit down, chewed on it a little. Rubbed my sweaty hands down the front of my housedress. I looked terrible, my short black hair uncombed and dirty. The cheap rubber sandals on my feet. I looked down at my bare legs. For some absurd reason, I had shaved them that morning, sitting on the edge of the tub. I was happy that at least my legs were smooth, even if the smoothness showed all my purple and blue spider veins.

It was the way Ernie emerged from behind the barn alone. How he stopped and looked back for a few seconds before turning around to look at me. He kept his eyes steadily on me as he approached, as if to make sure that I would stay put. When he stopped, he reached forward and clasped one of my hands. He didn't waste words.

"John's dead. I think he suffered a heart attack. He's back there," Ernie said, nodding toward the barn, "lying against one of the tractor wheels."

It had been a few hours since I'd seen him. I rarely went behind the barn when I knew my husband was back there. He'd been using the tractor as an excuse for years to sit back there and drink. Even if he had fixed the tractor, what would he have done with it? Why would I go back there? Why go looking for a fight?

I shrugged. "Should I call Sheriff Meyer?"

"I think so."

It was my turn to move, to turn around and walk into the house and call Al Meyer. I didn't want to move. I didn't want Ernie to let go of my hand.

"Do you want me to call him?" he asked.

He was considerate in the way he pulled his hand away slowly so that it didn't feel insulting. My mouth felt dry and tasted of wood. I tried to think of something to say just so I could look at him.

When we first moved up to Olina and were still reasonably social, we drove over to the Morriseau farm and introduced ourselves. We did not go into the house for a cup of coffee although they repeatedly invited us to. We simply wanted to say hello so that they knew who was now living on the place next to theirs. Ernie smiled and held out his hand. I was instantly captivated. He was the dark and handsome man of dreams. There was a calmness about him that was charismatic although I was sure that he did not realize it. My mouth was dry then too, but the rest of me became wet. I felt the sweat trickling under my arms. Could taste it on my upper lip. I wanted to leave right away, so sure that my husband and Ernie could see what I could not control. Then Rosemary stepped out of the house. She was tall and lithe with long black hair and skin like a model in a Rossetti painting. I could see that my husband was taken aback, that he had not expected our neighbor's wife to be so beautiful. They both were extraordinarily beautiful.

How little Ernie had changed. He smelled faintly of cedar and a freshly laundered shirt. He was still brown and muscled and ruggedly handsome, made even more so by hard work. My right hand lifted, and as if to stop an impending sin, my left hand caught it and brought it down before I could do what would have been embarrassing. To run a fingertip over his lips, before pressing one of my cheeks to his face. I crossed my arms obediently against my chest.

"Will you stay here until the sheriff arrives?"

"Absolutely. You better call Bill too."

I turned when I reached the screen door.

"Do you want something to drink?"

"A glass of water would be wonderful. Thank you, Claire."

I would never forget his answer. "Thank you, Claire." My newly dead husband lying against the hub of the tractor wheel never said thank you. Bill, in the way of all children who take their mothers for granted, never said it either.

As I was filling a glass with ice and water, I remembered a day during the summer when Jimmy was twelve. I had walked across our field and the adjacent Morriseau field to fetch Jimmy. It was hot that day too, and I needed Jimmy to do chores. Rounding the corner of the Morriseau barn, I saw Ernie bent over the engine of his truck without a shirt on. The perspiration on his upper torso glistened like dew and collected in the hollows and curves of his muscled back and chest before trickling down. I could not say anything to announce my presence, overwhelmed by my desire to palm his broad chest with my hands. To bend my knees and catch the tributaries of sweat with my mouth before they reached the waistband of his jeans.

I took the glass outside and gave it to him. Watched him gratefully drink the entire glass before wiping his mouth dry with a clean handkerchief. That's when I felt grief.

✖◆✖◆✖◆✖◆✖

I couldn't remember the sound of love or the feel of it.

It certainly wasn't taught to me by my own parents' example. Although my mother ceased to talk about how she came to meet my father or chose to marry him while I was still very young, I surmised later that she married my French-American father in a small moment of rebellion and because of love. Who could not have fallen in love with my father, Michel Chappeau? I looked at their wedding photograph and two other photographs of my father as a young man, and I thought he could easily have beaten Rudolph

Valentino in looks and charm. My father had black, curly hair and dark, long-lashed Gypsy eyes. His lips were full and sensual, and in later years he wore a mustache with the ends waxed and turned up into a handlebar. His cheekbones were high and slightly wide, and his large nose, although arched, was refined and not blunt or pugnacious like those of so many of the German men I'd seen in Milwaukee. My father joked about his looks, saying it was impossible for any French family who had been in America for at least a hundred years to avoid having some Indian blood. It gave him the kind of sultry looks attributed to Latino men. He was easygoing and loving, which didn't seem to fit what he did for a living. He was a banker. Clearly he was in love with my Irish mother, and she with him.

She was beautiful too, with strawberry blond hair that fell to her tiny waist and dare-me blue eyes. In later years the blue of her eyes became as cold as ice, and she could silence anyone with a sharp glance. I imagined their attraction to each other. But it didn't last.

My father wanted a large family. My mother often said she never wanted to be a broodmare, dying young from childbirth or from just being worn out. My mother wanted only two children, a boy and a girl. As if willing it, she had my brother, André, and then me, and that was it. No more lovemaking. My mother's God was the feared and wrathful old man of the Old Testament. My father was Catholic too, but his New World French Catholicism was less dogmatic and filled with the light and love of the New Testament God. They would not divorce for religious and social reasons, but my father found other ways to obtain the love he cherished. He was, for the most part, discreet so as not to hurt my mother, but she knew anyway and became more enraged through the years that her husband did not follow her example of celibacy. I used to think that if they had had access to the modern birth control of today, they might have remained a loving couple. But my mother's Catholicism was too rigid even for that, and she had a willfulness that increased with age and did not serve her well, eventually turning into hatred.

I once saw my father with another woman. A beautiful brown-haired woman who was at least a foot taller than my father. I was a freshman in high school and, having gotten my period, had left school early one day. I was sick with cramps, and one of the nuns suggested that the walk home might ease them. I had just shut the gate to the schoolyard behind me and turned to face the park across the street. It was then I saw my father sitting on one of the polished granite benches in the middle of the day, his arm around a woman's shoulders. He was kissing her, and it was clear that they would leave the park soon to seek a more private spot. Although I was almost doubled over with cramps, I could not stop staring at them, at the intensity with which my father kissed the woman's lips, cheeks, and neck and how she responded in kind, unbuttoning the top of her blouse so that he could reach her breasts. I saw for the first time what passion was and how it could overwhelm all inhibitions and judgment.

My father did not see me. I was not hurt for my mother's sake but for my own. My brother, André, physically took after my mother's side of the family. But I was my father's daughter. I looked and was every inch a Chappeau, and my father loved me for it, calling me his *petite chérie*. When I began to menstruate, my mother was no longer able to hide her hatred. She saw me as she did my father's women. He was generous with me, kissing and hugging me often and giving me beautiful dresses and small presents that my mother immediately took away. When I turned sixteen, he gave me one of the most beautiful dresses I'd ever seen.

"Stop it! She'll get conceited! She already thinks too much of herself!" she shouted at my father. "Do you want her to end up doing nothing with her life except to become some man's plaything?"

My father was about to leave the house when she began shouting at him. He turned around at the door and said quietly, "Is it so terrible to have some joy? Or to give joy? Am I not allowed to give my daughter what a father should give her? Claire's too smart to end up being anyone's plaything. But love. I would never deny her that. What happened to *you,* Sylvia?"

Although my father loved me, he was not stupid. When I came of age and was noticed by boys, he became strict and fiercely protective, frightening the boys who came to our door.

"Claire," he said, two weeks before I was to graduate from high school with honors, "it shames me to say this, but most men are evil. Particularly toward women. And you are both pretty and smart. It is the rare man who can appreciate that combination in a woman. Don't give yourself away. Think well of yourself, and choose carefully."

He was smoking a cigar, and I noticed that my father didn't look well. His lovely olive-colored skin was washed out. I did hear his words, but I could not forget the sight of him kissing that woman in the park. Or the rapture on her face. I wanted to be touched like that.

I made love on the sly to a young medical student when I was nineteen and in college. It was all that I dreamed of. God, it was bliss. It was like going to heaven or how I imagined going to heaven would feel. It was passionate and crazed, and I learned that my young body could bend and turn in ways I never thought possible. We made love in the wildest of places: closets, empty classrooms, in a park near campus late at night, and once in one of the medical school's laboratories with cadavers in the refrigerated room next door. I laughed later, thinking it was a kind of anatomy class for him, and wondered how in the world I didn't get pregnant. But he was near the end of his formal studies and went back to New York to fulfill his residency. He did not ask me to marry him, and I did not presume that I could ask him. I was supposed to wait to be asked. I was supposed to be a good girl—unassuming and sweet, just like my name.

My father died just before I met John. A burst blood vessel, the doctor said, or more accurately now, a cerebral hemorrhage. He was found slumped over his large banker's desk with blood coming out of his nose and mouth. I imagined my father looking at accounts and concentrating on balances when that small explosion in his brain suddenly made the world go dark for him, and then nothing. I cried for so long that my mother couldn't stand it anymore and yelled at me. Then I grieved silently. I think there were women privately crying all over Milwaukee. That was an odd comfort to me. Whatever my father's sins may have been, seeking love was not one of them. If my mother would not mourn him, then his daughter and all his lovers would.

I was so vulnerable when I met John. He promised to renew my dreams and ambitions, and I believed him.

The funny thing is, John wanted the dream of a farm, but it didn't want him. He never caught on to the basic idea of living a rural life: that it took patience. He expected instant success and when it didn't happen, when the boys and I couldn't provide it, his disappointment came crashing down on us. It enraged him, I think, that I provided all our vegetables from the garden, eggs and chickens from our coop, and that I excelled at those things. And that Jimmy, not he, provided so much fish and meat for our freezer.

I realized I hadn't really fallen in love with John. What I had fallen in love with was a uniform, for what I thought it stood for: someone to protect me, someone with respect and honor, and someone who was brave and who respected freedom. My freedom. I stumbled for years, thinking that he had to know he was hurting me and hurting our sons. I had been taught to believe that every person has an inherent sense of remorse or a conscience. But in time I found out that one-dimensional people can often act three-dimensional when they are in pursuit of something. When they get what they want, they settle back down into their shallow personalities and do ugly and shallow things.

After that our life together began its slow descent except for the two times I gave birth. My mother refused to hear of my unhappiness just as she refused to acknowledge her own. She was as clichéd in her statements as any staunch Catholic mother of her time could be.

"You were married in the church. You took a *vow*," she said venomously, clearly happy that her daughter had done even worse than she had and would suffer the same fate of going without love. "There is no going back. Just make the best of it."

My generation of women was never told what to do if the marriage went *bad*. We were the new generation, the progressive generation just after World War II. Marriages were not supposed to go bad for us.

We still had some feelings toward each other when Jimmy was conceived. But I'm not sure how Bill happened. A drunken roll over the top of my body one night when I was asleep? Bill was certainly not conceived in love, although I adored both my sons from the moment they were born, considering them the only worthwhile things that ever came out of my husband. I looked at my husband after Bill was born and realized that he was no longer handsome, no longer lovable in any way.

By the time of Bill's birth I had ceased to think about love as being related to sex. Forgotten the swelling of breath or the rapid chest pounding of desire until I saw Ernie Morriseau.

Just two weeks before John's death I had dreamed of Ernie's fingertips walking the bumps of my spine with the delicacy of a cabbage moth. I woke up. The room was dark, and I was alone in my bed. I cried, unable to recall what it was like to have such hands on my body. To have a sensual and welcome interruption to my sleep. Just to be *touched*.

Then the shame of it. Rosemary Morriseau had been nothing but kind to me. For years I wanted to stone Rosemary for her lucky twist of fate, for her movie star beauty and strength, and for what appeared to be a hardworking but charmed life. For having a husband with such a voice and such kindness. For having a man who was as handsome as she was beautiful. I often stood transfixed, staring at him until I had to look away before he became aware of it.

But crying can last only so long and then comes exhaustion. And after that a tranquillity and a thankfulness. I had slept alone ever since that August night when I heard the voice in the field and obeyed it. A long peal of laughter. Voiced hilarity that trumpeted out of the dark and terrified my husband so much that shit had poured down his legs. I found his pants the next day by the bird feeder. Who would have thought that laughter could be as effective as a gun? That it could deflect my husband's desire to terrorize me. After that night, if John slept at home, it was on the couch in the living room. I did not have to endure his body next to me in bed any longer. His sour, oily touch. His sallow skin and fleshy, loose horse lips. He could not in fact summon the courage even to hit me after that night.

He was afraid of me.

><><><><><><><><><

I stared out the window long after Bill was gone. I considered it a blessing that Bill was drunk in the hope that it might cause him to cry. He had never cried over his brother's disappearance, so sure that he was alive. That was the worry that weighed me down over the past eight years.

If drinking caused him to cry, then it would also relieve me of that ugly and shameful part of my history that I thought was over but that loomed in front of me like a necessary ghost. Necessary because I would repeat that history if I had to, to make my son cry. I would hit him as I did years ago when he was a little boy and didn't deserve to be shaken like a rag doll or have his hair pulled until his small head was wrenched back, all because Bill had, maybe, spilled a glass of milk.

What child, I thought bitterly, *wouldn't spill milk, wouldn't shit in his pants or wet the bed, wouldn't act out in a household where threats hung in the air like wet laundry until fists pulled them down?*

I crawled back into bed and pulled the sheets up despite the heat. I always cried after I hit Bill, cried when I heard his terrified sobs, cried because my little boy had done nothing wrong except exist to be a receptor of a long line of pain. And I cried too because I felt almost powerless to stop it. When Jimmy left, the truth finally locked my fists to my sides and found its way out of my mouth. I walked away, talking aloud to myself and the invisible whoever and whatever inhabited the space around me.

Bill had always been an introspective child. A different child. Unlike his brother, who could be verbally picked at and teased into a rage, Bill remained quiet and nearly impenetrable to verbal taunts. After Jimmy left, my husband tried the same humiliating tactics on our younger son. He pulled out those medals and dangled them off his fingertips when he was drunk, most often during a meal, and proceeded to tell stories I knew were lies. Bill calmly ate his food heedless and undeterred by the nearly indecipherable words of his father. When he did look at his father, it was with a momentary lift of his eyebrows and brief detached interest. Sometimes Bill looked at John with puzzlement, but most often he noticed him with an "oh there you are" attitude. Eventually my husband would give up, his lips pursed with confusion, his eyebrows wrinkled with thwarted anger. John was unable to determine whether Bill was spurning him or mocking him or simply didn't care or was too stupid to react. Knowing my husband, I watched him wordlessly reach the conclusion that Bill was too daft to understand the concept of the medals or what they stood for. What they meant to becoming a man, to being a man. What they meant to John.

Since John paid little attention to the details of our children's lives, he did not know that his younger son had an astonishing IQ. That Bill read books and painted pictures and could memorize whole songs just like his brother after hearing the song only once or twice. When he was quite young, he sat like a meadowlark on the fence railing by the chicken coop and sang songs he had learned from the nuns who spent time with the smaller children after church. Wistful and fluty songs. Robust and affectionate songs. I taught him the French songs I had learned in Catholic school, and I could hear his little voice from the house. "Frère Jacques, Frère Jacques, dormez-vous? Dormez-vous? Sonnez les matines, sonnez les matines, ding dong ding, ding dong ding."

My husband did not observe or know of Bill's loves. He did not know that Bill had learned to survive by merging with what he loved best: the sky, the birds and animals that lived on or near the fringes of our farm, and even the soil itself underneath his nails. He tirelessly took care of wounded or orphaned animals, watching for hours the menagerie of animals he kept in his bedroom until they were well enough or old enough to live on their own. The large animals that lived in our woods could not be caught or did not need Bill's ministrations, and so he did not have the same chance to observe them. Instead I occasionally watched Bill study his father when John wasn't aware of being stared at or ruminated over. I imagine Bill considered his father a large and incomprehensible species of being, a kind of animal gone bad that not even Bill could feel compassion for. Bill's professorial concentration, his pale and thoughtful face constantly reminded me of something.

It came to me one evening when Bill was ten. Silently defeated by the lack of response from Bill or me, my husband had left the dinner table. He went outside to the car, to drive to Pete's Bar, where someone was always drunk enough to listen to him. I dried the dishes and watched Bill draw in his sketchbook at the cleared table. I put a cup away in the cupboard. A porcelain cup with many cracks in the glaze. Looking at that cup caused me to turn around. Despite the smoothness of his kissable, cherubic cheeks, the pale brown of his long lashes or the fineness of his light brown hair, and the cowlick near his forehead that refused to lie flat, my son looked old. Not just old but sagacious. He paused in his sketching and looked up at me. I silently stared back at him. With the robes of an ancient Nazarene around him, my ten-year-old would look exactly like an apostle. Better yet, a prophet. A man of God.

I suppose some women would like to think of their sons as God or sons of God. I had no such ambition, nor did I want my sons crucified. Looking at Bill that night, I was afraid. I had a ten-year-old holy man on my hands. How do you raise such a son? Bill had even been born unconventionally. I had not wanted to be put under, as I had for Jimmy's birth, not knowing or seeing what they were doing down there. So I endured the labor pain, the episiotomy to accommodate his head, and the painful stitching afterward, just to see Bill emerge. One of his tiny hands was clenched around the umbilical cord as though the placenta were his blanket and he was determined to drag it with him. They pried his fingers away from the cord and cut it. And he *cried*.

"Well!" the attending nurse said. "He didn't like that."

I always thought it would be Bill who would turn out fragile enough to lose his life. As did other people, I mistook his quietness, his observation of the world for fragility and helplessness. He had vulnerability. That was true. But of such a quality as to make people step away from him, not toward him. As though he possessed an understanding of them that they didn't want seen. I knew that look. I saw myself reflected in my son's eyes all the time.

But Bill lost the magic somewhere in the spurt of adolescence and simply became old. He encased himself so that it became increasingly difficult for me to talk to him, to sense his thoughts. He didn't laugh anymore. He reminded me of those chicks in the incubator that, for reasons of uneven temperature and humidity, were conceived into shells too hard for them to break through. I often found them too late, the tip of the egg tooth on the beak peeking through a small hole in the shell. "Died While Pipping" was one of the categories under "Problems in Incubating" in my chicken handbook. On occasion I triumphed, delicately peeling away the shell from a still-alive chick so that it could stretch out and fluff up into activity and into life.

Bill was all I had left. I could not fight the cultural demons, tangible and intangible, that had killed my older son. But I could fight that which I had inadvertently taught to Bill: to deny the truth in order to endure the small horrors of our daily lives. I was sure that if I had summoned the courage to leave my husband years ago, there would never have been such a string of events in our lives. My older son would never have enlisted. My husband, left alone to his self-destructive ways, might have died sooner, thereby freeing up the farm for us. Bill would have been a happy, normal teenager and not a boy so deaf to the reality of life that he was at that moment wandering in the dark woods sleepless and drunk.

I turned on my side and stared at the window again. It all was a matter of timing. I wasn't exactly sure how I was going to do it. To peel around the small opening of the egg tooth too soon might hurt the chick inside. But I would risk it because I knew. Better to live with some hurt than die silently in a shell.

XXXXX ERNIE WAS UNCOMFORTABLE around Claire although he was careful not to show it. He had the sense that she saw some extraordinary goodness in him that he did not believe existed. True, he was far from being like her husband, but men like John Lucas were the extreme. John Lucas made other men squirm. Men who tried to be good, who lived every day with those intentions. Ernie felt that way too, but he was unable to name it until he cautiously walked to the back of the Lucas barn. He saw the green Oliver tractor with its missing steering wheel and the open toolbox tipped against one wheel.

"John?"

When there was no answer, Ernie ran his hand across the ridges of the big tire facing him. He did a half turn and looked down at the power takeoff, noted how greasy and dirty it was. Then he tapped the top of the other big tire before doing another half turn. His foot stopped in midair, and he sucked in his breath. John Lucas was slumped against the wheel hub with his mouth hung open as if to yell and his eyes staring out into his own field. Ernie didn't need to touch him to know he was dead. He could smell him. That sour bowel of a chronic boozer.

"Yup, he's dead," Alfred Meyer commented matter-of-factly after he had arrived and ambled out to the barn with Ernie.

"Natural causes?"

Meyer snorted.

"Are you joking? Smell him. Yeah, I would say natural causes with a little help. Probably a heart attack. He's lucky he died this way," Meyer added, spitting out a stream of tobacco juice. "He's borrowed money from anybody and everybody, but they were always too afraid to ask for it back. I always thought he'd end up dead from a fight in Pete's Bar."

"He's always been like that. Troubled, I guess."

"I suppose. I noticed Claire doesn't seem too heartbroken. Can't say as I blame her. I never did like him."

"That makes two of us."

Ernie stepped around John until he stood in front of the dead man. He stared down at him. He could not understand John Lucas's seeming ingratitude at having two sons, nor did he ever understand the fate that bestowed children on a man who didn't want them. It was, Ernie reflected, as though John had lived in his own world, his own time zone, his own *age*. It was then that Ernie understood what it was about John Lucas that bothered him and that bothered other men, who, in brief conversations when John Lucas's name was mentioned, could not find the words to describe the man. John Lucas had stopped time in his head so that he was a cemented twelve-year-old. He was a reminder of secret deeds done in boyhood and even in early manhood. Ugly acts of bullying or cruelty. Men felt that old violence anytime they happened to glance at John Lucas. That tall and mean drunk was a persistent pinch, a twang in their heads that reminded them that they had possibly not outgrown those mean displays of machismo. That one day they would embarrass themselves or hurt their families because it would bubble up unexpectedly. An old hormonal response they were incapable of controlling. Claire Lucas bothered them too. The scarves and sunglasses that hid her bruised face and the wariness she displayed whenever she was in town made them feel ashamed as grown men that they stood by and felt powerless to stop her pain. John Lucas walked their streets like a film character, haunting them when they saw him in the bar, working at the mill, or driving on the road. He was a wrong turn personified. A wrong turn they might have taken, might still take.

Looking down at John Lucas, Ernie knew that one did not need to die to become dead.

"He stinks. Charlie won't have to use embalming fluid on him," Al Meyer commented before leaving Ernie and lumbering back to his car.

He would always remember seeing Claire as he walked to the house after his discovery of her husband. The wooden clothespin in her mouth. How she took it out as he approached her. Her smallness. Claire had been pretty once. He imagined her as a vivacious young woman who went dancing every Saturday night, who could have been at any number of the dances in Milwaukee that kept people occupied during the war. He imagined her as a daring dancer, small enough to be swung and cradled in her partner's arms, energetically covering the floor, doing the jitterbug. He imagined her laughing with girlfriends, enjoying every minute of that release they all felt after the war.

He wanted to hold her then because of the secret slaughter of her life. It was visible in her prematurely wrinkled face, the cheap and ugly housedresses that she wore, and the shuffle of her bare feet in dime-store rubber sandals. Her hunched shoulders. How her eyes reflected despair as though her life were a rope insidiously slipping through her fingers and she was falling and falling. Ernie felt his own depression settle deeper within him when he saw her walk the perimeter of her field and saw her gesturing to the air and talking. She did not have the frank toughness of his own wife, nor had she been blessed with Rosemary's beauty. But she had her own life, and she did not deserve the way it had turned out.

He thought about it for a few seconds. If he reached forward, would she run away? Even if she didn't run away, he wondered, would she break like thin crystal if he touched her? He decided against it. He was afraid that hugging her would only make things worse, and it might frighten her.

Her reaction to her husband's death did not surprise him as it might have shocked and surprised others. If Ernie had not seen death up close or been responsible for killing, he might have been shocked too. But he believed that there were some people who deserved to be dead, who inflicted unnecessary pain, who were impossible to mourn but easy to breathe a sigh of relief over. People who were in such deep pain themselves that a quick bullet to the head would be as merciful as killing a rabid dog before it bit others. Whatever had happened to make them that way could not be undone after a certain age. It was the only compassion he could feel toward John Lucas. A general feeling of pity.

XXXX IT WAS AS MUCH A shock to me as it probably was to my mother when I spoke out loud, when I realized that I could speak and be heard. I have feelings too, which is weird. Although not pain in the physical sense. I have the memory of pain, the burning of my body. My mother once said the same thing about giving birth: that she could remember the pain but could no longer feel it. But humor has never left me. Sometimes my laughter echoes through the trees although I'm not sure anyone can hear it.

I laugh a lot. The history of my short life is fuckin' funny. Joining the Marines was not the smartest move I could have made. I was so conned. At first I thought the Marine Corps and my drill sergeant were just an extension of my old man, and in some ways they were. I was never good enough for him either, and he reminded me of it since the day I was born. Somehow he thought it would toughen me up. I believed him before I figured it out. I had hoped that at some point I would be good enough for him and then he would love me. Well, once I learned to shoot at twelve and got bigger at fifteen, I figured out part of it, and that took care of that. I refused to believe in his lies, in his little *stories*. I didn't love him, and he didn't love me. After fifteen he didn't scare me anymore, and in fact I scared him. But he'd done his damage. If it hadn't been for Ernie, I wouldn't have thought I was worth being alive. I might have ended up dead anyway like Terry. Besides being a 4-F because of all his smoking, Terry was generally just a lowlife. I can see that now. I watched him get drunk that spring of 1968, hit the gas, and plow his car into a telephone pole. I would never have wanted him

187

in Nam with me. Terry would never have protected me. He only would have watched out for himself. Most bullies do that.

I was one of the most physically fit grunts, but still the first six weeks of basic training were beyond hell. I got the piss beaten out of me through every sadistic drill the Marines had thought up over the years. Sergeant Davidson called me a pussy so many times that I got paranoid, as though the continual suggestion might actually make it true. I would look at myself every now and then just to make sure I still had a dick. Davidson threatened to write me up as *unsatisfactory,* which was nothing new. My old man's vocabulary never extended that far although he said the same thing when he called me a dumb-ass. We all were treated as though we were a dented can of peas that couldn't be put on the shelf for sale.

That changed when we got down to serious rifle training.

I blew their minds. I picked up a rifle, any rifle. I could shoot with my eyes closed. I could see through thick woods and cover and focus on the smallest target in the time it took Davidson to raise his finger and pick his nose. A marshmallow on a branch. Half a marshmallow. Then half of a half of a marshmallow.

"Pretty boy can shoot," Sergeant Davidson drawled. "Our man Elvis here might be worth something after all."

Davidson quit calling me the worst of the names he used on all of us and chose me, among the select few, to go on for more weapons training.

"You're a natural leader," he told me one day, and all I said was, "Yes, sir." But how nuts is that? I could shoot. How did that make me a leader?

The goal of the military is to take your brain, wipe it clean of anything you have ever cherished, and write its own bullshit on it. I had grown up with my old man's mind games. I was not as vulnerable as some of the guys. As much as I hated the Corps in basic, I discovered that unlike my old man, it did give me some skills to survive by. And something I'd felt only when I spent time with Ernie: a sense of pride. Not necessarily American pride, but pride in belonging to the Marines. They wanted me. Was that so bad? It was not so much the Corps as it was the guys I met and trained with. I got a whole slew of brothers when I joined up, with only a few of them being assholes like in any family. I was worth something to them. They were worth something to me. That was the secret of survival. If I was conned, then the Corps was conned on another level. Once we landed in Nam, we could see that the Corps was dicked around just like any other branch of the military by LBJ and Westy. By McNamara, who my buddy Rick nicknamed McNightmare. But when we first landed on Okinawa, we were treated like the sons of Zeus. Then a week before some of us in the Fifth Division were scheduled to rotate into the Khe Sanh Combat Base, Sergeant Fuller laid it down real and gritty.

"Martinson! Wipe that shit-eatin' grin off your face. This is not a Boy Scout trip!" he roared. "Some of you are not comin' back. Do you hear me? But at the same time you will come back. The Corps will never leave you. But I want you to understand one thing. You are *never* to leave one another. Do you understand me? *NEVER!* If you stick together, most of you might come out of this shithole alive. And another thing: Always keep your rifles *clean*."

Marv Martinson had bad dreams that night. Rick and I had to wake him up, to keep him from yelling so much. I wasn't going to buy all of it. I was gonna go home, come hell or high water. I think I survived as long as I did by thinking about Bill.

Barricaded inside the KSCB, I would think about how my brother had a way of traveling inside his own body. How he seemed born with the ability to ignore our old man. He had no illusions. He didn't love the old man and didn't need his approval. I wanted to know what that was like, to travel so lightly, to need so little. Only after I got drunk or stoned did I even get near to what I thought that experience was.

I became good friends with one of the Bru scouts. We called him Peanut Butter Pete sometimes because he loved peanut butter so much. But his real name was Kho. He was my age, which shocked

me at first. He looked older, and he had kids. Once his daughter became sick, and he left us for a few days. When he came back, I
asked him if his daughter was better. He said she was, but that was
all he said. I wondered what she was sick with and how she got better. Then our chaplain explained to me that the Bru believed that
when someone is sick, a bad spirit is living in that person and causing the sickness. So Kho's family cooked rice and other food and
put it on a little altar in their house to feed the bad spirit. I guess
they hoped the bad spirit would crawl out of his daughter and go
after the food. When I thought about it, it made sense.

Kho told me that there were spirits everywhere. Once when
we were returning from a short patrol, we came to the edge of a
rice paddy. Kho made us stop, and he covered his mouth and shook
his head. We were not to talk. I thought it was because he saw a
North Vietnamese. But it wasn't that. The people from his village
were harvesting the rice. Silently. Nobody talked. It was weird seeing all those women working without saying a word. The way their
small hands slid up the stalk and stripped off the seed heads without
dropping any of them. Kho told me later that to talk while harvesting the rice would anger the rice spirits, and they might cause the
crop to fail the next year.

I thought about Bill then. About the way he could not go to
sleep until I crawled into my own bed. He thought there was a
monster under his bed. It didn't matter how many times I shone the
flashlight under there to show him that there was nothing but dust
bunnies and mouse turds. He was stubborn. He said that something
pinched his toes at night, and it lived underneath his bed.

I teased him. "Maybe it's your damn mice. Or your hamster.
Maybe they're getting out of their cages at night and biting your
feet."

"No!"

Christ, he was stubborn about it.

I thought about Bill's funny ways. I was ashamed on those
nights when I thought about him. I don't know what came over me

when I was mean to him. When I hung him by his ankles from the bridge, knowing that if someone had done it to me, I'd have beaten the pulp out of him. Or the time that Terry and I dumped a whole bottle of Tabasco sauce in a glass of grape juice and gave it to him. Bill took a big drink of it and started to choke. I was terrified, but at least I remembered not to give him water to clear it. I poured milk into his mouth. Water would only have spread the pepper sauce whereas milk helped neutralize it. A fact I learned in first aid and that bubbled up just then when I needed it. Bill ran and hid in the upstairs closet, his mouth and throat burning. I could hear his gasps between crying. I told Terry to go home. Then I went into the barn loft and beat hay bales with a baseball bat until I broke it and finally cried. What was wrong with me? To make it worse, my brother always came back to me, looked up at me with those eyes the color of aspen bark. So hopeful. As though he could see some good in me when I was just a lousy bastard.

Some nights when I felt afraid, I would think about him fighting with that wooden sword that I had made for him in shop class and that snapping turtle shell he used as a shield. There was never anyone out there in the barnyard. Just my brother, spinning on the balls of his feet and shouting threats to some imaginary enemy. I would watch him from my window in the barn loft and shake my head. I told Mom once that I thought Bill was retarded. She got mad and then laughed.

"Retarded! Do you know what his school tests say?" she said. "You're smart too, but Bill's IQ is supposedly near genius level. So much for his being retarded. He's just different. Always has been."

Then she laughed and hugged me. "You are both smart boys."

All those boxes from home. Cookies, sweet rolls, venison sausage, candy, and clean underwear. I didn't have the heart to write to my mother and tell her that I could buy underwear at the PX cheaper than what she had paid for them at home. I knew Bill helped Mom pack the boxes, and he did what only Bill would do. The entire box was usually lined with cedar leaves from our swamp and sometimes with leaves of wintergreen. All the food had a faint aftertaste of cedar, but that was okay. It did something to the rest of the guys too. After the box was empty, the smell of cedar lingered and possessed them. Nobody wanted to throw the empty boxes out. They had to smell them and even rub their faces against the cardboard. In addition to the cedar, each box always had a little something extra that Bill had found. One box had a shed garter snake skin wrapped in tissue. Another box had a mud turtle's shell and a smooth skipping stone from the river. The box I received just before Christmas had Mom's fruitcake in it, and a Canada goose feather had been placed on top of the cake. I was made to understand that I wasn't allowed to open those boxes until most of the guys could be present. It was as though they all wanted to belong to that box somehow. I could pretend to be a Marine, a fighting man without ties to distract him, but I was James Peter Lucas and I was from northern Wisconsin and my brother sent me continual proof of our home.

Kho was there too. He would not touch the snakeskin or the turtle shell, the stone or the goose feather. But the cedar he put up to his nose just like the rest of the guys. Cedar is like that. You can't get enough of that smell.

"Your brother," he said to me one night as we sat out near the razor wire, "holds many spirits in here." Kho tapped his chest.

I didn't know what to say back. Kho didn't look as though he expected me to say anything. I thought about it. I was raised to think that we all were supposed to have souls, and it's funny but when Kho tapped his chest, I realized that I had always thought that souls did live in the chest area. At least that's where the nuns implied the soul lived, and we all were supposed to have souls although my friend Terry told me something different.

"Girls have souls," Terry whispered, leaning over in class. "Boys have guts."

But I never believed I had a soul. If I couldn't see it or feel it, then it didn't exist for me. Still, after what Kho said, I had to wonder. Then I thought about those people with their brains in their asses. I suppose they are sitting on their souls too. Kho was right when it came to Bill. I think that was where Bill traveled to when he was quiet. His soul filled with spirits.

I found a way to puncture a hole in the turtle shell so that I could tie it to my gun belt. Everybody had some sort of lucky charm he carried. Most of them were harmless but significant. There were a few guys, though, that lost it. Mostly the Special Forces guys who went nuts after their second tour. I can't even say out loud what they carried or kept as souvenirs. What they shot at for the hell of it. I kept my gun with me at all times, knowing that it wasn't just the VC or the North Vietnamese I had to be afraid of.

✕✕✦✦✦✦✦✕✕

It's been a long time since Nam. I didn't have control over people then, what they thought or said or did. Now I don't have control over what people see. I can't see myself. That hot July day when I just wanted to look at my old man. I had no idea what it was he saw. But it scared my father to death. *To death.* And wherever that is I don't know. I didn't see him go anywhere after his jaw fell open, after he grabbed his chest and his face caved in except for his eyes. They stayed wide open. If I had known the effect I had on him, well, I would have looked at him sooner. But at least now it's done. My mother and brother are free.

1982 and 1983

When the vacant sapphire sky
finds an alley of black trees
I feel you haunt an unknown layer
of my heart. How can I set in order this debris?
It's all I am.

—Roberta Hill, "A Song for What Never Arrives"

XXXX IT'S JULY. THE DOG LIES on the porch, catching the hot July wind in his mouth, tasting it between his pink tongue and the roof of his mouth before panting it out again. I watch him determine in a second what the messages in the wind are—who's coming, who's been where, who's alive, who's dead—and then he sends his own message when he lets the wind go, to whatever animal will savor and understand it the way he does. Angel's done this a million times. He's an old dog. So I imagine he has much to say.

I'm washing the supper dishes, listening to some of Jimmy Lucas's old records, watching the dog, and ignoring the heat. The records are stacked like a vinyl layer cake, losing a layer every time a record falls and is played on the stereo. Right now Roy Orbison is singing one of my favorite songs. "Blue Angel."

"Hey!" I yell, rapping the kitchen window with a soapy knuckle. "He's singing your song."

Angel briefly looks up at me and then, swatting a horsefly away from his mangled ear with his front paw, resumes his panting. I stare at the dog, stretched out on the porch floor. And I remember the day we found him fifteen years ago.

We were driving home from a Friday night fish fry when I thought I saw something moving in the shadows beside the road. Ernie slowed the truck down. I motioned for him to stop and rolled down my window.

Something big and dark was trying to drag itself back into the ditch, away from the headlights. At first I thought it was a bear cub and looked up at the trees along the road for the sow. Ernie opened his door and stepped out. Then he stood there, leaning against the open door and taking long drags on his cigarette. I waited. My husband just continued to stare at the ditch. Finally I leaned over in the seat.

"Are you meditating or what? You want me to check it out?" I whispered.

Ernie dropped his cigarette and smashed it with the heel of his boot.

"Wait a minute," he said. "I think it's a dog."

He slowly walked around the front of the truck and to the edge of the ditch. I poked my head out of the window just in time to hear a low growl. My scalp tingled.

"Be careful! He might have rabies," I whispered again, and grabbed the flashlight out of the glove compartment. I got out of the truck and shone the light down into the ditch.

Ernie was right. There, in the watery mud of spring, was a dog, his breath whistling through his blood-caked nose. He was about six months old but was already a big animal. The light caught the glistening blood running down the side of his head, and he weakly pulled himself around so that he faced us. He was as black as a night without stars. Blue-black. One eye shone white and luminous in the light, but the other was swollen shut and covered with clotting blood. Ernie stepped forward for a better look. The dog barked and tried to lunge forward.

"Christ!" Ernie said, stepping back. "It looks like he's been shot in the head and shot in his left hip . . . and I think he caught some birdshot in his chest. Whoever it was couldn't shoot straight. That's why he's still alive . . . and in one piece. Good-lookin' dog, though, huh, Rose? Think he's part Lab?"

The dog looked away from Ernie and focused on me with his one good eye before I could answer. I stared at that dog. He stared at me. His eye burned a path through all of the hidden memories in my head. Standing on that dusky gravel road, I felt the sudden chill

of knowing what the reality of his wounds meant. The same meaning that accompanies a calf born too deformed to live or a piglet
whose back has been broken by the carelessness of its mother's
bulky roll in the pen. It is not a mean decision but one that comes
with the harshness of rural life and expensive veterinarian bills.
Ernie had anticipated what was coming and had already retrieved
the shotgun from the back of the truck. I ignored the gun and
squatted, resting on the balls of my feet.

"You're right. Looks like almost all Lab. Poor fella," I crooned.

He stopped growling and whimpered. Then Ernie cautiously
moved toward him again. His good eye left me and zeroed in on
Ernie. He growled, this time baring his teeth. That's how I knew it
was a man that shot him and threw him into that ditch. His head
must have been searing with pain, like someone stuck a knife into
it, but he could still tell a woman from a man.

I loved him in that instant.

"Stop," I said. "Not this time. I can fix him up."

"Oh, Lord, Rose," Ernie said. "It's pretty bad. He's never
gonna be the same. He's gotta be in a hell of a lot of pain too."

I started to get up and prepare myself for a good fight with
Ernie. But as I stood up, a sudden warmth that felt almost blessed
infused me from my belly up to my chest. I am not a religious person, but I can't think of any other way to describe it. It was like that
circular feeling I had when I anticipated being a mother and remembered what it was like to be mothered, that feeling of having
been chosen without having to ask. And this dog chose me.

"Well?" my husband asked, turning to face me.

Then the name just popped into my head. "Angel," I said.
"We're going to take him home and call him Angel."

"Angel?" Ernie said, giving me a funny look. "He looks more
like a Bruno to me."

"Angel," I repeated.

Ernie shrugged and walked to the bed of the truck for some

twine. Angel's good ear stood up like a small wing. I kept talking to him until he slumped back into the mud. He gazed into the flashlight beam and became mesmerized enough by both the pain and the light so that Ernie could grab his muzzle and tie the twine around it so he wouldn't bite us. Then we took him home.

I don't know how he lived. Whoever tried to blow his brains out had missed the best part, the telling part. Angel has fits every now and then, chasing his tail around and around, and sometimes he gallops in his sleep, his legs scissoring through the air and going nowhere. His head appears a little lopsided when you look at him straight on, and the shredded remains of his one ear wave in the breeze. They are soft, though, when you touch them, like strips of black chamois cloth. He let me touch him from the very beginning. But it took Angel a long time to trust Ernie. I've always been secretly proud that Angel took to me right off. I'm good with animals and children, but Ernie's better.

Angel's memory is whole and enduring. I don't think any of the buckshot got into that part of his brain even though I can feel with my fingertips the round bumps of lead coming to the surface when I rub his head. When he loves, he loves completely, recognizing someone he trusts even after years of not seeing him or her. He lopes down the driveway in an easy way, his big tongue hanging out. This is the way he greets women and children. Yet his hatred is just as complete, just as absolute. He hates men, all men, except Ernie and our neighbor Bill Lucas and his brother, Jimmy, even though Bill's a grown man now and not the little boy who spent so much time visiting us and even though Jimmy has been dead for fourteen years, somewhere in Vietnam.

Angel's my dog. He sits in the cab of the truck with his big muzzle poking out of the window, tasting the wind as we fly down the road.

I'm almost done with the dishes. It's seven o'clock, it's hotter than hell, and I've got the blues really bad. I look out the window in the hope that I'll think of something else besides crying when a flash of color catches my eye from the Lucas field. Then I see Bill Lucas in the field. Angel sees him too and scrambles to his feet. His good ear rises like a flag, but he doesn't bark.

"There goes your friend," I say softly, but of course the dog can't hear me through the window.

Bill stops then. Just stops and stands there and faces the big swamp. Angel continues to watch him silently. He lifts his nose. I turn my head for just a minute, and that's when Angel barks, once. I look back just in time to see Bill get swallowed into the thick cover of those swamp cedars. This is the fifth time this summer I've seen him disappear like that into the swamp. I stand up on my toes to catch a glimpse of him, but he's gone, and the only thing I see now is my husband by the toolshed, watching Bill just like me, just like the dog. Once last summer I saw Bill up close at the Standard station where he works and was shocked by the oily stubble and savage look of his face. His eyes are no longer the soft gray color they were when he was a kid. They are a rock gray now, and like a split rock, they are small but with jagged edges.

We wait and watch, but nothing. Ernie's shoulders sag when he realizes that Bill will not reappear, and he trudges off toward the barn, fifty-eight years of exhaustion in every step.

We will not talk about this. My husband does not know that I know he watches the Lucas place, looking for signs of life, a vigorous wave of a hand or the yellow halo of the yard light when night falls. The little boy who used to visit our farm, eat dinner with us, and play with the dog grew into a remote and painfully shy young man. We see him rarely and almost always at a distance. And the oddest thing is that his name is never spoken between us . . . as though he were dead instead of his brother, Jimmy. Which is nonsense because we do *see him*, working, walking, or driving, even if it isn't often. It hurts Ernie that Bill does not come to our place anymore or accept visits easily from us. But Ernie doesn't talk about that either. He deals with his pain like most men, treating it as though it doesn't exist and therefore cannot be talked about.

I, on the other hand, have never been known to stay quiet. When I'm in pain, I cry a blue streak, and when I'm angry, I yell like hell. And when something is bothering me, I talk. A lot.

But I don't have another person to talk to easily outside of Ernie, who has been punishing me with silence for the past two weeks and who has even struggled to keep his feet from touching mine while we sleep. I don't even know what I'm being punished for, that's how nonexistent our conversations have been. I've given up trying, fearful that I might use the most intimate details that people who have lived together for a long time can carry like swords. But I still need to talk to somebody. Most of our neighbors are a good two, three miles away and busy farmers like us. So I talk to the dog, whose eyes have taken on a kind of old man wisdom to match his graying muzzle.

Some days it's hilarious. Angel patiently trails behind me as I do the housework, ducking behind a chair when I vacuum, sitting by the bathroom door as I scrub the toilet and floor, or lying on the porch while I peel vegetables or count eggs, all the while listening to the constant run of my mouth.

It is only at night when I let Angel out of the house that he leaves me for a few hours, running out the door and into the nearest patch of woods with the determination of a reconnaissance pilot, his black coat giving him a natural camouflage at night. In the past I had only an inkling of what he did on these forays, what any male dog would do, and him especially, pent up all day in the house with me. But lately I've suspected that Angel's nightly journeys are not meaningless wanderings or chance matings, and if he could talk, he would tell me things that my husband never does. It frightens me. Other women who are isolated and lonely drink or pick fights with their silent husbands or take up with other men or maybe just suffer silently. I talk to the dog. And watch a little boy who was never mine and who has long since grown up and abandoned me.

Then this morning at breakfast, my husband, who has borne like a Buddhist monk the hardships of being a World War II veteran, a farmer, and a mixed-blood man in northern Wisconsin, does talk to me, only to hurt me. He put down his coffee cup and said, "I just can't do it anymore, Rose. I used to be able to lift a bale of hay in each hand, and now I can barely lift one with two hands. I can't sleep worth a shit, and things that used to mean so much to me don't anymore. I just don't give a damn."

What could I say? For other people the meaning of life does not rest on being able to lift a bale of hay. But we're farmers. Everything rests on that bale of hay. Actually it was the look on his face, not what Ernie said, that did me in this morning. The message was loudly broadcast with those dark brown, bloodshot, and tired eyes. That bale of hay should have been passed on to younger hands. We are Rosemary and Ernest Morriseau, good farmers, but farmers *without children*.

I sat as though slapped speechless. My lips moved, but no sound came out. Ernie stood up as though he didn't notice, maybe he didn't care, and walked out the kitchen door.

"I give a damn," is what I couldn't spit out. "I tried." And it got worse as the day went on. I could barely keep my head up, could barely talk for fear of tears.

Now the dishes are done, and the dog is scratching to be let in. I open the door, and Angel strolls through the doorway, his nails tapping like drumsticks on the linoleum. Then, my only friend, he sits and looks up at me.

Suddenly I can't look at the dog, and I can't breathe. I stumble out of the kitchen and into the living room, but Angel trails me. When I reach for and slump into the old brown recliner by the window, I am temporarily relieved of the burden of Ernie's words, of

Ernie's silence. I cry, hiccuping and sputtering like a three-year-old. I cry for hours until it gets dark, until my eyes become puffy and my head aches. Angel rubs his scarred head against my knee for a while before settling down next to the chair. I'm grateful for even that touch.

I love this dog, and this dog loves me. But when did my husband and I stop doing the dance of love? What have I done, what crime have I committed, that warrants being ignored? That justifies not being touched? And when will I stop being punished for the children I could not give birth to?

◆◆◆◆◆◆◆◆◆◆

I met Ernie at a VFW dance in Milwaukee. I was an Army nurse who had just finished a two-year stint in the Philippines, and Ernie was a shrapnel-filled soldier. I was sipping my favorite drink of depression, a gin and tonic, and spiraling downward when I smelled cedar. I turned around to stare into a pair of the most velvety brown eyes I'd ever seen. He had a chest like a gladiator and thick black hair. His voice was warm and deep.

"War's over. Wanna dance?" he asked, and smiled that enormous slow smile that made me put down my drink, suddenly crazed to wrap my arms around that huge, cedar-smelling chest and hold on for as long as I could.

We both held on like two long-lost buddies from childhood. He was from northern Wisconsin like me. We got married and left Milwaukee to take on his family farm in Olina. Then I tried having babies.

The doctor said my uterus was damaged, but he couldn't figure out how. I told him I'd been sick, on and off in the Philippines, with what was thought to be some kind of intestinal flu.

"Well," he commented nonchalantly, "maybe that did it," and motioned for me to get dressed. Then he said to quit trying. But I tried.

Just when I would start to think that this one was going to hold and would get ready to shop for baby clothes, I'd feel that damn ache in my lower back. Then the contractions would come on fast, and before I could get to the hospital, twenty miles away, my lovely baby would slip and fall out, looking like clotted peony petals shaken from the stem into a pool of blood.

I remember the last baby. I was in the bathroom, feeling that downward pull and squeezing my thighs together to hold it in.

"Don't leave me. Don't leave me," I kept saying. Chanting it, Ernie said, long after the baby was gone and he'd taken me to the hospital. Ernie had been kind enough after the first three miscarriages. But as they continued, he made love distantly, his body going through the motions as if vaguely to obey the adage that hope springs eternal. But what sprang from him died in me.

Then Ernie and I got two sons by default, at least for a short time, and Ernie and the ghosts of our own children were temporarily appeased. First Jimmy and then Bill, driven out of their house by their father's rageful drinking and their mother's mental descent into another world, began to visit us. I didn't give a damn about John Lucas, but Claire was like too many women I'd seen and grown up with. Women with brains three times the size and depth of their fathers and husbands, but trapped and nowhere to go with that kind of intelligence but sideways or down. I tried for a long time to get close to Claire, but she avoided me as though I were painful to her. I used to watch her walk in one continuous circle around the edge of their back forty acres while Jimmy was in the Marines and Bill was in school, her hands talking to the air and her face slanted toward the sky.

"She's losing it," I said to Ernie once when we discreetly watched her from behind our barn.

"You don't know that for sure," my husband said, surprising me. "Maybe she really is talking to someone."

"Do you see anybody else out there?" I asked sarcastically.

"I'm just sayin' there's a lotta things we don't know about," Ernie answered, and shrugged.

"Especially in that family," I cracked, and even Ernie had to nod.

But I felt lousy saying it and shut up after that, not wanting to tempt the spirits. *There but for the grace of God,* I thought, *go I.*

Long before Jimmy left, I rationalized the boys' time at our house as thinking that Claire probably needed a break from the kids, and I willingly opened up our house and my arms to Jimmy and Bill, letting the love pour. But that was not enough. Jimmy became a teenager so hell-bent on escaping his old man that enlisting in the Marines looked like a sure chance in a million-dollar lottery in comparison to his life in Olina. Then Jimmy lost the lottery. In her grief, Claire Lucas woke up and, realizing that she had another son, kept little Bill close to home after that. And Ernie and I lost both of them. I don't know who I cried more for, Ernie and me or Jimmy and Bill.

Then, when Bill was seventeen, his father died of a heart at-tack. I could not find any warmth in that kid's hand when I shook it after the funeral mass. It was as though he didn't know or remember me. But the look on his face was one that couldn't be mistaken. While Claire appeared bewildered and exhausted, her son was obvi-ously relieved instead of sad.

"You'd be relieved too! He won't have that stinkin' mean drunk for a father anymore," Ernie commented bitterly on the drive home.

When Bill turned eighteen, he began working full-time for the Standard station. Not long after John's death Claire became the re-ceptionist for the Forest Service. She seems much better now, but she still won't return a wave or accept any sign of friendship from me.

<hr />

I'm almost ready to drift off to sleep when I hear the steps creak. Angel wakes up and cocks his head toward the staircase. I wait and watch. My husband's shuffling body fills the doorway. He is wearing what he always wears to bed, a pair of blue pajama bottoms and nothing else. It's too dark for me to see his face, but I know something is wrong by the way his big shoulders are slumped forward.

"You know," he begins quietly, "my grandma Morriseau told me before I was shipped out to the Pacific, that I would know if anyone close to me had died. Here at home or over there. I told her I didn't wanna know. She said, want to or not, I would just know, especially if I kept my mind open to it. I thought it was just old Indian superstition. Nothin' ever happened during my service that made me think about what she said. Except my buddy Frank. His old French-Canadian Catholic mother told him almost the same thing. We laughed about it."

Either I'm so tired or it's really been a strange day. This morning he tells me he doesn't care anymore, and now it's almost midnight, and he's telling me about his reservation grandmother, who's been dead for almost forty years.

"But," he says, his voice dropping an octave, "I had a bad feeling when Jimmy left for basic training."

I am instantly wide awake.

"Jimmy?" I ask. "What about Jimmy?"

Ernie goes on as though he hasn't heard what I said.

"I didn't pay any attention to it," he says. "I figured I felt that way because of the kind of war it was. But when I saw him, I knew I had done a bad thing. I could've invited him over to dinner with Billy that night, remember? Before he shipped out the next day? But I didn't 'cause of what he did to that turtle with that stupid-ass Baker kid he used to hang out with. I could've gone after him, talked to him about what he was getting himself into. I could've talked him out of it. I came so close," he says, and then repeats, "so close."

"Ernie," I say. "Don't you remember? We didn't know that Jimmy had even enlisted until that night Billy came over for dinner.

Remember, when John came over to pick up Billy, he told us. Remember you were so mad because John was *proud* of it, and you said he was just getting rid of his son before the kid took him down. Don't you remember?"

"I *saw* Jimmy," he says, his voice dropping to a whisper, "the day before we heard about him. Remember, it was so warm that winter? I was shoveling manure. Well . . . that's when I saw him. Angel"—he gestures toward the dog—"saw him first and howled like crazy. Jimmy was standing in the back field. But he didn't say a word, not a word. He just took off his helmet and dropped his gun. Then"—Ernie swallows— "he turned around and walked into the swamp. That's when I knew . . . that Jimmy had died."

My husband, by nature, does not exaggerate. Still, I find his words hard to believe until I remember that Ernie didn't cry like me when we heard the news that Jimmy was MIA. At the time I thought it was because he had accepted it as a consequence of war. He'd fought. He knew the chances. Now it all makes sense. For the past fourteen years, he has been trudging through his daily life not silenced by hard, solitary work but by grief.

"I wanted to tell you," he says, suddenly shaking so much that the air seems to crack around him. "Then this morning when I saw the look on your face . . . so lonely, *so lonely,* it hit me what a goddamn bastard I've been. I'm sorry, Rose. I'm so sorry."

Then Ernie covers his face with his hands and, hunching over, lets out a long, deep sob that echoes through the room. My heart hits the wall of my chest.

I don't remember the last time Ernie cried. It must have been years ago. I've cried plenty, and I've heard lots of other women cry too. But women cry even in their worst pain, with hope and relief. They cry like wolves and coyotes do, howling to talk to their mates as well as to the rest of the pack. But there is something about the way men cry that sounds so hopeless, so anguished, as though the very act of crying were killing them.

I can feel the tears start up fresh in my eyes. "C'mere," I say, and open my arms to stop the waters. My husband stumbles toward me. The recliner moans under our weight as Ernie sinks into my arms. Angel bolts up and trots over by the TV. Alert but oddly calm, he hunkers down in front of the TV. He lifts his nose to sniff the air and then opens his mouth to taste it. Our big black dog, satisfied with what his nose and tongue read, lowers his lopsided head to rest in a pool of moonlight on the floor. I wrap my arms tighter around Ernie, touching with my fingertips the scars and pointed shrapnel still under his skin. He nuzzles his face deep into the crook of my neck to hide it while he cries.

I wish there were some way I could tell Jimmy that Ernie cries for him. I wonder if John Lucas ever grieved so for what was his flesh-and-blood son. We thought not at the time. He'd brag in town about Jimmy's being a war hero and tell stories as though he'd actually been there with Jimmy, fighting in Vietnam. Ernie and the other veterans in town never talked like that. They'd done it. They knew war wasn't a movie. It was hell personified, and for them to talk about it was to give it new life, to raise the dead. And I'd covered up so many shattered bodies in the hospital in the Philippines that I had dreams. Terrible dreams that lasted for twenty years. I dreamed that my limbs were being torn off or that I was being held at gunpoint, unable to speak Japanese, finally being bayoneted through the chest. My worst dream, though, was of a large white sheet descending on me from above, and I was still alive and fighting to keep that endless white cotton from smothering me. John Lucas just couldn't know. Whatever it was that made him drink, it wasn't the crap of war.

The dog exhales a deep lungful of air, but his eyes stay open, luminescent in the white light. I stare at him until I realize that I have forgotten to let him out for his nightly wandering. Then it dawns on me that he has not made the slightest familiar sign of wanting to go outside.

My head suddenly clears from years of shameful and cloudy debris, and my skin prickles.

Oh, yes, I want to say out loud. *Yes, yes, yes.*

Grandma Morriseau was right about such things.

Up until now I would've traded Angel to have had at least one child come out of my rickety womb. I was at one of the lowest points in my life when we found Angel lying in that ditch. I believed, since the first time I saw him all shot up and spared him an early death, that I had saved him. That all my stored-up and unused maternal love and care could at least save him, a mere dog. I was *determined* to save him. But all the tears in the world can't hide the truth.

If anyone was saved, it was me.

When I have given and given and danced with love until I am exhausted, when my husband has remained silent and, some days, as bitter and brittle as a winter's day, this dog has given to me. When I have felt fragile and vulnerable, when I have wondered if Ernie would still fight for me and over me, over an aging fifty-seven-year-old farm wife instead of the slender and long-legged beauty that I once was, it is Angel who sits beside me in the cab of the truck while I sell eggs to homes on some of the worst back roads in this county; it is Angel who guards the farm and me from aggressive salesmen, from all the possible evil that people are capable of bestowing out of the blue. It is Angel who has kept me from talking to the air like Claire Lucas and whose very presence has kept to a distance the haunting ghosts of my never-born children. It is Angel who circles the perimeter of the farm at night, black and mysterious, who tastes the wind and listens for sounds that we cannot hear. And it is Angel who saw Jimmy Lucas first, and who I suspect, because I will never really know, is able to talk to Bill Lucas while Ernie and I cannot. It is this big, black, scarred-up dog lying in front of us that has for years carried a spirit that is not his own.

My husband has stopped crying but makes no move to uncoil himself from my arms. Someday I shall tell Ernie what I know. I shall tell him that it was a good thing, not a bad thing, that he saw

Jimmy. That Jimmy chose him. That we cannot save anyone. That we choose to be saved ourselves.

"Love," I shall tell my silent husband, "is never wasted."

And I shall tell him, looking at Angel, now sleeping by the TV, that we have never been alone.

✕✕✕✕✕ IF HE STAYED VERY STILL and gave no indication that he was awake, Bill could see through one cracked eyelid the black dog passing between the trees about ten yards away. He was not frightened, only cautious that any sudden movement would scare the dog away. He was familiar with his neighbors' dog, had played with him when he was a boy, had seen him roaming the boundaries of his farm in the early morning, and indeed knew the dog shadowed him whenever Bill was in the woods. He was an old dog now. Even from the distance of ten yards, Bill could see the frost of age on his muzzle. The dog's appearance gave Bill an inexplicably eerie yet familiar feeling. But he was never afraid.

Not like the night during the previous summer, when Bill had awakened halfway through his drunken slumber only to see a party of coyotes staring at him in the moonlight from the south end of the ridge, their eyes iridescent and haunting. His resting heart jerked like a cranked lawn mower, and he jumped up, shouting and waving his arms. The coyotes yipped and scattered down both sides of the ridge. Bill listened until he could no longer hear the papery sound of their paws on top of dried pine needles. When he calmed down, he realized it was only a group of yearling pups from that spring's litter by a female that had denned successfully at the base of the ridge for several years now despite a trap-crushed leg that had healed crookedly. They were curious and not threatening.

What had frightened him so badly was the sense of *waiting* he felt when he first saw them, motionless between the trees. The same silent waiting of crows and ravens in the treetops as they watched a winter-beaten doe die after giving birth in the spring.

He had spent many nights on the ridge during the past six years. It was the only high, dry land on his family's property that faced the deep kettle lake on the north side, rising out of the surrounding cedar swamp like the massive back of a brontosaurus long dead, and covered with red and white pines and birch.

"Search and destroy! Search and destroy!" James would cry as he chased Bill up the ridge in a mock game of war. Armed with his turtle-shell shield and wooden sword, Bill could never make it to the top with his brother chasing him. James would grab his ankles while Bill tried to keep from being pulled down the slope, releasing his sword and clawing the ground with his hands. Then his brother would run his fingers up Bill's legs, up to his chest, and tickle Bill under his arms until the towering red and white pines echoed with the sputtering and hiccuping laughter of a little boy. That was if his brother was feeling good.

If his brother was feeling mean, he would drag Bill down the slope until Bill's face was skinned and bleeding and his hands were raw. Breathing hard, James would crouch over him and yank the turtle shell from Bill's right arm and steal the wooden sword out of Bill's right hand. James would run up the slope until he reached the top. Turning around to stare down at his whimpering brother below, James would raise the turtle shell and sword and breathlessly chant a portion of the Eucharist prayer. Only James would change the possessive pronoun. "The kingdom and the power and the glory are *mine,* now and forever!"

The prayer, never meaning much to Bill in church, radiated with meaning as the God that was his brother, that looked like Elvis, shouted it from the top of the ridge. To Bill, trembling with fear and love below, the power of his brother's deep voice caused the woods to become silent. Caused the ridge to become a mountain and the mountain to become sacred. The ridge was his brother's, and it was where his brother would live forever.

Although Bill was a grown man now, he still clung to his childish belief. It was here on the plateau of the ridge that he slept most
nights within a stand of four red pines that seeded themselves in almost perfect geometric harmony with one another, forming a natural square room. If he wasn't sleeping, then he was drinking and
finally sleeping some more. He had his brother's shotgun, a Remington 870 Wingmaster pump, which he kept with him whenever
he was in the woods, the barrel nuzzled against his cheek when he
slept. It was the gun that Ernie Morriseau had given to his brother
when he was twelve years old. He was not old enough to go along
when his brother joyfully left their house, dressed in hunting clothes
and carrying the shotgun. In his jealousy, Bill went over to the Morriseau place anyway and spent time making cookies or helping Rosemary in the kitchen.

He had a vague sense of why he always took the gun with him.
Someday the pain might become so bad that he could not outdrink
it. His life was going nowhere, and even the simple pleasures he had
loved as a child held nothing for him. Even worse, the very thing
that had kept him alive, kept his hopes up, seemed to have disappeared even at night. Bill had not dreamed since he was nine years
old. When he looked in the mirror, he saw the Tin Man from *The
Wizard of Oz*. His skin was gray, and when he pounded on his
chest, it sounded hollow. All he had left was the numbness of beer
and the remaining physical sensation of something *out there*.

✕◆◆◆◆◆◆◆◆✕

"What are you looking for?"

It was a foggy gray morning two days ago when his mother appeared, standing at the edge of the field nearest the barn and holding a kerosene lamp even though it was daylight. She startled Bill
when he emerged from the cedars, wet, cold, and hung over. At
first he could only stare at her, not entirely sure that she wasn't an
apparition. She worked as a receptionist for the Forest Service, but

their paths coming and going on the farm rarely crossed. He knew she was there, though. His clothes were always washed and put in his drawers; there was always food cooked and ready to be eaten in the refrigerator. The house was clean.

It shocked and simultaneously amazed him that she knew exactly where he would exit from the swamp, that she had apparently waited and had not gone to work. It also made him angry.

"The sun," he answered sarcastically, pointing up at the sky. "Haven't seen the damn thing in days."

Her dark eyes narrowed, and she tilted her head back slightly.

"Wally Wykowski," she said as her son walked past her, "told me that you're going to lose your job and that it is a shame because you do excellent work."

Bill stopped and turned around. "Wally can fuck off."

"Bill—" she sighed "—I wish you wouldn't use that language. This is a small town. There aren't many jobs. We might be forced," she continued, waving her hand toward the house and barn, "to sell this place if you can't earn a living and help me. You know I can't pay the taxes on it alone."

His head hurt so badly that he could barely hear her. He looked down at his feet but not before noticing that she was wet and shivering and had a streak of mud on her cheek.

"I never see you," she said. "You're never home. Do you need anything? Money?"

"I don't need any money!"

"Look at me," his mother commanded. She grabbed Bill's arm. "I know," she said tersely, "what you're looking for. I live here, remember?" Her fingers pressed into his arm. "It's not worth it to drink yourself to death."

In an effort to divert her, he laughed. A fake and horsy laugh. "I told you," he said, shaking his arm loose, "I'm looking for the sun."

He felt a sudden urge to puke. In an attempt to quell his stomach, he stared back at his mother and realized that her hair was

completely white and not its former black color and that she was
stooped. He saw the misery in her face. The defeat in the way her
arms hung limply. Then his stomach erupted, and he bent over,
emptying into the wet grass what little liquid was left in him. Bill
felt her hand cup the back of his head.

"Yes," he heard his mother say through his spitting and coughing, "you are."

✗✗✗✗ ERNIE MORRISEAU WAS CAUTIOUSLY SCALING the barn's gambrel roof that morning, hammering the tar-coated shingles so that they overlapped and were waterproof, when he heard the distant brassy honking of geese above him. In his haste to look up, he fumbled with his hammer and lost it. He watched it slide down across the shingles before falling to the barnyard below. He swore loudly before looking up in time to see a very small flock of Canada geese pass over him on their way south. He thought he'd counted twelve of them until Ernie noticed that something was amiss about their flight pattern, and he rapidly re-counted the flock. Eleven. There was an obvious gap in the right string of the V-shaped flock between the fourth and fifth birds. A lost bird.

Ernie listened as each goose intermittently sounded off, the cracked bell of their voices calling out as if to leave a trail of sound like bread crumbs for their lost member to follow. He knew the geese would maintain this space for the missing goose for the rest of their migration. As Ernie watched them, he wanted to believe too that the lost goose would find the others. But it was November, and the entire flock was unusually late in migrating. The more probable truth was that the goose was dead. Ernie continued to stare at the geese even as tears blurred his vision and the flock resembled a strand of hair floating in the distance.

He raised his arm to wipe his face on the upper part of his sleeve but stopped when a movement in his neighbor's field caught his attention. Ernie hoisted himself up for a better look and settled his body halfway over the pinnacle of his barn roof. He knew who it was before he saw him, and he watched intently as Bill Lucas's tall and gangly figure emerged from the corner of Ernie's field. He watched as Bill swung one long leg and then the other over the fence into his own forty-acre field. This was the first time Ernie had seen him emerge in the morning. Usually he saw Bill at dusk. It had become a twilight ritual begun last spring, Bill walking the field and Ernie watching him.

He was mildly relieved. It had always bothered Ernie that he never saw Bill come back out, although he knew the young man was fundamentally safe in the woods and swamp. In Ernie's mind, Bill would always be the sensitive and inquisitive boy who used to visit his farm with his older brother, Jimmy. He could not quite reconcile this image with the Bill Lucas who was a Standard station car mechanic, who still lived with his mother and was rumored to have inherited his father's absorbency of beer. Ernie had acted on his worry only once, waiting until Bill disappeared from sight before walking across his own field in an attempt to follow Bill. He stopped when he reached the middle of his field, his stomach cramped with memorable fear and apprehension. He turned around and walked back to his barn, telling himself that to follow Bill was a terrible invasion of his privacy.

Perched on top of his own barn like a swallow, Ernie timidly raised one hand as if to wave, fanning his fingers out to let the wind pass through them. But then his chest began its slow rumble of grief. As he began to shake, Ernie quickly dropped his hand to steady himself on the barn roof.

Moments later his wife stepped out of their farmhouse to find out what had caused her husband's swearing, only to see the silhouette of his weeping body draped over the top of the barn roof.

"It *will* get better," his wife said later that night, both of them squeezed together in the old brown recliner like two loaves of bread. "Think of crying," she whispered into his ear, his face burrowed into the crook of her neck, "as medicine. It feels bad now, but it will make you feel better in the long run. There is nothing wrong with crying."

Ernie felt the vibration and muffled rise of sound in his wife's throat before it enunciated itself in his ear. She was right, but he was still appalled that at the age of fifty-eight, he should cry with the same painful urgency as a newborn with colic. It was as if the grief had stored itself up, a small lake behind his eyes that had reservoired in his chest for years, its shoreline slowly rising until it overflowed the upward barrier of bones and tissue and gravity. He rested in his wife's arms until she gently pushed him out of the chair and guided him upstairs to bed.

The exhaustion of crying coupled with his work on the barn roof caused him to sleep deeply for only a couple of hours. He woke up feeling the pleasant warmth of Rosemary's thigh against his own. She shifted in her sleep to lie on her side, and he aligned his body with hers, slipping one hand underneath her exposed arm so that he could caress her breasts and belly. She woke up and turned over to face him. They made love leisurely. Then he had slipped into that watery, vague state of early-morning sleep most apt to produce dreams when he thought he heard a shotgun go off. Although she never woke up, his wife stirred in her sleep as though she had heard it too. He sleepily opened his eyes just enough to see that it was two-thirty and then drifted back to sleep. When he woke up again, it was to the hammering ring of his alarm clock at five-thirty.

He sat up and shivered. It was the opening day of deer season, and although he looked forward to it, getting up in the cold darkness still took some effort. He quietly got out of bed and groped his way down the unlit staircase to the kitchen. He had stuffed most of his hunting clothes into a large plastic bag filled with cedar boughs and left the bag in a corner of the kitchen the week before. He discovered, after opening the bag, that he had forgotten to include a pair of thick wool socks and quietly felt his way up the stairs to the bedroom. He was blindly feeling through the dresser drawer when he heard the sheets rustle and the click of the bedside lamp.

"What are you looking for?" his wife asked behind him.

"My wool socks," Ernie answered at the same moment he spied them in the far corner of the drawer. "Found 'em."

He turned around and held up the socks as if they were trophies. His wife smiled, her long salt-and-pepper hair fanned out like a spiderweb against the pillow.

"I better get rollin'," Ernie said, bending down to give her a kiss. She reached up and held the bottom half of his face in her hand. He patiently waited, caught by the pressure of her fingers on his cheeks. "Do you want me to stay home?"

DID I WANT HIM TO stay home? Yes and no. I contemplated his question. Looked into his dark brown eyes and stared at his cheeks and chin with its mix of black and gray stubble. My face was chapped from the stubble on his face, from hours before, when I had awakened to his hands cupping my breasts. He asked me while I could still taste him in my mouth, always that taste and smell of sweat and cedar. The first taste of him when we made love the night we met. I wanted to say, "Yes. Stay home with me. In bed." It had been so long since we'd made love, and I felt dreamy and luxurious from his touch. Girlish.

But it was a good sign that he wanted to go hunting. This past summer I lived in daily fear that I might walk into the barn and see him hanging from the rafters. I watched him struggle to get out of bed in the mornings, unable to raise his face to a beautiful sunny day. I fought to keep from being sucked down into the eddy he had become and, at the same time, wanted to reach down and pull him out, even when he lashed out unintentionally and hurt me.

Every marriage re-forms itself over and over again with each crisis. We've been lucky. Most of our years were spent under fairly happy circumstances except for the lack of children and the wound that festered from it. Thinking about it now, I think it was appropriate that our breaking point would come during the season of summer. Like heat rash, every painful truth and secret in our life together surfaced under the searing light of the summer sun. One of the biggest secrets of all. None of our friends had any inkling of what we'd been through. Not just this past summer but the whole fourteen

years before. If they knew, they would say that I was crazy to let
Ernie go alone in the woods with a gun. If they really knew, they
would say that Ernie was crazy, period.

Once he started crying, I knew he would survive. I make sure
that I am never very far away. Ernie cries when he needs to, sometimes once a day. And soon he will surface completely from his
tears. From what causes those tears.

I would be more worried if he hunted with other men. Thank
God, Ernie prefers to hunt alone except for years ago, when he
hunted with his father and his uncles and then with Jimmy Lucas. In the Morriseau family, hunting meant something very different, and it bears little resemblance to the craziness of deer season in
these times: Sundays spent hunting in the morning, stopping for the
noontime NFL game and several six-packs of beer, and then going
back out to hunt until dark. I can't tell you how many hunting accidents happen on Sundays.

I've seen the aftermath of accidental shootings because I'm a
volunteer nurse and paramedic, riding with the Olina ambulance
whenever a call comes through. I've seen shotgun blasts at close
range where a deer slug makes a quarter-size tunnel through a human body. That's to be expected with a shotgun. But rifle bullets are
different, and even then there is little similarity between a .22 rifle
bullet and a .30-'06 bullet. With a high-powered .30-30 rifle and a
scope, a hunter can shoot an animal at a considerable distance, sitting comfortably on top of a truck or in a deer stand. At first all you
see is a clean hole in the chest of the man or boy who has been
shot, but a strong clue is the large puddle of blood he is lying in. It
is when I turn the body over that the devastation can be seen and
smelled. A .30-'06 long-nosed rifle bullet without a full metal jacket
enters the body neatly and almost pierces it with the fineness of a
sewing needle. But when it exits the body, it does so with such
force that it blows open a crater, splintering the spine and exposing
spilled and ruptured intestines. The fresh smell of blood and bowel

can make whatever you've eaten crawl up into your throat instantly. It is even worse when the victim has caught the bullet in the face and head. Then he is almost unrecognizable. I lost three new volunteers the year before, after they saw the shattered head of the Penter boy.

The hunter who has ill-fatedly pulled the trigger usually does not vomit or cry but stands near the dead man or boy with a lost and uncomprehending look. There is emotion on occasion, especially when it is a father who has shot his son or a brother who has shot his brother or a son who has shot his father. He falls to the ground, incoherently praying and apologizing, and has to be picked up and carried to the ambulance as well. Sometimes he just faints.

I surprised myself when I volunteered five years ago to do ambulance duty. After taking care of men or what was left of them in an Army hospital in the Philippines during the war, I didn't think I could handle it anymore. I didn't think I'd have the edge. But the township was having a terrible time finding volunteers. Someone has to do it. It takes practiced detachment because if they are still alive, you have to work fast and think rationally to try to save them.

Don't get me wrong. It is never easy. I wait until later, until I can get home, and then I rant and rave at the stupidity of it before collapsing into tears.

But it is about crying.

It is those men who do not cry that are in danger and dangerous to hunt with. Those men who often drink instead of cry. It is those same men that at the last minute suddenly realize that in the haze of their hangovers it is their buddies' heads they are staring at through the rifle's scope and not the eight-point bucks standing just beyond them in the snarl of brush. Those are the men who shoot and kill, sometimes anything in front of them. Sometimes, I think, they pull the trigger because their rifles are raised and they don't know how to put them down without firing them. As though once they've set their eyes on those beads at the end of the barrels, it is shameful not to fire. It is strange. I eventually see those same men because they have either drunk themselves to death or have pointed the barrels at themselves. And they die never knowing why.

"No, go ahead," I answered, releasing his face. "But come home before it gets dark."

XXXX BILL HAD NOT SHOWN UP for work or slept for three days straight. The sky had remained a silvery gray since the beginning of the month because the sun never showed itself. It was typical November weather, and on the third day the sun finally set in the west unseen. Bill left his house and walked to the barn in that peculiar dim light just before nightfall that his mother had always referred to as owl light because it was then that the mottled brown and white barn owls silently lifted from their perches on the barn windowsills and glided over the fields in search of mice.

Bill was tipping back the last can from his second six-pack of beer and leaning against the southwest corner of the barn when he heard a bark. Just one. He spotted the dog through the overgrowth of grass near the middle of the field and slowly lowered his arm, releasing the beer can into the grass.

"Angel!" he called, and then whistled.

The dog barked twice but did not move.

Bill whistled again. The dog responded by lifting his muzzle to sniff the air. After a few minutes the dog lowered his back haunches and sat.

"Annngel! C'mere, boy!" Bill drunkenly crooned in one last attempt to get the dog to come to him. But the black dog remained seated and continued to watch Bill.

"Fuckin' dog," he muttered. In a burst of rage he crushed the beer can in his hand and threw it at the dog. It fell far short of the dog's position. Angel's ears went up, but the dog did not move.

"What do you want from me?" Bill screamed at the dog. "Why

are you following me? What the fuck did I ever do to you! You'd be dead," he continued, shaking his fist at the dog, "if it wasn't for me! I never hurt you! So how come you don't come when I call you?!"

Bill picked up his shotgun, loaded it, aimed, and fired at the dog. When it became apparent seconds later that he had missed, Bill reloaded. But when he raised the gun and hooked his first finger around the trigger, there was no longer a sitting dog but a man.

Bill nearly dropped the gun. The man stood still. Bill staggered forward, straining to make out the man's features in the diminishing light. As soon as Bill stepped forward, the figure stepped back. Bill stopped moving.

"Ernie?"

It was the only man he could think of who would have a reason to be in the middle of his field. He panted, heard the sound of his own frantic breathing.

"Hey!" Bill yelled again, fear making his voice audible this time. "Ernie, is that you?"

The man briefly turned his head as though to look at the swamp bordering the field. There was something about the slope of the man's head and his long neck and the familiar ease the dark figure seemed to have in his surroundings. Bill stepped forward and raised his arm, realizing too late that he was still gripping the shotgun. The man immediately spun around and began to run.

"Wait!" Bill yelled. The man continued to run, and without thinking, Bill ran after him, still clutching his shotgun.

"Wait!"

The field had not been plowed under that fall, and his legs became entangled in the thick, overgrown grass. He tripped. The loaded gun flew out of his hand, and Bill heard it go off. He was positive, even in his sleepless and beer-soaked state, that it had fired into the grass. But when he picked up the gun and scrambled to his feet, he saw a burst of flames engulf the man running ahead of him. He watched in paralyzed horror as the burning man danced and screamed in pain. Then the man fell, and the fire disappeared.

Bill spent hours desperately searching the field even when it became so dark he could not see his hands clearly, let alone anything else. There was no body, and even the dog had vanished. Although he could not be sure, the merest suggestion of what he might have done sent him into a zigzagging stride out of the field. He did not realize the direction he was taking until he hit the barbed wire fence dividing his farm from the Morriseau farm. He heard and felt the barbs puncture and rip his jeans as he rolled over the top of the fence. Felt the immediate pain of gashed skin on his thighs. He landed on the other side of the fence, the gun still in his hand and the breath knocked out of him. His boots were snagged in the lowest string of wire. Terrified that if he surfaced above the grass, he would see the burning man again, he lay there for several hours.

But in the early-morning hours he kicked his boots free from the barbed wire and did get up. Bill didn't remember how he got there, just that he ran and ran, cedars slapping him in the face, his boots wet from crossing a narrowed inlet of the swamp, until he found himself at the base of the north slope of the ridge. He saw a black clump of something in the nearest red pine, and his hopes were momentarily lifted. Then he saw what it was. In the extreme pain that causes a righteous and reckless abandonment of conscience, he loaded his shotgun, pointed it up at the homemade deer stand, and fired shell after shell into it. Then he savagely ripped the ladder off the side of the red pine before throwing the hot-barreled gun to the ground next to the tree and running up the slope of the ridge.

✖✖✖✖ WHEN ERNIE LEFT THE HOUSE half an hour later and stepped into the circle of light cast down by the yard lamp, he knew that Rosemary was standing by the bedroom window watching him. He was dressed in blaze orange pants and jacket with his deer tag displayed like a billboard on his back. In one hand, he carried his father's Marlin 1895 rifle, its barrel safely pointed toward the ground. Just before he reached the edge of the illuminated barnyard, Ernie stopped and pretended to check his pockets. Then he straightened up and, turning slightly, blew a kiss to his wife before stepping out of the artificial light and into the presunrise darkness.

A layer of hunter's snow, wet and perfect for tracking, had fallen during the night. He stopped walking after a few feet and looked down his driveway at County H, the blacktop road in front of his farm. He could walk H for about a mile to get to the red pines woods and big cedar swamp he usually hunted in, but it would take longer. It would be shorter to cross his own field. He stared into the darkness.

In the many hunting seasons before Jimmy Lucas had left for Vietnam, Ernie would wait for him in the early morning in this very spot. He would hear his young neighbor first before seeing him, hear his footsteps and heavy breathing from having run across the fields between their two farms. Then Jimmy's face would surface under the yard light, flushed a deep red as though he had popped up from a long underwater swim. First his windburned eyes would focus on Ernie, and then Jimmy's lips would crack into the seductive grin that made many people in Olina compare him with

Elvis Presley. It had been years since an early November morning held that happy face. They had hunted together since Jimmy was twelve, and it had never occurred to Ernie then that he would not be hunting with Jimmy into his old age.

Uneasily Ernie turned and studied the outline of his barn, barely visible in the predawn darkness. The coffee in his stomach burned, and a familiar tingling sensation crept up his legs, threatening to keep him frozen in place. He kicked one leg forward like a wooden soldier, and then the other, stiffly moving toward the field just like the deer he was looking for, with his head raised and his eyes wide open, alert for any sudden movement.

Ernie was halfway through the field when the sun peeked over the eastern horizon and a raucous chorus of crows clustered in the tops of the huge white pines at the field's edge greeted him. With great relief, Ernie stopped walking and listened to their familiar cries pierce the silence of the woods and field.

Ernie liked crows. He affectionately regarded them as he would a beloved but sinning relative. They were not as noble as geese, but they had their place. Crows were the barhoppers of the bird world, flying from tree to tree, looking for something to eat or drink, and gossiping at every stop. Their eyes missed very little. Deer season was a holiday feast for them. Ernie gazed at their black bodies perched within the pine boughs. He knew how to decipher the language of crows. Their rusty early-morning cawing was done at casual intervals and did not contain the hysterical shriek of danger. The field was safe. A sudden flush of happiness hit him. His father had taught him the lessons about crows. When Ernie gutted his deer, he left the gut pile on the forest floor as his father had always done, to appease the crows. "Because," his father had said, "crows talk."

On impulse, Ernie laid his rifle on the snow-dusted ground, stood up, and raised his arms into the air. He stretched his fingers to hold the sun's warmth the way he had when he was seven, in imitation of his father. While his mother openly expressed her feelings, her eyes often twinkling with mischievous humor, his father was a man not often given to emotional displays. Although he was a mixed-blood man of Ojibwe and French ancestry, Claude Morriseau was almost stereotypically Indian, reserved and stoic about life's pains. Ernie later understood that it was less about being Indian and more about adopting a strategy that allowed his mother and father to live peacefully outside the reservation and even succeed at farming in the cutover land of northern Wisconsin. The German fathers of Olina Township could not find an avenue on Claude Morriseau's face that led to his emotions and therefore an opening for weakness. But Ernie knew his father's feelings ran deep, and nowhere was this more apparent than in his great love of mornings.

Claude Morriseau believed that morning was the holiest time of the day. He told Ernie that if he could make it through a bad night, morning would reward him with his life. The first thing Claude Morriseau did every morning until he became crippled by a stroke was to walk outside to greet the sun, even on days when clouds blanketed it. If they were hunting in the thick cover of woods when sunrise began, his father would stop walking, lay down his rifle, and raise his face and arms to the rays filtering through the canopy of leaves and needles. This was a practice unique to his father. None of Ernie's extended family on the Heron Reservation exhibited this quiet reverence for morning.

Ernie tilted his head back to receive the warmth of the morning sun on his face. His bad night had lasted for years and finally, with this kiss of early-morning sun, was nearly over. He felt surprisingly very *alive*, just as his father said he would, and as if to prove it, his heart drummed loudly inside his chest. Beat with a memory of long ago.

"I carry you in my heart," his father had written to him in an unexpected letter while Ernie lay wounded in an Army hospital in Hawaii during World War II. Those words, so uncharacteristically sentimental, wrapped themselves around Ernie and cradled him as if he were a small boy. He had tucked the letter under his belly so he could pull it out to reread it when the pain from the shrapnel in his back became unbearable.

Ernie happily waved at the sky once more before picking up his rifle. He wiped it off with a rag from his pocket and began walking again. The crows became silent as Ernie advanced toward them. When he was about to step over the sagging section of snow fence much used by the deer, the big black birds loudly announced his presence before flapping into the sky. Ernie waited until it was quiet again before crossing over the faded redwood fencing and entering the swamp.

He took a deep breath and inhaled the heavy, sweet smell of cedar. Although his clothes were previously scented with cedar boughs, Ernie reached out and stripped a nearby branch of its flat needles anyway. He crushed and rubbed them between his hands and then smeared the scent over his face and the front of his chest. He had hunted this swamp and its edges since he was very young, and it never failed him. Although he didn't search for deer directly in the swamp, he had, in past years, surprised a few big bucks while trudging through it. It had always been risky shooting a buck in the swamp, but it was even more so now that he was an older man. He did not have the quick reflexes anymore to move with the speed and silence necessary to get a close, clean shot, nor did he have the energy to run on the spongy swamp bedding to track a wounded animal. And he did not have a younger man to help him. He was handicapped in such an environment, and Ernie was sure the deer knew it.

He sighed and looked down at the tannin-colored water pooling around the soles of his boots. They could use the venison, but they didn't really need it. Just a few weeks before he had sent one of their heifers to the meat locker, and their two freezers were full of beef. But it felt so good to be in the woods again, felt so good to *feel* good that he didn't want to go home either. He could not have imagined what a fall would be like without hunting, yet he had not hunted for the past five years, afraid in his deepening depression to be alone with a rifle or shotgun. It had been a mistake, he realized now, to stay away from the woods. The fall hunt was a timeless tradition in his family, and it was the time of year he felt both the closeness and the loss of his own father most intensely.

Ernie shaded his eyes from the sun with one hand and looked over his end of the swamp. In the middle of the swamp was the ridge, a dumping of glacial moraine that rose like a humped spine. It was on the north slope of the ridge that Ernie had shot his first deer when he was twelve and where his tree stand was now. He contemplated its pine-covered hump and decided that it was time to see it again after so many years. Even if it was to sit quietly in his stand among the huge red pines near its pinnacle and gaze down at the smaller of the two kettle lakes.

But by the time Ernie had gotten three-quarters of the way across, he began to have nagging doubts about walking up the north slope. Not that he wasn't capable of doing it. It was a small ridge, and its sides, though a climb, were not treacherously steep. If he took it slowly, it would be as pleasant a walk as any on flat land. He had begun moving toward it with the happy memory of hunting it with his father, thinking it had been forty years ago when he was last on the ridge, until his faulty memory made him suddenly recall differently. He stopped and stared at the big red pines, deeply bothered that he had forgotten what had been a momentous day. It was sixteen years ago, not forty, and it was not his father but Jimmy Lucas who had last hunted with him on the ridge. It was the fall of Jimmy's senior year in high school, the November he shot the big twelve-pointer that many people had seen in the area but could never find during hunting season. Like a fist smashing through a wooden door, the area of his brain that kept all pain locked away opened up. The memory bled and pooled in his eyes.

xxxxx THAT DAY THEY HAD POSITIONED themselves at the base of the ridge in the hope that they would catch the deer either coming down or going up the slope.

"I think he's in there," Jimmy had whispered to Ernie, jerking his head toward the swamp. It was before sunrise, and Ernie could feel the warmth of Jimmy's breath on his cheek.

"Maybe," Ernie whispered back. "But remember what I said. If you shoot him in the swamp, you better make sure it's a clean shot. Otherwise it's gonna be you spending your day trying to find a blood trail in that soup."

They stopped talking and quietly moved into their positions, leaning into red pines that were twenty feet apart. Ernie was doubtful that the buck was in the swamp. It was too wet for deer to bed down, and they usually reserved the swamp as a last effort to shake off a predator.

It was half an hour before the darkness gradually became gray and, within a matter of minutes, lightened up enough for both of them to see the white pines towering in the distance on the edge of the Morriseau farm. At first the boreal cedar growth appeared quietly empty. Ernie watched as the mist thinned with the gain of light and whole patches of canary reed grass and moss became visible with the lift of fog. Then they heard a snort and saw the flagged tails of three does as they emerged from behind a large white cedar. Neither man raised his gun. Both had doe permits, but they had tacitly agreed to try for a buck first. Ernie watched with surprise as the does bounded out of the swamp in single file on the well-worn path that led through the white pines into his field. He had swiftly concluded that there weren't any more deer coming out of the swamp when out of the corner of his eye he saw Jimmy slowly raise his rifle. Ernie looked back at the cedar.

A huge rack followed by a sizable head, neck, and body materialized in front of the tree and made it look small. Ernie stared at the buck. Like the trophy animals of badly written outdoor stories, he appeared ethereal in the mist, and Ernie wondered if the swamp fog was fooling his eyes. An animal of that size had survived many hunting seasons and was most likely the dominant buck in the area. The buck was so preoccupied with the whereabouts of the does that he had not registered the presence of the two men. He seemed to be almost drunk on the scent of his does and lifted his black muzzle, his nostrils flaring, to catch the direction they had taken. Jimmy scoped and aimed. In the seconds that followed, Ernie surprised himself by hoping that Jimmy wouldn't pull the trigger. Then the shot was fired, and it whistled as it spliced the air. The huge buck surprised them, going down immediately rather than running a ways as many deer were able to do even with a bullet-shattered heart. And Ernie knew that Jimmy's aim had been perfect. As it should be. As he had taught Jimmy. Ernie expected Jimmy to whoop, but the boy only lowered his rifle and stared in astonishment.

Ernie walked over and slapped Jimmy on the shoulder. "There's your twelve-pointer!" he said jovially. "You were right. I would never have thought he'd bed in the swamp."

"I didn't know if he'd bed in the swamp either." Jimmy faltered. "I only guessed it . . . Jesus . . . he's bigger than I thought."

"C'mon," Ernie urged. "Let's drag him to hard ground."

They each grabbed a hind leg and pulled, the buck every bit as heavy as he looked. They propped the animal on its back at the base of the ridge. Before Ernie made the abdominal cut with his knife, he bent over the animal in a moment of silence just as his father had always done.

Jimmy took off his jacket and folded it before reaching into the buck's belly and pulling out the entrails: the red-brown liver; the coiled ropes of intestines; the nearly empty stomach of a buck in rut, too preoccupied to eat. Sweat ran down Jimmy's forehead and cheeks and dripped back down into the buck's abdomen. When he pulled out the shattered heart, Jimmy looked at it for a few seconds before placing it alongside the rest of the gut pile.

When he was finished, he wiped as much of the blood off his hands as he could in the grass before carefully reaching in his coat pocket. He took out a hand brush and a bar of soap. He walked until he came to a depression in the sphagnum moss that held water and washed his hands. Then he came back to where Ernie was sitting next to the buck. He sat down and took the Hershey bar that Ernie held out to him. He peeled the wrapper off the chocolate. Ernie noticed that Jimmy's hands were scrubbed until they showed no trace of blood.

"I always thought it was crap," Jimmy said, staring at the gut pile, "that some guy wrote up in *Outdoor Life* about finding the trophy buck of his dreams, only to end up not shooting it because it didn't seem right. But I almost didn't shoot him. Now I wonder if I did the right thing."

His face betrayed his usual affected teenage toughness, the Brylcreemed black hair with its small ducktail in the back, the dark eyes and slightly pouty full lips. Sitting next to him, Ernie could almost feel again the difficulty of being a teenager, the grappling with hormones that promoted the premature desires of an adult but without the knowledge or experience to handle them. Shooting the buck had punctured the veil of toughness on Jimmy's face, and Ernie pretended that he didn't see the rapid blinking of Jimmy's eyes.

"It's always that way," Ernie explained. "I don't think any good hunter feels totally sure. When I shot my first deer, I thought I was going to cry. I couldn't look at its eyes. Those long lashes. There's something about deer that doesn't seem real . . . like they're spirits. I still feel like that sometimes. My father told me that day that it was a good thing to feel that way. That I recognized the seriousness of killing. I was lucky. My father was a good man and a traditional man. He believed in hunting to feed your family and only that. Remember," Ernie told Jimmy, "now that this big guy is gone, it will give the younger bucks a chance to mate with the does."

"Well," Jimmy commented, looking down at his boots, "we can always use the meat. I think that's why Mom lets me hunt with you."

Ernie nodded. Almost everyone in Olina knew that John Lucas's entire paycheck was often in danger of supporting Pete's Bar and Grill in town rather than his family.

"Are you gonna mount the head?" Ernie asked, although it was something he would never do.

"I guess before I shot him, I thought I would," Jimmy answered. "But I don't have the money, and Bill would be mad as hell at me."

He turned to Ernie, his face suddenly brighter. "My little brother is somethin' else," he said with a quick grin. "He fights with make-believe warriors, swinging at the air with that stupid wooden sword and that turtle shell he uses as a shield. But I don't think he'd really ever kill anything. You know if he could, Bill would try to take care of even bigger animals in our bedroom. It's a damn zoo in there now!"

Ernie laughed, the sound echoing across the swamp.

"Christ!" Jimmy exclaimed. "The other night I crawled into bed, and as soon as my head hit the pillow, two deer mice came running out from underneath it. Scared the shit outta me! I called him a little bastard. Then Mom yelled at me for swearing. But I'm the one who's got mouse turds all over his bed!"

Although Ernie had never stepped inside the Lucas home, he could imagine the mice, birds, snakes, and whatever else inhabited the boys' bedroom and the noise and smell that filled Jimmy's nights.

"Don't be too hard on him," Ernie said, his laughter trailing off. "He's a good kid."

"Yeah," Jimmy replied. "But he sure doesn't like people. He's always been funny that way. Kind of a loner. He hates my friend Terry. Course Terry is an asshole sometimes. Picks on Bill bad if I don't stop him. I think if Bill could, he'd stick that wooden sword right through Terry."

Ernie knew about Jimmy's friend Terry—chain-smoking backwoods hood—and he silently agreed with Bill. *Stick that sword right through him.*

Ernie glanced up at the sky. He thought it was about nine, but the sun never broke through the clouds, and the sky remained its characteristic November gray. Still, the temperature had risen to the mid-forties, and they could hear the quiet drip of melting snow. Without turning around, Ernie knew that the north slope of the ridge had lost its white cover of snow and was now a slippery wet bed of brown pine needles and birch leaves. He pulled a thermos full of coffee out of his field jacket. He was pouring some into the thermos's cup when Jimmy spoke.

"Is killing a man like killing a deer?" he asked.

Ernie nearly dropped his cup. He put the thermos down and steadied the hot cup of coffee between his hands before answering.

"How do you mean?" he asked, stalling for time.

"Well, when you were in World War Two," Jimmy asked, "you probably had to kill some men to defend yourself, didn't you?"

"I did."

He could tell by the way Jimmy dropped his head that he was uncomfortable.

"It's not that you can't ask," Ernie said quietly. "I don't know how to answer. It's not the same, but at the same time it is because you're taking a life."

Ernie paused and looked at Jimmy. The confusion and embarrassment were apparent on his young face. How was Ernie going to explain the Battle of Leyte in the Philippines as a way of justifying why he had killed other men? He was part of the U.S. Eighth Army, the soldiers brought in, they were told, for the task of "mopping up," which in effect meant killing off any remaining Japanese on the island. In an effort to distance the men from thinking of the Japanese as human, their commanding officers told them that the Japanese were a stain on the whole of humanity. It was as though they were being sent in to clean floors. Only it was their rifles and artillery, not a bottle of Pine Sol that would do the housekeeping of war. He was not a violent man, had never been one, and this had not served him well in the Army. He found it hard to fight the Japanese with any sort of rage. It was merely self-defense and luck that kept him alive. He knew that Jimmy, despite his embarrassment, wanted to hear stories of heroism, *his* heroism.

Out of the corner of his eye he could see Jimmy, now eager to hear what Ernie had to say. What could he say? War was full of little stories. A man's dress shoe found in the mud on his ascent up the island. A woman's brooch made of ivory. Once a jawbone that was clearly human and small, perhaps a child's. Mostly, though, Ernie thought that war was alternately boredom and anxiety with occasional bursts of real fear. Sitting in the mud and rain and rain and rain. The fuzzy growth called jungle rot that made his feet stink and swell. K rations that made you forget what fresh food was like. The god-awful odor of his own body when they'd been unable to wash for days. The horrific stench of rotting corpses, most of them Japanese, piled upon one another and covered with thunderclouds of flies. If there was any action, it occurred all at once. Those little signs of life were forgotten momentarily in the roar of artillery going off, the shelling and falling shrapnel, and his own desperation to stay alive. Then the skirmish was over, and he was back to sitting in the mud and the rain and wishing that he could look up and see a clear blue sky, pines, and the fiery color of sugar maples in fall.

He wasn't sure why he made it home alive when so many other men didn't, men he knew and thought about from time to time. They had not been told just how many Japanese were left on the island. They popped up out of nowhere like jack-in-the-boxes. It was the worst dogfighting he'd ever experienced. Hand-to-hand

combat using his non–Army-issued bowie knife, instinctively knowing just where to stab under the rib cage and work the blade and
handle up toward the heart. Sometimes he used the stock of his rifle
like a big stick, swinging until it made contact with a head. The
noises that came with such fighting. The cracking of bone and the
sucking sound a knife made going into a human body.

He tried not to think about that one terrible day that had
caused him to be sent home with enough metal in his back and legs
to draw an industrial magnet.

✶✦✦✦✦✦✦✦✶

They were humping up a slope. The humidity was such that they
were wet all the time. It made their helmets feel like molded steel
on their heads, compressing their brains. There was so much water
in the air that they breathed noisily, as though asthmatic, straining to
sift out the airborne oxygen. Frank was saying something to him
and laughing. Frank's last words were "steak sounds good right
now." There was a sudden burst of rifle fire and the whine of bullets
whizzing past them. They dropped to the ground, and Frank returned fire. When it was quiet, he ran up the muddy trail, thinking
that he had killed the Jap who had fired at them. Ernie, beginning
to follow him, had turned around to see if the rest of their platoon
was behind them when the explosion lifted him off his feet and sent
him flying forward as though a burning hand had shoved him in the
back. The pain was horrific, and he tried to breathe against it and
the thick smoke and debris. He could not hear or see Frank, so
Ernie got to his feet in his desperation to find him. Someone else
pushed him back down and held him. It took them an hour to
cover the thirty feet, searching for more land mines. Only then was
he permitted to get up, and he crawled behind the munitions expert.

How could you tell a seventeen-year-old boy what it was like
to find a man's head? His friend's head. How he cradled Frank's
head and sobbed, closing the lids over the blue eyes with his trembling and blood-covered fingers. Frank was as close to a brother as

he had ever gotten. He roared like a wounded bear when they tried to pry Frank's head out of his arms, and he kicked at anyone who dared try again. They left him alone until he was lifted and placed on a litter, still holding Frank's head. Ernie didn't recall feeling any pain in his back even though it rubbed against the canvas of the litter. It was only after they got him to an evacuation hospital and he was given a shot of morphine that they were able to take Frank's head out of his arms.

How lucky he had been. He had caught an almost fatal blast of shrapnel in the back, and miraculously not only had he survived but none of the hot metal had sliced into his spine, rendering him paralyzed. Ernie tried to feel grateful, but there was a nagging suspicion that he hadn't been brave enough. That he hadn't taken enough risks or aided better those who had died.

He didn't trust himself with a rifle or shotgun after the war and almost didn't go deer hunting after he had married Rosemary and come back to Olina. Claude Morriseau sat in a rocking chair in the kitchen and sensed his son's discomfort, his confusion. His speech was slow and measured.

"You did what you had to do," his father said while he watched his son put on his cedar-scented hunting clothes. "You are still a good man."

Then his father said something that contradicted what they had been taught to chant during basic training. His father leaned forward.

"This," his father said, drawing the words out slowly and tapping the barrel of Ernie's rifle with a calloused finger, "is a tool, nothing more. It is not you. Think when you use it, but don't love it. Then you won't kill stupidly with it. Only foolish and weak men," his father whispered in the dim light of the kitchen, "love their guns."

✗✗✗✗✗✗✗✗✗

Ernie shifted his body so that he would face Jimmy directly.

"When somebody is comin' at you with a rifle and bayonet,"

Ernie explained, "you don't have time to think about killing. You just do it. It's either you or him."

"Did you get any medals?"

Ernie nodded. "I have a Purple Heart because of all the shrapnel in my back, and I have a Bronze Star for bravery. Rosemary," he commented, gesturing toward his back, "is still cutting out the shrapnel with a razor blade. It works its way to the surface, even after all these years."

"Dad has medals too," Jimmy said bitterly. "He takes them out and waves them at me when he thinks I need to be taken down a few notches. But you know," he added, looking at Ernie quizzically, "I don't think he ever fought in WW Two. I don't have any proof. It's just a feeling and the fact that he shoots so badly. I think it's all a pile of crap. I think that's all I've ever heard from him. Crap."

"Well," Ernie answered lamely with a wave of his hand, "some guys handle it differently."

But Jimmy's perception knocked Ernie momentarily off course. Ernie too was sure that John Lucas had never seen action in the war, despite his stories told at Pete's Bar. But he would never say that to Jimmy. It was not Ernie's place to expose John Lucas to his son.

He sighed and poured more coffee, which he offered to Jimmy. He watched as Jimmy threw back his head and drained the cup, and he refilled it when Jimmy held it out.

"I wasn't the only one," Ernie added, hoping to divert the conversation away from any more war-related questions concerning himself. "Rosemary was an Army nurse in the Philippines. There were a few times when she had to run down to the beach to help them unload wounded men and the Japanese were strafing the whole beach. One of the nurses was killed that way. Rosemary came down with some sort of fever and was sick for a long time."

"She told me that."

"Oh! You've been asking her questions too?" Ernie grinned and reached over to punch Jimmy's shoulder lightly. "Speaking of Rosemary, let's get going. She's probably baked a coffeecake."

They dragged the buck home on foot, trudging across the field toward the Morriseau farmhouse. Rosemary's face appeared in the kitchen window, and they could see her wave before she dashed outside to meet them in the barnyard. They hung the buck from one of the huge beams in the barn before heading into the warm kitchen for more coffee.

XXXX IT WAS THE GUTTURAL CRY of a heron that yanked Ernie back into the present. He had to shake himself as though he'd fallen asleep standing up, and that was when he noticed the spit that had trailed out of his open mouth onto his jacket. He finished crossing the swamp. It took another five minutes of slowly walking the base of the north slope of the ridge before he reached the place where three deer trails crossed and where he had hunted the most. Ernie was fifteen feet away when he looked up expectantly and caught his breath.

His deer stand was gone.

Rather, it was no longer perched in the large red pine above Ernie's head but scattered in pieces on the slope around the tree. Even the wooden ladder he had built up the trunk to reach the camouflaged small platform had been pulled out of the tree and tossed into the snow. At first Ernie thought the culprit was a bear. When he got closer, he saw the platform had been shot up at close range and the ground around the red pine was littered with yellow shotgun casings. Then he saw the gun. Five feet away from the tree and dusted with snow was an older-model pump shotgun. Ernie stared at it, pulsing with anger and confusion until his common sense got the better of him. He looked again at the snow around him and saw the tracks. The gun looked familiar. It was a popular shotgun, a Remington 870 Wingmaster that had sold well during the late 1950s and early 1960s. He picked it up and wiped it off, then pumped the gun to eject any rounds and looked into the breech to make certain it was empty. He balanced the barrel against his shoulder alongside his own rifle and began his slow ascent up the slope.

The tracks did everything but run in a straight line, and interspersed with them were the familiar paw prints of Ernie's own dog. He had trudged two-thirds of the way up the ridge when his right foot slid on some wet needles, and he went down on one knee. He quickly but painfully straightened up, using the Remington as a staff. He stared at the shotgun again. No wonder it was familiar. He had once owned it and given it as a gift. He ran his fingers over the stock and found the worn letters carved near the end of the butt. *JPL*. James Peter Lucas.

His gut cramped up. Ernie turned his head from side to side and did a swift visual reconnaissance of the area. He scanned the trees and brush for any signs of green canvas, for the slightly askew pattern of camouflage or the rounded top of a metal helmet. What he had feared facing that morning was back again, and he could almost smell it.

He instinctively loaded his rifle but kept the safety on and the barrel pointed at the ground. He leaned the old Remington against the nearest pine before turning his attention to the tracks that disappeared when they reached the top of the ridge. His mind felt muddy, and he rubbed his forehead as though to massage his brain into action. Ernie slowed his breathing so that he could hear better. The woods were silent except for the chattering of chickadees and a nuthatch's occasional *zweeee* call. Ernie quickly counted; fourteen, almost fifteen years since Jimmy died. He had wanted to see Jimmy again, to talk to him, but now he was terrified, his stomach cramping. Jimmy was close by. He didn't want to turn his back on him, but he was afraid of him. Even if he wanted to run, Ernie could not safely turn his back on Jimmy now.

"Jimmy!" Ernie shouted up the slope, and listened as his own voice echoed through the silence of the trees.

"Jimmy! It's Ernie."

He waited for fifteen minutes, never taking his eyes off the top of the ridge.

"Jimmy! I know you're up there!" Ernie shouted again. "I'm not angry . . . you know . . . about the stand."

Ernie waited for another fifteen minutes. Then, when he was about to give up and chance turning around, he heard the snapping and rustle of brush being pushed aside. He had been so preoccupied with his last vision of Jimmy that when the silhouette of a man appeared on the top of the ridge, Ernie's heart kicked against his ribs, and he had to stifle a gasp.

Bill.

The tall young man was emaciated, and his big, bony hands dangled out of his coat cuffs helplessly as though broken. His hair was wet and covered with leaves and dirt, as was his red and black plaid jacket. But what really stunned Ernie was the look of Bill's face. Rather than having the florid meatiness of heavy drinkers, his face had the white waxiness of suet, and his eyes were sunken into the sockets of his skull.

"You've come to get me, haven't you?"

Ernie paused.

"No, Billy!" Ernie exclaimed. "I didn't even know you were out here."

"I'm the one who did it," Bill answered in the monotone of exhaustion. He dazedly stared down at Ernie.

"Ahh," Ernie said with a wave of his hand, "don't worry about the stand. I can make a new one. That one was about to rot off the tree anyway. That was nothin'. Just a little horseplay, huh?"

"I'm the one," Bill repeated flatly. "I did it."

"I don't care who did it." Ernie tried to persuade Bill. "It was only a deer stand. Just forget it. I'll tell you what," Ernie went on, adopting the soft tone he used on sick animals. "Why don't you come home with me? Rosemary would love to see you. How 'bout it?"

"You've come to get me," Bill said again, and shifted his gaze toward the rifle in Ernie's hand.

"No, no," Ernie answered quickly. "I was going deer hunting." He bent down but kept his head up and his eyes focused on Bill as he placed the loaded rifle on the ground. Then he stood up and began to walk slowly up the slope toward Bill. "What do you say, Bill? You don't look like you're feelin' so good. I'm gonna take you home with me, okay? Okay?"

"No!" Bill shouted, and Ernie immediately stopped moving toward him.

"I did it! I'm the one!" Bill shouted again. He obsessively began to rub his hands over the dirty jacket covering his chest.

"Billy," Ernie asked, confused and frustrated, "what are you talking about? What did you do?"

Bill tilted his head back to look up at the canopy of the pines while his mouth desperately tried to work the words out. Then he looked down at his neighbor's face, and the kindness he remembered from childhood released the years of stored grief. He stumbled down the slope a few feet before falling down hard on his rear.

"It was me," he suddenly sobbed, making no attempt to get up. "I killed my brother."

Ernie let go a deep breath as though he had just been slugged in the stomach. He bent over slightly, resting his hands on his thighs.

"Bill," Ernie tried to say evenly, "that's impossible. Jimmy's been dead for fourteen, almost fifteen years. You were only nine years old. You didn't kill him. He died in Vietnam, remember?"

"No," Bill cried, gulping in between breaths, "I saw him. I didn't mean . . . to shoot him. I thought it . . . was the dog. I was mad 'cause he wouldn't . . . c-c-come to me." Bill hiccuped. "Then I saw James. And he ran away from me. I kept yelling at him . . . to wait . . . but he kept runnin'. I d-d-didn't mean to shoot him. I tripped . . . and dropped the gun . . . and it went off. He was burnin' . . . and runnin' . . . and then he fell. I looked all over . . . the field . . . for him. I've been waitin' . . . and waitin' . . . for him. I was happy," Bill sobbed, "to see him. If I'd a known . . . it was him . . . I wouldn'a fired at him. I tried to find him. I c-c-couldn't find him . . . anywhere. He ran away from me . . . and I shot him."

Then Bill raised his knees up and rested his forehead against his kneecaps. Ernie stared at the sobbing young man. His hands trembled, and sweat trickled down his wrists to wet his palms. *Is killing a man like killing a deer?*

✖✖✦✦✦✦✦✖✖

He'd never forget that day. Never forget the smooth handle of the spade in his hand. The dog's howl. The sight of Jimmy standing in the middle of his field. The pain so severe in his head and chest that Ernie thought he'd die there, kneeling in the snow.

How after that it insidiously began to invade him. That creeping of muck that covered his senses and that he couldn't put a name to for fifteen years, that gradually robbed him of the simplest joys, the simplest details. The drift of clouds over a full moon, the click of the dog's nails on the floor, the graying of his wife's hair, and the growing loneliness reflected in her eyes. Just when he thought he had no other option but to end the pain by swinging from his own barn rafters, Ernie trudged down the stairs one night in July and walked toward his wife sitting in the living room, his mouth open, the words of 1968 finally reaching the air. He would never forget her outstretched arms, ready to catch him as he lurched toward her. And catch him she did. In the past five months, she didn't let him go back down, pulling him to the surface again and again, holding him when he cried. He never once saw doubt in her face over his story or a furtive glance that might have indicated that she thought he was crazy. Ernie begged her not to say a word about what he'd seen, and Rosemary did as he asked her, folding the story into herself. But he hadn't counted on Bill.

Ernie cautiously began trudging up the slope toward Bill. When he got to within three feet, Ernie dropped to his hands and knees and crawled up next to him. He lifted and pulled Bill toward him until the young man's head was cradled in the crook of Ernie's left arm and his body lay across Ernie's lap. He pulled out the gun rag from the pocket of his hunting jacket and wiped Bill's nose, wiping again when he saw he'd left a smear of gun oil on Bill's cheek.

"Billy," Ernie said quietly as the young man slumped against him, "Jimmy's been dead a long time."

"Not to me," Bill cried, shaking hard in Ernie's arms.

"No," Ernie said, gently rocking Bill back and forth. "I know he's not dead to you. He's probably been with you," Ernie said, looking down the slope at his rifle lying in the snow, "all this time. Here," he added, sweeping his free arm at the surrounding pines, "all this time." Then he quit talking and listened to Bill's deep sobbing punctuate the silence of the woods.

Ernie raised his head and stared at the November sky. This was the year he had begun to love autumn again. He liked the canning of fruits and vegetables and the last-minute winterizing of the house and barn. He liked the dark furrows of dirt after he plowed the fields to ready their absorption of melting snow in the spring. He loved the smell of woodsmoke from his fireplace, an ancient smell that clung to his skin and made him grateful for a warm house. He loved the stark and skeletal outline of the hardwood trees against the mottled gray skies and the intense yellowing of the tamarack needles in the swamp. He loved the increasing silence and the space it encompassed above his head, space often filled with the passing flocks of migratory birds whose voices it seemed had been with him even before he was born. He strongly believed that it was the season in which life did not die but transformed itself, flew to another part of the world, went underground, went to sleep, and in some cases throve. It was the season of the spirits and the spiritual, the season most embedded with tradition and ritual for him, the season of his father. At the age of fifty-eight, Ernie still missed both his parents, but especially his father.

Feeling Bill's head slip from the crook of his arm, Ernie hoisted him up so the nape of Bill's neck was resting against Ernie's chest. He brushed the wet hair from Bill's forehead and gazed at the small blue veins in his eyelids. The color of his skin was startling. Ernie lightly pinched Bill's cheek. It did not redden but stayed a waxy, nearly albino white. Ernie realized with horror that he could lift the skin from Bill's cheekbones. He had lost so much weight that the skin on his face folded in places, giving the twenty-three-year-old man the appearance of being decades older. With one hand, he methodically rubbed Bill's cheeks to warm them. Bill was fair-skinned and did not have his brother's olive brown complexion. Ernie remembered teasing Jimmy when he started shaving, tapping him lightly on one cheek when he noticed a nick on the boy's face. Rubbing Bill's cheek harder, Ernie tried to remember at what age Jimmy had first made himself known to the Morriseaus. Was it five?

✕◆◆◆◆◆◆◆✕

He had sought them out. Ernie and Rosemary did not question his wandering over to see them until the visits became frequent. They surmised from rumor and observation that all was not well at the Lucas home. Jimmy ate fried egg sandwiches with Rosemary in the mornings and tried to help Ernie in the barn in the afternoons. By then Rosemary was calling Claire to ask if Jimmy could stay to supper. Soon it was little Bill, tagging after his brother on their neighborly visits. Ernie remained slightly gruff with them, wanting to maintain a distance from the boys, while Rosemary lavished maternal care on them. They were not his sons, and he was acutely aware that their father did not like him. Ernie in turn did not like John Lucas.

Even with the boys over at their place so much, it still came as a surprise when Claire Lucas unexpectedly phoned Ernie one August day. "Jimmy wants to hunt, and I'm exhausted from saying no.

I don't want my husband to teach him how to hunt. He doesn't have the time," she breathlessly added. "Would you be willing to teach him how?"

He heard her nervousness, the way her voice dwindled down after speaking from one intake of air. It had taken all of Claire Lucas's strength to ask him. "Claire," he mouthed silently to Rosemary, who was kneading bread dough. Her eyebrows shot up in surprise. It was as though a ghost had called them, so rarely did they see Claire Lucas. He hesitated before answering, wondering if John Lucas knew of his wife's request.

"Does he have his own gun?"

When she paused long enough for it to be an answer, he interrupted. "Don't worry. I have a safe gun he can use and some hunting clothes."

He lied. He did not have a gun he would trust with a twelve-year-old, and they certainly did not have hunting clothes that would fit Jimmy.

"I don't know about this," he commented, shaking his head after he hung up the phone. "I don't want that drunk bastard on my doorstep yelling at me. He should be doing this. It's his son. What if something happens? Then we're liable."

Rosemary stopped kneading the dough, straightening up from the table to brush a stray hair away from one eye with the back of her hand. It left a floury sash above her eye.

"Honey, you can be so dense sometimes. Why do you think the boys are over here so much? Do you really think that John Lucas cares? And for Claire to ask you . . . well, that speaks for itself. She is the other parent there," Rosemary reminded him, "and she has asked you."

She dropped the mound of dough into the buttered bowl and covered it with a flour sackcloth.

"We can afford to buy another gun and some hunting clothes," she said calmly, scraping the dried dough off her palms with a thumbnail. "This will be good," she added with a smile, "for you too."

Whatever hesitation Ernie had felt disappeared with his wife's response. He rose to the challenge, fueled by memories of his own father and by the sobering fact that he had no children to pass on what his father had taught to him.

The distance between them dissolved on hunting trips. They suffered through cold, rainy weather, hunkered down in a duck blind, drinking coffee, eating brownies, and laughing while waiting for rafts of mallards, wood ducks, teals, and bluebills to drop out of the sky and land on an oxbow of the Chippewa River. They hiked through stands of poplar and aspen, their faces scratched by the slap of branches and their pants covered with burrs, trying to keep up with Butter, the yellow Labrador that Ernie had then. He was an old dog but full of mischief. They never knew when that sudden explosion of feathers that was a flushed ruffed grouse would occur because Butter was a dog bent on his own wishes.

Once, when Jimmy was fourteen, the dog enraged a sow bear, having tampered with one of her cubs by chasing it. Ernie and Jimmy scrambled for the nearest big trees. Ernie instinctively put himself between Jimmy and the black bear, raising his shotgun and aiming while Jimmy climbed to safety first. They stayed up in the branches of their trees until the bear had sufficiently rebuffed the dog and retrieved her cub before running off. The dog sat under Ernie's tree, his mouth dripping foamy saliva in what appeared to be a fool's grin as he peered up into the branches at Ernie.

Ernie took Jimmy fishing too. They fished the Namekagon, the Brule, the Flambeau Flowage, and even Lake Superior for whitefish and steelhead. Wherever they went, people mistakenly took them for father and son. Except that Jimmy was much taller than Ernie's five feet, nine inches. Other hunters and fishermen slapped Ernie on the back kiddingly about his height compared with his "son." Ernie corrected them while Jimmy smiled and said nothing.

By the time he became seventeen, Jimmy had grown into a more skilled and sensitive hunter than many men three times his age. Ernie was a good teacher, and Jimmy was a good student. That, as Ernie saw it now, was his biggest mistake. Jimmy became too good with a gun, too confident that he could protect himself.

Bombs. That was one of the many obvious differences between hunting and war. There wasn't a bullet made that could disarm a technological rock of hell. Or something so lethal that it could be tossed at you as easily as a baseball. Jimmy fought in a different war. While the bombs and artillery had gotten sleeker, and the grenades more effective in their timing, it was the reason for Jimmy's war that was never clear to Ernie.

SOME OF THE BEST MEN I'd ever known were in the Marines with me. Even some of the officers. But the grunts like me were automatically considered stupid if we didn't have a college education. Some of the guys in Fifth Division didn't even have their high school diplomas. But that didn't mean they were *stupid*. They were poor. They came from poor families. More poor than I thought was possible. The Corps seemed like an island with pineapples and coconuts to those guys. Some like Cracker Jack had been facing jail time. He told me that he'd had his nickname since childhood because he craved boxes of Cracker Jacks and the small prizes that were in them. When he didn't have the money to buy them, he began stealing them from the store, and as he got older, he stole bigger things. When he got caught stealing a car, he was given a choice: prison or the military. He said he picked the Marines to get his ass kicked and his head screwed on right.

I did have my high school diploma. My mother also drilled it into my head by dragging me to the bookmobile that reading was as necessary as breathing. She was right. I had no idea what kind of country Vietnam was. I was terrified, and the only way I knew how to get rid of some of my fear was to figure out just where I was going and who lived there. I always was a history buff. So I read everything I could about Vietnam in what little free time I had during basic. I spent one night screwing a prostitute and getting a case of clap that everybody laughed about. But the rest of the time I read. It helped in some ways. Made it worse in others.

Dienbienphu kept surfacing in the talk among the officers at

Khe Sanh. I knew exactly what they were talking about although I never let on. It was like saying the Battle of Little Bighorn except it happened in Vietnam. Led by Giap, the Vietnamese slaughtered the French in 1954. I could read my CO's thoughts. The French were nothing in comparison to what Giap wanted to do now. If Giap could mastermind that one, he could do it to us, and what a notch in his belt that would be. Slaughtering soldiers from the most powerful country in the world. The Khe Sanh base was just one big corral, and we were a lot of pigs. That's what we were looking at: being gutted.

I learned a lot of good and bad things in the Corps. Those bad things contradicted nearly everything I had been taught that was any good before I joined up. One good thing stood out above the rest: *Don't take what doesn't belong to you.*

✗◆◆◆◆◆◆◆◆✗

It was close to Christmas when one night Marv asked me, "Do you know why we are here?"

It wasn't a dumb question. He would never have asked such a question before we left the States. But once we landed in Nam and realized the big shittin' lie we had been dropped in, it had to be asked. You had nothing to lose by asking. Especially if you were stuck at Khe Sanh.

"To fight Communism," I said, giving the standard answer. I was reading *Huckleberry Finn* for the umpteenth time and drinking a beer we had pinched from a supply we had found in another bunker. I had my copy of *The Man Who Killed the Deer* with me too. Ernie had given me those books as well as many others. I had left the rest of them at home. My .45 was napping on my belly. I kept it available when I was relaxing because of rats. The biggest rats I'd ever seen, and they carried anything and everything you didn't want to get, rabies and fleas that carried diseases like typhoid. Being bitten by a rat was a war wound just like getting shot or bombed. They lived and squealed in the sandbags, and some nights they even fell on us while we were sleeping. That was as bad as being shot in my book. What hell it was at night sometimes. I'd feel a thump and then that wild scratching on my face and chest as they scampered to get off. That squealing. I woke up like a three-alarm fire, hollering like hell. I swear the fuckin' Viet Cong trained those rats. God, I hated 'em. I shot every fuckin' rat I saw.

Marv persisted. "Yeah, I know that. *But they want it.* At least the Vietnamese do. I'm not sure about the Yards. I don't know what the hell Communism really is," he said again. "So, really, why are we here?"

Marv had been in college for one year when he got drafted. He was smart. He was just shell-shocked and not thinking. Ignorance *was* bliss in some situations and probably necessary. I had *Huck Finn* on the brain at that moment, so I broke it down into terms that I thought would get a laugh out of Marv.

"Beeecuz," I wisecracked in a southern drawl, "a bunch of ol' men have der hands in dis cookie ja. And we aw heah to make sho each one of dem gets a cookie."

"What do we get?"

"Medals."

"I'm suppose to get bombed for a medal?"

" 'Fraid so," I said.

When he didn't answer, I looked at him. His mustache was ragged-looking, and it appeared as though the razor had skipped over his face rather than made a smooth run. Despite his beard growth, he looked as young as my brother. And as sad. It's funny how you can love someone so much in such a short period of time. When you know you shouldn't because he could die at any time. And that's what we were there for. To kill and be killed. At least Marv didn't have a choice. But I did it to myself. Like signing a contract with the devil. Rick had enlisted too. I was the stupid fucker that let the devil get him.

"Listen," I said, shutting my book and holding it out to him, "read *Huck Finn*. It will take your mind off of things. Reading is good for you."

"But will it save my life?" Marv asked sarcastically.

"Well," I answered somewhat seriously, "yes and no. Yes and no."

✕✕✕✕ A MONTH AFTER ERNIE HAD accompanied the Navy chaplain and the other officer to the Lucas farm, he told another lie. He told his wife that he was making a day trip to Madison to get some parts for their Farmall tractor that he couldn't get anywhere else. To make sure that the trip would not be in vain, he called the reserve office and made an appointment with the officer who had not gotten out of the car to say good-bye.

✕✕✕✕✕✕✕✕✕

"I can't tell you without the family's permission."

"I'm not going to tell anyone," Ernie replied.

He leaned forward and put his elbows on Hildebrandt's desk. "His father never gave a shit about him. I know you didn't tell his mother everything. I'm not leaving until you tell me."

"It's not that easy—"

"I fought in the Philippines."

Ernie stood up, unbuttoned his shirt, and peeled it off. He turned around so the officer could see his back.

"I was not in the Marines. I was in the Army. I won't talk to any jarheads if that's what you're worried about. Does that help?"

Ernie put his shirt back on and turned around. He managed a small smile. "I assume that the Marines and the Army still don't get along real well."

Hildebrandt opened the file in front of him and unfolded a map. "These are just some notes from basic training and from the field. Private Lucas belonged to the Fifth Marine Division and was a member of India Company, Third Battalion, Twenty-sixth Marines."

He pointed to a section. Quang Tri.

"He was at the Khe Sanh Combat Base. On January twentieth," Hildebrandt said, moving his finger slightly, "the Fifth Division, Bravo Company, temporarily lost hold of Hill Eight-eighty-one North, and the Fifth Division, India Company, moved from Hill Eight-eighty-one South to Eight-eighty-one North to help gain Hill Eight-eighty-one North back. Private Lucas was apparently right behind Lieutenant Miller as they stormed up the western side of the hill. The report says it was foggy that day, and in the early afternoon the fog lifted. That's when they discovered they were surrounded by the North Vietnamese Army. Lieutenant Miller was shot and killed. Private Marvin Martinson reported seeing Private Lucas running after Miller and then ahead of him. That's when Martinson lost sight of him. An F-four dropped napalm, and it was so close that it singed Private Martinson's mustache. Martinson said he heard an explosion too."

Ernie stared down at the desk. "What else does it say?"

"His record states that Private Lucas excelled in basic training and was one of the best marksmen to pass through Camp Pendleton. A Captain Kendall noted that Private Lucas would have done well at Annapolis and that he was surprised that Private Lucas was not college-educated. He was a sniper in Vietnam. It appears he was extraordinarily good at it. He was very well liked."

There was a long pause. Ernie could hear movement out in the hallway.

"Listen, I have to be straight with you. I think Private Lucas is dead," Hildebrandt added, his voice wavering. "I think he took a direct hit of napalm. I pray to God that he was shot first."

Bile crept up the back of Ernie's throat, and he coughed to clear it. "Were you in Vietnam?"

"Yes. Ironically, I was at the Khe Sanh Combat Base in '65 and '66. The base sits on a plateau. But around the plateau are the highlands. If you didn't know what was hidden in all that beauty, you would think that you landed in paradise. Since I left," he said, "they've been fortifying the base camp with more and more Marines. Have you seen the papers?"

Ernie shook his head.

"Khe Sanh was only a preliminary target. The NVA was massing up toward Hue. All hell is breaking loose right now."

Ernie stood up. "I appreciate your honesty. I'm sure you were very helpful to the men in your unit."

Hildebrandt stood up as well. "I don't know about that. I am a priest, and I was a makeshift medic. I was not supposed to engage in combat or carry a weapon. But I did carry a forty-five."

Hildebrandt ran a hand over his bristly crew cut. "I thought being in Vietnam was bad. But these visits I have to make . . ."

"You must be close to being discharged. Can't you find a parish somewhere?"

"Actually I could have been discharged a few months back. So it's voluntary at this point. And I'll be volunteering to get out very soon."

Hildebrandt walked around the desk so that he could usher Ernie out.

"You cared a great deal about James Lucas."

"I did."

Ernie stopped just outside the chaplain's office door. He turned and looked at the chaplain. "I'm the one who taught him how to shoot so well."

✕✕✕✕✕✕✕✕✕✕

He watched Ernie Morriseau walk down the narrow hallway until he turned the corner and was gone.

In a week he would inform the bishop of his archdiocese and then file his discharge papers from the Navy Chaplain Corps. He didn't know what he'd do after that. It was as though the visit to the Lucas home had opened a hole in his brain and Marcus had crawled through it. He was on Hildebrandt's mind every day, and he felt the weight of Marcus as surely as if he were carrying the man on his back. He heard the words of St. James: *"and the prayer of faith shall save the sick man, and the Lord shall raise him up; and if he be in sins they shall be forgiven him."*

He shut his office door and sat back down at his desk. Stared out the window. He remembered being given Marcus's dog tags so that he could wash them before they were placed back with the body and zipped into a body bag. The chain necklace draped over his hand and fingers in a familiar pattern, and he stared at it as the water washed the blood and little bits of tissue away. He stared at the rectangular metal plate with Marcus's ID number. The tag that represented Marcus. A man's life on a metal tag.

The bizarreness of it. He had dog tags too. He was a priest and a soldier. Why hadn't he seen it before? Thought about it before. The military unwittingly issued necklaces with tags that represented only five of the fifteen Mysteries. Not the five Joyous or the five Glorious. But the five Sorrowful, punched into the metal by a machine and given to each man. Or, in Marcus's case, to each boy.

Just yesterday he was on the University of Wisconsin, Madison campus and had to dodge demonstrators. The protests were growing daily. There was one sign held up not by a young student but by a middle-aged woman. He assumed, even before reading the sign, that the official military picture pasted on the tag board was her son. The sign said:

DEAR PRESIDENT JOHNSON,
MY SON DIED FOR YOUR SINS.

That sound of humming in his ears. Hildebrandt listened as though Private Marcus were right next to him, buzzing that familiar tune in his ears. A nursery rhyme. "Down will come baby, cradle and all."

✕◆◆◆◆◆◆◆✕

Ernie left Madison, knowing what he already had known but having it more or less officially confirmed. Jimmy had died a horrible death, burning until he was nothing but ash scattered across that hill. He thought nothing could hurt him as much as what he'd seen in World War II. The friends like Frank LaRue who died there. But the knowledge that it had happened to Jimmy stabbed him with a pain like no other. He drove home, hunched over the steering wheel of his truck, trying hard to breathe evenly against the information he had been told that afternoon.

✕◆◆◆◆◆◆◆✕

"Ernie," Rosemary had repeated to him last week, "listen to me again. At that age children think they are immortal. They do the exact opposite of what you want them to do. My mother said I was unnatural and selfish. My father said he never thought he'd see a daughter of his go to war. Your parents were very unhappy when you enlisted. And so happy when you came home alive."

He knew Rosemary was right. There was nothing he could have done or said that would have changed Jimmy's mind. The simple fact that Ernie and Rosemary had survived the war was encouragement enough for Jimmy to think he could do the same.

"Bill," she reminded him, "is still alive. We could try to see him."

✕◆◆◆◆◆◆◆✕

Looking down at Bill, Ernie knew they had almost waited too long.

He heard Bill moan and saw more tears trail down his face. Bill looked like his father, but Ernie would not believe, could not believe that he had his father's traits. Not the small boy he remembered. That wooden sword. The huge turtle shell encapsulating his left arm so that it looked as though he had no arm at all. The shy Oliver Twist smile of yearning and the small face pressed into the screen of their porch door at lunchtime.

He stroked Bill's forehead and remembered something else. He used to be able to locate Bill anywhere on his place just by listening. The aria of a child's voice in song, fading in and out.

Ernie rocked him for the next three hours until his crying died down to an occasional whimper. When Bill fell completely asleep, Ernie moved from beneath him. He gently pushed Bill off his chest onto the ground. Ernie stood up and stretched the cramped muscles in his arms and legs. He looked down the slope and saw his rifle on the ground and the old Remington leaning against the tree. He'd have to leave the rifle and the shotgun and come back for them. Squatting down, Ernie hefted Bill into his arms, amazed by the initial lightness of his tall but impoverished frame, and began the long walk home.

✗✗✗✗ THE DAY STARTED OUT SUNNY and then went gray at noon. At 4:00 P.M. the light began to fade as it does in November. I was dull and slow from lack of sleep. I was staring out the window, remembering Ernie's hands on my breasts, when I pared the skin off my left thumb while peeling potatoes. I dropped the peeler and shook my hand like a child trying to throw the stinging pain away. While I was holding my thumb under cold water from the faucet, I heard the dog whining and scratching at the back door.

Angel had been gone all night. It was a good thing he came home when he did. The minute I opened the door the wind slapped me, and I slammed the door shut after the dog was inside. The temperature was dropping. I didn't notice the blood until the dog walked across the kitchen floor to his watering dish. He left a trail of red beads on the linoleum. I bent down and examined him while he noisily lapped up water. He shifted his weight slightly when I touched his right side. He had been peppered with birdshot, the little BBs wedged into his skin. I watched in astonishment as our dog finished drinking and then, circling nose to tail three times, dropped into a relaxed heap on his blanket. I was shocked. Someone had shot our dog.

My nursing bag was in the truck. I knew I'd have to wait until Ernie was home, to hold the dog down while I squeezed the BBs out with my smallest forceps, but I pulled my barn jacket on anyway and went outside.

The first flakes of what turned out to be a snowstorm hit me in the face, and I turned sideways to avoid the needle-pricking feel of them. It was then that I saw the remote but recognizable figure of Ernie at the far end of our field. I remember smiling, thinking that Ernie must have had a successful day because of the way he was walking. So slow. I reached into the truck and grabbed my nursing bag and started back to the house. Something made me look again. I realized there was something odd about the way Ernie was walking. His pace was so labored. I stood and waited. He was carrying something large, and I thought that was too strange to ignore. He usually came home first and got the truck to haul his tagged deer home from the edge of the field. I wondered what possessed him to carry his deer. How could he do it? Two hundred pounds of deer?

I waited. My vision became clearer as Ernie made progress across the field. That was when I cried out. I clutched the nursing bag to my chest and began to run. I had on only my household slippers. When I reached the barn, I simultaneously heard Ernie shout and fell down. My nursing bag dropped into the muddy snow, and my arms flailed like the wings of a wounded duck before I hit the ground. I pushed myself up and heard Ernie shout again.

"Go back!" he yelled. "Get ready to open the door!'

I slipped and slid my way back to the porch, shaking my slippers free of snow when I reached the steps. My feet burned. I trotted in place to keep them from going numb while I waited. Ernie stopped every so often to shift the weight of the man in his arms. The wind picked up speed, and the snow began to fall more heavily, coming down in white sheets. I could barely see Ernie even though he had reached the barn.

Just in time, I thought.

✕✕✕✕✕ THAT NIGHT AND THE WEEKS that followed gave rise to our private scars and unspoken grief, some of it floating in the air of the house, some visible enough like braille on our faces and bodies so that it could be read with fingertips. Some of it spoken aloud.

✕✕✕✕✕✕✕✕✕

I shall always remember the way Ernie had to swing sideways because Bill was so tall and how even then one of Bill's boots caught on the tension spring of the screen door and stretched it as if it were a rubber band. I squeezed between the two men and the screen door and, with a clenched fist, hit the heel of the boot, popping the foot loose above the spring.

Ernie placed Bill on the same twin bed he had slept in when he was a child and was permitted to spend a few rare nights sleeping over. Then Ernie slumped into the yellow chintz–covered rocking chair in the corner. His arms were so sore, he said, that he wasn't sure if he'd ever be able to lift them above his shoulders again. I had to hold my breath as I pulled off Bill's rank outer clothes, then his boots, socks, pants, and shirt. I fingered each piece of clothing before dropping them to the floor and then looked at Bill's nearly naked body. No blood anywhere.

"He's not shot."

"I never said he was. I found him on the ridge," Ernie said, and sighed. "Or I should say he found me. He's dead drunk."

I considered Bill as being closer to dead. The pelvic bones jutting up like river bluffs. The lower abdomen so sunken that it could have held water and a few minnows. There was little fat on him. Even his butt cheeks were as flat and as thin as Swedish pancakes. His underwear would have slipped down his legs effortlessly if I had stood him up. I looked at his face. The cracked and chapped lips and hair as dry as ripe corn tassels. The white spittle gathered in the corners of his mouth. The swollen eyelids red-rimmed and crusted with eye sand. His was not the body of a happy drunk, a drunk of evenings and parties. He did not even have the body of a middle-aged drunk. Bill reminded me of those men I saw as a child. Impoverished and despairing men of the Depression, homeless and starving slowly because they had no will to live and no appetite for food. Whatever money they acquired all went for beer, wine, whiskey, and toward the end raw alcohol, which often killed them. They were found dead on the outskirts of Cedar Bend, sometimes in the alley behind the old hotel, and once a group of them were found frozen to death in Washaleski's barn. They all had that pickled-in-formaldehyde look, green-tinged white skin from their self-inflicted drowning. I ran the years in my head. Bill was twenty-three years old.

I drew a hot bath for Ernie while he set up an electric heater on one of the bedside tables. Before I shut off the faucets, I filled a large bowl with sudsy water and carried it into the bedroom. Ernie had brought up a chair from the kitchen for me to sit on, and I took out a washcloth and bath towel from the linen closet. As my hand pressed the green washcloth below the surface of the warm water, I could hear Ernie groan as he lowered himself into the tub and then whistle as his cold limbs hit the steaming water.

I began washing Bill's head, tilting it from side to side, stopping to place two fingers on one of the arteries of his neck. His pulse was weak but not as bad as I thought it would be. Bill's eyes rolled underneath his eyelids, but they did not open.

There are the normal ABCs of the human body. What should be there from birth and then a record of normal life experiences as they impact the body. A scraped knee scar from climbing a tree, the fleshy bumps left from chicken pox pustules that were scratched repeatedly, and the pincushion of a vaccination shot on the upper arm. The last time I'd seen Bill naked was when he was six years old. He sheepishly allowed me to undress him and give him a bath after a day of play spent in our muddy farmyard. The shivering thighs and the small bud of a penis contracting so that it was almost hidden between his legs. The sweet timidity of a little boy.

I didn't bother to pull Bill's underwear off. His briefs were so grimy that I took the scissors from the bedside drawer and cut them free. I tilted the shade on the bedside lamp so that I could see Bill better. I bent down and wet the washcloth again and then stood up. It was only when I heard Ernie washing himself, the splash of water as he soaped up his own washcloth and rubbed it vigorously over himself, that I realized that I hadn't made contact with Bill's skin. That the washcloth in my hand was dripping soapy water onto his genitals. I stared as the water trickled over the skin and disappeared between his thighs.

A naked body can also tell stories to the practiced eye. After what we'd been through the previous summer, I wanted to be free from the weight of secrets and bad dreams. I wanted Ernie to be well, and I wanted peace. And here was yet another secret. One that burned my eyes and hurt so bad that I couldn't detach from it. I didn't know what to do. *I didn't know what to do.*

I heard more splashing from the bathroom. I wasn't sure how long Ernie would stay in the tub. I quickly finished washing Bill. I remember how the heat came out in waves from the red coils of the old heater. How it emitted a sound that was like a baby's rattle. I had to take my red cardigan off because the sweat was pouring down my face and stinging my eyes. I ducked into our bedroom and grabbed a pair of Ernie's pajama bottoms from a dresser drawer. I swabbed Bill down with the towel, slid the pajama bottoms over his feet and up his legs. His legs were so long that the pajama bottoms ended just

below his knees. I brought the cotton blankets up from the foot of
the bed and tucked them under and around his long body until he
was swaddled so tightly that only I would be able to uncover him.

I remember walking down the stairs to the kitchen to get two
cups of coffee. The dog slept as though the birdshot sprinkled on
his sides were a forgotten irritation. I wrote a note to myself and
taped it to the refrigerator door: "Angel—shot of penicillin tonight.
BBs in A.M."

I walked up the stairs and handed a cup to my husband soaking
in the tub before I sat on the toilet cover and watched him. His
chest glistened with water and did not reveal his fifty-eight years as
it did on some men. His pectoral muscles were taut from hard work,
his shoulders and arms contoured and firm. If our night had been
different, I would have stripped and stepped into our large antique
tub, and eased myself down until my back was against his chest. As I
had done in the old days after making love. I mindlessly lifted the
cup to my lips. The first sip burned the roof of my mouth.

Ernie took a drink of his coffee before resting the cup on the
edge of the tub. Leaned his head back and gazed at me.

"Now we know what he was doing out there all this time."

I thought of what I'd just seen and could not fully take in or
even speak of.

"Well," I murmured, "we know some of it. We may never
know all of it."

Ernie took another sip of coffee before placing the cup down
on the tile floor. I stared at the familiar keloid scars on his brown
skin from shrapnel wounds. I could see two gray bumps on his right
shoulder, the skin stretched thin as though they were erupting pim-
ples. After taking care of the dog in the morning, I would then go
to work on Ernie. I always lanced the bumps with a razor blade and
squeezed out the nugget of metal. I was the archaeologist of my
husband's body, extracting history from thirty-nine years ago. It
seems perverse, but I save those nuggets, putting them in a jelly jar
and keeping the jar on the shelf with my other preserves.

I turned and stared out the bathroom window. The snow was coming down faster, so white that I wouldn't have known it was nighttime. It was a November storm that would cover everything, all the gut piles left in the woods from the first day of hunting. It would have covered Bill if Ernie had not found him. Or if he had not found Ernie.

I had the equipment and the saline bags to start an IV in Bill. When he could eat without throwing up, I'd have to start him on something mild for his stomach. Cream of rice or cream of wheat. We would have to take turns sitting with him. The delirium tremors would start in a day or maybe sooner. If we were lucky, he'd have only mild ones, given that he was so young and not a career alcoholic yet. Until I could figure out what to do or what to say, I would be the only one to wash and dress Bill. I was thinking of asking Ernie if we should take Bill to the detox center in Cedar Bend in the morning when he spoke.

"Have you called Claire?"

I shall never forget how at that moment, as though Ernie's voice had summoned her, Claire banged on our back door.

How she walked inside the kitchen almost unrecognizable, dressed in her late husband's outdoor clothes. Huge Sorel boots on her feet, men's red-and-black-checked wool pants with suspenders, and an oversize parka covered with snow. I reached forward and pulled back the hood.

"I need help. I can't find Bill."

That breaking of fine china voice. A mother's voice near the point of hysteria.

"We have him. Ernie found him."

Claire remained motionless and stared at me. I repeated it a little louder as though she were deaf.

"We have him. Ernie found him."

I cautiously reached forward and grasped the zipper of the parka. When Claire showed no resistance, I unzipped the parka, took it off, and threw it across the kitchen table. I unbuckled the suspenders on Claire's wool pants and removed the thick leather mittens and their woolen liners from her hands. Claire lowered herself into one of the chairs so I could pull off the oversize boots.

"Lift up."

She obediently braced her hands against the sides of the chair and lifted her rear. I rolled the pants down from the waistband. Then I grabbed one of Claire's hands, felt how cold they were.

"How did you get here?"

"My car got stuck at the farm. I walked across the fields."

I got up and poured another cup of coffee.

"I want you to drink this," I said, putting the cup in Claire's hands, "and then I'll take you upstairs to see Bill."

✕✕✕✕ CLAIRE AND I DRANK THREE pots of coffee that night and didn't sleep at all. She sat in the chintz-covered rocker on the right side of the bed. Ernie sat in another rocking chair at the foot of the bed, and I sat on the left side, on the kitchen chair.

Ernie replied to Claire's questions with as little detail as possible but enough to soothe her. That he had found Bill on the ridge while he was hunting. That Bill was drunk and crying, and that when he calmed down and fell asleep, Ernie was able to carry him to our place. Just as the snowstorm was beginning to hit.

"Bill was out there by himself?" she asked.

Ernie sat up, smacked out of his exhaustion for a moment. I didn't dare look at him.

"Yes, he was. Was Bill hunting with someone else?"

"Oh, no," she said quickly. "He didn't hunt. He just liked being in the woods. I was just worried because this is hunting season and people do trespass on our land."

We let it drop at that. I could tell Ernie was bothered by Claire's question, but he was exhausted and struggling to stay awake. The warmth of the bath, the rhythmic rattling of the electric heater had put him in a hypnotic state. Finally I watched as his eyelids dropped and then shut. He slumped, his head falling to one shoulder, and was out.

We sipped our coffee in silence at first. Claire occasionally reached out to caress Bill's cheek. I had brought my knitting up from the wicker basket in the living room and pretended to concentrate on adding rows to the sweater I was making.

How strange it was. In all the years that we lived less than a mile apart, this was the longest time I had ever spent with Claire. The first time I'd ever been that physically close to her. She always declined my invitations to come over for dinner, my offers to help, and she never returned my waves when I saw her in town. Even so, I knew we were alike in some ways. We were not the barrel-shaped, knee-slapping women sitting at Clemson's Bar and Bowling Alley, having one too many beers and laughing in rough, smoky voices, waiting for their league's turn to bowl. Nor were we women who participated in 4-H or the PTA. We didn't wear our hair in towers of shellacked meringue that got washed and styled only once a week. Beehive hairdos that had gone out of style years ago except in Olina. Some of those women stretched their styling and washing to once every two weeks, and it would not have surprised me if bugs were hidden in the honeycombs of those columns. Claire used to have black hair like me. But it had turned completely white, and she wore it in a short pageboy that was becoming to her. My own hair was a mix of silver and black. I had always kept it long because Ernie liked it that way.

We had the same taste in books. I know because I saw her name on the library cards of the same books that I borrowed from the bookmobile.

There were differences between us, though. I had gone to nursing school, which was an education and a trade in those days. From what little I picked up from the boys when they were young, Claire had gone to a private liberal arts college in Milwaukee. She still went to church on Sundays. Ernie and I hadn't stepped into a church in years. I had, all things considered, a wonderful husband. She had had the husband of a B-rated horror movie.

But Claire had children. I did not.

I watched her out of the corners of my eyes. Watched her sip her coffee.

I had wondered for years what her story was and why we never saw company at their place. Company, as in relatives. You would have thought that some of her family would have visited after Jimmy was declared MIA. Or at John's death. The boys never mentioned grandparents or aunts and uncles. I didn't ask them. They were children, and I didn't want to make them feel uncomfortable.

I had sisters and made yearly trips to visit them in Oregon, or they came to visit us. I wrote to girlfriends from the service, and we often called one another at holidays. But then I thought about my parents. My mother. The brothers that I never saw.

My mother had lived just twenty miles away in Cedar Bend, and I visited her only when I absolutely had to. It was a relief when she died. Her cruelty was in her passive acceptance of wrongs committed against us and in her failure to love her three daughters as she did her sons. She didn't think we were as worthy as our three brothers. Her expectations of us were to stay put, get married, work like beaten horses, have a houseful of kids, and take care of her and Dad in their old age. The farm was never to be ours.

My older sister, Betty, was the first to leave. A week after she graduated from high school in 1935, she got up early one morning and dressed and left a note on the kitchen table. Her note said she'd contact us once she got settled wherever it was she was going, and she signed it "Betty." That note was a code to Jeannie and me. Like a honky-tonk song, Betty was really saying, "I'm looking for love and someone who'll want me." But she did love her sisters. When we woke up that day, we saw two chocolate bars propped up against the mirror on the dresser. We cried and then ran out to the hayloft to eat our precious chocolate. I learned then that sometimes leaving is sweet.

A few years later Jeannie and I did the same thing. Left early one morning and didn't look back.

That's why I understood Jimmy's decision even though it gave me grief.

I was as hell-bent to get out of Cedar Bend as he was to get out of Olina. I worked my way through nursing school and then did the unexpected. I joined the Army in '43. I wanted to travel,

and it made me feel proud to serve my country. I was going to show
my mother and father that I was smarter and braver than my spoiled-
rotten brothers, all of whom found a way to dodge joining up. I was
initially trained for nursing in North Africa. But in the eleventh
hour they sent us to the South Pacific. I worked from Guam to the
Admiralty Islands and then to Leyte, becoming part of the Fifty-
eighth Evacuation Hospital.

I hadn't planned on returning to northern Wisconsin. I came
back to Milwaukee, where I had gone to school, to look for a civilian nursing job. I was no longer so proud or so brave. I felt sad
and hollowed out. I thought I had fallen in love with a doctor. But
after the war he returned to his wife. The wife I didn't know
about. He had given me a pair of silk stockings as a good-bye gift.
In my grief, I blew some money on a wickedly beautiful dress and
shoes to match in San Diego. When I arrived in Milwaukee, I heard
there was a VFW dance for returning veterans. So I put on my
dress and shoes and went to the dance to sap over my wounds and
memories. I didn't want to meet anyone. I just wanted to get drunk.
In style.

After the doctor I did not believe in fairy-tale love. I thought
love was something that had to get built up over time like a house
that needed constant remodeling. Lust was different. It helped ease
the loneliness at night just like a good bottle of wine. A temporary
bandage on the brain and a lot of fun between the legs. But when I
looked at Ernie and heard his voice, a lot of what I thought I knew
about myself disappeared. I just knew I had met the man I would
marry. If he hadn't asked me, I would have asked him. In those days
they called it fate. Now they call it chemistry or pheromones. We
fizzed and popped at first, but we've never gone flat. Maybe underground but not flat.

Ernie insisted that we stop in Cedar Bend first and see my parents. I didn't want to, but Ernie felt it was only right. I think he
knew what would happen.

"How could you?" my mother growled when we were alone.

I had predicted that she would shit peanuts, but it wasn't over the dress. I had married an *Indian*. Even worse, a *local Indian*. It was bad enough growing up feeling worthless as a girl, but facing that German prejudice and arrogance after all that I'd seen and been through was the last straw. Her words bounced off me because I didn't care what she thought. But it would be over my dead body before I'd let her hurt Ernie.

"Too late now," I smarted off, holding up my left hand. "I thought you *might* be happy for me."

"You girls never did have the sense God gave you!"

I marched through the kitchen to the door. "Don't worry," I said sarcastically, slamming the screen door on the house I'd grown up in and hated, "we won't visit and *embarrass* you. My last name is now Morriseau, not Niedemeyer."

Ernie drove to Olina with one hand on the wheel and the other hand wiping the tears from my face. I was afraid to meet his parents after that. After all, racism goes both ways. I was afraid they would not think me good enough for their son. How wrong I was.

You would have thought I was the one who had brought their son home alive. His mother had a face as round as the moon and copper penny eyes. When she smiled, it radiated through the darkness I felt, and she laughed right away as though Ernie had brought them a huge surprise. I towered over her, but she reached up anyway and hugged me around my waist. His father was more reserved, but when his big hands wrapped around mine, it was with such strength that I didn't think he'd let me go.

The sweetness of having such parents. His mother gave me a lifetime of maternal love in the five years that I knew her. Even while she was dying from congestive heart failure and I was caring for her, she would rub my hands from time to time.

"The babies will come," she whispered. "Maybe a little late like Ernie, but don't worry. They'll come."

I glanced at Claire. I thought about her own mother. Did she talk to her? Did she talk to her sons?

Jimmy had pestered me to tell him stories about the war. Tagged after me with the tenacity of a badger. So I told him the funny stories and not the bad ones, although I did tell him that I'd been sick for a good six weeks when we were on Leyte. I told him how we used our helmets to wash our underwear in, to carry water in, and how the nurses even used their helmets like shovels, digging small tunnels underneath the zigzags of low-grounded barbed wire. How we would wake up with snakes on the dirt floors next to our cots and how I had to kill the first snake with one of my boots so that the other nurses would feel brave enough to do it. How once we ran out of containers to carry our rations of rice and I took off my bra, put my shirt back on, and had them fill the cups of my bra so that I could carry my rice back to the hospital. Jimmy went into giggling fits on our kitchen floor when I told him that. He was fascinated by the fact that I had gone through basic training too and could shoot a carbine rifle. That I outranked Ernie, being a lieutenant while Ernie was a corporal.

And he asked me to tell him the story of how I met Ernie over and over again. He thought it was magic that Ernie and I grew up twenty-five miles from each other, were in the Philippines at the same time, and didn't meet until that dance in Milwaukee. He wanted to know what we wore and what we talked about. I had kept that dress and opened the closet to show him. He called it my movie star dress. When Jimmy was still small, I sometimes caught him looking into our closet and holding the hem of that dress. I even had to tell him the songs we danced to, which of course wasn't easy. I couldn't remember, and I wasn't about to tell him that I'd been really drunk. So I told him some of the songs that everybody danced to then: "Jivin' the Vibes," "This Love of Mine," "Take the A Train," and "It Don't Mean a Thing If It Ain't Got That Swing." I pulled out my albums and played them on the record player. Jimmy loved music.

I wondered why Jimmy craved our stories so much. Didn't Claire tell him stories? Or was her life so painful that she could not repeat it or remember any of the good times? I knew there was a complexity to abusive marriages, that the women in them did not enjoy the suffering. Did not ask for it and often found themselves trapped before they knew it. But I often wondered: Did he ever push her too far? Far enough where Claire picked up a skillet or a hammer and tried to smash his skull in?

I took a sip from my own cup of coffee. We probably would have heard about it if she had. A man of his size would have killed her for making such an attempt. But on the off chance that she had succeeded, Ernie and I would have defended her all the way to the stake if it had come to that. Any belief I had in redemption was killed in the Philippines along with all the men whose heads I cradled as they died and the pain I saw in the people who lived there. All the Filipinos and the Chamorros, caught between two forces they wanted no part of, who came to us looking for food. They were often shot, and their women raped. Occasionally a Filipino or Chamorro woman, made a refugee because her village had been bombed, gave birth in the hospital. The baby was passed from nurse to nurse. We could not believe the smallness of its hands or the kernels of its toes. The beauty of its crying. The wounded men who were conscious called out to see the baby as well. The men stared at the baby's face in disbelief. Birth was not in our line of work, so when it happened, it carried more than a sense of the miraculous. It was an act of opposition to what was going on around us. I'd watch the mother nurse, and it broke me to see that small face blissfully pressed into her breast.

Justice during war takes on a concrete meaning. There are no courts to make fair and judicial decisions, to prosecute the obviously guilty or safeguard the innocent. It is one thing to shoot and kill or be killed in combat. It is entirely something else if you kill and cripple innocent people caught in between. If you torture them, rape them, and keep them prisoner. If you kill children and their mothers. You do that during a time of war, and justice can be immediate. A bullet to the brain is in store for you.

I could never help thinking whenever I was called out with the ambulance during hunting season that it was a pity that John Lucas hadn't been dispatched while hunting. It was too hard to sort out those deaths. They were almost always ruled accidents. I know almost for certain that if Jimmy had come home from Vietnam, that might well have happened.

I put my cup back on the bedside stand. "He's going to have delirium tremors soon, and he may even have seizures," I said. "I think he may need to be in the detox center in Cedar Bend. Do you want us to take him there in the morning?"

She put her own cup next to the heater. "I don't think," she said, caressing his face again, "that Bill has insurance any longer. I think he may have lost his job at the Standard station."

She looked down at her hands, picked at the cuticles of her nails as though *she* had lost her job and were ashamed.

"The county would pay then," I said.

"I'm not sure that would be good for Bill. For other people to know."

I watched her turn slightly in her chair and stare out the bedroom window at the falling snow. The room was so quiet except for Ernie's occasional snore and a moan from Bill. *For other people to know.* Always that fear of other people's knowing her business that had prevented her from asking for help. I suffer from the sin of pride too, but I'd have taken John Lucas down with me in a fight if I'd had to and not given a crap what the community thought.

I could tell by the way she stared out the window, the way her lips pursed together, that she was working up something to say. Then she said it, and it struck me as if she had reached across the bed and slapped me.

"You always had what I wanted. A wonderful husband. A good life."

She turned and gazed at Ernie, who was not looking his best at that moment. A bit of drool dribbled onto his shirt. I was used to other women eyeing my husband and in fleeting moments falling in love with him. Ernie was the kind of man you fell in love with within seconds. After all, I fell in love with him in the course of one night. And *what* a night that had been. He had been gorgeous and even now was still handsome. But more important, he was a good man. He is a good man. Someone who thinks deeply about his actions. At times too deeply. There is no pretense or hostility in his manners. But in being the closest one to him and his wife, I have been hurt by Ernie. Husbands and wives hurt each other in ways that others don't see.

I was sure that Ernie saw as little of Claire as I had. It never occurred to me that Claire would desire my husband. Of course. Why wouldn't she?

I put my hand on my chest and swallowed.

"*Claire.* You *had* children. We *couldn't* have children. Our life has not been golden. I love Ernie," I said, nodding toward my sleeping husband, "but he's not perfect either."

Claire bit down on her lower lip, and I knew that it was a reflex to keep her lip from trembling. "You did have children," she said. "You had my children. My boys loved you."

She was right. But to hear it said stopped me in my tracks. I had never meant to hurt her. I had thought I was helping her, that the boys wandered over to our place because their mother was too busy or too much in pain. But truthfully, I did love her children. More than that, I coveted them.

"And I loved them," I said, finding my voice. "But I was not their mother. Are you saying that I took your children away from you?"

Claire looked at me straight on then. For a few seconds the two of us just stared across the bed at each other. Despite years of abuse, she still appeared delicate and birdlike. With the contrast of her snowy hair, her brown eyes appeared darker than ever. If her hair had been a smoky gray instead of white, she would have resembled a junco.

"I would have said that years ago," she said, trying to stay composed, "but it isn't the truth. You didn't even have to try. My boys wanted to come to you. I can't blame them. I suppose," she added, clasping her hands in her lap, "that you and Ernie think I've been a bad mother all these years. Even now." She tilted her head toward Bill.

I stood up and put my knitting on the chair.

"We have *never* thought that. *Never*. In pain, yes. But bad, no," I answered adamantly. I placed one hand on Bill's forehead, to feel if it was hot. "Bill is going through a troubled time," I said. "But not because of you."

I reached across the bed. "Give me your cup. I'll get us some more coffee."

Claire spoke just as I was taking the cup from her. "I was relieved when he died. I haven't missed him at all. I didn't miss him when he was alive. I often thought . . . but I had children," she said defiantly as though daring me to ask what I had wondered earlier. "I'm sorry about a lot of things, but I'm not sorry about his death."

I had always known it. But it strangely lifted my spirits to hear her say it, to know that there was some part of Claire that her husband could not beat down.

"Nor should you be," I said.

As I walked down the stairs to get more coffee, it occurred to me that we had the easy part. We had the treasured role of an aunt and uncle or grandparents. We did not suffer the boys' tantrums or fights, they did not mouth off to us, we were not responsible for making them do their homework, nor did we have to worry over bad report cards. We did not have the daily discipline of raising a child. We had the gift of their love and their good times. Claire had their love too, but she also had the work and the pain.

Did anyone, I thought as I poured coffee into our cups, *love Claire without asking something from her?*

✕✦✦✦✦✦✦✕

We offered and Claire accepted our care of Bill.

✗✗✗✗ ERNIE WOULD REMEMBER THE DAYS and nights spent sitting by Bill's bed. The muscle spasms that rippled down Bill's belly and legs. The intermittent gagging and crying from withdrawal although it was not nearly as bad as they had anticipated. Ernie's hands shook as he tried to weave a plastic straw through Bill's chapped lips and past his teeth to wet his dry mouth with a little water. When that didn't work because Bill's jaws were so locked together, Ernie used a mouth sponge. He parted Bill's lips with two fingers and pressed the sponge against the clenched teeth so that some of the water trickled into the well of Bill's gums.

Rosemary had inserted an IV line into a vein on Bill's right arm that first night. But Bill ripped it out of his arm repeatedly during his hallucinated thrashings. They finally tied his arms to the bed, and Rosemary reinserted the line, taping it down in several places on his arm.

Ernie had to wait until the next day after the snowstorm passed to go back to the ridge and search for the guns. He had worn snowshoes to give him better traction on the deep snow, but upon reaching the base of the ridge, he realized with horror that he had left a loaded rifle behind, and it was now buried under snow. He found the old Remington still propped against the tree, appearing as though it were a snow-covered stick. The ridge was not only snow-covered but had a glaze of ice covering it. He did not want to step on a loaded rifle. He squinted against the sun, trying to determine just where he might have put the rifle down. Then he noticed a three-foot-wide ribbon of impacted snow and about halfway down a patch that appeared to be thrashed. He walked up the ridge on the right side of the packed snow until he reached the mangled snow. He ran his hands gingerly over the spot, pressing down just enough to feel for steel. He found the butt end of the rifle first and dug around the entire rifle before lifting it up. The safety was frozen into place, and he warmed it with his bare hands until the ice melted. Then he moved the bolt back and unloaded the rifle.

He walked back down the slope with a gun in each hand, but when he reached the bottom, he turned to look back up. There wasn't an animal that made such a distinctive mark, and he had found no footprints. It was exactly how it appeared to be. As though a child had taken out one of those newfangled sleds that looked like a large metal tray but were called saucers and enjoyed a fast and snowy ride down the slope in the night.

✗◆◆◆◆◆◆◆◆✗

Four days after he'd found Bill, Ernie walked upstairs one afternoon to relieve Claire and Rosemary so that they could get a chance to eat and rest. Half an hour later, while he was wiping down Bill's face, he heard a loud wail from outside. He dropped the washcloth and ran to the window. The two women were standing in the middle of Rosemary's vegetable garden in snow up to their knees. His wife had her arms around Claire, holding her up. He stood for a few minutes and listened to the desolate crying. He watched as Claire began to slip, dragging Rosemary with her until both women were kneeling in the snow. He assumed it was delayed grief on Claire's part, that she had just realized how close she had come to losing another son.

Claire saw him standing in the window. Shook her head. She did not want him to come down.

✗◆◆◆◆◆◆◆✗

Bill wasn't silent either. Ernie could not shut out Bill's cries or the effect they had on him. Those memories from the war roiled up.

He thought about all the men he carried on litters to the evacuation hospitals on Leyte. They cried out for their mothers or they cried to God. He remembered how difficult it was to keep the litters steady as they moved down slopes of mud in the rain. Canvas was thrown over the tops of the wounded men to protect them from the rain, but he could still hear them screaming in pain when they were jostled.

He would never forget the British officer. Red-haired and blue-eyed. Freckles the color of iron-stained soil on his face. The remainder of his body was little more than a head and torso, but he was not dead yet, and he was not unconscious.

"Look at me," he commanded. Ernie told his buddy carrying the other end of the litter to stop. He balanced one pole on his knee and lifted back the flap on the canvas.

"Shoot me," the officer said with such calmness. Then he added as though his mother had nudged him, "Please."

✕✦✦✦✦✦✦✦✕

When the tremors ceased, the three of them took turns feeding Bill spoonfuls of cream of rice cereal and Gerber's baby food. Pureed apricots, peas and carrots, tapioca pudding.

Ernie would remember the weeks after Bill was up and moving around and eating solid food. His clothes did not fit him, and not even his jutting hipbones could hold up his jeans. Claire's voice rose above Rosemary's offer to buy him new clothes. It would be a waste, she said, because he would gain the weight back. And where would they find a belt but in a boy's size, and what would they do with such a small belt afterward? So his jeans were held up with a piece of twine woven through the belt loops. Bill helped with small chores on the farm. In the afternoons they drove over to the Lucas place, to work on the chores needed to keep the place up there.

✕✦✦✦✦✦✦✦✕

Nothing worthwhile moved in a straight line. After all, Ernie had crawled out of the muck of himself last summer, but it remained in his head as a small patch of quicksand, always threatening to take him down again. It was true of Bill's recovery too. But that was a misnomer. Bill would never completely recover. He would learn instead to cope.

✕◆◆◆◆◆◆◆◆✕

Early that spring Bill heisted Ernie's truck and drove into town to drink at his father's old haunt, Pete's Bar. Ernie and Rosemary drove into town in their sedan. Rosemary waited in the car while Ernie, both angry and grateful that Bill was drunk enough that he couldn't fight back, hauled Bill out of the bar. But it didn't stop Bill's mouth. Ernie clenched his teeth against invectives he hadn't heard in a long time. Bill's voice punched and echoed through the silence of a small-town night. Ernie considered himself fortunate that it was near midnight and only the few dedicated nightlifers were about. There was one expletive that Bill seemed particularly fond of calling him and that Ernie had to endure hearing the six miles home, with Rosemary following in the sedan.

"I think you have a new name," Rosemary said after they'd gotten Bill home and put him to bed. They sat under the yellow light at the kitchen table, too exhausted to even drink their coffee. Ernie tented his hands over his forehead. He was more tired than he ever thought was possible, and his arms ached from wrestling Bill into the truck.

"Let me guess," he said, rubbing his hands down his face and looking at Rosemary. "Fuckin' bastard."

His wife smirked.

"I'll have to set him straight the next time," Ernie wise-cracked. "It's fuckin' half-breed. Not fuckin' bastard. My folks were *married*."

They laughed then until their lungs burned, until they coughed from lack of air.

Rosemary and Claire went with Ernie and Bill to the first few weeks of AA meetings in Cedar Bend. Then it was only Ernie and Bill driving to Cedar Bend every Monday night.

Early in May Bill tipped again. He told them he was going for a walk after dinner. When ten o'clock rolled around, Ernie walked outside and contemplated how far Bill might have gotten on foot and if he had walked the six miles into town.

Tough love, they preached at the weekly meetings. Tough love. *Jesus Christ!* he fumed. *Tough on who?*

He decided to heed the advice. Let Bill fall down wherever he was. But of course Ernie could not sleep. He paced his kitchen floor until he went outside and walked up and down his driveway.

He remembered on his second time down the driveway. Claire had warned him. The Lucas farm was a veritable liquor store, all of it buried underground. He didn't have to imagine John Lucas doing it. Ernie could see the tall and slope-shouldered man rooting around in the dark when he could not or did not want to go into town. Combing the ground and then digging with the obsessiveness of a red squirrel looking for a lost stockpile of pinecones. Claire had estimated that the entire field behind their barn held bottles beneath its surface. She had gone through their barn with a hay rake. She found and drained twenty bottles of Ever Ready, buried and insulated by old hay and hay bales. At least the barn was clean. But a whole field? How was he going to find all that booze? He looked down at the dog patrolling beside him. He wondered if he could teach Angel to scent alcohol like the pigs they used in Europe to sniff out truffles.

He sat down on the porch steps with the dog. He had a hunch and was proved right when he heard Bill before he saw him, coming from the direction of the Lucas farm. Claire was right. High-proof alcohol, it seemed, could be preserved for eternity in a gopher hole, despite the frost line.

When Bill saw Ernie, he ran into the small patch of cedar swamp just north of the house. Ernie chased and tackled him, and they fell down in the mud, the dog barking wildly from the edge of the barnyard. In an attempt to pin Bill's arms behind his back, Ernie missed one of Bill's flailing fists. It careened off his cheekbone, just missing his left eye. He dragged a howling Bill out of the swamp and into the barnyard, where he could see him under the light. Bill twisted out of Ernie's grasp, and the two men circled each other underneath the yard light.

The dog would not stop barking. Ernie was afraid that Rosemary would wake up, if she hadn't done so already. So he stood still, and finally so did Bill. They eyed each other from ten feet away. Bill was tanked, but he did not wobble or weave. His feet remained solidly planted to the ground. He was shivering, though, his arms wrapped around his chest. Mud was caked over one side of his face, gumming the eyelashes on his left eye together so that he had to squint.

Bill glanced at the dog. The dog's barking had diminished to a whining growl, but he remained agitated, walking between the two men.

"For as drunk as you are, you run pretty fast."

Ernie bent over and rested his hands on his thighs, but he kept his head up and his sight pinned on Bill. The twenty-four-year-old certainly looked better than he had six months ago. Although he remained slender, it was not the skeletal look of a crow-picked deer carcass. Food had put enough flesh on his frame so that Bill carried himself with the languidness of a long-limbed cowboy.

Ernie wiped his brow. He could hear the wind of his own breathing as it struggled to regain its normal rhythm through the pipes of his lungs. He could not figure Bill out. During the day he was deceptively quiet but easygoing and helpful. Occasionally he betrayed that calm by nervously pulling on his thumbs. But if he got a hold of some hard liquor like the bottle of Wild Turkey Ernie had found, he was just that. *Wild.*

Jesus! He got worked up.

Ernie remembered seeing Jimmy drunk a couple of times, but it was nothing like this. Bill seethed and foamed with the rage of a rodeo bull. Bill was looking at him now with an expression that could not be mistaken. Hate.

Ernie took a deep breath, lifted his head just like the dog when he wanted to sniff the air. If he got any closer to Bill, he'd get loopy just on the exhaust coming out of the kid's mouth.

Tomorrow he'd have to do something about that field, about the supply resting in its soil. It was evident that John Lucas had taken great care never to run out of what made him tick. He had apparently buried his treasures down far enough so that the freeze of winter would not shatter all of the bottles. Ernie wondered how long Bill had combed through the grass to find a mound. How long did it take him to dig up even one bottle? Then he briefly pondered if hard liquor aged with the changing seasons. Could the whiskey in the bottles have evaporated enough so that instead of being a hundred proof, they were two hundred proof? Alcohol distilled so much that it could kill its consumer. Or anybody close to that consumer.

He straightened up slowly. He was too old at fifty-nine to be physically fighting.

"Hell, Bill, what is it this time?"

Bill's face crumpled. A thin stream of saliva ran out of the corner of his mud-crusted mouth and rolled down his chin.

"You!" he screamed. "You were always there for James. You went hunting with him! You never took me! I was alone over there!" He stopped and roughly wiped the mud away from his lips with one hand. "You think it was a picnic living with the old man? At least James had you! I didn't have anybody!"

Ernie groaned inwardly. He hadn't thought and shouldn't have spoken as he had. He didn't mean to sound uncaring or fed up, but he was tired. Still, he should have been more careful.

The dog paced between the two men. Ernie opened his mouth

to apologize, to try to explain those lost fifteen years, but Bill beat him to it.

"You wanna know what happened after James left?"

Bill walked until he stood directly underneath the yard light. Then he undid his belt, pulled the zipper down on his jeans, and shoved both his underwear and his jeans down to his knees. He pulled off his T-shirt. Tilted back his shaking head and bit down on one corner of his dirt-smeared mouth. The cracking in his voice.

"Take a good look."

Ernie stumbled forward and held out his hands as if to shield his face. It couldn't be what he thought it was. He could feel the pulsing underneath his left eye, the throb of what he knew would be a shiner in the morning. He lowered his hands and stared at Bill's nakedness. He thought Rosemary had been strangely possessive, insisting on being the only one to help Bill with his bedpan and then, when he could stand and walk, being the only one to escort him to the bathroom. She had been the only one who gave him his baths while he remained bedridden.

It couldn't be what he thought it was, and he had to fight to keep breathing while his eyes took in what was shown to him.

Rather than the normal-size testicles of a grown man, Bill had lumps the size of small walnuts. Across those lumps were brownish red circles like full moons. Bill had the same lunar scars on his upper thighs and in the creases where his thighs met his groin. On the head of his penis.

Ernie blew air out of his mouth and gulped it back in against the sudden rage that sucker-punched him. Although he did not utter it, a scream ripped through the creases of his brain and bottled up near his ears. The pressure in his ears. He thought he was going to blow up.

He had been so preoccupied with Jimmy, with the possibility of his appearance again, with his own guilt and paralyzed grief for fifteen years that he had done to Bill what it appeared everyone else had done to Bill. They did not question his silence but relinquished the quiet boy to a dark corner, and because he did not speak out, they thought he was all right and forgot about him.

Ernie had trouble focusing on Bill, but he limped toward the young man anyway until he stood in front of him. Still breathing hard against the pain in his chest, Ernie bent and gently pulled up first Bill's underwear and then his jeans. Zipped up his fly and buckled his belt. He wrapped his arms around Bill's waist and rested one cheek against Bill's bare chest. And sobbed.

Neither one of them could recall how they got inside the house and made it up the stairs. Ernie only vaguely remembered taking Bill's boots off before tucking him into bed. Bill cried and would not let go of him, would not let Ernie leave the room. So Ernie wedged himself next to Bill on the twin bed and held him until they both fell asleep.

They did not hear the muffled dragging going up the staircase. Or realize that they had left the bedroom door ajar. The arthritic old dog took one step at a time, hauling his stiff and painfully knotted hind legs up behind him.

Rosemary found them all the next morning. Ernie and Bill asleep on the bed. Angel asleep in the corner behind the door.

✕✕✕✕✕ ON THE FIRST DAY HE awoke with complete clarity, Bill became aware that he was not in his own bedroom but in a bedroom faintly familiar to him. He tried to raise one hand and discovered that both his arms had been tied to the bed. He turned his head and saw the IV stand and the saline bag hanging from a hook with its tube trailing to his right arm. He tried jerking his arms free, but it was no use. He did not have the muscle strength to try more than twice. Then he saw Angel.

The dog was lying in the corner by the door. Bill dimly recalled a night in which he'd seen the dog in the field, but he could not be sure that it had been just a dream. The dog coughed and yawned. His breathing was a wheeze and a rattle, as though the air passing to and from his body had to pass nearly insurmountable obstacles. He could not believe the dog was still alive. *If I'm twenty-four,* Bill thought, *then Angel must be at least sixteen years old.*

He watched as the dog got up stiffly and stretched. Noticed that his muzzle and the hair around his eyes were ivory. The dog recovered from his stretch, yawned again, and sat. He stared back at Bill.

✕✦✦✦✦✦✦✦✦✕

Ernie did sport a shiner and a pouch of fluid under his one eye the morning after his tussle with Bill, but he only weakly kidded Bill about a possible career in boxing and then told him to rest. Ernie didn't eat breakfast. He mumbled something about town to Rosemary and got into his truck. He was gone all day and most of the night.

Despite having a self-inflicted headache that would drop a moose, Bill did all the chores that day in Ernie's absence and was grateful when it was time to go to bed. He was so tired. Just as he was pulling off his boots, he heard a whine and a scratch at the door. He let the dog in, and Angel limped to his usual corner behind the door. Bill stripped down to his briefs and climbed into bed but did not go to sleep right away. He listened to the labored breathing of the dog and shifted to lie on his side, to quietly observe the sleeping animal. But Angel was not asleep. His large dark eyes caught and reflected the moonlight coming in through the window.

✕◆◆◆◆◆◆◆◆✕

"This dog has been through hell and back," Rosemary commented that morning as she watched Bill wipe away the eye mucus that crusted the corners of Angel's eyes. "Do you remember when we found him?"

Bill couldn't remember, but he lied because he didn't want Rosemary to think he'd forgotten.

"Yeah. He's an old dog."

She leaned down from her chair and scratched the dog under his chin. "Angel knows me better than anyone," she said. Thoughtfully pausing, she added, "Even better than Ernie sometimes. I can't bear the thought of losing him, but he can't live forever. And the aspirin I give him for his arthritis can only do so much."

With the dog's crusty eyes watching him, Bill suddenly did remember the nearly half-dead six-month-old puppy that Angel had been and his tenacious will to survive. They'd found him in a ditch.

Bill could not look at the dog any longer and turned his face into his pillow. Bill had done the same thing a year and a half ago, taking the corner too fast and spinning the car into a full circle before it slid, back end first, into the ditch. Then he passed out. Wally Wykowski had found him after having driven out to the farm, wondering why his mechanic hadn't shown up for work.

A couple of weeks ago his ability to dream suddenly returned,

and he did not have good dreams but nightmares. Images so vivid
they spiked right through him and caused him to wake up yelling.
One night he woke up covered in a sweat that chilled him and that
pierced his senses. What he saw and felt was neither a dream nor a
nightmare. It had been real once.

✗✗✦✦✦✦✦✦✦✗✗

That smell in the middle of the night of diesel oil and beer and of
days-old sweat. The big hand between his legs, squeezing down
with a viselike force. The pain was so intense that his eyes rolled to
the back of his head. He dimly saw the glow of the cigarette, felt it
burn into his thighs. Then on the tip of his penis, and he screamed.
A hand was slapped over his mouth. The hand with the cigarette.
Hot ash was flicked into his face. Always the same thing said. A
chanting in the middle of the night.

"There is only one man in this house.

"Only one man.

"Only one man.

"Only one man."

Then Bill could remember nothing but waking up. His bed
was often wet, but sometimes he made it to the toilet on time, and
that was even worse. His groin cramped, and he pissed fire, the
stream of urine coming out of his body in pumped jerks.

It did not occur to him that he could tell anyone because he
did not know if it was real. It had a nightmarish quality, something
that couldn't be explained in the daytime. Yet when he looked
down at himself, it was shamefully visible on him.

✗✦✦✦✦✦✦✦✦✗

He wanted a drink so bad that he considered drinking the awful
salty stuff that Rosemary cooked with. He knew where she kept her
cooking sherry, and he swung his legs out of bed. He was reaching
for his pants when the dog blew air loudly through his nose and

clacked his jaws as though he were cold. The dog stared at him and clacked his jaws again. He'd never heard a dog do that before, and it frightened him. Angel had stretched out so that he was lying in front of the closed door, and Bill wasn't sure if the dog would let him pass.

✕✕◆◆◆◆◆◆◆✕✕

"You weren't the only one we had to take care of that day," Rosemary said, making conversation at the lunch table. She was uncharacteristically edgy, and he noticed that she looked out the window at the driveway a lot during the course of that day.

"Angel had been gone all night, the night before. He showed up just before Ernie brought you home," she went on. "His right side was covered with birdshot. Somebody had shot him. We still don't know who or why. Thank God it was birdshot," she added, looking down at the dog lying near their feet, "and not a deer slug."

He had told Ernie that he couldn't remember much from that night, and it was the truth at the time. That night came to him in bits and pieces, out of the blue and mostly while he was working during the day. But it came to him now in one big chunk. He remembered raising the gun and being angry at the dog. How the dog had stood up and become a man. Then fire and burning.

He crawled back into bed and pulled his knees up to his chest. Tomorrow he would have to tell Rosemary. He had shot the dog.

He wished his mouth were not so dry. He wished Ernie were home.

The dog took a deep breath, exhaled noisily, and rested his head on his front feet.

✕◆◆◆◆◆◆◆◆✕

He scrutinized the dog in the moonlight. He remembered Angel as being so black that he had merged with the night, and the only way the dog had made his presence known was through his breathing.

Now his coat appeared flecked with stars, small white hairs interspersed through his body, and of course, the ivory muzzle. The changing season of old age. Winter coming on the dog.

Bill wondered why the dog didn't hate him or give any outward sign of it. The dog had to have known it was him, smelled him, and of course, he sat in the field and watched him. Wouldn't Bill have hated someone who had shot him?

He thought about Angel lying in that ditch fifteen years ago. He had been put there to die by someone else until Ernie and Rosemary had pulled him out.

"It wasn't easy getting him out of that ditch." Rosemary laughed. "He growled and tried to lunge at Ernie. We hypnotized him with a flashlight. But he was so weak too. Ernie was the brave one who tied the twine around his muzzle. It took him a long time," she said, "to get used to Ernie."

"He likes him now."

"Oh, sure. But it took awhile. He still likes women better. And children who don't tease him. You just prefer us gals, don't you?" she crooned to the dog, rubbing the top of his head. "He never forgets anything," she added.

✕◆◆◆◆◆◆◆✕

Bill wiped his face. He had dug his own ditch. Steeped in the mud and shit of his life while it seemed everybody whizzed past him. Ernie and Rosemary and his mother had pulled him out even while he fought against them.

He sat up and, leaning forward, looked out the window.

Bill was staying in what used to be Ernie's boyhood bedroom. He could see the barn and the field behind it from the window. He briefly tried to imagine Ernie as a little boy and what Ernie saw out of that window fifty years ago.

Then he thought of his father. It was going to be hard to stay sober. What else would help him against the memory of that remorseless, cold-eyed man or the chanting Bill still heard in his sleep?

What would brace him against the hatred of the man and the marks he left as though he had branded his son with an identity he could never erase? His father had been one mean fucker, and stories about him still hovered in the community. Hovered over Bill.

Bill looked at the dog again. Angel had never lost his hatred of most men. His reaction to their presence was still so strong that their first priority was to get to the dog first when someone drove onto the Morriseau place, just in case Angel bit someone. What the dog had been through was visible on him. The lumps on his head. The one ear tattered as though it had been put through a paper shredder. How it waved in the wind like a shot-up flag.

Bill wiped his eyes again.

Some dogs wounded as badly as Angel had been either became so savage they had to be put down or they cowered and shied away from people, crying even if they were touched lightly. Angel had done neither. He had never walked as though he were wounded. He had acquired a ruff around his neck with age and a slow stroll that made his big shoulders ripple with authority. That announced his territory and his determination to protect those within it. Had Angel been a wolf or coyote, his scars and his age would have identified him. To have survived those injuries and have reached that age in the roughness of the natural world would have elevated him. Made him larger than life and a legend.

He would be the talk of the woods and a presence that would cause fear in most hunters.

✕✕✕✕ ERNIE WAS GONE MOST OF that day and into the night. Not because he couldn't face Bill but because his rage was so severe he could not risk its unwarranted explosion on those he loved.

He killed time before nightfall by driving up to Lake Superior. He had taken one of his rifles with him, but after reaching the hardware store in Washburn, he realized that using bullets would be dangerous. He was about to the leave the store when he caught sight of a shelf full of baseball bats. He bought six of the cheaper wooden ones but reconsidered and went back into the store to purchase two of the more expensive heavy alloy bats. Then he drove on to Bayfield, where he bought a whitefish sandwich and thick-cut potato fries from a lakefront restaurant. Sitting on one of the docks, he ate his food and watched the ferry cross back and forth from the mainland to Madeline Island.

It was midnight when he reached Olina again and parked by the cemetery on the edge of town, shaded by very old and lofty elms. He gathered the bats under one arm and, using a tiny flashlight from the truck's glove compartment, walked through the newer section of the cemetery.

The headstone was as clean and polished as the day it had been set into the ground. An expensive gray granite. He had to give Claire credit, though. The only words chiseled on it were the name. No date of birth or date of death. No terms of endearment. Still, it galled him. The money spent for a meaningless piece of stone. Money that Bill and Claire needed. And the harshest joke of all,

John Lucas was buried in an area of ground known as the Sacred Heart Cemetery.

He picked up one of the wooden bats and raised it above his head. He listened for a moment, to make sure that he was alone. Then he brought the bat down and struck the headstone. It splintered after the third strike, and he tossed the handle aside. He picked up another bat, and then another, beating the headstone until they broke.

It was the metal alloy bats that did the most damage, and he regretted not purchasing more of them. He stepped sideways and thought of what he'd seen the night before. The maimed genitals. The humiliation and agony on Bill's face. He swung so that the tip of the bat smashed into the chiseled name. He shut his eyes against the chips and wedges of granite that flew with each strike. When the first alloy bat was so severely dented that it was useless, he picked up the second alloy and last bat. Exhaustion stopped him before he had destroyed the last bat. His shirt was soaked with sweat, and he felt something heavier trickle down his chin. He had bitten his lip.

He stood for a while until his breathing was steadier. Squatting down, he gathered up as much of the splintered wood as he could and the two alloy bats, and headed back to the truck. He took the long way home and stopped to dump the remains of the wooden bats into the Chippewa, where they would secretly float away.

He hid the alloy bats in the far corner of the hayloft in his barn before going into the house and taking a shower. Then he crawled into bed next to Rosemary and fell asleep.

✗✗✗✗ "WHY DIDN'T YOU TELL ME?"

We were in bed talking in the dark. It was two nights after Ernie found out. I had rubbed ointment into the bloody split on his lip.

"Because," I answered, feeling fragile myself and near tears, "I was afraid of what it would do to you."

I wasn't happy either. I resented being the one who knew, who had to tell. It reminded me of writing letters for dying soldiers. Putting their last words to their families on paper in my penmanship. I was sick of being the body through which bad news had to pass. It wasn't entirely true, though. Ernie had been the one who had had to tell Claire about Jimmy and then about John.

But there was another reason I hadn't told Ernie. A very good one. Bill did not tell me or give me permission. I stumbled on it while he was unconscious. I had no right to speak of it until Bill did. That's what Ernie had to know.

"Bill had to tell you," I whispered into his neck. "Not me."

But I did tell Claire. Or rather I showed her. That fourth day while Bill was still drifting in and out of consciousness. We were sitting across from each other, in our same chairs, listening to Bill's breathing. I stopped knitting.

"Claire," I said, standing up, "I have to show you something."

I slowly rolled the blankets down. Unsnapped the top of Bill's pajama bottoms and tugged them down his legs. She stared at his bared hips.

"What *is* that?" She reached forward and touched one of the red marks with a fingertip.

"Those are burn scars. I think, from a cigarette."

She cupped his penis in her hand for a moment.

"I didn't . . . I didn't . . . *know*," she said in a small voice. "Bill would never let me see him naked. I don't remember when he got funny that way about it. He would never wear shorts," she continued in a daze, "even on the hottest days."

I heard Ernie rustling around in the kitchen downstairs. I pulled Bill's pajama bottoms back up and covered him once again with the blankets.

"C'mon," I said, "let's go for a walk. We need some fresh air."

Claire stumbled going down the stairs, and I caught her by the arm. I had to put her coat and boots on. Her mittens. Then I dragged her outside with me. When we waded through the snow to the garden, she fell against me, and I caught her again. Her lips opened, and her teeth bit down into the fabric of my coat. I felt the sound in my shoulder before I heard it. That intense wail of a mother in pain. She began to slip from my arms, and I didn't have the strength to hold her up. So we went down on our knees.

<hr />

It was almost as I feared. When I saw the small article in the *Olina Herald* about the vandalism of John Lucas's grave, I knew exactly who had done it. The headstone was severely chipped and cracked down the middle. The front was smashed so that John's name was obliterated from the stone. Sheriff Meyer was quoted as saying that he thought it was someone that John had owed money to years ago but that he didn't have any leads.

I went through the motions of the day Ernie smashed John's headstone, smiling like an idiot as though nothing were happening and making lunch and dinner. Talking to Bill, who was severely hung over. Bill asked me where Ernie had gone, and I lied, saying he had gone to look at a used tractor for sale near Rice Lake. I had no idea what Ernie was up to that day or where he was, but I knew what had happened the night before. The dog's barking woke me up. I watched from our bedroom window and bit my knuckles, wondering if Bill and Ernie would fight some more and whether I should go down there to break it up. I couldn't have predicted what happened next. But it made sense. How do you explain something like that? Bill could not say what was done to him. He had to show Ernie.

I was grateful that John Lucas was already dead. I know Ernie would have killed him. I don't know how—hanging him from a rope, beating him, and then maybe shooting him—but he would have killed him. And I would have lost Ernie for doing what was only right, what was just. Still, killing John Lucas wouldn't have relieved Ernie or erased the physical remnants of what had been done to the most consecrated part of a little boy.

Claire said nothing to us about the wrecked headstone. But she told the priest that she would not pay for another one.

Ernie had trouble getting out of bed again, and he had that dead fish look about him for a while. But he did get up. He had to. Bill was with us, and that was a blessing. Sometimes you can do the impossible for another person when you cannot do it for yourself.

While Ernie spent time with Bill, I spent time with Claire. We walked our field and her field countless times, wading through snow and then through the mud of spring. I had lived in this area all my life and on the Morriseau farm for nearly forty years. But I never took the time just to amble through it. I let Claire lead us on the walk, and it was always the same. She could name all the birds, knew what plants grew on the edge of the fields and why some of the cedars grew in their twisted way. Claire wordlessly showed me how walking the same route over and over again had a meditative effect. How she had survived those years of loneliness and pain by putting her feet on the ground and moving forward. It hit me that walking in a circle means you never come to a dead end. You just keep walking the circle over and over until whatever it was or is that bothered you slows down or becomes unwound. And then, maybe, drifts away.

I finally understood why she had stayed after her husband's death and had not returned to her hometown of Milwaukee. It was never his home. It was hers.

XXXXX THEIR HOUSEHOLD THAT WINTER, SPRING, and summer of 1983 became one in which three people resided at the Morriseau place with a fourth, Claire, drifting between the two farmhouses, staying some nights with Rosemary, Ernie, and Bill. Rosemary had a short bout with her own polluted memories. They drifted up through her sleep and caused her to kick the covers off the bed. One night, before he realized what was happening, she had pushed Ernie off the bed with such force that he hit his head on the bedside table before landing on the floor. Then there was Bill's constant flood of nightmares. One of them, both of them, and sometimes all three of them found themselves running into Bill's bedroom when they heard him crying loudly in his sleep.

A week after he smashed the headstone, Ernie borrowed a six-bladed plow meant for cutting deep furrows and began the hard work of unearthing what amounted to liquid grenades left by John Lucas in the field. He wired a wooden box behind the seat of the tractor. Whenever he unearthed a bottle or the blades sliced into and smashed a bottle, Ernie stopped the tractor and let it idle while he picked up the bottle or the pieces of glass and put them into the wooden box. If there were any contents in a bottle, he used a glass cutter to slice off the rusted top and drained it into the soil. Only half of the field was pockmarked with booze, and for that he was grateful. Most of the bottles containing less than 80-proof alcohol had shattered. But that half was so loaded with buried forts of shattered bottles and then some bottles that were miraculously intact that Ernie filled six empty oil drums with bottles and glass.

"You won't be able to walk barefoot in that field for a few years," he warned Bill and Claire, knowing that he had left numerous shards of glass.

While he monotonously worked the field over, he tried to grasp a way to begin again with Bill. He envisioned what his own father would do. Watching the blades cut and fold the top layer of dirt, snarled with brome and timothy weed roots, he realized that his boyhood had been happy and peaceful because Claude Morriseau did not dwell on the actions of others, particularly if they meant him harm. His father was not without compassion. But rather than let hatred eat him, Claude Morriseau stepped away from people who could not be helped, distancing harm so that it petered out on its own volition or turned back and bit its owner.

In those days and especially among his father's people on the Heron Reservation, such an act toward a child was dealt with in a manner consistent with the horror of the act itself. The reservation was a sovereign nation and had its own court system. Even then the perpetrator was often not brought forward. They made sure, of course, that the guilty was indeed guilty. And then they made sure that he disappeared.

✕✕✕✕ HOW COULD I LOOK MY SON in the face, knowing it was I, his mother, who should have protected him? I never thought I would face pain as terrible as that day when I was notified that Jimmy was missing in action. Of not knowing what had gone through his mind before he died. Or how long he had suffered.

This was worse in some ways. I threw up for days afterward and could not eat. I tried to remember if there were any clues that I hadn't picked up on. What hadn't I seen?

What possesses a man to torture an area of the body meant for pleasure and for giving life? A sacred area. How could he do it to a little boy? His own son?

It would shock people to hear me say it, but my dead son has benefits that my living son does not have. It would have been kinder to have just killed Bill rather than calculate and deliver this secret torture night after night. To leave him with visible scars and a humiliation and pain that would deny him the right to seek love. There were clues, though. I have scars too. They call it rape, but back then I thought of it as survival. To squeeze my eyes shut and let him do what he wanted. It never occurred to me that he would do the same to Bill.

I could not bear to think of Bill's nights. I did the only thing I could think to do, as a bulwark against such knowledge. I walked at night, around and around our field and then sometimes the Morriseau field. I walked down the driveway and once that spring all the way to the river. I contemplated my life that night, leaning over the bridge. Hearing the dark water below and wondering if my body

306

would float unimpeded all the way to Eau Claire or get snagged on a submerged log just a mile or so down the river.

I was walking back from the river in the dark when I heard footsteps on the gravel walking toward me. Then I saw the light from one of our kerosene lamps.

"Mom. What are you doing out here?"

"I needed to go for a walk."

"In the dark, Mom?"

I said nothing. He lifted the lamp higher to look at me.

"Are you mad at me?"

Was I mad at him? That was too much. I cried so suddenly and so hard that I could not stand up. Everything that tormented me ran to the front of my brain and pounded until my forehead, my cheeks, and my eyes bulged with pain. I went down like a tripped kid onto my hands and knees. I didn't have to look to know that my palms and knees were scraped and bleeding and that I had pebbles jammed into my skin. I was grateful that the gravel hurt so much. It was not enough suffering. I deserved to feel pain for what I did not do, and I wanted Bill to be angry with me.

"It is," I choked out, blindly reaching forward to grab one of his ankles, "the other way around. You should be mad at me."

"Those Lucases," people would say if word got out that we were seen sitting and crying on the side of the gravel road near our farm in the middle of the night. "They have always been crazy."

"The worst," he whispered to me, "is that I can't figure out how he got into my bedroom. I locked the door every night and put a chair in front of it."

I wondered too. I remembered John as being gone most days and evenings. Did he come back at night when we were asleep? Or maybe he never went to work but hid underneath Bill's bed?

When I asked him how long he thought it went on for, Bill said, "I don't remember. It stopped, I think, when I was being carried somewhere. And then someone laughed."

My son released me with those words. Such a gift. That he

could remember that night and that laughter. I had at least, un-
knowingly, ended his torture. I almost told him about the voice in
the field, the voice that told me to laugh. But Bill had enough to
struggle with, and I did not want to burden him with the additional
thought that his mother was really crazy.

✖✦✦✦✦✦✦✦✖

"How can I help Bill?"

It was such a humble question. As if bringing him home from
a near death of hypothermia in the woods were not enough. Ernie
was in such deep misery that it announced itself in his body. He
walked as though physically gnarled and twisted from torture. I did
not have to be told who had smashed John's headstone.

I didn't want him to have a headstone in the first place. We
could hardly afford it. Nor did he deserve to be buried in consecrated ground. That was when what little Catholicism I had left in
me reared up like a spurred horse.

"Your husband was baptized a Catholic." Shocked at my vague
suggestion that John not be buried in the Sacred Heart Cemetery,
Father Wallace admonished me. Of course Father Wallace was thinking of himself. His puffy face with its explosion of broken red and
purple capillaries was a strong sign of his own excess. If he could
deny it in himself, then he could certainly bless a fellow drunk with
the same blindness.

It was on the tip of my bitter tongue. "Throw him," I very
nearly said, "into potter's field."

I had to think of the outcome, though. Social norms in Olina
dictated that I should bury my husband in the proper way. Father
Wallace would take up a collection for the headstone if I didn't
come up with the money. That would cause gossip, and I had to
think of Bill. I did not want people to poke my son with painful
questions.

I envied Ernie. I understood why he had done it. I only wish I
had thought to do it as well.

When John was alive, I visualized murdering him every day. How to do it and not get caught. It was only right. We deserved to live our lives with the release and pleasure his death would bring. There was no court of law that could know how we lived or what he did to us. They could not exact justice on him in the way I could, or Bill could, or Jimmy could, if he had come home. Or even Rosemary and Ernie.

✕✕✕✕✕◆◆◆◆✕✕

I thought a lot about Ernie's question because I asked myself the same thing.

I could have helped Bill much sooner. Those years I kept him to myself. Those years when I did not allow him to wander over to the Morriseau place. As if to punish me for my selfishness and my fear, fate allowed Ernie to find him when I could not. I did not tell Ernie and Rosemary what I did before I walked through the fields to their house. I did not tell them that I trudged through the swamp and woods. It was beginning to freeze, and I had to grab the lower branches on some of the trees, if there were any, to walk up one side of that ice-covered ridge. Most of the time I had to crawl, and when I reached the top, he was not there. I walked sideways going down the other side, but I fell anyway and slid straight down. I was desperately trying to grab at anything to stop my descent when I hit something hard midway down and felt it through the rear of my pants. I could barely see it, but after I wiped the snow off it and read its shape with my leather mittens, I knew it was a gun.

You can imagine what went through my head. I tried calling for Bill. I became frantic and screamed his name. It is useless to do so in a northern snowstorm. Snow muffles sound and buries it like it does everything else.

"Help me, help me," I kept saying, but all that ever answered me was the wind. There is that moment that has happened to me many times in my despair and that always feels new with each crisis. I sit there feeling small and unable to think. Feeling stupid and ashamed. Crying because I don't know what to do. Then something takes over in my body. Instinct, I think. I just got up and started moving as fast as I could. I fell again and slid the rest of the way down that slope. I stood up and hiked through the freezing swamp bedding. It was cold, and the snow was coming down in blankets. It is a miracle that I didn't get lost and die out there.

I reached the Morriseau porch feeling much like Zhivago when he finally makes his way, frozen and exhausted, back to Lara in that little village in the Urals. I pounded on their door. Rosemary opened it, and that butter yellow light that seems to inhabit country kitchens filled my face. I was speechless with gratitude and nearly out of my mind with terror.

✕✦✦✦✦✦✦✦✕

Another thought came to me one day that May when I was cleaning up after dinner at their house. It did not feel like work. The evening sun was warm on my face as I cleared the table, and I was basking in the simple pleasure of a shared meal, thinking of how wonderful it was to sit and eat and talk and laugh like normal people at a dinner table. Although Bill was in a good mood and told jokes, there was a moment when something surfaced in his face during dinner that reminded me of how he had looked after Jimmy's death. Of how wise I used to think he appeared.

We ate dessert, and then Bill and Rosemary went outside to weed the garden.

I caught Ernie by the arm before he went outside to join them. "You want to know how to help Bill," I said. "He has never been a child. What would you do to make a little boy happy? To help him?"

✗✗✗✗ AFTER A LONG HOT DAY of putting new siding on the Lucas farmhouse, Bill took Ernie up to his bedroom and showed him the bed Jimmy had slept in and his own bed. He took out his shoebox of mementos, and they sat together on the bed and looked wordlessly at the Polaroid of Bill's brother. At the leather pouch containing the fringe from the bedspread. A mud turtle's shell. The worn leather collar from a dog Bill and Jimmy once had. The thick packet of letters sent from Vietnam.

"He never told me until the night before he left that he was leaving."

"That's the same night we found out," Ernie said. "Remember you ate at our house and your dad came to pick you up?"

Bill flipped the picture over and stared at the writing on the back. "He told me that he had signed up that winter and that he never thought the day would come when he'd have to leave. That never made any sense to me. How could you sign up and not know you were going to leave?"

"I don't know, Bill," Ernie answered. "Your mom says she didn't know until that night as well. I can't figure that one out. It didn't seem like something your brother would do. I don't mean enlisting. I mean, not telling anyone."

"I thought he l-l-left," Bill stammered, his voice cracking, "because he didn't l-l-like us anymore. Because we w-w-weren't ever happy."

Ernie pulled Bill's head to his shoulder. "Nah, Bill. That wasn't it."

◆◆◆◆◆◆◆◆◆◆

Ernie thought of all the trite sayings they listened to during their Monday night AA meetings. "Let go and let God" was the worst one. It made Bill squirm and Ernie bite his lips. The meetings were good in that Bill got to see other local people struggling to keep sober just as he was. But the heavy emphasis on God needled Ernie so badly one night that he thought he'd have to leave. Bill must have sensed Ernie's irritation. He calmly asked, "What if you don't believe in God?"

"Hey! That's a good question. I was wonderin' the same thing," a brawny woman about Ernie's age chimed in.

"Well," one of the senior members said, not comfortably, "think of it as a higher power then."

Bill decided to focus on "One day at a time." Ernie thought that was a better idea too. After all, that was the unofficial creed of life in northern Wisconsin, where jobs were seasonal at best and the tourist trade fluctuated with people's desires and pocketbooks. It could be said of farming as well with a slight modification: "One rock at a time."

"That's where," Bill said, pointing to the small cemetery they always drove by on the outskirts of Cedar Bend on their way home, "the 'Let go and let God' people are."

"Lucky bastards," Ernie cracked, thinking of the dismal price of beef and whether or not he'd have enough hay for the coming winter.

◆◆◆◆◆◆◆◆◆◆

Ernie gazed up at the bookshelf above Jimmy's bed while Bill cried. *Walden Pond. The Ballad of the Sad Café. The Heart Is a Lonely Hunter. For Whom the Bell Tolls. Go Down Moses. Everything That Rises Must Converge. Catcher in the Rye.*

"Hey," he said nodding to the bookshelf, "where's *Huckleberry Finn*? And there's another book that's missing. Oh, I know. *The Man Who Killed the Deer.*"

"I don't know. Those books didn't come back with his other stuff."

Bill got up and put the shoebox back into his dresser drawer. He sat down next to Ernie on the bed.

"I gave him those books. Have you ever read them?"

"No. James was more of a reader than I am."

Bill was telling a white lie. Ernie remembered seeing him read books and carry books. Remembered how he had snuggled next to Rosemary as she read books aloud to him.

"That's not true. I used to see you reading all the time." He nudged Bill good-naturedly.

"I guess."

"You guess? I know. You should start again. It would take your mind off things."

Then Bill got up again and opened the closet. He took out the Marlin .30-30 rifle and handed it to Ernie.

"It used to be James's. I don't hunt. I think the rifle probably needs cleaning."

✖✖✖✖✖ HE HAD LIED TO ERNIE. Of course he used to read books. His mother had always read books and continued to read books. His brother had read voraciously. And Bill used to lose himself in books as well. He just stopped reading his senior year of high school. If Ernie had pressed him, he would have shaped and stretched the lie and told Ernie that he didn't know why he stopped. But he did.

He couldn't hold a book with shaking hands. He didn't want to read when he felt numb and weightless. A book would have crashed through all that. He did try. The beer bobbing in his veins caused a throbbing in his eyes. The words appeared to skip across the page and not make any sense.

✖✦✦✦✦✦✦✦✖

Late that August his mother and Rosemary went on a shopping trip to Madison. His mother was so excited. She waved her hand out of the open car window all the way down the Morriseau driveway. Ernie made Bill go to bed that night, saying that he would stay up for them. They came home late. Sometime in the night she must have entered his room. He woke up the next morning and saw a book on his bedside table. *Death Comes for the Archbishop.*

He thanked her at breakfast and was startled when she beamed. It wasn't until a week later, when a thunderstorm kept them all inside, that he picked up the book.

"One summer evening in the year 1848, three Cardinals and a missionary Bishop from America were dining together in the gardens of a villa in the Sabine Hills, overlooking Rome. . . ."

He read through the night.

Bill could feel the dust of the Acoma mesa. He wanted to crack piñon nuts between his teeth and stand on top of the mesa, all ten acres of it, and look at all that blue sky and the distance. The seemingly unending distance.

Huddled in his bed, Bill was only vaguely aware of the rain that slapped the window glass. The thrashing of the pine boughs in the wind. He was in Acoma. He could feel the night coming on there after a hot day and the slow gathering of the Acoma people. Their singing and chanting. How they gathered as a large family and approached the abusive priest reading his breviary. How they bound his hands and feet. He tried to imagine those small people carrying that obese man and throwing him off a cliff.

He reread that book several times. Then he moved on to the books on his brother's shelf. Ernie gave him new copies of *Huckleberry Finn* and *The Man Who Killed the Deer*.

He had forgotten the interior pleasure of sitting quietly and absorbing a story that lifted him effortlessly away from his own life and at the same time strangely affirmed that his own life was real to him. People shared his own feelings long ago. Books held those people whose lives were not so far from his own. Books said that life mattered in its beauty and its ugliness. His life.

"I want you," his mother said one evening, "to go to college. I wanted Jimmy to go to college. He was smart, and so are you. College," his mother said with a dreamy look, "is not at all like high school. It is like having the world brought to you, and you can study anything you like."

She got up and opened one of the kitchen cupboards. Placed a jarful of money on the table. "I found this when I was cleaning out the barn. You can use this to buy your first semester of textbooks."

He stared at the jar. So many nights when he was short of cash for beer or cheap whiskey, it never once tickled his memory. That money hidden in the corner of the barn.

"I think your dad probably hid this and forgot all about it.

Funny, isn't it?" His mother giggled. He looked up at her. She had a satisfied "I-got-him" look on her face. He had a flash of that look from long ago. *Things will get better.*

Her giggle snagged him. It was a joke. A joke on him. And so funny.

"Not Dad," he gasped, slapping the tabletop. "James. I got that money from James. I forgot all about it."

"He sent you money?" His mother was stunned.

"Yeah. All of that," he said, wiping his face on his shirtsleeve.

"When you were eight and nine?"

"Yeah."

"And you kept it?"

"Yeah."

"Good Lord!" His mother covered her mouth. She tried to hold it back with her hand, but her giggling bubbled through the crevices between her fingers.

Bill howled. "James told me not to let *Dad* use it on a beer dream!"

That did it. His mother dropped her hand from her mouth and let loose with raucous laughter. Bill slapped the table again and joined her.

A somber mood settled over them when they both were too tired to laugh anymore.

"I want you to understand something," his mother said. It was her choice of words that once again conveyed her intent. It made him sit up and listen.

"Small towns are often like chicken coops. They don't like or accept difference or change. If one hen is molting or is hurt and the rest of them aren't, they will peck at that bird until she is bloody. I've seen hens that were molting," his mother said, "get pecked to death."

She ran her hands down the sides of the large jar. Rubbed it up and down as though it were a genie's bottle.

"In a small town," she said, "talk is like that. It can kill you if you let it. Sometimes you need to leave and finish your changing somewhere else before you can come back. Then they have nothing to say about it because they don't know where you've been. That frightens them. Then they shut up."

She pushed the jar into the center of the table and then leaned toward Bill. "Will you at least try a year of college? I think you'll be surprised."

He glanced at the jar of money.

"I'll try."

✖✖✖✖✖ BILL WAS NOT A HUNTER like his brother. But he loved the river. *Loved* water.

They sat one morning, their legs dangling off the old logging bridge above the Chippewa, and ate fried egg sandwiches that they had made before leaving the house.

"We used to come down here. Except Terry was with us most of the time." Bill peered down at the water. "We never did go fishing. James said he'd teach me to fly-fish, but he never did."

Then he lifted his head and smiled at Ernie. "James always said you were the best."

"Best gone to rotten. I haven't fished in a long time. But I'll teach you how to fly-fish. Do you still want to learn?"

✖✖✖✖✖✖✖✖✖✖

Ernie started him on an old fly rod right away and watched in the evenings as Bill clocked the rod back and forth. He had a natural swing to his cast, a flick of his wrist that made him appear to be waving a wand. Within two weeks, Bill had mastered the rudiments of fly-fishing and was well on his way to becoming far better than Ernie. Nearly every night they fished either the Chippewa or the deep and clear kettle lake near the ridge that was a trout heaven. Ernie went foolish with his money, just as he had for Jimmy, and bought Bill a six-hundred-dollar Orvis fly rod and reel. Before mid-summer they had expanded their fishing territory by taking weekend trips to the same spots Ernie had taken Jimmy: the Namekagon, the Brule, the Flambeau Flowage, and Lake Superior. On weekday

evenings they crouched over newspapers laid out on the ground behind the barn, gutting and cleaning fish. They glanced up every now
and then to watch Claire and Rosemary walk through the fields before dinner. Once Ernie heard a shriek from the field, and only
when it was followed by his wife's familiar laughter did he re-
lax. Ernie had never heard Claire laugh before. As if reading his
mind, Bill commented, "Mom's been lonely for a long time."

The silver from his new braces glinted in the sun. Ernie smiled.
It was an incongruity to see teeth braces on a grown man. Bill filled
out his frame of six feet, five inches and towered over Ernie far
more than Jimmy had.

⊱◆◆◆◆◆◆◆◆◆⊰

Ernie took Bill to a doctor in Madison that summer. Ernie went in
first to talk to the doctor, and then Bill was summoned in for a
physical exam.

As Ernie sat in the waiting room, he thought about Bill's life
and where it would go. Bill had perhaps chosen the more difficult
path in life. Ernie knew Bill could have escaped this grief, left home
like his brother, left it all behind. Ernie thought of how he viewed
his own classmates who had stayed in Olina and never gone anywhere: provincial, cowardly, redneck, and small. To go away and
then come back was something different. A person gained perspective that way. But Ernie had to think twice about his notion when it
came to Bill. To stay in one place required discipline in many ways
more rigorous than holding yourself together when surrounded by
a new land and new people. It might be harder just to stay and
live with the foundation your family might have laid for you, rotten
or not.

The doctor came out of the examining room and gestured to
Ernie to come into his office.

"His genitals function normally in that he can pass urine and
get an erection. But," the doctor said, shaking his head, "I doubt he
will ever be able to have children. Testicles damaged like that can

barely produce any sperm. I can run more tests, but I can tell you just by looking at him that they would be a waste."

"What about surgery?" Ernie asked

"To open the ducts from the testicles?"

Ernie nodded.

"There's not even a fifty-fifty chance. And why put him through that?"

<hr/>

He came close to telling Bill about Jimmy several times but at the last minute backed down. Ernie wavered between whether it would do more harm than good, and Bill didn't appear to want to talk about it.

There were several times that late summer and early fall when Ernie happened to glance at Bill, especially when they fished the Chippewa, and saw Bill reel in his line and pause. Watched him stare and focus on something down the river. Ernie quietly inched his way through the brush in the hope of glimpsing whatever it was that Bill seemed mesmerized by. Once Ernie thought he heard whistling. He looked up from the fly he was tying on his line to locate it. He felt a cold mist settle on his face and thought it was river spray. But when he wiped his face with a handkerchief and then looked down, he saw that he was standing in shallows that threw no water, no mist.

When they weren't fishing, they hiked the ridge. Stood on its pinnacle and looked down at the lake on its north side. It happened more than once, his nostrils picking up the sharpness of it. Finally he asked Bill, "Do you smell smoke?"

"Sometimes."

Bill looked at the lake and chewed his lower lip.

"Huh," Ernie grunted, thinking it was the new guy who bought the neighboring farm just beyond the lake. Ernie thought he was burning leaves or wood, except that the smoke had a sulfuric edge to it.

✖✖✖✖ HE HAD ONCE INHABITED his mother.

Bill thought about this as he watched her eat. They were having supper alone as they had in the old days. Mesmerized by the motion of her hand, by the clink of the fork as the tines hit the plate when she pierced a piece of broiled chicken, he stopped eating. He watched as her arm brought the food up to her mouth. It was one of those things he could not remember. His mother eating. It slowly dawned on him that he had no memory of it because he had not seen her eating food. She always sat and watched him as he ate his meals. *When did she eat?* he wondered. She must have eaten something or else she would have starved and would not be sitting with him at the table now. He gazed at her face. She *was* thin in those days. As a child he had often thought she was hollow. In those days she appeared to be sustained only by coffee and by the invisible reserves in her own body, her flesh eating upon itself.

He had once gnawed on her as well. Wasn't it true that babies were parasites on their mothers? He had lived in her once. Small as a pea, he had floated in her habitat. She had been his soil, sky, water, and air. Now through testing and ultrasound, women could know the sex of the babies they carried. But did his mother have a sense back then that she was a woman walking with a baby boy inside her? That twice in her life, for nine months, she was both male and female?

He watched her sip from her glass of water. Their silence was pleasant and comfortable. It had almost always been just the two of them. He could dimly remember James at the dinner table, his joking or sometimes his quiet anger. But mostly it was just the two of them.

✖◆◆◆◆◆◆◆◆✖

His mother was right. There was a side effect in trying to stay sober in their small town that he did not like. He noticed people more—what they said and what they did—and it was generally a painful and bewildering experience. They identified him in town as *that* Lucas boy. Not like his brother, the dead Vietnam vet who had looked so much like Elvis, who had been the Romeo of his class, and who had moved with ease and jocularity among others. Bill was pointed out as the *other one*. The son of John Lucas who still generated bar talk seven, almost eight years after his death.

Now there was talk in town about him.

Wally Wykowski took him back. Working at the Standard station did not make him feel proud or accomplished as it had when he was seventeen. It was boring and simultaneously irritating, even hurtful at times. Local people he'd been familiar with all his life kept their distance, and he could hear their whispers. Saw their elbow nudges. They didn't have to say it to him directly. It was apparent when they visibly chewed him over and then dismissed him. *Like father, like son.*

"Ignore 'em," Ernie told him. "And they wonder why they don't make ends meet. Should flap their tongues less and work their hands more."

So Bill tried. He considered them as he did his father. Bothersome elements like tornado warnings or heavy winds. But he had never belonged to his father and was persistently perplexed that people connected them just because of his drinking.

"Whose little boy are you?" He remembered being teased by Mrs. Schaefer, who owned the hardware store with her husband, Sheldon. Bill was still quite young, just barely out of his white toddler walking shoes. It was during a rare moment when both his parents were present. He took his thumb out of his mouth and silently pointed at his mother.

Bill had always thought of himself as the son of Claire Lucas. As though his father had had nothing to do with his creation. He was her son. She was his mother. She was the country in which he had grown up and still lived in. It may have been a country full of rocks, seas whose tidal waves threatened to drown him, periodic droughts, and seasons that shifted from hot to cold and sometimes warm. But simultaneously it was a country full of wonder and promise and mystery. Always a place that never let him forget that he was native to it and wanted him despite the upheaval.

It was to his mother he went after that night in September.

The new elementary school teacher in town had brought her Volvo in for a prewinter tuneup. Then she came back for some windshield wiper fluid, and after that, a pack of cigarettes. She finally asked him out, and he shocked the rest of the men in the station by casually saying yes. She was of average height with shoulder-length blond hair and bluebird-blue eyes. They went out for a couple of weeks, and he thought they had fun together. That she liked him. It was long enough for him to feel somewhat safe with her. To let down his guard.

⬥⬥⬥⬥⬥⬥⬥⬥⬥

Her mouth on his neck. The unbuttoning of his shirt. Then she removed her blouse, revealing a lacy bra. He fumbled, trying to unhook her bra from the back.

"The front," she whispered, and lightly bit his ear.

The breasts that filled his hands. She unzipped his pants and pushed them down to his knees. He pulled her to him so that they were lengthwise on the couch. He became so lost in the dreaminess and intense sensation of arousal that he didn't feel her slide his underwear down. Then she moved down his chest and bent over his pelvis to take his penis into her mouth. He momentarily came out of the haze of his arousal and began to sit up, but it was too late.

She froze and stared at his genitals. *"What is that?"*

He saw the distaste, even the horror on her face. He panicked and squeezed his eyes shut.

"Is that a rash? Oh, God. Do you have herpes?" she fired away. "And *why* are your balls so small? You weren't going to tell me, were you?" she shrieked.

He pushed her away and yanked up his underwear and then his pants. He reeled and crashed against walls on his way through the dimly lit rooms of her rented house, feeling as big and as ugly as Frankenstein. He nearly fell out her front door and stumbled down the broken cement steps before running for his car.

⊠◆◆◆◆◆◆◆◆⊠

Bill frantically drove away from Olina and toward Cedar Bend. It was two in the morning when he got home, carrying a third six-pack of beer. He bumped against the kitchen table and knocked over a chair. He had been so drunk that he didn't realize the light he was moving toward in the living room meant that his mother was sitting on the davenport.

"Bill," she said faintly, "what happened?"

He dropped the six-pack on the floor. Heard the thud as it hit the wood, and he knew that he had dented and scratched the floorboards.

"Here," he heard his mother say and felt her pull on one of his hands. "Sit down."

He sat down and looked at her hand, a pearly shell inside his large paw. She was so small beside him. A little bird. A very tired little bird.

"What happened? Are you all right?"

He saw the years ahead through the inebriated wash of his brain. It was now 1983. He'd live at home with his mother and work at the Standard station. He'd avoid people in town. He'd never, *ever* date again. He could never forget that look of horror and disgust.

"Nobody," he sputtered, "will ever want me."

He leaned over, buried his head in his mother's lap, and let his sorrow drain into her thighs.

✕✦✦✦✦✦✦✕

Bill had been terrified to go to work after that and to even walk through town. He imagined the teacher whispering to other teachers, the whispering growing until it became a roar in town. "Bill Lucas is deformed."

But if she did talk, he was not aware of it, and nobody said anything at the station. He avoided her completely although she did not do the same for him.

"Don't cry over that one," Wally remarked one day after she left. She had brought her car in for an oil change, and Wally had another mechanic do it. Bill retreated to the picnic table behind the station and sipped a Coke. He waited until he was absolutely sure she was gone.

"Word has it that she has screwed any and everybody available, and I guess she's now spending her nights driving to Cedar Bend. I think"—Wally chuckled, chewing on a peppermint-flavored toothpick—"she got Ray too. He's been pretty ornery lately."

Bill said nothing.

"Funny," Wally went on, "she looks sweet, and you'd think she'd have more sense, teaching little kids and all. But I guess she's a real bitch. Uses 'em and tosses 'em. She's only here for the fall and she's plowin' these fields before she moves on." Wally slapped Bill on the shoulder. "She wasn't good enough for you, kid."

✕✦✦✦✦✦✦✕

Bill sometimes scrubbed himself raw in the shower. But it was the inside he couldn't reach, and he had a funny mental picture of himself: a green garden hose shoved down his throat while his pants were dropped around his ankles, drinking and peeing himself clean. Nothing made him feel at home with himself. Nothing except for spending time in the woods or on the river. Or on the ridge.

He frightened his mother whenever he left the house and walked through the field, into the swamp and toward the ridge. He could sense her watching him from her bedroom window. He did not want to hurt her, but he could not help it. There were days and evenings he had to go back. He could not say exactly why, but he was instinctively driven there.

It was November again, two days away from the first-year anniversary of when Ernie found him. He sat in his usual spot on top of the ridge, centered in the middle of the four red pines that had always been his imaginary room. He stared down at the kettle lake.

He knew what it was now. He thought that being on the ridge would help him regain what he saw and felt when he was younger, before he began drinking at the age of thirteen. He watched as a breeze rippled the surface of the lake. The lake reflected the color of the sky. A gunmetal gray.

A huge glacier, his mother had told him when he was five, created the lake. A glacier, she said, was a large bed of moving ice, like a giant mattress that could crawl. She said the glacier had many hands underneath it, some of them huge. Think, she said, of all the legs on a centipede. Only the glacier, she said, had hands. On every palm side of the hands were crusted boulders and sharp rocks. As the ice moved across their part of the world millions of years ago, the hands scooped and scoured out small holes and sometimes larger holes, which then filled with water. Lakes. Glacial moraine lakes. He had always imagined the hands as looking like the oven mitt that his mother used when she cleaned out the oven. One side was covered with a layer of steel wool. She had also told him that the ground underneath his feet was alive, and he remembered believing it because he felt it then.

He stretched out and stared up at the fading afternoon light filtering through the trees. He was conscious of his back as it made contact with the ground. His mother said the ground had a heartbeat, and if he was quiet enough, he would feel it and hear it.

⁘◆◆◆◆◆◆◆⁘

They were outside that morning, and his mother was squatting on the balls of her bare feet, picking up rocks from the driveway. He watched her roll them between her hands and study their shapes before dropping them and picking up some more.

"Do you know what makes dirt?"

He shook his head. His mother was funny. He knew the formal word for it. *Eccentric.* While other Olina mothers talked about cooking, their hair and makeup, Tupperware parties, Mary Kay parties, or who was doing what in the community, his mother in her bare feet was talking to him about dirt on a cold November morning. He did notice that those shopping trips with Rosemary were paying off. His mother had nicer clothes, and she clearly felt better. Although her hair was white and her face carved with old worries and fears, she was still pretty in an oddly delicate way.

"It's when geology and biology get mixed together. Organisms and rocks. Or an easier way to think about it is rocks and bodies. Isn't that fascinating?"

He smiled. Her bliss was contagious.

"Yeah, Mom. It is."

⁘◆◆◆◆◆◆◆⁘

He sat up. He'd have to leave soon. The sky was becoming a darker gray. He shivered. It reminded him of one February night when the moon was luminescent enough to change the sky from black to twilight gray. James had pulled him out of bed and taken him outside in the middle of the night, saying only that it was a *night for foxes*.

On the field behind the barn lay a hard crust of snow that glittered under a full moon. Bill could hear several short, high-pitched barks coming from the field, and James had lifted him onto his shoulders so that Bill could see better. At first he saw nothing. Then James pointed and said, "See 'em? See 'em dancing over there?"

Sure enough, a vixen and dog fox were chasing each other on top of the hard crust, running in playful circles and lifting themselves up on two hind legs as though to dance with each other. As the two boys watched, the vixen abruptly stopped running and crouched low as the dog fox maneuvered his body behind hers, roughly nipping the back of her neck. He then mounted the vixen, thrusting hard, and remained locked into his mate for what seemed like hours instead of minutes to Bill.

He tugged at his brother's hood. "What's wrong? Why are they fighting?"

"They aren't fighting. It's their mating time. You know. To make little foxes."

Confused and uneasy, Bill watched as the dog fox suddenly released himself from the vixen and then nipped the back of her neck again.

"I heard them barking. That's how I knew," James whispered to Bill, letting him slide off his shoulders.

Bill lingered for a moment by the fence post. It was a magical night with the wind blowing through the shelterbelt of pines so that it sounded like a flute and the moon shining down on the fox pair as though to illuminate their performance.

"You're gonna freeze out here," his brother said, returning to hoist his brother up on his shoulders again.

Bill relaxed into the rhythm of his brother's gait and watched the sky as his brother slowly worked his legs through the deep snow. Sister Agnes had told him that God lived in the sky with the Virgin

Mary and their son, Jesus. Sister Agnes had told him that the Virgin was kind and gentle and loved little children. James told him that it was all a pile of crap, the stuff they tried to make you believe in Catholic school, but Bill did think the statue of the Virgin Mary in church was beautiful. Looking up, Bill had taken off his mitten and waved, just in case she was watching him.

❌◆◆◆◆◆◆◆❌

He brushed the pine needles and other leaf litter from his jacket. He laughed aloud. Only a nerdy backwoods kid would keep his innocent belief in the Virgin Mary after watching a pair of foxes screw their brains out. "Mating is part of a wider scope of natural stimuli that affects even humans," he recalled his high school biology teacher saying.

He flopped back down and rolled over on his side and stared at the lake again.

❌◆◆◆◆◆◆◆❌

A week ago he had taken his mother fishing on the river. He paddled and watched as she trailed her hand in the water, periodically lifting it and letting the drops run off her fingers before placing her hand back into the water. She seemed to be in good spirits, but he could tell something was bothering her. She waited until after they were done fishing and he had loaded the canoe on top of his new but used truck parked near the bridge.

She unbuttoned the top pocket of her field jacket and pulled something out.

"I've had these for a few years now. But I kept them because I didn't think you were ready."

She pressed them into one of his hands. He felt metal and a chain. He opened his hand and stared at them.

"A veteran who had gone back to help search for POWs in 1978 saw this around the neck of a little mountain boy. Very near what used to be the Khe Sanh Combat Base, where Jimmy was. Actually it was the Navy chaplain who came to the house that day with Ernie to tell us about Jimmy."

Bill fingered his brother's dog tags, their edges thick as though they had been partially melted and the metal chain they were connected to.

His mother leaned against the side of the truck. "Do you understand what this means?"

He knew why she picked this moment. She thought it would stop his forays back into the woods and to the ridge.

"I know James is dead." He sighed. "Can I have these?"

His mother nodded and reached into her pocket again. "And these."

She gave him the medals. A Purple Heart. The Bronze Star.

"They don't mean much. But at least Jimmy earned them."

She paused.

"Your father's stories were never true. He never fought in WW Two."

"I figured."

Bill put the dog tags and the medals in his own coat pocket. He reached through the window and pulled out two cans of pop from the cab of the truck and gave her one. They drank in silence and listened to the river. Bill watched the last of the yellow birch leaves fall and drift onto the surface of the rapidly moving water.

He wondered what his brother would have been like if he had lived. Would he have come home like so many other Vietnam vets? Visibly and invisibly wounded? In a few months, during the grip of late January, it would be the anniversary of his brother's death.

"How did you know," he asked, startling his mother, "that James was dead?"

She poured the rest of her soda onto the ground and gave the empty can to him.

"*Missing in action* is an ambiguous phrase."

She crossed her arms and looked back at the river.

"Think of what action means when you are fighting a war. It means that bombs and guns are going off. It means that something has happened to that person that is unmentionable and not visible. There is action, and in the middle of it, they cannot be seen or found. That's the way I've always thought of it."

"Isn't it possible," Bill cautiously ventured, "that he was taken prisoner?"

"No." She shook her head. "I knew this about your brother," she said. "He would never have let himself be taken as a prisoner. He knew what could happen to a prisoner of war. The torture. He could never have tolerated that. Never did."

Bill drained the rest of his can with one swallow and threw both cans into the box of the truck. He glanced at her and wondered if she felt his brother in the way that he did. But he couldn't ask.

She set her face in such a way as to end the conversation. He knew that look well. She was not going to talk anymore. He used to think she did it on purpose just to yank his strings. But lately it came to him that she was of a generation and culture that didn't talk much and that his mother was an aberration, talking more than her parents ever did. She could only give away so much information at one time. It exhausted her, riding against that ingrained stoicism, and she needed to break and rest before she could say more.

✕✕✕✕ IN THE MIDDLE OF NOVEMBER of '83 the dog became more incapacitated, limping outside only when the need to urinate or defecate became intolerable. He barely made it beyond the porch steps. The piles of excrement from his aging dog's body left a scent so overpowering that even after they were shoveled away, Ernie had to spread lime repeatedly over the spots. One night a week before Thanksgiving, Angel settled on his blanket and would not get up, nor would he eat or drink. Although Rosemary had always been the most attached to the dog, it was Bill who seemed to take Angel's impending death the hardest. Bill had moved back home at the end of summer, but he spent the last five nights of Angel's life in a sleeping bag on the Morriseaus' kitchen floor. Angel died early in the morning three days before Thanksgiving.

Ernie sat helplessly in the kitchen and watched as his wife and Bill knelt over the stiffening dog, their bodies wrenched with grief. He had always considered it a miracle that the dog lived in the first place. He did not ask Rosemary how much she paid or what strings she pulled to get the dog's body cremated so that they could have his ashes for Thanksgiving morning.

They had invited Claire and Bill to their house for the holiday. Ernie helped Claire in the kitchen while Rosemary and Bill bundled up. Ernie waved them off from the porch, but he watched them for a while as they somberly crossed the field and entered the swamp. Bill carried the canister with the dog's ashes in his arms, and Ernie was pretty sure he knew where they were going.

A couple of hours later Claire and Ernie were setting the table when they heard loud singing and bursts of laughter approaching the house.

Ernie looked out the window and saw Rosemary and Bill striding arm in arm. The song was familiar. His wife's head was nearly tucked under Bill's armpit. Ernie glanced at Claire, who stood next to him.

"Orbison. 'In Dreams,' " she said.

"I haven't heard that song in years."

Claire smiled and shook her head. "Jimmy's records. Bill must have found them."

1998

◆◆◆◆ HIS SON PLAYFULLY CHASES the dog in the yard, and Bill watches the boy as he delights in following the dog. The lanky Lab and collie mix occasionally stops and barks at the boy as if to challenge him. His son stops too, laughs, stomps his feet, and the dog begins running again. The sun is warm, and Bill is relaxed, slouched on the steps of his porch. The past years seem like a lifetime ago, and watching the little boy who is his son makes him acutely aware of where he is now and where he has been.

◆◆◆◆◆◆◆◆

His mother was right. Small towns and the life in them could be cruel and self-defeating. He discovered in that first year of sobriety that there were many in the community who did not welcome his recovery. He had cheated them out of talk and out of the role they had willed upon him. He denied them the failure they wanted to focus on against the misery of their own lives. They wanted him to enact and carry on his father's misdeeds for the rest of his life. The message was as plain as his first-grade Dick and Jane reader. *See Bill run. See Bill fall.*

One day at the end of his shift at the gas station he blew his nose and noticed for the first time that the mucus was as black and tarry as the oil he cleaned out of car engines. He stared at the gummy and toxic substance wadded in his handkerchief and thought about how it was robbing his life little by little. That night he filled out his admissions and financial aid forms for the University of Minnesota. Although his grades from his senior year in high school were barely above a C because he had rarely shown up for class, his SAT scores were excellent.

Still, leaving was hard. He would never forget the sight of his mother, Rosemary, and Ernie as they stood in front of Bailey Hall on the St. Paul campus, getting ready to climb back into the Morriseaus' sedan and go home. He saw how love caved in their shoulders and threatened to collapse them at the knees. Ernie blew his nose. His mother absently wrung her hands. Rosemary shifted from foot to foot. They would do anything for him, so desperate were they to make things right and give him some happiness. They wedged themselves as much as they could against the past, acting as though they were killdeers, faking broken wings to trick the bad memories and bad spirits away from him so that he could run to safety. He was homesick and could not speak. He hugged them all and then picked up his duffel bag and quickly walked inside the dorm before he changed his mind.

✖◆◆◆◆◆◆◆◆✖

It had been the right thing to do.

College filled a part of him that had been starving. He felt himself rise with each challenging course. He loved studying. It was the best drink of his life. Every A he earned was a sword against the real and imaginary enemies in his head. He wanted them off the cliff that was his life. He wanted his brain to be free of all the unwanted garbage that was buried in it. The only dirt he wanted near him was the real thing. As if she could read his mind, his mother sent him a pint-size pickle jar full of dirt from the farm. He placed it on the windowsill above his dorm room desk, and it solidified what he would do with the rest of his life. He double-majored in soil science and wildlife biology. They were the two things that never betrayed him: animals and where they lived, what they walked on.

He thought about going out west, but the pull to go home was stronger. He heard the words in his sleep: *Don't ever leave here.* He knew his chances of getting a job with the U.S. Fish and Game Service in northern Wisconsin were almost impossible because it usually assigned its new biologists elsewhere. But he had a plan. He sent in his first application during his freshman year in college, and he applied every year until he graduated. He specialized in the flora and fauna of northern Wisconsin. He was born to it, he argued in his cover letters. He knew exactly what the damage was and how he intended to undo it. He decided that he would study constantly, that he would not date and thereby keep anyone away from pushing him off his chosen road.

⟫◆◆◆◆◆◆◆⟪

Elizabeth had red hair. He could not name its particular shade, and he pondered it frequently when they talked. She accused him of not paying attention to her, but he was listening. There was something familiar about that particular shade of red hair and her amber brown eyes.

He liked her too much. It made him afraid. They met in a soil science class, and despite his fear, he was drawn to her. She was double-majoring in soil science and geology. She liked dirt just like his mother did, and although they shared some other things in common as women, they were different. He told her he just wanted to be friends.

"You are full of layers," she said one day. They were eating pie and drinking coffee at Vescio's restaurant in Dinkytown near the East Bank of the campus.

"Don't dig too deep," he answered cynically, "or you won't like what you find."

The grin vanished from her face. "Every time we start to have fun, you say something like that. Why?"

"Sorry. I just meant"—he fumbled—"that I'm not a saint. I have my bad elements."

"I wasn't talking about elements," she retorted.

He didn't answer and ate the last piece of his lemon meringue pie. He thought the meringue resembled and tasted like plastic. The waitress dropped off their bill.

"Is this real meringue?" he asked.

"No. It's called flacto-macto," she replied curtly, and was gone. *Flacto-macto.* He looked at the crumbs left on his plate. What was that? What had he just eaten?

Elizabeth persisted.

"I wasn't talking about elements," she repeated. "I was talking about *layers.* Good and bad. Everything," she added as though daring him to contradict her, "grows from layers."

✕✦✦✦✦✦✦✦✕

He liked her too much. He was more than afraid. He was terrified.

But one night it occurred to him that although he never needed people much, there would be a day when his mother would die. When Ernie and Rosemary would die. The three most important people still living in his life would not live forever.

They were friends for a year before they became lovers, and then two years later they married. Looking back, Bill was amazed that Elizabeth kept trying. He pushed her away and pushed her down with the weight of words thrown hard, only to pull her back up in confusion, to soften his tone and apologize frantically.

✕✦✦✦✦✦✦✦✕

One night they were sitting together on her couch, drinking Seven-Up and relaxing after having seen a movie. Elizabeth was talking about her parents' divorce and the fact that she never saw her father much. She stopped in midstream during her monologue about her father. "Huh. I just thought of something. You never talk about your father. Or a father. Did you have a father?"

He had told her about his mother and about Ernie and Rosemary. He had talked about his brother as though James were still alive. When he told stories about James, he never tripped over his words. It wasn't as though he didn't feel pain. Of course he felt pain. His brother was dead, and the loss of him was a tragedy that did not diminish. But Bill did not believe in heaven or hell. He believed in systems, natural and unnatural. He believed in zones. And there was more than one zone of death.

He realized that people who were much loved and who died had a way of clinging. Rather than fade, they grew in another dimension, became epizoic, although not harmful like a disease. He had helped that process by casting his brother in a fertile zone that he knew best. In his mind, his brother had crossed the river and was walking in woods. It was his natural habitat.

But his father? In those silent minutes before he began speaking to Elizabeth again, he imagined that Holocaust survivors or anyone who had been tortured, nearly murdered, or hurt in ways by other people filled with hate had to do something with those unforgettable memories in order to survive. As he had done without realizing it. Just as he had willed his brother to love and life, he had willed his father to death. He put him in a most unnatural place in his mind. A museum's airless closet where his father's remains became mummified. Where none of Bill's memorial juices could hydrate him again.

Still, it was hard to find the words to describe what was marked on him. He did not look at her while he talked. When he did turn his face toward her, expecting to see disgust, he saw something else.

Awe.

✕✕✕✕ "GIVE THE DOG A REST!" he calls out to his small son.

His son is so happy today. As though nothing has happened. Last night he had a bad dream. The same bad dream as always. His cries are so piercing that it takes only one or two to wake Bill up. As his son suckered to his chest, Bill wondered, as he always did when he got up to soothe his son, if the boy remembered the first eighteen months of his life. If the mystery of those months would be known someday.

Most of the time he rocks his son back to sleep. But sometimes Bill has to crawl into his son's bed and hold him until he goes to sleep again.

✕✦✦✦✦✦✦✦✕

He remembered the night he fought with Ernie. How he woke up beside him the next morning. To see a male face inches from his own, sound asleep and rough with silver-tipped stubble like an old bear. On rare occasions James would crawl into Bill's bed when he was having really bad dreams. When he felt Ernie's breath on his face that morning, he remembered the hot comfort of his brother's breath.

He woke up this morning, feeling his dark-eyed son pat his cheeks and smelling the chocolate cookies on his breath from the night before.

"Wake up, Daddy," he sang.

✕✦✦✦✦✦✦✦✕

Through persistence and complete stubbornness, Bill did get the job he wanted in northern Wisconsin, alternating fieldwork with grant writing to keep his research projects alive. Liz lucked out as well, acquiring a job as a soil scientist with the County Extension Service. After they were married, Liz did not use birth control in the hope that maybe Bill was not sterile. But nothing happened. He was secretly relieved.

"We could adopt," she said.

He shook his head. She would not let it go, and it led to one of their few bad fights.

"You will not turn into a monster. Or your father," his wife whispered to Bill that night in bed. He was glad it was dark and she could not see his face.

He said nothing.

Her sigh was as heavy as water.

"This big place needs kids. Your mother needs grandchildren. And some child," she said, walking one hand up his chest until she could tap his chin with a finger, "deserves to have you as a father. No one," she added, and her voice drifted above him, "expects you to be perfect. Except you."

They did not speak about it the next morning, eating their breakfast in silence. It was Sunday, and he and Ernie had planned to fish the Chippewa before the really cold weather had set in.

They pushed north on the river against the current in Bill's new ultralight canoe. Bill could see that Ernie was favoring his left arm, and he knew that Ernie's right shoulder hurt from paddling. Ernie was in his seventies, and Bill wanted him just to sit and enjoy the river for once and let Bill do the steering and paddling. But Ernie insisted on paddling too.

They no longer entered the river at the old logging bridge, preferring to drive in on an old fire lane farther south. It meant backtracking a bit on the water, and they eventually paddled past the sandbanks and shoreline that Bill and his brother haunted as children. It was quiet except for the noise their paddles made cleaving the water. As they approached the banks, Ernie pulled his paddle in and stared at the shoreline.

"You know, this past spring I came down here to see if the turtles had nested," he said over his shoulder to Bill, "but I went there for five days straight, and I didn't see one snapper. Not even any drag marks or signs of digging. I guess," he went on before Bill could say anything, "I didn't think it would change. They've nested there since I was a kid. But maybe something is wrong with the river."

Not the river, Bill thought. The logging bridge had always been a place for teenagers to hang out, but in addition to beer cans littered on the road, Bill found used condoms, syringes, cigarette butts, and the scant remains of joints. Then there was that persistent rural belief that snapping turtles were unwanted predators like badgers, wolves, and coyotes. Many of the locals shot snappers on sight, always justifying their actions by saying the turtles were hurting the walleye population or preying on too many wild ducklings. Bill also surmised that kids had raided the nests for years now, throwing the eggs against the bridge for sport, and that any of the old females that would have returned were probably dead.

"Not the river," he said out loud, "although the water quality could be better. Our water biologist, Charlie, says snappers can survive in some pretty funky water. They still live in the Mississippi in Minneapolis."

Ernie shrugged and put his paddle back in. They glided under the bridge. The noise of their paddling echoed, and Bill thought he could hear their breathing bounce off the rusty brown sides. They paddled for quite a ways until Bill saw the slump of Ernie's shoulders.

"Hey! Let's shore up first," he said. "I'm hungry."

They sat in a grove of white-barked birches, lovely even without their leaves. Ernie chewed on the venison sausage sandwich that Liz had made, tasting the tang of cheddar cheese against the peppery meat. Bill watched him.

"Were you ever afraid to be a father? I mean, whenever Rosemary got pregnant, did it scare you?"

"Nooo," Ernie answered slowly. He paused from eating. "I was afraid after the first miscarriage and then every time she reached about the fourth month. One time she even made it to six months. I was more afraid that Rose would die from complications of a pregnancy or that another one wouldn't make it. And after a while I got angry and blamed her. It was stupid of me. It wasn't her fault. Fear"—he sighed—"and disappointment can make you do stupid things."

Bill took a bite of his sandwich, but he could feel Ernie watching him. "Liz wants to adopt children," he said at last. "We've been arguing over it."

Ernie nodded. He had resumed eating, and Bill could hear the slight grinding noise of Ernie's jaws. Ernie lifted his coffee cup and took a drink.

"Well"—he coughed to clear his throat—"I think it's natural for her to want a family. But if you don't want to be a father, then you shouldn't be one. Or," Ernie added quietly, "are you afraid?"

Bill stared down at this boots. "I don't know exactly. I don't know. . . ." His voice trailed off.

Bill didn't want to talk about it anymore. He poured more coffee into his cup from the thermos. Then he remembered something, spurred by their earlier conversation as they passed the sandbanks.

"Do you remember what you told me the night you killed that turtle?"

Ernie put his cup down. He shook his head.

"You said that your father told you that turtle made the world," Bill said, taking a sip from his own cup. "I've wondered about that for years. How did a turtle make the world?"

"I don't remember killing a turtle," Ernie said, bewildered. "Are you sure I killed a turtle?"

"Don't worry about it. I'll explain it later. You didn't kill her in the way you are thinking. Just tell me the story."

Ernie pressed a hand to his aching shoulder. "That's one story I can remember well. It was my favorite story when I was a kid. My father could always make me laugh. I tried to memorize it, but he told it to me so often that I remember it or at least most of it. My father said not to worry, that each storyteller adds a bit of himself in telling it."

Ernie thrust out his cup. Bill poured coffee from the thermos into the tin cup and, nudging Ernie's arm, dropped two ibuprofen tablets into his hand. Ernie swallowed the pills and washed them down with hot coffee.

"You know," he said slyly, "I had to go to the kitchen and get something sweet for my father before he'd tell me the story."

Bill shook his head. "Your blood pressure. Rosemary would kill me," he said, reaching inside his field jacket and pulling out a Hershey bar.

"A Hershey bar! I always carried Hershey bars when I went hunting with your brother."

Ernie popped the chocolate into his mouth and took another drink of his coffee, savoring the melting taste of chocolate and coffee. He stared out over the river and briefly waved a hand toward it.

"This used to be all water once. Either a big lake or an ocean. At that time all the animals lived in water, but many of them could ride the waves or would surface like mayflies to breathe and look up at the sky. They knew a spirit woman lived there. Sky Woman is what they called her.

"One day a moist wind blew across their faces, and they knew it was her breath and that she had been crying. They looked up and could see that she was tired and unhappy. That made them all feel bad. They got together and tried to think of ways to make her happy again. Then they thought of something, but before they did anything, they asked Loon to go beneath the water and call for giant Turtle, who lived below. Loon had to go down several times to persuade Turtle to help them. Finally Turtle rose to the surface of the water and agreed to offer his back as a home for Sky Woman."

Ernie put out his cup for more coffee.

"That sky," he said, nodding upward, "is the gray that always tells me I've got work to do on the house before winter."

He took a sip of his coffee.

"All the water creatures called up to the sky and invited Sky Woman to come down and live with them. She agreed and left her house in the clouds and settled on Turtle's back. They all climbed up on Turtle's back as well. Once she had made herself comfortable, she turned to the animals around her and asked, 'Who of you can get me a handful of dirt from the bottom?'

"Beaver volunteered right away and dived down. He soon came back up, coughing for air and saying he couldn't do it. Then Fisher tried, but he couldn't do it either. Marten and Mink tried too, but they said the water was too deep. They urged Loon, knowing that he could stay under the water for a long time, and Loon dived down. He stayed under for quite a while, but then Loon too came popping up like a cork. He said it was too dark down there and that he couldn't see where he was going, much less find the bottom. They all hung their heads down because they were so ashamed. Here they had invited Sky Woman down from the sky, and they could not perform her one request.

"Then they heard a small voice. 'I will try.'

"It was little Muskrat, and they started laughing.

" 'You! Ha!' said Mink. 'I'm a lot stronger than you. I have more oil to make me glide through the water. And I smell the best!'

" 'You mean, you stink the best,' said Muskrat, because like Mink and Fisher and Marten, they all had musk glands. But while Muskrat was proud of his musk, he realized that only others of his kind thought the smell was beautiful.

" 'Mink is right,' said Fisher. 'We are much stronger than you, and we couldn't do it. You are the weakest among us. It isn't possible. Don't cause us to waste time.'

"Sky Woman looked at little Muskrat. Muskrat looked at her.

" 'I will try,' he repeated, and with that said, he dived off Turtle's back and plunged beneath the waves. They laughed and joked while waiting for Muskrat to come up just as they had done, with no dirt to offer. But time passed. They kept joking, but their laughter began to sound hollow. Finally they became afraid and felt bad that they had picked on Muskrat because they feared he had drowned. When they had just about given up hope and were ready to apologize to Sky Woman, Muskrat floated to the surface, and it was only the quivering of his whiskers that told them he was alive. In one paw was the lump of soil that Sky Woman needed.

"While Mink and Fisher and Marten patted Muskrat on the back to get the water out of his lungs, Sky Woman took the dirt and painted the rim of Turtle's back. Pursing her lips, she breathed upon it and gave it life. The animals couldn't believe their eyes. The soil grew and covered Turtle's back and formed an island where even more creatures could live, and eventually the People. Sky Woman spoke to Turtle.

" 'Thank you for helping me build my home. I shall call this place Mishee Mackinokong, which means the Place of the Great Turtle's Back. As a reward, I shall give you the ability to understand and speak the languages among the other beings, great and small. They will come to you so that you can interpret their thoughts and send them to others. This must be done slowly and with the clearness of spring water. Everyone will know that it is through you that thoughts should be given and shared.'

"Turtle bowed his head with honor and then swam away."

Ernie paused and sat up so that he could relieve the cramp that had now traveled to his lower back.

Bill involuntarily shivered and drew his legs up to his chest to stop it. "What about Muskrat?" he asked. "Didn't he get anything?"

Ernie laughed. "I asked my father the same question. He said Sky Woman winked at Muskrat. Never"—he grinned, wagging a finger at Bill—"underestimate a muskrat. When the beaver and the rest of them move out looking for better places, the muskrat stays and survives all the same."

Ernie looked up at the sky again and then back at Bill. "We better get moving if we're gonna do any fishing today."

They hadn't even gone a quarter of a mile toward the oxbow where they fished when Ernie spoke over his shoulder. "Say, whatever happened to that turtle shield you used to have as a kid? And that wooden sword Jimmy made for you?"

He hadn't meant to, but Ernie's sudden recollection kicked Bill and threw him back. For a few seconds he was not thirty-nine years old but eight again. The grief erupted so unexpectedly that he could not speak. Grateful that the pain in Ernie's shoulder prevented him from turning around to look at him, he lowered his face and clenched his teeth.

He could almost feel the wooden sword in his hand, the spin of his body, and the hot dust under his feet. The rope of the shield as it rubbed against the skin of his forearm. The bright yellowness of the sun in his eyes until he moved his arm. The larger-than-life shadow cast on the ground by his shield and how protected he used to feel, hovering inside that shadow.

He heard wood hit the side of the canoe.

"Billy! You're losing your paddle."

The broad end of the paddle was bobbing alongside the canoe. He grabbed the handle before it slipped into the water too and pulled the paddle up. Ernie had managed to turn around enough so that he could see Bill out of the corner of his eye. Bill was on the verge of saying "I don't know" when he stopped and remembered how the shell had traveled down the river as though pushed delicately by many hands, the sword held under the rope. How he had watched it until he couldn't see it anymore. He was about to answer Ernie when the older man spoke.

"You know, Billy," Ernie said over his shoulder, "we haven't talked about some things, mostly because I didn't wanna push you. But I have to tell you this. Life has to go on. You think you can stop it, but you can't. I tried to stop seeing what was right in front of me for those fifteen years after your brother died. And I ended up hurting Rosemary and you and even your mother. And I hurt myself."

He sighed.

"I should have told your brother a lot of things. I should've driven over to your place that night your dad told us Jimmy had enlisted and stopped him. I have to live with the things I didn't do. Or didn't say. But I'm telling you not to make the same mistake. Don't be afraid. You're a good man," Ernie added. "My father would have thought so too. And he would have told you to live life."

XXXXX HE AND LIZ HAD TRAVELED quite a bit in the few years after they were married, with their honeymoon being the first long road trip they took across the United States.

But nothing had prepared him for Bogotá. As if it were a premonition, Bill had hiccups from time to time on their flight down to Colombia. He could only remember the flight and parts of the trip, perforated by the visceral memory of those chest-pounding hiccups. Their cab ride from the airport to their hotel gave him the disquieting feeling of being lost and out of control. The cabbie drove with speed and a lack of rules. Driving in Bogotá was simply about getting from point A to point B, even if it meant hitting someone or something.

If they had gone with the intention of finding a child, they were mistaken. Their children found them. The two girls drew them within days, the magnetism on their little faces so strong that Bill felt as if he and Liz were compelled to take them. It was as though they had been chosen and did not have a choice. The babies knew they were coming and could smell them as parents when Bill or Liz picked them up. Isabella squawked whenever they left her crib side, so they spent their first two days soothing her, unaware that they were being seduced. It was the opposite with Maria. She was three cribs away from Isabella, and her wispy brown curls were charmingly attractive. She looked at them sleepily and contently but loudly passed gas in their presence, smiling as though she had released perfume. Her eyes never completely shut when they were there, and she casually looked from Liz to Bill and then back to Liz.

Both girls were alert and even smiled when tickled. Both were six months old. Bill helped Liz with most of the paperwork but could not sit for long and got up to wander through the orphanage. His height frightened some of the older children, so he walked slowly and spoke softly.

The orphanage was segregated by age, and he found himself walking most often down the corridor that he thought of as the Peninsula of Babies. He walked the corridor at least four times up and down before he became aware of a noise behind the sniffles and intermittent crying. He could hear a small body lurch from one side of the crib to the other as it followed Bill's movements.

Bill stopped midway down the corridor and saw the eighteen-month-old boy. He held on to the railing of his crib as though it were a boat about to be launched. The toddler did not move as Bill approached the crib. When Bill gently rubbed the boy's knuckles, he lifted the hand Bill had touched only for a moment before clasping the wooden railing again. The boy did not speak or cry. Bill ran his fingers through the boy's curly black hair, smiled, and caressed one of the boy's brown cheeks. He dabbed with his handkerchief at the white crust of formula on the boy's lips. But nothing Bill did could elicit anything other than seriousness on the child's face.

That night Bill dreamed that he saw the boy inside the crib floating on an unfamiliar surface of water. The crib bobbed. The boy silently held on to the railing, his almond-shaped eyes wary yet expectant.

"I want that boy too." He pointed toward the crib the next day. Elizabeth, fluent enough in Spanish to conduct conversations, asked the caseworker about the boy. The caseworker said the child had been abandoned by the service entrance to the building six months before and been nearly unconscious from dehydration and hunger when he was found. He did not speak and had only recently learned to pull himself up into a standing position. The caseworker tried to dissuade Bill. The boy was sick, the caseworker said, tapping his head.

Bill was sure the boy was not autistic or sick in the way the caseworker implied. He could not even explain it to his wife. Every day he went there, and every day the little boy was standing up and holding on to the crib railing. Every day he tried to get the boy to smile and failed. Their last month in Bogotá was spent haggling over the little boy. It was against the rules. Two children were the maximum for adoption. Bill called the adoption agency they had worked through in Milwaukee, which then referred him to an attorney who specialized in foreign adoptions. After many more phone calls and wiring their bank for more money, the orphanage was persuaded to make an exception and let them have three children.

✕◆◆◆◆◆◆◆◆✕

He was only dimly aware of the cramp in his legs on the flight home. Liz held the two sleeping girls for the first hour while the boy stood up on Bill's thighs and braced his hands against Bill's chest. They stared at each other for half an hour. Then, for the first time since Bill had seen him, the boy's eyelids began to drift downward. His legs gave way, and he gave in, slumping against Bill's chest to sleep.

"He's stubborn," Liz commented. She shifted the two girls in her arms. Then she laughed. "My God! I don't know what to expect next from you. We were going to adopt only one child. Now we have three. We have *a litter.* This," she exclaimed, "from a man who was terrified to be a father! How are we going to do this?"

Bill shrugged. He couldn't explain what had come over him. He felt almost beatifically calm. "We'll just do it."

XXXXX HIS SON IS WINDING DOWN, unable to keep up with the dog. His brown feet are even browner, covered with the dust from the sun-warmed and scuffed-up soil of the barnyard.

"Wear your shoes," his mother used to say to Bill. "Or else"— she followed up with the threat—"you'll get worms."

His son did have worms. Bill was changing his diaper on a couch in the Tampa airport and saw what looked like rice on the child's butt cheeks and in his feces.

"We'll have to wait," his wife said, "until we get home. I don't want to drive around Tampa looking for a doctor or a clinic. I just want to get home. Even if we got the medication now, we might end up with a very sick kid on the flight into St. Paul." She squeamishly wrapped the diaper in a small garbage bag and put it in the trash bin in the women's rest room.

All three of them were slightly malnourished, and for a worrisome two days of testing, they thought the two girls might have tuberculosis. Three months after they brought the children home, his son spoke. Or rather he chortled. He had pulled himself up to the low windowsill in the living room one day and ecstatically pressed his face into the glass. Bill quietly crept up behind him and looked out the window.

Birds. Birds feeding at the bird feeder.

His son, dirty and sweaty, flops into Bill's arms to rest. They sit together on the porch steps and watch the dog gratefully settle underneath the shade of the big elm by the chicken coop. His son has the endearing legs of most little boys. Thin pieces of wire with bone knots for knees.

Bill can't remember ever being able to walk up to his father as his son just did. With the knowledge of what to expect. Knowing Bill will hold him and touch him safely. He rubs his cheek against his son's black hair. He can hear his mother and his wife talking inside the house. Hears his mother's shrieking laugh and then his wife's low chuckle. He thinks about the way Liz touches him.

His wife caresses him, and he experiences pleasure and his body feels good then. She aligns her body with his and slides underneath him like a canoe. He is lifted, and at the moment of climax, he feels as though he has transcended the white clapboard house and is flying. He feels holy in that moment. Afterward his wife rubs the liquid from both of their bodies into his groin, and the smell is both sweet and salty. She is careful, when she awakens him from sleep, to touch him someplace else before working her fingers across his body. Only then does she cup and fondle his penis.

His testicles remain small, but the burn scars are fading with age. Still, it does not release him from the self-loathing that surfaces on occasion. As if his body were still dirty. He fears touching his wife, his children at those moments. He tenses up when the children touch him. He tries to hide it from them, but they work harder to get his attention. They hug him forcefully and more often. They reach for his hands and pull on his thumbs. He is amazed at what they inherently know. That if they touch him, they can lift him out of the isolation that would lead him backward and lead him to drink again, burying bottles like his father. They crawl into his lap before their baths and crowd his chest. He can smell the milk on their breaths and the loamy dirt in their ears. His fingers scratch against the grit in their hair, and he knows they will leave a small sandbar in the tub after the water has drained away. Their fingers travel over the land of his face as if they have walked a long way to speak to him.

It is not just Bill.

He watches as they touch his mother. She has become a woman he does not entirely recognize from his youth. Elizabeth sensed Bill's need to help his mother and was adamant that she not move out of the house. They remodeled and added onto the house so that his mother could have her own set of rooms, but those doors are rarely shut. His mother kisses and hugs her grandchildren every day. She greets them with the freedom to know she can. Even if she's been away for only a few hours, they surround her as if she were the sun and they little moons that had drifted out of her orbit. They have fights over which one of them gets to sit on her lap.

"You can take turns," she says, obviously delighted at being so treasured as to be fought over. They bring her stacks of books, and she reads to them tirelessly.

Every now and then, though, he will catch his unknowing mother as she watches the children at dinner or in the bathtub or at play. He sees a sudden stricken look, a quick but paralyzing pain that freezes her face for seconds. Or when Liz hugs him or kisses him, he sees the small envy on his mother's face as she witnesses their casual affection.

Still, his mother tells him daily how happy he has made her. Sometimes in the noise around them, the constant talk at the dinner table and occasional cries of childish disappointment, he locks eyes with her. Or when they are on a walk through the woods with Liz and the kids, he falls into step with her. He knows that they remain as they always have been. Just the two of them. They know each other's histories and the wounds they still carry. Scars that can be torn open with a wrong word or a gesture meaningful only to them. They are aware, even when they hug each other, of that space between them that was once filled with someone else.

◆◆◆◆◆◆◆◆◆

His two daughters skip out of the house, and suddenly his son regains his energy and lifts himself free of Bill's arms. His children chase one another, running so hard that he can see the deep red in their faces as they gulp for air on the run. Sometimes they get so absorbed in their surroundings and one another that they do not hear their parents calling them. He knows exactly what they feel. Invisible and invincible. Immortal. Their imagination conquers all. For that period of time they are lost in a world of their own making and want for nothing else.

It is a hot and humid day, and he has no energy to do much of anything. Still, it is pleasurable just to sit and think and watch what is going on around him. He looks at the dust in the driveway, at the tiger lilies that bend languorously, heavy with their finger-length buds that will bloom soon. He closes his eyes for a moment, and he can see himself as an eight-year-old again, playing in the yard. He can almost hear his brother's record player blaring from the barn. He dreams often, sometimes during the day like this but most often at night. The dreams that disturb him the most are the ones that cause him to wake up with a question that he loses in the second after he reaches consciousness. He knows something was asked of him, yet he can't remember or answer it.

He opens his eyes.

His children laugh, and the sound spirals upward. Bill watches them run toward the faded red barn and then behind it. He knows they play in the exact same spot where he and his brother used to play. Where they cannot be seen but can be found. They have discovered this on their own.

His children's curiosity is endless, and in their roaming, their little fingers touch everything. Grass, trees, flowers, fences. Every inch of the barn they explore again and again. The lake and river water they tickle and splash with their hands. Their fingertips on his skin. Although he can still look at the barn or specific places on the farm and see painful images from the past, they are fading, and the farm is becoming a new place every day because of his children. Because of their touch.

It will not be long and they will be asking the questions that will be difficult for him and Liz to answer.

In the Darwinian world of his work, where only the strongest survive, they belong to the enigma of humans. He knows that Isabella's and Maria's mothers left them at the orphanage and, not long after, were found dead. He assumes it is the same with his son's mother, and soon enough he will have to explain the harshness of the world to them. The despair and poverty that destroy the conscious act of love. He will also tell them of the kindness of people. They are alive because biology does not always determine destiny and goodness can arise from the most hellish of conditions. Even the natural world is not as ruthless as it seems. Hollow logs allow raccoons an escape from a predator. Skunks can spray those that threaten them. There are even places in the woods where small children can hide if they need to. His children have discovered this too without being taught it. Their need to hide is all in fun, either from one another or to pop out and scare their parents. They have to work harder to hide from their grandmother. Bill is amazed that his mother often knows just where the children are in the woods.

What he will have trouble articulating to them is what he didn't know until recently. That children flower out of any soil that will nourish them. That his wife was right. That the layers of his life have enough nutrition in them for his children to take root and that at times he has only to be present and his children siphon what they need from him without his being fully aware of it. He cannot imagine life without them. They redeem and make holy everything they touch. They redeem and bless him.

There is a burst of laughter and his three children suddenly come into view. They run toward him as though he were the prize.

He has told his wife nearly everything about his life. But not everything.

Bill watches as a breeze that he does not feel on his own face suddenly lifts his son's curly black hair.

Somewhere he hears a deep barking he thinks is coming from

his own dog, but when he locates Enrique—he doesn't know how the children came up with that name—the dog is sound asleep or in his favorite spot under the tree by the chicken coop.

One day his two daughters, standing ankle deep in the river and holding on to their cane poles, began to whistle. He did not teach them. Neither did Liz. Ernie said nothing, but he tilted his head back. Bill knows that Ernie heard it too. That third whistle, high above the girls' halting notes.

2000

XXXX IT NEVER FAILS TO AMAZE me what people can survive. Wars, disease, affairs, gossip, unemployment, drinking, husbands and wives, their parents, their children—good and bad—or their lack of children. Or, thinking of Angel, what animals have to live with, being at the mercy of humans. How they survive people period or even show what we think are signs of love for us.

I thought Bill would be a bachelor for life, consumed by his research and career and of course too damaged to seek love. But we underestimated him. He shocked us his senior year when he brought a woman home for Thanksgiving. A red-haired spitfire who was down-to-earth. We all liked her right off the bat. And she was *crazy* about Bill.

Six years ago we pooled our money with Claire so that Bill and Liz could fly down to Colombia and spend the few months it took processing the paperwork before they could bring home what we thought would be one child.

When we picked them up from the Minneapolis–St. Paul airport, they had two six-month-old baby girls and an eighteen-month-old boy.

"We had no choice." Bill pantomimed helplessness, throwing up his hands. "I can't speak or read Spanish. We signed the papers before we knew. How was I to know that *tres* means 'three'?"

"Do you have names?" Claire asked after recovering from her laughter.

"Not yet," Liz said.

We have a picture on our fireplace mantel of the day they were baptized. Bill told us to dress up, but he didn't say where we were going. Ernie, Claire, and I were in our car, and we followed Bill and Liz in their van.

Claire and I gamely followed them in our heels down a sandy slope to the Chippewa River, holding on to each other so that we would not fall down like undignified broads on our aging asses. Ernie sweated and tugged at the tie he hadn't worn in years and frowned at the new loafers on his feet. Bill's best friend from college, Alan Willis, who is a landscape photographer, joined us.

There is nothing more blessed than standing near a river in spring. Especially one that is still somewhat wild. I have struggled for years to name the color of spring. That green. It is a yellow green, but even that doesn't describe it accurately. And on that day the sun played off the leaves in such a way as to make you wish you could live forever.

I was given one little girl to hold, and Claire was given the other. Then Liz placed the baby boy in Ernie's arms. While the photographer took pictures, Bill filled a pottery cup with river water. He was never one for long speeches. He poured a little bit of water over each child's head.

"Water is life," is all he said.

Then they shamelessly reduced the elderly to tears. The girls were named Isabella Rosemary and Maria Claire. The little boy they named James Ernest.

All three of them are the luscious color of milk chocolate, and it is visibly apparent when they are with their mother and father that they are adopted. But when we go out of town or go out to eat as a whole group, it is Ernie that people think the children really belong to.

✕✦✦✦✦✦✦✦✦✕

Still, Ernie is not happy.

Jimmy remains a mystery.

Happy endings are like buying lottery tickets. It's a crapshoot, and you can keep buying them in the hope of winning, but it doesn't happen very often. Still, you can die hoping.

There are some happy endings. The happy ending you want may not be the happy ending you get or need. I did get to be a mother and then a grandmother through circumstances I could never have foreseen or predicted, through the default and then generosity of first one woman and then two. Ernie is the only grandfather those children will have via Bill, and although he is not as demonstrative as I am, I know he treasures Bill and his family more than his own life.

But there is that lost child.

I watch Ernie sit on the porch and shiver. He stares at our field. He'll catch pneumonia at his age. He is still troubled, and there seems to be nothing I can say to him to ease his conscience. For years he read everything he could about Vietnam. To try to understand it and therefore gain some peace of mind, but it only made it worse.

"I just want to see him one more time. I want to know why," Ernie said to me the other night after dinner. He was wrapped up in a shawl I made for him. "How come I've never seen Frank LaRue? Patterson or McDougal? Or Scofield and Krenshaw? They were my best friends. They all died young. In the war."

Ernie went on before I could answer. Angry this time.

"That goddamn Westmoreland. All of them. Johnson, McNamara, Nixon, Kissinger. Even Kennedy in the beginning. But Westmoreland and Johnson just had to have their battle at Khe Sanh. What dumb-asses. The North Vietnamese must have laughed like hell over that one. We bombed the shit out of that area and threw away lives. Westmoreland just couldn't get past World War Two and the big battles. After two hundred years of history he never did understand fighting Indian-style. Giap did, though. He loaded up that area with soldiers so that Westmoreland thought the big threat was there. Westy took the bait. Left Saigon and the lower half of Vietnam wide open. Like lifting a blanket off a baby in a crib. Jimmy and the rest of those guys were just *bait,*" he spit out. "Jimmy died for *nothing.* Jesus Christ!" he cried. "By 1966 they knew it was wrong. *Why didn't they stop?*"

This anger and bitterness never go away. Ernie does not feel that way about our war. He has let that one go. But this one he'll take in his fists to his grave.

"Why did Jimmy show up that day? What did he want from me?" he asked.

I love my husband, but he is a man. Even among the best of them, he's still dense sometimes. This world would have gone to hell in a handbasket if it hadn't been for women. We've always had to interpret the signs for them.

I pulled my chair up next to his and cupped his face in my arthritic hands. "Why do you think Jimmy showed up that day? To punish you?"

His lips trembled. I knew that was it. What he carried for years.

"Did it ever occur to you that he was coming to tell you first? I think that's why he never told you he enlisted. He knew you would try to stop him. Just like he knew his own father wanted to get rid of him bad enough to sign those papers."

I stroked his white hair and marveled at how handsome he still was at seventy-six. But the pain. I can't stand to see him in this pain.

"I think he wanted," I said, "to spare you whatever outcome his decision would have. Then the worst happened. Like many sons in trouble, he needed to tell the father who would have protected him. Always remember," I said, feeling his tears wet my hands, "that he came *to you* in your own field."

✕✕✕✕ OH, BILLY. BILLY BABOON.

Don't fuck it up! I wanted to scream at him that day, especially after he took a shot at the dog. It was so unlike Bill that I had trouble believing it. But I saw it, and I wondered why I hadn't seen it before. The way Bill walked, the way he held himself. As though his skin were in danger of sliding off.

I'd have given anything to be in his shoes. To be able to smell the sphagnum moss, the white pine, and the cedar in the swamp and to touch it. To chew on fresh wintergreen leaves and see wood anemone in the spring. To walk down to the Chippewa on a summer's day and go fishing. I felt longing. Something I never thought I'd feel after I was dead. But watching my brother turn into my old man was too hard. I saw my mother's helplessness. What could she do? Point a gun at his head and tell him to stop drinking?

I had to do something. I had to scare him. Just like the old days. I had to scare him so bad that he would turn around and run back toward his life. And not give up.

✕◆◆◆◆◆◆◆◆✕

I am tired. All that is me has slowed down and is leaving. I did what I had to do. The Yards believe that their ancestors, their dead loved ones, live in the highlands, sometimes as good spirits and sometimes as bad spirits, but all of them belonging to the land. I too am that way. The Bru and the rest of the Yards will fight like hell to stay there, and they should. It is their land and their soul. Their burned and bombed soul. But someone had to stay there and make it green again.

I lost my copies of *Huckleberry Finn* and *The Man Who Killed the Deer* at Khe Sanh or they were pinched. But it was something else Twain said, that Sister Maria read to us in class. She was my favorite teacher in high school because she had such a wacky sense of humor. She read it to us, knowing that Twain poked at religion. I never forgot it.

Twain said, "I think we never become really and genuinely our entire and honest selves until we are dead—and then not until we have been dead years and years. People," he said, "ought to start dead and then they would be honest so much earlier."

What had seemed like a bunch of fuckin' nonsense to me at sixteen made perfect sense after I was dead.

⬥⬥⬥⬥⬥⬥⬥⬥⬥⬥

If I have not been a good son or brother in life, then I hope that I have been a better son and brother in death. I have existed in this way for a reason that I still don't fully understand, but the energy that is me is finally falling apart. As it should. I can drift away, unhinge myself just as we used to unhinge snapping turtles to get at the meat. This is what seems to be happening. The molecules of my being are drifting into the pines and cedars, sinking below the surface of the water. I can feel myself get carried down the Chippewa. Feel myself settle onto the skin of those people I loved and left.

In this way I will never leave them again.